# WATERS
### OF
# SALT & SIN

## UNCOMMON WORLD
## BOOK 1

# Waters
## of
# Salt & sin

## Uncommon world
## book 1

## Alisha Klapheke

Text copyright © 2017 by Alisha Klapheke
Cover art copyright © 2017 by Merilliza Chan

Library of Congress Cataloging-in-Publication Data
Klapheke, Alisha
Waters of Salt and Sin/Alisha Klapheke. —First edition.
Summary: Low-caste salt sailor Kinneret sets out to find a lost island of silver so her sister won't starve and so she can have a chance at her high-caste best friend's heart, but when a madman captures her sister, Kinneret must change course or lose the ones she loves.
ISBN 978-0-9987379-0-4 (trade)
ISBN 978-0-9987379-1-1 (ebook)
[1. Fantasy. 2. Magic—Fiction.] I. Title.

Printed in the United States of America
10 9 8 7 6 5 4 3 2 1
First Edition

For my family and friends, both near and far

# CHAPTER ONE

A BREATH BEFORE SUNRISE, THE sea was a half-lidded eye, pale blue and white beyond the town walls and lemon orchards. The sea and me, the only two awake this early. Or so it seemed when I climbed to the roof of the tavern. The streets were only dark mud and shuttered windows. I should've been out scouring too, looking for a fallen dumpling or a bit of orange-spiced chicken. But I couldn't help myself. The glimmering saltwater winked at me and I gave it a lazy smile.

"Soon," I whispered before heading back down.

I had to finish the rope I'd labored on all night, because though magic was good for a lot of things, unfortunately, twisting coconut fibers wasn't one of them.

My hands used to bleed when I did this kind of work. Not now. Now my palms were like moving stones, pressing, rolling over the two sections and twining them around one another until they were long enough to tie off a sail.

My younger sister Avi snored lightly on our straw mat in the port tavern's undercroft. I opened her hand. Someday—if I managed to keep her alive until someday—those angry blisters would disappear and she'd have rocks for hands too. I touched the area around the worst of them gently. Though she was fourteen, I rubbed her arm like Mother used to do when we were little. Soon enough, she'd be beside me on the sea, rushing to finish our day's work before night fell and the salt wraiths came. But she didn't love the risk, the delicious challenge, or the waters like I did.

"Kinneret?" Avi's eyes opened, red and bleary.

"No. I'm Amir Mamluk," I joked, pretending to be the steel-eyed woman who held the town in her ruthless grip, only a few steps below the kyros in power. "I am in disguise as your sister so I can enjoy the pleasures of low-caste life. What's first? Prying barnacles off the hull or watching my hard-earned silver disappear into rich men's pockets?" I clapped my hands like an idiot as Avi bent over laughing.

"You're a madwoman, Sister." She looked past me to the light. "You should've shaken me awake sooner. Did you get your sailing papers stamped?"

I waved her off. "I will. Tomorrow."

"All right." A black spot marred the edge of her grin. She'd lost a tooth last week. The empty place looked wrong next to the pretty yellow-brown hair she'd inherited from Father.

Avi leaned over to touch the shells she hid under her side of the mat. She didn't know I knew about them, so I stood and turned away, giving her a moment. It was her own ritual and whatever gave her peace was fine with me.

Gathering the fibers I hadn't used last night and the new rope, I forced a worthless tear back inside my eye and tried not to hear her little whispers.

"Mother. Father. The kitten. The cat. My broken bird."

She'd found a shell for each of the ones she'd lost. A curving one with ridges, as dark brown as our mother's skin had been. A spotted one for Father. He would've liked that. He'd loved the unusual.

As I tied on my sash, the tiny bells jingling, she drank from the bucket and wiped her mouth with the back of her hand.

"Eat that bread there." I jerked my chin at the stool that served as our table.

"What about you?"

"I ate with Oron late last night," I lied. I was a great liar, but I didn't rejoice in it. Lying was the skill of the desperate, something I intended to stop being as soon as possible.

"He actually ate?" Avi said around the nub of bread. "I thought he was on an all stolen wine diet."

"He wishes. Said so right before he went down to the boat." This time of year, depending on the crowd at the dock, my first mate sometimes slept onboard to protect our only real possession. Harvest brought a lot of strangers who wouldn't worry about consequences.

Smiling, Avi shook her head and handed me the bag of salt I kept tied to my sash. I shook it, felt its soft bottom. There was enough for some Salt Magic if we ended up needing it today.

"What shipments do we have?" Avi asked.

"None. We're scouting new port locations again."

"Hope it goes better than last time. Is Calev going to predict our weather for the trip?" Avi grinned.

As a member of the native community of Old Farm—and the chairman's son to boot—Calev was born high-caste, raised to oversee his people's lemon orchards and barley fields, and basically treated like a kyros around town. *The brat,* I thought, a grin tugging at me.

But despite his powerful family and his position, he had the hardest time predicting weather, a child's first lesson on a farm or at sea. He just couldn't seem to gather the clues hidden in the thrush's song, the clouds' sudden curl, or the moisture in a breeze. Seriously, he was rubbish at it. His eyebrow twitched when it frustrated him and it was—

"You're the prettiest when you smile like that, Kin."

I shoved her gently. "Shut up, you. Come on. We need to go."

My relationship with Calev was complicated. And dangerous now that we neared the age of adulthood. Avi really did need to shut up about it.

At least until I found some way to snake my way into a higher caste.

I unlocked the door and held it open for her, pretending there wasn't a pile of both human and animal waste we had to step over. Soon, the middle-caste merchants would open their booths in these dirty streets to trade goods and gossip under the white-hot sun.

Ugh. There was the sailmaker's son.

He was still burned over the deal his father gave me when Calev came along to buy our new sail.

"Kinneret Raza the Magnificent, friend to high-castes." He pretended to whisper, but his words were plenty loud. "But only if you have eyes and a backside like that Old Farm boy Calev. For him, she pretends that bag of salt at her sash is for seasoning food. It's a miracle he doesn't see you for what you are. Witch."

A ringing filled my ears. If the wrong people heard him, we'd wish our only problem was finding something to eat today. "The real miracle is that pest birds haven't nested in your continuously open mouth, between your rotting teeth."

His gaze lashed out at Avi. "Soon I won't be the only one with an Outcast's mouth, witches."

I raged toward him and he lifted his leg to kick me off, but Avi jumped in the way. The tip of his sandal struck her leg, and she winced.

"You better stop it," Avi shouted. "Or you'll be sorry."

He laughed and went on as I bent to check Avi's leg.

"It's a scratch," she said. "It's nothing."

"That horse's back end is going to be nothing if he ever touches you again. You should keep quiet when he is around."

"Oh, like you do, Sister?" She raised both eyebrows.

I snorted. "Well, I'm Kinneret the Magnificent, remember?" The ridiculousness of the title burned like a brand.

Avi put a hand on my arm and pulled me to standing. "You are magnificent to me."

I hugged her and felt her shoulder bones like driftwood under my arms. My temples throbbed. She was little more than a skeleton. A chill slithered down my back. How long could we live like this?

A woman who'd been Outcasted, sat at the bend in the road, begging. Bells hung from her knotted hair, the edges of her dung-crusted tunic and sash, from every fingernail. The metal seemed to weigh her down, making her back slump like someone years older, bones rising beneath her rags. As a high-caste man walked by, his five bells lightly ringing, she tucked her feet under her, hiding the scraps that used to be sandals in a series of rickety movements.

The high-caste whipped around and pointed at the Outcast.

In addition to never being allowed to enter their families' homes—or anyone's for that matter—they weren't permitted to hold a job, wear more than rags, or cover their feet with shoes. At the man's gesture, the woman closed her eyes and removed her sad excuse for sandals, shoving them into the gutter. The high-caste nodded and continued on, obviously pleased with himself.

I'd heard the town's last amir caught her doing Salt Magic to win a boat race where the prize was a hefty bag of silver. But I wasn't going to let that scare me off what my mother had taught me.

An image of her hands covering mine, salt glistening on our skin, blinked through my mind. I could be sly with the magic she'd given me. I could be clever with the way I used it. No one needed to know.

As we started toward the dock, a couple of high-caste women paraded by, their skirts clean and black and beautiful.

One sneered at Avi's skirt. "Filthy scrappers. Look at the blood on her clothing."

The other one frowned. "They were probably fighting like dogs."

*Idiots.*

I never bought anything that wasn't red just so no blood would show on me. But the high-castes were wrong. It wasn't fighting that normally brought the blood I hid. It was making rope, hauling sail, lifting, scrubbing, scraping. And I'd never let them see my blood.

As we continued on, Avi raised her chin like a proud woman twice her age. She should've had her woman's bleed already. It was lack of food that scared it off. I knew what came next. Her hair would go. The rest of her teeth, her skin.

I knew Calev would gladly give us a loaf of bread or some lemons. But the questions I asked myself were always the same. What about tomorrow? And the day after that? I couldn't beg off him.

No.

I wouldn't let him bring us food every day like we were cripples. The thought turned my empty stomach and I kicked at the dirt. Mother and Father had made this life work. I could too. When the fevers had them, I'd promised I'd take care of Avi. Maybe I'd get another headland farmer to use us to ship surplus barley across the strait.

But that didn't put figs in Avi's mouth today.

"What are you doing?" Avi whispered as I walked up behind a woodcutter's cart.

Manure and fresh timber masked the scent of what was almost certainly a bag of barley cakes near the left wheel—the woodcutter's noon meal. I threw a tiny rock toward his horse's back leg. The horse jerked and the cart lurched to the side, the woodcutter shouting at his animal as I snatched the bag faster than a falcon can grab a chicken.

I ate one before Avi could argue, hurrying around the cart and hiding the bag in the folds of my skirt. And though she frowned at me the entire walk to the dock, Avi ate her fill for once.

FISH LIVER OIL WAS BOTH the worst and best smell in the morning. Best because it meant I was near my boat. Worst because, well, it was fish liver oil.

The fisherman selling the stuff crossed his arms. "I won't give it for free."

"But you dump most of it anyway," I argued. "It's rancid."

"*You* need it. So I want something for it."

Of course he did. This was Jakobden, after all. A port town full to bursting with people who cared for silver and fame, and nothing as low as a generous spirit.

"Do we really need it?" Avi asked.

I whispered in her ear. "The stern stitching is begging for a coat."

I felt the coins in my sash. Four coppers. It was all I'd saved toward a better boat, a better sail, a better anything. Then my gaze dropped onto the bag in Avi's hand. There was one barley cake left. It would leave me without a noon meal, but the lack of oil could sink us under the wild waters of the Pass, the strait we sailed every day.

Avi saw my eyes and handed me the bag. I held a cake out to the man.

"Fresh this morning," I said. "It's more than you deserve."

He frowned, then snatched the cake and pushed it into his sash for later. After he ladled some oil into our small, wooden bucket, we headed down the near deserted dock toward the red and purple boat our parents had left behind.

Sitting side by side on the dock's uneven planks, we took turns dipping our brushes into the foul-smelling oil and painting it over the coconut fiber stitching that held the stern in place.

Seawater slapped the space between the boat and the dock as I called out, "Oron!"

No answer.

"Why do we love him again?" Avi asked, grinning.

"If he didn't handle sails like the Fire, I wouldn't...no...I'd still love him. The beast."

I didn't affectionately call him 'the beast' because he was both a pale-skinned northerner and an unusually small person—I wasn't a horse's back end like the sailmaker's son—but because of his taste for drink, his sharp tongue, and his tendency to nap like an oversized cat.

Footsteps pounded down the boards, and I turned to see an official striding toward us, his tunic and sash billowing in the wind. Worry tied a neat knot around my heart. This might be about the rent and what I owed. It might be about any number of crimes. And the Fire knew, my word against a middle-caste's would be mouse dung to silver pieces.

Avi dropped her brush into the water and her lips pinched together. "I told you we should've gone for the stamp and seal."

I groaned as I helped her fish the brush from the water. These dock officials were the worst.

"Just *Kinneret* them," Avi whispered. "Like you did to the woodcutter."

"Hush," I said, shaking my head.

"Sailing papers," the official spat, looking down at me.

Standing, I gritted my teeth and pulled my out-of-date papers from my sash. "Everything is good here." I held them to his face, then quickly folded them again.

He ripped them from me. "These are expired. You cannot sail again until you have an updated stamp. Report immediately to the town hall." Spinning, he hurried back up the dock.

"Guess I'll finish this up while you go," Avi said. I didn't like how she looked. The skin around her mouth was pale.

"I don't want to leave you."

"You have to. You know you do."

"I'll kick Oron awake first," I joked. Sort of.

He may've been the one who came to us in our worst hour, and close as an older brother or an uncle, but he still needed a good shove every once in a while.

She stood and wiped her hands on her skirt. "I'm fine. I'll do it. Go."

I had to smile. She sounded like Mother.

I rushed away, hoping she really was as strong as I thought she was, and praying my own stubborn will might be enough to keep us from the life of a dead-eyed beggar.

# CHAPTER TWO

I WALKED UNDER THE TOWN hall's arched doorway, passing a hand respectfully over the Holy Fire burning in the bronze bowl. Though I really didn't feel anything for the Holy Fire faith—the flames had never granted me any new ideas—everyone except Old Farms was expected to follow its tenets, and I certainly didn't want to join the Outcasted for such a small thing.

An Old Farm representative—with a beard that made him look like Calev's father Chairman Y'hoshua—came in behind me. Instead of passing his hand through the Fire, he slid his dagger across his finger and dropped a bead of blood into the bowl. He didn't even glance at me before pushing past to meet with one of the amir's officials near the front of the busy room.

I got in line to renew my sailing license as a man and woman wearing the red leather of the amir's fighters entered and paid the Fire their respects, their palms glowing for a moment and showing their faith. They moved on, squishing my toe with a heavy shoe.

"Don't worry about it," I growled out, rubbing my toenail with a thumb. "I love being stepped on."

The clink of silver coins and the din of gossip bounced off the domed ceilings and sloping walls, and my sarcasm was lost to the noise.

A flatbread seller's tray flavored the air with nutty cardamom and cinnamon. My stomach roared, and I ignored the merchants' wives idly chatting and downing golden dumplings like every bite didn't cost what I made in two moons.

When I finally neared the front, Old Zayn shuffled in the door, a hand on his scanty beard and his gaze zeroing in on me. He lifted his shaggy brows and waved. As usual, he'd remembered something, and judging from the gleam of crazy in his sweet, old eyes, it was a doozy of a something.

But I didn't have the sun for that. I needed to get out of here before my landlord found me and decided I needed one less finger. Giving Old Zayn an indulgent smile, I waved back and held up my index finger, meaning I'd talk in a bit.

My caste bells jingled, and the merchants' wives sneered.

Putting a hand over my bells to quiet them, I imagined myself as kaptan of the *amir*'s gloriously enormous, black-sailed ship, and gave the snooty crowd a pirate's grin.

Someday. Somehow.

But I had to laugh at myself. A girl, two steps from starving, daydreaming about running the town leader's ship? I was crazier than Old Zayn.

Berker Deniz, a middle-caste ship kaptan with as much charm as a bleeding blister, crossed the tasseled rugs. His feet kicked the hem of his silk tunic and a weasel's smile cut across his mouth. He didn't make eye contact, but headed for me like a dog on a scent.

"Move back, low-caste." In the mess of people, he tried to step in front of me. It was his right to do so, by law.

An itch I could never scratch started up under my skin. Considering I'd helped free his barge from the rocks last moon, he should've let me keep my place. I pretended not to see him. From the corner of my eye, I watched his face flush. It made him even uglier.

I was glad for my darker coloring, a blend of every blood that had lived in Jakobden and even across the Pass. When I blushed, no one noticed.

"You're just like your mother was," he said. "No honor."

I whipped my face to his. "What do *you* know about my mother?"

He grabbed my arm and pulled me back, taking my place in line. The merchants' wives eyed me, their ten bells shining from their sashes, marking them as middle-caste. One whispered something to the other, and my cheeks burned as I jerked away and settled for the spot behind him.

"Go ahead and argue," Berker hissed. "I'd love the officials here to order you to kiss my feet in apology."

*Breathe. Breathe.* I wanted nothing more than to throttle the beast and force him to kiss my flying fist. "I'll move up someday and people like you will be sorry," I whispered.

He laughed under his breath. "I saw you and that high-caste boy together at the docks last night."

I sucked a breath as Calev's face blinked through my mind.

Berker snorted, glancing over his shoulder. "Just as I suspected. You lust after him."

My face was hot as coals. "He is not…"

The room grew hazy and I grasped for Berker's sleeve to stay upright. Lack of food was making me lightheaded. Berker's mouth dropped open, then twisted into a grimace worthy of his sliminess as he stared at my fingers on his fine tunic.

"I scout port locations for Calev's people," I said, letting go quickly. "That's all. My twice great-grandmother was Old Farm."

"Interesting you would bring up an Outcast as part of your argument."

How did he even know that?

I mean it was public record, but still. Besides Avi and me, who cared that a long ago woman had an affair with one of the amir's house slaves and was Outcasted. How much did Berker know? Did he also know she lost her children to Quarry Isle, where her bloodline slaved until Father proved his worth at a testing—

alongside Mother—and that Old Zayn paid for their rise to low-caste?

Why did it seem like Berker was always at my back, biting at my heels? For a grown man, nearly as old as my father would've been if he were still alive, he acted like an overgrown and seriously annoying puppy. A puppy that could ruin my life.

"Calev isn't always visiting *me* by the docks," I said. "His father sends him to Old Zayn to learn weather. We aren't doing anything taboo."

Berker dusted his striped sleeve and sea salt fluttered to the floor. "Not yet."

He was referring to our fast-approaching coming of age. "We're only associates."

"Well, it didn't appear that way when I saw you. Sometimes I wonder if you low-caste scrappers almost want to be Outcasted."

Our local ruler, Amir Mamluk, claimed keeping upper-caste bloodlines strong—making certain only highs bred with highs and so on—kept the right people in decision-making positions in Jakobden and the surrounding area.

A view worth its weight in dung.

"Sounds like you know a lot about my low-caste mother. How is that, when you've always been a middle-caste barge kaptan?"

"Your parents and I were on the slave island together."

The breath went out of me. My expired license crumpled in my fingers, the wax seal biting my palm. I knew Old Zayn had taken my parents from the island to apprentice on his boat, but that was about all. I'd never heard about Quarry Isle and Berker. My parents had mostly kept their pasts to themselves.

"What are you talking about?"

"Your mother was a liar with no honor."

My hands shook.

"You're just like her," he said. "Being dishonorable will get you nowhere."

My mouth popped open.

Maybe this was why he made sure to push in front of me and gossip about me to his fellow middle-caste kaptans. He'd known and hated my mother for some invented reason. My teeth ached from clenching my jaw. No way he was right about my mother. He was the liar.

"You must earn your way to the top, like me," he said.

"Last time I checked, middle-caste wasn't the *top*."

"I nearly forgot," he said. "Didn't you once run a shipment for that new grain farmer on the headlands?"

"That's my biggest run each moon."

"My apologies. I'll be running his goods from now on. He had a bumper crop and needs more than your little raft."

My knuckles pressed against my skin as I fisted my hands. Raft? That had been my parents' boat and it was the cleverest craft out there. A lot of good it did me if I didn't have enough clients.

The license official raised a palm to Berker. "Good day, kaptan. We have important matters to discuss."

Before joining the official, Berker hissed, "Remember where you belong, Kinneret Raza." He frowned at the bag of salt hanging from my sash, beside my dagger. "Salt Witch."

Praying and giving salt to the sea was an older practice than even the amir and her fighters' Holy Fire prayers. Why was one perfectly fine—expected even—and the other taboo? The only big difference was they used fire to develop new ideas and I used salt to alter current and wind patterns. It wasn't cheating anymore than other prayers.

"I am here to pay for the removal of a bell," Berker said to the official. He held a handful of silver coins high and spoke loud enough for the world to hear. "Please consider my request."

I made a gagging noise. I couldn't believe Berker was moving closer to the top. If he made it to high-caste, he could buy and sell land, take the first fruits from every harvest, and have an even better view as he looked down his squid nose at me. But surely that would take him an eternity. That was a lot of silver.

The license official smiled, and with a lot of extra hand-waving, removed a bell from Berker's pale orange sash.

Berker retrieved two more handfuls of coins from his bag. "I would like to remove four more bells. Please consider my request."

It was like the wind had dropped to nothing on a busy shipping day. I could barely breathe. I certainly couldn't move.

The license official went to his work and everyone, except me, stomped their feet in praise.

Berker now wore five bells on the shoulders of his tunic. He was high-caste.

The license official raised his rough voice. "I have the distinct honor of announcing that as of today, Berker Deniz is the new kaptan of Amir Mamluk's ship!"

My legs became seaweed, and I caught the wall to keep from falling.

All around me, congratulations rose toward the painted ceiling. Sandals pounded the floor tiles.

A mean laugh snapped from my lips. I shook my head, picturing the ship's tall sides and its sails big as the night sky. Fire burned through me. My gaze lit on the fine linen and silk of everyone's sashes and the deep blues and blacks of their tunics. Their sandals without holes and fleshed out stomachs and limbs.

They didn't see the injustice, because they didn't want to.

I shook, my teeth grinding, and the bells of my sash jingling. My dreams were broken, cracked at mid-mast and beyond repair.

Words spilled out of me. "The lack of bells doesn't make someone a good kaptan. He may be high-caste, but he's a high-caste idiot!"

All heads turned, and before I could worry about what I'd done, the guards rushed forward and shackled my arms with their iron-strong grips.

# CHAPTER THREE

L ET ME GO." I TRIED to peel their fingers off as the room erupted into hissing and whispers.

"Stop struggling, low-caste," the guard on my right said as they dragged me toward the door. "Don't want to work off all the tasty bits. Our prison rats are sadly underfed."

Before I could make a colorful remark about feeding his generous backside to the vermin instead, Old Zayn scurried over.

"Please, let me take her," he said in a clear voice. Everyone froze, then looked from him to the license official. "She's not been right since her parents' death. Neither her nor her sibling. Nor her sibling."

People called Old Zayn mad because he repeated himself. He might've been. But I was fine with his madness—it was always tempered with kindness and a flood of childhood memories. I was especially fine with his madness if it rescued me from this mess.

"They died over five years ago," Berker snapped.

I squeezed my hands tight.

"Have mercy." Zayn bowed awkwardly. "I'll make certain she doesn't speak out again."

The official frowned. I was going to rot in a cell.

"Please," Zayn pleaded. "It's harvest. Time of plenty. Be merciful." He made the sign of the Fire on his forehead.

"Fine then." The official ran fingers over his beard, the Old Farm representative standing beside him watching everything. "But if she causes trouble, the amir will hear of it, and her life and yours will be in Amir Mamluk's hands."

While I waited by the door, Old Zayn secured my updated sailing papers. Seas, I had Calev's kind of luck today, catching Old Zayn in one of his lucent moments right when I needed him. The old friend ambled over, thrust the documents into my sash, and pulled me into a corner. His wide tunic sleeves almost covered his raisin hands.

"Thank you, Zayn." It wasn't enough, but it was all I had. He'd risked his own freedom to keep me out of trouble.

A smile ghosted over his whiskered face. "You're like your mother, but ten times worse. You'll never settle for a small life, will you? Will you?"

More about my mother. My heart gave my ribs a nudge at the memory of her bright eyes and strong voice, but I didn't have the sun for this. I had to go to that farmer and get back his business.

"I need to—"

"Wait," he said, looking at the line of people past the elephant tusk.

No one was peering at me anymore. They'd gone back to their lives. Berker had disappeared.

"Ayarazi exists," Zayn whispered.

The strange word echoed through me like a song I'd forgotten.

"That's a children's story." I touched his arm gently. "Mother and Father used to tell me about it. The lost island of silver is filled with pretty horses and green grass and a mist that'll freeze your toes off if you don't clean your dinner plate and wash behind your ears. It's a myth; a sweet, exciting one, but a myth just the same. Now, may I walk you home?"

His eyes flashed. Intelligence lived in their cloudy depths.

And maybe a dash of anger.

22

"Did I seem out of my wits in there?" He jerked a thumb toward the license room.

"No," I admitted. "But you come and go…"

A seed of maybe sprouted in my mind. Ayarazi—*moon land* was what the amir's fighting sailors called the lost island of silver—didn't exist, but maybe he knew of another island, a place I might sail to and find silver or copper coins in ship wreckage or something of the sort.

"I made a promise to your parents," he said.

"What?" This was the first I'd heard of this.

"I promised I'd watch out for you. You're set on rising above your status," he said. "Aren't you?"

My gaze flew to his face, and I imagined Calev's shining eyes, his jet hair, his hands. "More than anything."

He nodded. "And you want more for your sister and that dwarf you pity…"

"Pity? Oron—the best sailor I've seen and I've seen a load—has saved my life and Avi's about a thousand times. But go ahead and pity him." I could picture him, tying back his thick locks of purposefully tangled hair and looking up at me with his face of scars and sarcasm. "Oron loves silks. Adores northern ice wine. But pity? Pity is his absolute favorite."

"Yes," the old man said, smiling, misunderstanding me completely, going on like I'd said nothing at all. "I've watched you your whole life. With your fire, if you found riches, you'd put them to good use. Maybe you'd even marry well, marry *him*, and cease my worrying about you two. Outcasting is shameful. Shameful. One of the worst things the Empire encourages, in my opinion. As if your blood changes when you move up or down. Stupid! I should know…you two are meant for one another…remind me of your mother and father…"

My throat went dry. "Zayn. Please. Focus. What are you trying to tell me?"

He grinned. "My greedy, foolish cousin died. He never found the map. But you could. Now that he's dead and won't be coming after you with a rusty yatagan." He tapped the sore side of my head with a dirty finger that smelled like goat. "Smart girl. Smart girl."

"Zayn. Out with it. What are you talking about?"

"There's a story in my family. And in it hides the clue to finding the lost island of silver."

# CHAPTER FOUR

ZAYN'S HALF-ROCK, HALF-MUD home was a tumble of rusted fishing hooks, line weights like lead bags, and nets. The place smelled of charcoal and dirt. A hot breeze poured through the window where Calev often stood with Zayn, working on learning the weather's hints.

A moon after Zayn warned Old Farm of a hard frost and saved the lemon harvest, Calev's father sent the man a crate of the fruits, carried by his eldest son. Ever since, Calev visited regularly to work on reading the sky and earth for crop-killing surprises. I loved the arrangement because Old Zayn's hut wasn't too far from the dock.

Beside the window, maps smothered a spindly table. Some of the maps were drawn on yellow parchment, others on wrinkled paper, and more still scratched onto wide pieces of tree bark. Layouts of the sea, the borders of our town, and the swathe of rich land where Calev's people farmed along the southern edge of the jagged coast.

"What is the clue, Zayn? I don't have all day to gossip with you. Avi is waiting. You know how she gets." She was fourteen going on forty-five. Oron better have roused his lazy self to help her with the oil.

He made a tutting noise. "Sit. Sit. This is nothing that can be rushed."

A dingy hammock swung over the dirt floor. There was no evidence that this man was formerly high-caste. No silken tunics left over or fine furnishings. The only clue that he once scribed for the amir was the quill and ink pot sitting on the maps.

He gestured to a stool near the table and I took it, hoping I wasn't wasting sun being here.

Zayn ran a hand under his nose. "My cousin searched for the map every day. Every day, he returned to his home empty-handed. You remember seeing him once. I'm sure. A bald man, raging into and out of here. He said he'd murder you in your sleep if I told you."

"Hold on. What map? You have to explain this all to me." He had to be cracked. Ayarazi? It couldn't be real. He hadn't had family living here with him in a long while. But that's how his mind was, in and out, with days disappearing and reappearing. I did remember the cousin though.

"My ancestor was a scribe for the Invaders."

I blinked. "That was over three hundred years ago."

"He learned the Invaders knew the lost island of silver's location."

The Invaders hadn't attacked Jakobden in generations. They were from the far West and mainly ravaged the northern climes and the Empire's outskirts on that side of the world.

"He recorded clues," Zayn said, "and hid them in a wine jug that sank in a wreck along with my ancestors' employers."

"This...this is madness." I pinched at one of the bells on my sash, my foot bouncing. I needed to leave, to get on with my day. This was nothing more than daydreaming.

"Treasure hunting is not always so good for a soul. Dangerous work." Zayn picked a clod of dirt from the map and chewed his lip, making his beard stick out on his chin. "I don't have it in me to search. Takes a certain drive." He bumped a knuckle under my chin. "You have it, Kinneret. Inside you. Inside you."

I touched my bag of salt for magic and ran a finger over the fraying, leather ties.

I did have that desire, that drive Zayn spoke of. I felt it, hot and unrelenting, in my veins, my heart, my head. I met his gaze.

"I'm sorry, Zayn. You're right about some things. About the caste system being wrong. That the lunar cycle would last an extra day last year. You always know the best place to catch those foul eels the high-castes strangely adore. But this? This is...I can't just take off into the waters on a story."

"Because you think you'll rise up on your own? How?"

I lurched back like he'd hit me.

Why was he trying to hurt me? Zayn had never been anything but kind, repairing our sandals when his hands were working right, passing gossip to me about which farmers might need a cheap grain transport. So why the meanness? He'd always been my friend.

"You know I'm right, Kinneret. Think."

Even if I kept scraping together every last bit we didn't spend on food or supplies, I'd never have enough to raise us all up. Thinking of my pitifully empty sash, I rubbed my temples and took a deep breath, my heart shushing with the most dangerous feeling in the world. Hope.

It couldn't be true. In 300 years, someone would've found it. Wouldn't they?

I stared at Zayn's old quill and ink pot and thought about what my old age life might look like. Would I live in a hut with only wishes to keep me company, and dirt for a floor while some other girl wedded my Calev and had brown-eyed babies? My pulse beat in my ears. That feeling, hope, it tugged at my chest and spun a dream into my mind.

Calev and I dancing at a harvest celebration. Avi clapping to the music. In this imagining, my younger sister's skin glowed with health.

I looked at my arms and fingers, chapped and sun-scorched and bony. Hope. Was that all it took to risk looking like a fool, to risk wasting light to run after an old man's fantasy?

I never, ever wanted to see Avi brush the last of her hair with her fingers and come away with a fistful of sunny locks. I ached with all the tears she'd already shed. How could I stand more of them?

Closing my eyes, I whispered, "Say I did believe you. Say I was…up for this madness."

He stood, smiling. "Tell me again why you want it. I must be sure…the risk…maybe you should wait."

My eyes snapped open. I could at least try. If it didn't work out, well, I'd be no worse off.

"What's to wait for?" I was getting carried away by the idea of it now. I almost wanted him to stop me, to clamp a gritty hand over my flapping lips. "More of being kicked around? More of watching Avi starve? Tell me what you know, Zayn, and I'll do what I can for all of us."

I battled the possibilities back and forth inside my brain. A fly buzzed at my face and I swatted it away.

Breathing out his long nose, Zayn clasped his hands behind his back and stared into the pile of maps. "Just remember what you have, Kinneret Raza. Before you go off into the wilds, risking all—"

"I have nothing. I have a future in a boat with holes I can't afford to patch."

"It is decided then," he said.

He ran a finger along a map of the choppy waters I sailed daily. "The wine jug with the map will be somewhere near here. Where the current paints a teardrop on the surface of the water."

My skin went cold. "That's near the slave island."

Most slaves worked at Quarry Isle their entire lives, carving pale stone at night and sleeping a few day hours in a crowded pit they snidely called their Quarters.

Zayn told me they were whipped to bloody shreds when the slavers thought they weren't working hard enough. Food was nothing more than hard bread cakes, mealy and tooth-breaking.

Father told me thirst had hounded his every waking moment there. "My skin was so different then. Like a dried barley stalk," he used to say.

Mother never would talk about it. When I asked her questions, she crossed her arms over her chest and just shook her head.

Thank the Fire, Old Zayn had rescued them from that hell by hiring them before I was born.

"Yes, it isn't far off at all." Zayn's gaze flicked to me. "As I said, there are risks."

"How do you know he meant *that* current? Just because it has the shape of a tear?"

His fingers pressed into my short sleeve. "I don't know. It is a guess. A guess. But I think it's a good one. And you're the only one looking for it now. I have no other family who has heard the tale."

A good guess. I breathed out and turned one of the bells on my sash. "Is there definitely a shipwreck there?"

He shrugged. "I've told you all I know. All I know." He scratched at his scalp.

I put my hand on his, and his cloudy eyes studied me. "If I find it," I said, "I'll give you any part of it you ask for."

Waving his hands, he shook his head. "No. I have a season or so left in me. I don't have the sunlight to weather a change in status now. Not after all these years."

Before I could leave, my skin prickling with excitement and my thoughts whirling, Zayn pulled a coin-sized compass from his sash and handed it to me. The bronze was warm from his body.

"Stop and note your course from time to time." He smiled. The young man he once was peered out between his wrinkles. "You *are* capable of doing this, but remember, it's your choice. You can return if you don't cross too many boundaries. Too many. Too many. After that?" He held out his hands.

"After that, I'll be rich. I'll have all the choices." I went to the door, opened it, and squinted into the white sun.

"I hope so," Old Zayn said to my back as I walked away. "I hope so."

# CHAPTER FIVE

ILVER. LOADS OF IT. MORE than I could picture in a thousand of my low-caste, spit-on, calloused dreams. It would be raw. It could be cursed. But it would be ours.

Heading away from dockside, I padded down the baked dirt road toward Calev's home. Fallow fields of yellowed weeds chittered in the breeze beside stretches of barley. The sun would reign for another five hours. I had to move fast.

At the first of Old Farm's low, stone walls and wide-reaching fields, I eased past two men in calf-length tunics embroidered with lemons. I'd seen them with Calev's father many times. Their noses wrinkled at the bells on my sash and made them ugly.

I grinned at the men, teeth and all. Their Old Farm scorn couldn't touch me. Soon, I'd be wealthy—rich enough to buy a feast for my sister and Old Zayn. And I'd be on my path to becoming a full-ship kaptan, lord of a real ship, its hull heavy with bright lemons, bundles of barley, rainbows of silk.

Old Zayn might be softheaded, but I didn't think so. The details of his tale were too specific to be imagined. I had one life to live, and by the Fire, I was going to take it by the tiller and steer.

Passing through the estate's wooden beam entrance, I touched the ridged surface of the blue-striped *shamar yam* shell nailed to the supports. It held a written prayer, and I hoped some of its magic would soak into me. Maybe Old Farm practices like this had helped them survive the Quest knights' takeover, then the line of kyros since. It certainly couldn't hurt to embrace that kind of power.

At the edge of a shushing barley field, the earth's scent in my nose, I skittered to a halt.

Calev reined in his chestnut horse and waved, tossing his leg over to dismount. The warmth of the ground spread up through my feet and into my legs, stomach, and every inch of me. The harvest sun extended a beam over Calev's obsidian hair. Two workers nodded at their chairman's son. I breathed too quickly, willing my heart not to explode and expose my deepest secret.

I was in love with my best friend.

And he couldn't know until I had the silver to buy my way to high-caste. Only then could he consider me. Only then could I dream of his fingers drifting along my cheeks and his mouth dusting mine. I shivered. I would not make him an Outcast. He'd never be allowed to enter his family's home again.

Beside the fields, Calev spoke to a man and a woman, his voice a lighter rumble than his father's. "...and take the seasoned wood to repair the first storage barn. The cowshed doesn't need it now. Not with this weather."

He held up his hands toward the blue sky and turned his red-brown eyes to me. As the workers hurried to follow his request, he gave me his smile like a First Sun gift, so much better than any spice cake or present wrapped in fine paper.

"Kinneret." He took my hands, and I looked at his. The land lived in bits and pieces under his short nails. I grinned. Such a land lover.

The two men furrowed their brows at our show of caste-free friendship, and after giving Calev a respectful nod, continued on. The elders tolerated our closeness because I once saved Calev's life.

When we were both seven years, accompanying our parents at the bustling dock nearest Old Farm, Calev fell into the water. He couldn't swim—silly Old Farms didn't teach that until the children were ten years. I'd been swimming since I could breathe, so I dropped into the salty sea, grabbed him under the arms and dragged his skinny self to the rope ladder off our boat.

The elders would keep on tolerating us, to a degree, until our Age Day in one moon. On that day, everyone aged one year, and Calev and I would be eighteen. Adults. After that, if we were seen doing anything more than everyday business, we'd be Outcasted.

Calev tightened the deep blue headtie that rested above his eyebrows. The sturdy sandals he liked to wear on my boat stuck out from the bottom of his tunic.

"Could we go on a quick ride before the port-scouting trip?" he asked, running a hand along his horse's nose.

My mind threw out pictures of Calev's lean body in front of mine, sitting in his green tasseled saddle, the barley tugging at my skirt like paupers' fingers and no Berker anywhere in sight. But we didn't have the sun for a ride. I squeezed his strong fingers in mine.

"We need to leave now. And it'll take…" I tapped my lips, thinking. Who knew how long it would take to find the map? Maybe hours, maybe much longer. Zayn's instructions would get me to the spot, but with weather and the possibility of the shipwreck moving over the last hundred or so years…

If I told Calev seven days, he'd say *no*. One, and he might not warn his father of his absence. "Three days. At the most."

He smoothed a hand over his head. "Three? I told the council we'd be at sea just one." Looking over his shoulder at the fields, he grinned. "It's harvest."

"Not yet."

"Almost. And my father—"

"Let your brother handle it."

His brother appeared from behind a painted wagon near the tool shed.

33

"Eleazar," I said, "Calev has something to tell you." I jabbed a thumb at him.

"I do?" Calev asked, laughing.

"You do." I pulled him two steps up the path toward the side of the fork that led to the sea. "Come on," I whispered. "I need you."

From shallow water spearfishing to creeping onto full-ships to climb rigging, he'd always been with me. I didn't need a lucky frog's leg like other sailors. I had Calev ben Y'hoshua, eldest son of the chairman of Old Farm—the most profitable stretch of ground on the amir's sprawling lands. Everything Calev smiled on grew wings and flew on to greatness.

"All right, Kinneret. I'll go. But you might have to take me on as a crewmate when my father throws me out."

"Ugh. An Old Farm a sailor?" A laugh flavored my words. "It takes you way too much sun to get used to the swells." I pretended to be sick, bending and coughing.

With a gentle punch to my shoulder, Calev broke away and clasped his brother's arm in both his hands. "Father knows I'm leaving. It's been approved. I'll just be gone a little longer. Three days at the most."

Eleazar mumbled something and his jaw tensed.

Calev shook his brother's arm. "It'll please our ship's kaptan. You know Kinneret is good at this. Come on."

The side of my mouth jerked up. It was a good lie. Their kaptan, old as the sea itself, knew I was a master at navigating the Pass. He'd never admit it, but when I'd been caught going through his maps during a visit to see Calev, he'd told me I didn't need to spy. That I already knew the best routes.

A frown ran over Eleazar's freckled bottom lip. "I don't know…"

"The weather will change soon," I said, thoughts of silver and food and Calev's mouth swirling through my head. My life could completely change. I grinned, imagining Avi's happy smile. "We need to go. Now."

"Fine," Eleazar said. "I'll tell Father. As usual."

A shadow of guilt crept into my gut, but I pushed it down.

Wearing a butter-colored sash, a girl with the prettiest, darkest eyes walked out from behind the shed. My skin blazed and I swallowed hard. Miriam.

She didn't smile but nodded once to Calev. He straightened his blue and yellow sash and coughed.

The skin over my knuckles burned as I fisted my hands tighter. They'd be married in a year if something didn't change.

Eleazar raised his eyebrows. "Maybe you should tell your Intended about your plans."

Calev closed and opened his eyes, then smiled at her.

I willed my heart to keep beating. That smile. I was the one who'd found that smile first. Not her.

She peered back at him, her chin tilted prettily. *Pretty, pretty, pretty. High-caste, high-caste, high-caste.* My teeth ground together. I looked at the fields, wishing I was a blind woman so I couldn't see her beauty. I was well aware that my smaller, lighter eyes were mere field flowers next to the black roses she blinked at Calev.

I tugged Calev's arm. "We need to go now."

"If it's so pressing, maybe we should enlist my horse." He had a point.

We bid them goodbye and mounted up as I did my best to push, shove, and smash the image of Calev smiling at Miriam out of my mind.

Calev had tried multiple times to talk to me about his father and Miriam and how all that happened, but I made it clear I didn't want to hear about it. The more the situation was mentioned, the more chance of it becoming real. In my mind anyway.

Seated in front of me, Calev kicked the horse with his heels, bumping my feet. "Don't worry about it, Kinneret," he whispered. His breath smelled like lemons. "My father is so busy with harvest preparation, he won't even ask them about me. Not until they need me. Which shouldn't be until five or so days from now, if I'm guessing right."

I looked skyward. He didn't even realize why I was grinding my teeth into nothing. At least Miriam and Calev weren't hennaed yet. The Intention ceremony hadn't yet been performed. I still had a chance. Not much of one. But still.

The horse's hooves ate the ground between Old Farm and the dock. I reveled in the feel of Calev, warm and strong, against my stomach, legs, cheek.

When we'd hopped off, Calev slapped the mare to send her home. She was used to our comings and goings.

"What's this about?" Calev asked. "I'm all for avoiding harvest prep—it's exactly as appealing as a hug from Aunt Y'hudit—but usually I know what kind of adventure you're dragging me into."

Smirking, I eyed the sun. "I'll tell you when we're on our way."

The hill slanted down to the dock where my craft bobbed in the jittery water.

Calev blew out a breath. "Last time you surprised me," he held his groin protectively, "...ugh, those spotted leeches..."

"No leeches, I promise. You'll love this trip."

"That's good," Calev said as our sandals slapped along the dock's wooden boards. "I'd take a bucket of Aunt Y'hudits over those disrespectful creatures."

I threw him a spicy grin. "You didn't lose anything important to the blood-suckers, did you?"

He grinned like a thief. "I'm fully equipped. Don't worry."

I felt like I'd sailed over an enormous swell.

Following me, Calev leaped onto the swaying deck. His feet barely missed the glass Wraith Lantern that would protect us if we didn't make some sort of landfall before sunset. Avi had sewn a new fist-width wick for it yesterday. Her long fingers were perfect for lacing the wool, iron, and pale malhatc fibers in sets of seven and three and five.

As Avi untied us from the dock, I raised the stone anchor. The coconut-fiber rope scratched familiarly against my palms and salt-scented water dripped from its coils.

"Oron is asleep again." Avi pointed to the hull before giving Calev a hug. Her head used to bump the hilt of Calev's curved dagger, but now, she stood high as his shoulder.

After hauling anchor, we lowered the poles into the bay's water and pushed our way into the open water of the twisting strait. Looking at the ridge of rocks and the narrow openings leading to our destination, I grinned.

"I don't like that look, Kinneret." Calev lowered his pole onto the flat planks of the deck, which made a hollow sound because the only thing below was Oron.

I set mine down, and Avi helped me tug the halyard and hoist the gaff to the mast top. Our lateen sail spread like a triangular gull's wing.

"Tell me where we're going," Avi begged, smiling.

I breathed the salt air in, loving the way it pulled at my curls. Directly in front of us, the Pass was empty of other boats. A feeling shivered through me, a tease of a freedom I didn't have. I couldn't use Salt Magic to make silver appear in my palm. But by the Fire, I could sail my way to it. I forced my features into a vicious smile, a scorching grin forged to burn through anyone's doubts, even my own.

"I will tell you. Just not yet," I said.

Calev shook his head. "Let no one say you know nothing about theatrics."

My skirt brushing my ankles, I left Avi and Calev on either sides of the tiller and used the strong *josi* line to force the sail into a tip toward the bow.

With the canvas like a second sky above us, we sailed close reach, at an angle going slightly into the wind. With my eyes trained on the sail and the water beyond, we sped into the Pass. Behind us, the stone wall around Calev's home faded into the distance.

I was finished with the tease. I wanted real hope.

"We're going to change our caste." I released a glance like an arrow at Calev.

The wind lashed a few loose strands of hair against my cheeks as Calev frowned, thinking. The sun glowed through the sail's dark purple fabric, casting a shadow like a bruise. Calev's tanned hand perched on my shoulder and his frown morphed into a grin.

"Are we becoming the pirates we always wished to be? If so, you probably should've brought a few more weapons. Maybe a monkey. I always wanted a monkey."

Avi laughed and chewed her braid. Fifteen was too old for hair-chewing, but I wasn't going to talk her out of any childlike habits. She could do as she liked as long as it made her happy in this harsh world.

Oron crawled out of the hull. "Flying Seastingers, people. Must you squawk like birds? What do you have against a man taking a well-deserved nap?"

Calev fought a smile and ran a sun-browned hand over Avi's hair. "Well-deserved, Oron? Don't tell me you've been sneaking around doing kind things for the masses?"

Oron grabbed for a skin of wine at his sash. As a dwarf, and three hands shorter than Avi, Oron had to look up into Calev's face. "There are more ways than one to deserve a nap." He took a hefty swallow of his stolen beverage. "Kindness to others is one, yes. But you must also consider the pursuit of a pleasant life as a valid goal. Don't you agree?"

"We have big things to discuss, Oron," I snapped. "Perhaps naps should wait for nightfall." I gave him half a grin.

"Sorry, my dear. But night is reserved for actual sleeping."

"Why I put up with you is the world's greatest mystery."

"Here I thought the mystery was whatever you all were discussing so very, very loudly." Oron plucked what appeared to be a rumpled golden dumpling from his sash and handed it to Avi. I wondered who he'd stolen that from.

Oron gave me a look that reeked of suspicion. "What was this about monkeys and pirates? If you're planning a celebration with said folk, I'm in."

"It's us who are the pirates, she says." Avi grinned.

I shook my head. "Not pirates. We're treasure hunters." That wasn't quite right either. "No, not hunters, really. We won't need to hunt. I *know* the way. We're going to retrieve a map to the lost island of silver."

Calev and Avi's mouths fell open, and Oron simply stared.

I nudged Calev aside to take my place at the tiller. "Ayarazi exists, and we are going to be the ones to claim it."

# CHAPTER SIX

ORON'S WIDE BROW FURROWED. HE rammed a thick finger into his ear and jiggled it. "Did I hear her correctly?" He looked from me to Calev.

"Old Zayn told me where to find a map to Ayarazi."

Oron blinked. "When will I learn that a day with Kinneret Raza is never dull?"

The wind lagged, then gusted. The sail snapped grouchily as we rose over a swell and dipped down again.

Oron hurried to adjust the sail, his skilled hands moving faster and more sure on the line than anyone I'd ever seen on the water. When he'd first come to work for me, right after the fever took Mother and Father, I'd known he was a special person because who would offer to work for basically nothing? Only the kindest of souls. I almost felt like he'd adopted Avi and me. I hadn't known then how amazing he was with the sails. I sure as Fire knew now and I'd never let him go.

Calev clutched the boat's side, his knuckles whitening. "What are you talking about?" He was a little green around the lips.

I gave him the tiller and brought him my skin of ginger water. "The lost island of silver."

"But that's not a real place." Avi's throat bobbed as she looked down the road of water at the rocks like broken-down carts. The biggest of the obstacles were Tall Man and the Spires.

"I heard it is," I said.

Calev took a swig from my water skin. "From who?"

"Zayn."

Calev grinned. "So the kind, but seriously very crazy old man realized how much you'd adore a chance of riches with a side of possible death and/or mutilation and offered this information."

Oron tipped his head. "Nicely put. Only brushes with Death himself satiate our Kinneret here."

I shrugged them off. "It's not all that risky."

Calev squinted at the sun and held out the water skin to me. "At least this insane adventure is happening during the day."

Avi shook her head, all cynicism and muttering. "It's still dangerous." She eyed the upcoming black shapes jutting from the sea.

"We never come close to hitting those rocks, Avi," I said.

"Your idea of close is oceans away from mine," she hissed as I took the tiller to navigate.

As we dodged Tall Man, the boat's lee side heeled a bit more than I liked. I pulled the tiller windward, balancing her out.

"Even if it was night, Calev," I said, "we have the lantern's magic."

The domed and vented object sat behind me, lodged in a space between the tiller's housing and the side. I ran an absent hand over its glass surface. Father had made the lantern from a high-caste's discarded vase, and Mother had taught us how to weave the special wick. For as long as I'd been alive, the combination of the two had kept us safe from the Salt Wraiths, the evil spirits of those who'd died at sea.

"Lanterns aren't magic," Calev argued. "They're science. It's proven their light repels the wraiths. But repelling isn't always enough. Wraiths can be smart."

I ignored his all-too-common, close-minded view on the line between religion, magic, and science. To me, they were just different words for the same thing.

"Mother wouldn't have let this opportunity go by," I whispered, more to myself than to them. Berker's ridiculous slur about her being a liar wafted around like a bad smell.

Avi's steady gaze flicked to me. Her eyes were focused like she was about to pounce and rip my throat out. Mother and Father had always called it her lion look. She might not have been so good with Salt Magic, but my sister had her strengths. Determination being one of them.

"But we don't need an island of silver," she said.

"Speak for yourselves, dear friends," Oron said. "I need all the silver to do all the joyous things." He spun in a circle, jumping once and wiggling his backside.

Calev jerked his chin. "I'm with Avi. You don't need riches. Kinneret, someday you'll be the most successful small craft sailor on the Broken Coast."

If I didn't starve first. "Yeah. A successful ant in a field of horses," I muttered. "You don't know what it's like to have people push in front of you. To be refused service at the market because of bells."

To watch the boy you love be promised to a girl only because of her caste.

Maybe Miriam would be eaten by wolves on her northern trade trip with her father.

Calev frowned and glanced at Avi. I let the matter drop and smiled at the thought of Miriam running from very hairy, very toothy beasts.

To lessen our speed, we worked the halyard's pulleys and lowered the spar holding the sail aloft. After a good bit of tiller work and a few prods to the rocks with our poles, we made it through the Spires. Water splashed over the deck and wet our feet as I watched for the next obstacle—Asag's Door, a powerful eddy that had definitely earned its spirit-monster name. Another scattering of barely visible rocks sat at its end.

Not a league ahead, a sweep of lighter water showed where the door's current swept southward.

"The map lies near Quarry Isle." My voice came out louder than I'd wanted. "It's under a teardrop-shaped current."

Oron faced me, frowning, then looked around the boat, like he was searching for something. I rolled my eyes skyward at his drama.

"Where is your note of permission to pass from the oramiral?" he asked, blinking his big eyes.

The oramiral was the kyros's second cousin and totally and completely mad. The kyros let him reign over Quarry Isle and forced our amir to put up with the way he treated the slaves she took in wars with borderlands. It was a kink in the caste system, to be sure. Slavery was meant to prove mettle, not destroy the body and mind. It was an honor to have served. Only pure bloodlines of the desert race and the respected Old Farms were permitted to thrive outside the system.

"Did the amir herself give you leave?" Oron demanded. "Or perhaps, her new kaptan, Berker?"

"You heard about that?"

"When I'm not languishing in the arms of Lady Grape, I get around." He tweaked his ears with his fingertips. "These are not merely fantastic ornaments on my gruesome head."

My gaze traced the familiar lines around his mouth and the tilt of his eyes. I remembered, four years ago, when those eyes noticed the gaff break from the mast. He'd caught most of the sail and its support before it could land on Avi's small frame. He was the reason she could still walk.

"You aren't ugly," I said to Oron.

"Definitely not," Avi said.

"Not the point of this discussion, my dears."

Calev smiled. "Oron, your face is nothing less than legendary."

I glared at Calev.

"Don't aim those vicious eyes at him." Oron grinned.

"I didn't intend it as an insult," Calev said.

"Of course not," Oron said. "I like *legendary*. Makes me feel as if I really do belong on a boat with a madwoman who insists on sailing to an island born from the dreams of sailors."

The ancient wine jug was there, hidden under the water. I could feel it in the salt hiding under my nails and flaking from my cheeks.

"So we're simply going to sail right up under the oramiral's nose to the spot near the slave island where the goat man indicated and snatch some map?" Oron asked.

Avi made her way to my side, her eyes searching mine.

"It shouldn't be in the oramiral's waters," I said.

"A teardrop current?" Oron scratched at his tangled hair. "I know the place. It's dangerously close to his disgusting Quarry Isle. I'd argue it's past the boundary."

I always stayed well away from that section of the Pass. There were plenty of ways to ship goods and passengers from our lands, across the waters, and back again without nearing Quarry Isle.

"It'll be fine, Oron. We won't cross the boundary."

"But if you're wrong, and we do, he might not honor your bells. Or the fact that you're my employer. In fact, he'll surely nab me since I have no bells at all and am pretty obviously not Old Farm or of the desert race." He displayed a pale arm with a flourish.

"I said it's fine. We're staying in the free waters. No one will become a slave today."

Oron huffed and held his hands to the Fire. "As Kinneret wills, so shall the world move."

Avi chewed at the end of her braid, her eyes worried. She had to keep her nerve. I had to make this move.

Calev tapped his chin. "Avi, it'll be a few until we get there. Want to play?" He held up his hand and wiggled his fingers.

I mouthed a *thank you* as they began playing tally win. They waved hands over their laps and stopped at a count of ten. Calev displayed seven fingers, Avi two.

If I didn't change Avi's caste, along with mine, she'd lose Calev and it'd be like losing a brother. As he smiled at her, I knew he felt the same way about her. She was the sister he didn't have at home.

"Ah ha." Avi clapped once, but her eyes stayed tight, her lips pinched in worry. She pointed at Calev's fingers. "That's nine. Odd. My choice. You owe me a lemon slice."

"After all our suns playing games, I owe you lemons enough to fill the Pass," Calev said.

Avi worked at a laugh. "If we find the island of silver, I'll build a castle for my fruit. Everyday you can visit and play tally win and drink lemon honey wine."

"Paradise," Calev, Oron, and I said in unison.

Avi smiled, enjoying our ongoing joke. She came up with wild imaginings and we judged them either hells or paradises.

"A pirate ship filled with monkeys," she said.

"Hells," we responded.

"A silver gilt pirate ship only slightly crowded with tiny monkeys who smell like flowers and obey our every command."

"Paradise!"

Oron looked to his sandals, smiling, and adjusted the josi line so the sail captured more wind. Avi went to help or really, it seemed, just to lean a little on Oron. He patted her arm, then squeezed it gently, and the shadows around his eyes deepened.

I kept my hand on the worn wood of the tiller, willing everyone to stay positive.

Eyeing the direction we headed, Calev brought his knees to his chin. His sandals, hidden beneath the drape of his tunic, ground salt and dirt into the decking as he fidgeted.

"The men on the slave island would've already found underwater clues to Ayarazi if there were any," he said quietly. "The oramiral used a hundred of his prisoners to scour the sea floor when they first sent him down."

From what I'd heard of the man who ran the quarries, he wore his honorary military title *oramiral* with a killing sneer. What had he done for the kyros to garner that cushy post?

"I don't think the oramiral knew what he was looking for." And I did.

Frowning, Calev turned toward me, then rubbed at his stomach and swallowed.

*Poor thing.* The Lord of the Harvest humbled. "We're looking for a wine jug." I dragged my gaze from the angle of his sharp chin and back to the sea.

From the front of the boat, Avi held a hand up to block the sun gliding over the green waves and soaking the air.

A spray of water soared over us. "It holds a map."

"Who knew a wine jug could be put to even better use than its original purpose? Color me impressed." Oron's words were as sour as those lemons Calev owed Avi.

"Kinneret!" Calev jumped up. "The rocks!"

I growled and jerked the tiller, bumping him back and out of my way.

The rocks churned the water, whitening it to the color of a wraith's shadow. I'd missed my mark, and we needed to reverse course and go around Asag's Door the other way. The tiller fought me.

"Avi, ready to jib!"

When Avi, Oron, and I had hands on the sheet's lines, and Calev was at the tiller again, I kicked the knot holding the sheet in place. It slipped from its wooden knob and the sheet ran through our hands. The sail whipped up.

"Pull the tiller to starboard," I commanded Calev.

"But won't that—"

"Do it."

He did, and when the sail's tip flashed over the spar, we tugged the sheet and brought the sail into place. The pouch at my belt was heavy with salt. If this didn't work, I had options. Magical ones. I didn't want to use Salt Magic around Calev, but if worse came to worse...

We made it around the eddy and its rocks. Avi tugged her sash back into place and her bells jingled.

Calev sucked a breath. "That was...exciting."

"Please don't vomit," Oron said, edging a step away. "High-caste food stains."

I squeezed the tiller, wishing Oron had a much, much smaller mouth.

A ship appeared, and unfortunately, it didn't look like it was harmlessly toting lemons and wine.

"Did we pass the mark?" Oron's voice was wary.

Beyond Oron's head, sails the hue of sickness rose like the wings of an ancient flying lizard. The craft moved at a speed I'd never know unless I found Ayarazi and its silver.

Avi rushed over and handed me the spyglass. Through the tube, I saw a tall man at the prow. His yellow tunic billowed over his broad shoulders. I went cold all over. Was it the oramiral? He was rumored to be as handsome as he was cruel. His closest men were supposedly chosen for their height, so maybe it was only them and not their master.

"They're only running to the coast. They're not interested in us." My pulse ratcheted up.

Oron's song went slow and quiet. Calev put a hand on Avi's back in a brotherly way.

I adjusted our course, watching my sail and those of the oramiral's boat.

Calev pulled his dagger from the silver sheath hanging from his green sash.

*No.* Today was a lucky day. I had Calev. "It's not necessary," I said.

The dagger wasn't bigger than my hand and its hilt and sharp edge were decorated in intricate calligraphy. This was a piece of jewelry, not a weapon. Old Farms were known for their skills with daggers, but it was about ceremony, not killing. Calev was an innocent. And by the Fire, today would not be the day he saw blood.

"They only want to know why we're here," I said.

Avi trembled against me. "Shouldn't we try to sail away from them?"

"We couldn't outrun them on my best day, Sister." I wiggled the bells on her sash, then shook the ones on my own red one. "We remember so they remember."

It was the old line. If one's family had served, one should not have to serve again. It was respectful to have been a slave, then rise to middle or high-caste. Falling into slavery again was seen as a complete and total failure. A failure to rise, to survive, to swim strong in life on the Broken Coast.

Was there any chance the oramiral would hold to the old line?

Closing his eyes, Calev inhaled, his chest rising and falling. Oron pinched his lips together.

What would Father or Mother have done? I ran a finger over the sickle-shaped scar on my forearm—all that was left from the fever blisters that made my sister and I ill, but stole life from my parents.

A spot two fingers past our view of the oramiral's ship undulated with an odd current. "There it is."

Was the oramiral's ship getting closer? Or were they turning her?

Something stung my ear and I touched my lobe. My fingers came away bloody. An arrow.

"They fired on us!"

The arrow had missed me, going into the sea.

Oron swore and everyone ducked low.

"It was just a warning shot," I said.

Everything was going to be fine. It had to be. My blood shushed through my veins.

Oron grabbed the lucky frog's leg hanging from the cord at his neck as the oramiral's ship leaped over the waves, coming at us now with frightening speed. The sails arched into the sky, impossibly big, dangerously close.

Calev urged Avi toward the hull. Her braid trailed her like a lit fuse and Oron disappeared behind her into the darkness.

"I'll tell him who I am. They won't make trouble with me." Calev's firm hold on the dagger turned his farmer's fingers into a soldier's hand. But he was no fighter. It was all a ruse. A rich boy playacting.

"I'll tell him we're on a fishing day trip," he said. "You go below, too."

"I'm not hiding. Besides, if I can see him, he can see me." I tied the tiller off and tugged my blade from my sash. The beads of steel on the hilt gripped me back. "Drop sail. I'm not leaving without my map. You're right. They'll listen to you. And I'm not leaving."

Calev's wide sleeves fell back as he hauled the sail in, showing his lean muscular arms, browned from working outside. "You don't really want to argue about boundaries with the oramiral's men. They're—"

"Lay down your weapons, trespassers," a voice boomed from a speaking cylinder.

The owner of the voice hung from the oramiral's sails like a long, slim monkey. He flipped and landed next to his mates, most of whom wore the same slave bell contraption as he did. Metal circle around the waist of his tunic and his chest. Bar attached at the back, reaching past the head where the noisemaker clanked with every move. The slaves, dressed in fine, yellow silk, like the monkey-faced leader, drew back crossbows. The more ragged slaves, in gray tunics, nocked arrows. Together they formed a wall of flashing metal, wood, feather, and muscle, the one with the speaking cylinder in the middle.

With eyes like scorched wood, Calev raised his dagger, his arm brushing mine. He was beautiful, even in his terror. His gaze jerked from slave to slave, but his hands were steady. One strand of hair hung over his finely shaped lips.

I put my hand on his arm and lowered his weapon. "Just talk to them."

He squeezed his eyes closed and nodded. Avi sneezed from the hull and Calev took my hand.

"Bring them aboard," the leader said.

The biggest men of the bunch threw grappling hooks. My heart snagged on a beat. I ran at the flying links, as if I could somehow stop this. The hooks dug into the side of my boat like Kurakian fanged snakes. The slaves tugged the attached ropes and Calev grabbed me as our boat surged toward the full ship.

"I'm Old Farm!" Calev pushed himself between me and the three men leaping onto the deck. "My father is the—"

A slave threw an arm toward Calev's head, but Calev stopped the blow with his forearm, surprising me with his speed and power.

Avi screamed. When had she come back up? The wind gusted, and the sad piece of twine at the end of her braid tumbled into the waves.

"Get back down there!" I pushed her toward Oron's pale face. He stood at the hull's small opening.

"Too late." The second man grinned, standing on the starboard, then hopped down, grabbed Avi by the arms, and dragged her toward the side.

I tore at her, trying to get a hold. "Didn't you hear him? He's Old Farm! You can't treat him like this! The chairman is his father, associate to Amir Mamluk of Jakobden, and he'll—"

The slave kicked me in the stomach. The strike stole my breath, and I fell into Calev and Oron, who struggled with the other two slaves.

The slave threw Avi to his crew mates on the oramiral's ship. "We're not doing anything to the Old Farm, as long as he doesn't get in the way," the slave said. "We're just taking this one to punish you for crossing into forbidden waters. You're lucky we're not coloring the sea with your blood and hers, girl." He spat.

Dodging the spittle, I scrambled to my feet. My stomach clenched, heaved. "We're not in your master's territory. These are free waters!"

From the side of the boat, he reached down and grabbed hold of my hair. Fire lashed from my scalp and down my neck. He threw me back and my elbow cracked against the mast, shooting sparks up my arm.

He and his crew mates rushed to their ship, tugging the hooks free on their way.

"I won't let you do this!" Sweat bled down my cheeks. "That girl's family already served. She has the bells to prove it!" My voice was snake and storm and desert and it wasn't nearly enough.

"You'll regret this," Calev hissed, his face carved into angry lines and ferocious shadows. "The oramiral will never sell another piece of stone in Jakobden."

But they didn't care.

The ship roared away.

With scratched and bleeding hands, I clutched my rolling stomach, tore at my hair.

I had to be asleep. This could not be reality.

A small canon shot boomed, and after a puff of black smoke, the snarl of ripping fabric filled my ears. I stood, my ribs like firebrands and my head a pincushion. In the middle of the sail, a circle of sunset sky marred the deep purple. Threads danced from the hole like flames.

"Come back again," the slave's voice spun through the air, "and we'll take the lot of you. Best of luck with the Salt Wraiths!"

I fell to my knees beside Oron and Calev, who stood at the mast, fear etched into the way they held themselves, the way they didn't breathe, the way they looked at the ruined sail.

Night was coming. We had no sail. And my Avi, my sweet sister, was gone.

# CHAPTER SEVEN

W E'LL GO TO MY FATHER. He and the others will rescue Avigail." Calev stared into my eyes. His hands lifted like he might try to hold me, but he dropped them.

Y'hoshua ben Aharon might help. Maybe because I'd saved Calev's life when we were little. Maybe because I had a little Old Farm in me. Maybe because he didn't treat me like he did other low-castes. Maybe maybe maybe.

I stood dumbly, shaking and trying not to scream.

A memory of Mother teaching Avi to weave the wraith wick flickered in my mind. Mother's hand reached across the tiller to help my sister add another row of iron-laced threading. We'd bought the stuff after a trip to Kurakia, where Mother's sister, Aunt Kania Turay, lived.

Visiting her tower house and farm felt like walking on my hands. The sea hardly played a role in her days. I could never live as a Kurakian. I'd pulled at the neck of my shirt, feeling choked just thinking about a life without the sea.

"Keep the sevens of the outer part heavy on the iron," Mother had said.

Avi chewed her tongue as she worked the fibers into a neat braid.

"You're good at this," I said.

She smiled up at me and the sunrise glowed across her baby-fine skin. "I'm going to show Calev. You should do your magic for him."

Mother's eyes pinched a little at the sides. Then her face cleared. She touched my hand and Avi's. "You both have talents that will serve you." A spark glittered in her eye as she walked with me to the low-sided sea salt tray she'd left out on the dock beside our tied-down boat. She scooped a handful into the pouch at her sash. I did the same.

"Today, as all the women of our blood have done," she said, "you will learn to call the sea's wind."

I shivered like someone had dusted me with the waterflakes Calev told me fell from the sky in the North.

Father arrived and helped a man load our hull with lemons, and we set sail.

Leaning against port, Mother dipped elegant fingers into her salt pouch and they emerged sparkling white, a contrast to her warm, dark skin. The wind kicked its feet and helped the sea take some of its lifeblood back, the salt dancing up and out into the waves.

"I think the sea's wind is already here," I said.

"Ah, but it is up to you to ask it for a favor. Not easy when the sea is full of spirit. Now you will say this prayer—"

I took my own handful of salt and let the salt drift away. "Hear me, sea. Feel my will. Bend the wind so we may reach another land."

The deck swooped under my feet and Mother and I grabbed the side. Avi squealed and ran to Mother's side as Father shouted from the tiller.

"Kinneret Raza! Take care with your prayers!"

The water licked at the boat like a thirsty dog and the air wheeled us around so that the sail pressed against the mast in a foul, aback position.

After we'd worked into a good tack again, Mother took my salt-rough hands in hers.

"You have great magic in you, daughter. Respect it. Learn first. Then it will be a help instead of a hindrance."

"But you like trouble."

"There is a difference between trouble and danger." She smiled sadly and turned away. "I suppose you'll have to learn that for yourself."

The memory dissolved.

The horror of *now* clawed its way through me. I gripped my skirt in shaking hands.

"It isn't getting any brighter out here." Oron's voice was barely a whisper above the water lapping and the clink of metal trappings.

He was being foolish to keep my mind off Avi. I looked at him, wanting to see that unmovable strength Oron's eyes usually housed, but tears wet his eyelashes.

Calev shut his eyes, took a breath, then opened them. Fear and determination swirled in their walnut depths. "We'll get her back, Kinneret."

I swallowed and stood on weak-kneed legs. "She won't survive long enough to participate in the testing for the apprenticeships. She's so frail. I never thought…I should've…I need to make a plan. Gather allies. Something."

The purpling sky told me we didn't have the sun to properly repair the sail. I went straight for the salt in my bag, hating what I knew Calev would think of it.

He stopped me with a hand, his gaze sliding to the salt. "Can't we just fix the hole?"

I gave him a look. "We'll sew it up as best we can. We'll use the Wraith Lantern when the sun falls. But we'll need the magic. Or we'll be out here all night. And I don't think you want that."

Calev grimaced. Though Old Farms weren't in charge of Outcasting anyone, they didn't like Salt Magic anymore than the rest of Jakobden. Called it low and uneducated superstition. But Calev wasn't just any Old Farm. He was more.

I studied his face for clues. "You had to know I use the salt."

He eyed the sky and swallowed. "I did, but I hoped it was only that once."

"At the cape during the storm?"

His dark eyes were honest, his mouth a frown. "Use what you need to, Kinneret."

"It's no different from your prayers." I was pushing him, but it had to be done.

"Is that really how you see it?" His voice was gentle, earnest.

My eyes burned, but I willed those tears back inside my lids. If I cried now, I wouldn't stop and I'd be pointless to everyone.

Calev swallowed. "It's forcing your will. Our prayers show respect, use the proper language. We don't demand immediate displays of power like Salt Magic does. Even the Holy Fire is more humble than the salt. They at least wait for wisdom. There are no demands or heavy requests."

"It is the same...I..." I stuttered, my eyes swimming. "Calev. This is the skill my mother taught me. She used to cup my hands in hers and I remember watching her lips move in and around words and smiles. When I use the magic, it's like she's here again, holding my hand, her voice in my ear." Touching the raised embroidery on his sleeve, I blinked and blinked again, swallowing. "You have to agree—I need this now." I didn't know why I wanted him to be okay with this. But somehow, it seemed important that he was behind me.

He gave me a sad smile and put his fingers over mine. They stilled my shaking a little. "I'll try to understand," he said. "For you."

"That's all I ask."

Oron was already lowering the damaged sail.

Boards set loosely in place around the tiller gave us a place to sit out of the uneven and oftentimes damp bottom of the boat. I drew out a box of sewing supplies from under the wooden planks.

I'd call the sea and persuade it to move us the way we needed to go, get Calev and Oron safely to shore, then let my tears come, my rage overtake me, and my fear for Avi strip me to bare bones.

Shoving those thoughts to the back of my mind, I kept my hands busy by threading the stout bone needle.

Using a strip of extra cloth, we sewed the hole closed as best we could, fingers working against the setting sun. When the moon did come, it hung low in the sky like an old man's cloudy eye. When the cloud swam away from the orb, the brightness scattered gooseflesh over my arms. If a Salt Wraith came now, we would be trapped in its shadow, Infused, our minds twisted to lust for blood and death.

Helping Oron and Calev hoist the gaff and position the sail for beam reach, I stared into the darkening waters and pictured Avi's fingers wrapped around a quarry pick.

"Kinneret." Calev shook my shoulder, and I blinked. "We must go," he said. "How can I help?" His voice broke on his last word and he swallowed, his throat moving.

I realized I was standing there like a fool. Sucking a breath, I pointed at the bow. "Keep watch for rocks. Call out if you see anything." I didn't want to say *wraiths*.

Oron took the tiller. "I'll keep her even." His quiet voice chilled me. He didn't sound like himself at all.

"Thank you." I joined Calev at the bow.

The wind was nonexistent. We were becalmed. I forced a breath out of my nose. We'd never rescue Avi if the oramiral's men caught us or if we killed one another under a wraith's control.

The salt from my pouch was dry. Dry worked, but not as well as salt touched by fresh sea water. Blinking a strand of hair from my eyes, I bent, scooped a handful of cold water, and dashed it into the small bag. Sprinkling a fistful of the dampened salt into the wind—more than I'd ever used—I cooed a sea prayer.

*"Accept this gift, bold sea,*
*Breathe life into our sail,*
*Draw your currents near."*

Was there a limit on the sea's patience?

Maybe not.

The air, raised by the Salt Magic, shushed gently past my face, and the boat lurched forward. Calev slipped, and I caught him, hearing a thud from the tiller.

Oron had rolled off to one side. He swore as he righted himself. "My mother's third—"

"Where did you learn to talk like you do?" Calev's knuckles whitened on the boat's side, but I didn't think it was from Oron's foul mouth. His chin lifted as he scanned the thankfully empty night sky.

"Watch our lean, Oron," I said. We were heeling to leeward. A little more and we'd be thrown into the water.

"I was raised in a roadside brothel by a mother who fancied traveling theatre players," Oron said to Calev, his words whipping toward us as the wind rose even higher, and we sped forward. "I speak the tongue of the wicked and witty."

To keep our conversation off what had happened, to keep myself from jerking the tiller from Oron and turning us back and raging toward the oramiral to battle for my sister and lose, I picked up the distracting thread of talk.

"Surprised you never heard that one," I said to Calev. "It's his favorite line."

Moonlight slipped over Calev's hair. It rolled down his skull and sat on his broad farmer's shoulders like a death shroud. I tightened my sash's knot and pulled my sleeves lower on my arms.

"I'll take the tiller now." I moved to aft.

Asag's Door was quieter, though white caps still curled around the bases of the rocks. With the gusts and Oron at the sail, I pulled the tiller and guided us through the Spires. It was low tide now. The boat responded to me, shifting under my body like a horse. The sea had listened and sent us wind and soon we'd be home. If the Salt Wraiths let us be.

Calev came to the tiller with me and Oron moved to watch at the bow.

Calev tried to laugh. "Oron and I haven't have the opportunity to talk as much as I would like."

This was ridiculous, us trying to be brave and making jokes. Black shadows and streaks of moonlight used my imagination to turn the water and rocks into a slithering beast waiting for us to make one wrong move.

"He has the best foul language. I could pick up some tantalizing bits from him to shock Eleazar," Calev said.

I tried to smile, but all I could think was right now Avi was being led up the steep side of Quarry Isle. They would fit a bell contraption around her waist.

How were we going to persuade Calev's father to use his influence to get her back? Old Farm had never interfered with the oramiral. At least to my knowledge. It hadn't come up. Being people of the land, all Old Farms, except their full ship kaptan, stayed clear of the sea. Similar to my aunt's people in Kurakia, across the Pass.

*Avi. My brave little Avi. How are we going to rescue you?*

A grin trembled on Calev's lips but fled when Oron made a choking noise near the mast. We jumped up.

"They're here." Oron pointed to the western sky.

All the blood in my head drained into my feet. Salt Wraiths.

I whipped my flint and dagger out of my sash. We had to get the lantern lit. Now.

Calev held the Wraith Lantern's miniature door open. My flint sparked onto the wick, but it didn't flame.

A swooping noise like a tree limb swinging through the air stung my ears. The sparkling white of one Salt Wraith whisked between the moon and us, but far enough away that we could barely see it. Its soul-and-mind-possessing shadow didn't touch us, but it soared closer. I dragged the flint over the dagger again. The wick caught fire and blazed bright. Calev slammed the opening shut to keep the wind from putting out the strange flame.

Seeing the orange, black, and silver flickers, the wraith reared and disappeared in the distance.

Hanging the lantern on the mast's hook, Calev sighed. "That was too close."

"It might come back." As I made my way back to the tiller, I studied the fire encased in the glass. A flash of silver rose and fell, then a glint of orange.

"We need to squeeze into the hull." Feet first, Oron lowered himself through the square opening.

"We won't all fit in there." I raised my gaze to the sky.

"I told you we needed an on-deck compartment for ropes and water," Oron called out of the space. "If you'd let me buy the wood to build one, you could've tucked me in there. Being lesser in stature might be an advantage. Who knows? In one hundred years, we small people might be the only ones left."

A look dark as the Expanse's greatest depths crossed over Calev's face. "Let Kinneret in there first, coward."

I looked at Calev's hands as he stood beside me. "You're trembling too," I said. "I wouldn't cast labels around so easily."

"Courage isn't not being afraid," Calev said. "It's standing and fighting through your fear. Protecting those you love." His eyes softened. "Not that I have to tell you."

My heart skittered through three quick beats, and I looked away.

"I'll go down if I think it's necessary," I called out to Oron. "Someone has to get us home."

Whispering the sea's words over and over again under my breath, I worked with the magic to veer and tug, push and pull our craft toward Tall Man, toward home. Calev stayed by my side. The lantern's sunset light flickered over his cheekbones and his forearms. He looked made of flame.

Stars pierced the velvet sky. The moon watched, its candle-white glow melting onto the sea. Eventually, Oron climbed out of the hull. Calev stared at him, eyes slitted.

"Oron, will you see to the prow?" I asked. The tiller vibrated against my hand, a current fighting our direction. "I want your eyes on the waters."

Rubbing his small hands together, Oron nodded but didn't exactly hurry to his post.

"In case you decide to condemn me for cowardice, you should know I witnessed a wraith Infusing an entire full ship's crew," Oron said to Calev. "And yes, I can feel that scornful glare through the tunic on my back."

"What happened?" Calev asked.

The sail billowed in a gust and the ropes pulled against the blocks. The pulleys knocked against the mast like hammers.

Staring out at the sky, Oron crossed his arms over his chest. "A flock of nine came."

"Nine wraiths?"

Nodding, Oron said, "They spun around the vessel like the skin of the moon had been peeled away and tossed into the wind. The emotions whisked over me though I was a good league away on another boat. Rage, the desire to inflict control...it was..." He bent his head. "When the wraiths left, I watched their Infusion lights leave the sailors' mouths and leak back into the sky. We boarded their ship—I rode with a fishing crew then—there was nothing left alive. Men had hung themselves from the boom, their bodies swaying with the movement of the sea, their tongues swollen, eyes popped clean out. Blood covered the decking. I slipped in it. Drew up against a pile of men who'd either fallen on their own yatagans or been murdered by their Infused crew mates."

He ran a hand over the fat tangles of his hair.

"So when I go to the hull, you'd be wise to follow. We should all squeeze in there like happy sardines."

The whooshing sound returned.

Calev looked to me. Oron swore.

Another wraith.

The whispering began. Hissing, sighing, moaning in my ears.

I covered my head with my hands and the remainder of the salt I'd used rained onto my face and hair.

Oron was already back in the cabin. Calev grabbed my arm and dragged me toward the tiny space. We'd never fit. Besides, someone had to make sure the lantern didn't fall over or go out. If it did, the wraiths would swamp us and cover us in their whitewashed shadows—their way of possessing mind and body—and it'd all be over. We either had to be under the shadow of a solid roof in the hull or swamped in the Wraith Lantern's light.

I snatched the lantern and crawled into the hull behind Calev. Turning, he pulled my back against his stomach and wrapped his arm around me to help me hold the lantern up. His fingers lay on mine, his hips pressing into me. Both of us were shaking against one another as the sounds increased. Oron had to be suffocating behind us. The air was hot and moist with our breath. Our feet stirred up the pungent scent of old lemons and last year's barley, remnants of the shipments we'd made over our lifetimes.

We lifted the lantern as the wraith came screaming toward us. The light spun a web of colors over my forearms, but this creature was strong and some of its power crept under and over the flickering orange and silver. Emotions flooded my mind, rushing in like boiling waves, filling in every crack of my thoughts, my heart.

# CHAPTER EIGHT

I TRIED TO SCREAM AS Calev's hand fell from the lantern. He yelled, but it sounded far, far away.

*Anger. So much anger, burning, burning, burning in my veins, my hands, my head. Wild sadness.*

Then I was falling, and the sea was a gaping hole beneath us. A mouth. A well. An abyss, far under the earth's crust.

We would fall forever.

My hands slipped and moonlight darted into our hiding place, breaking the nightmare hallucination. I jerked the lantern up again, my fingers burning as I squeezed.

"Kinneret!" Oron shouted and moaned.

*Seething, swirling, my hands are not my own.*

I bit down on my lip, bringing blood to wake myself. *I will not be Infused. Their shadow isn't touching flesh. I'm fine. I'm fine.*

Calev's hands found my sides, shaking but firm. I closed my eyes, soaking in his warmth like it would save me. His body pressed against mine. Every bump and curve and bone and breath of him kept my heart beating, held my mind in check.

"Come closer," he said through gritted teeth.

The wraith screamed.

His body jolted.

63

"We can move back farther…" He breathed the words along my neck, making me shiver.

Another wave of blood lust washed over me. My breath hitched. I could not cry. If I fell apart now, we'd be lost. They didn't know how to use the salt. We were still too far from shore for swimming. And the currents would take us to the Expanse. There'd be no coming back.

I whispered the sea's words again, chanting them into the rise and fall of the wraith's emotions. The boat surged, close to the wind, the sea answering me, the Fire helping me.

It wasn't working. All I could see was blood. Hate roared in my ears.

Then it eased, cooled, lessened, and I could breathe again.

The sweeping sounds receded. The anger drew away.

The wraiths were leaving.

I collapsed, leaning out of the hull's opening. Calev helped me the rest of the way free and pulled me to standing. His tunic smelled like sun-warmed earth and crushed lemon leaves. I buried my face in his neck, wishing he would always be my safety, my place to come home to, instead of becoming that Old Farm girl's Intended.

"Near death experiences do lend themselves to salacious behavior, but do you mind waiting until we reach the shore?" Oron found his feet and dusted himself off. "Unlike my dear old mother, I'm not open with all things love. I rather like to be included when such activities are afoot." He peeked around Calev's arm, his brows raised. He took my hand in his, kissed it kindly, and pressed it to his forehead. "You were so close to it and still you didn't succumb. I'm not half the man you are, Kinneret."

"That's the truth," Calev said quietly.

My heart grew a little at their praise. But Avi's face flashed through my mind. I wasn't half the woman she'd someday be. I would rescue her. Doubt wasn't even in the same universe as me.

A sapphire cloud smothered the moon, promising rain and a veil of protection from the wraiths' infusing shadows. The mainsail had come loose and it flickered like a serpent's tongue, but with a bit more magic and a few more prayers, we sailed into Amir Mamluk's most southern port on the Broken Coast.

We were home.

The boat bumped the docking and Oron tied us down with Calev's help.

"I'll go to the amir. I've brought some of her surplus across the Pass, and a few passengers. Plus my low prices bring all the kaptans' charges down. Well, once in a while. People like Avi and me are good for Jakobden. Right?" I pressed a hand against my pounding temple. "I'm lying to myself, aren't I? Why would an amir care about us?"

Calev's normally smiling lips twisted and he stared down at the rope in his hands.

"Tell me something good." I knocked the tiller into its resting spot and climbed out to stand beside them, my heart shushing blood too quickly into my fingertips.

"No, maybe you're right. It is in her best interest to have talented Pass sailors." He met my gaze, his eyes steady as the horizon. "But shouldn't we try to talk my father into helping us first?"

I sighed, feeling like I held a sack of oats on each shoulder. He was certainly very careful not to say *my high-caste father*. A bitter taste stung my mouth. But his suggestion was a wise one. And it wasn't his fault he'd been born high and me low. It'd never been his fault.

"Yes," I said. "We should."

"That'll be entertaining," Oron said as he leaped off the boat and followed us up the hill. "The chairman of Old Farm might teach me a few new naughty words when he learns his eldest tangled with the oramiral and now the whelp who started the whole thing wants his help."

I stopped. He had a point.

"Shut it, Oron," Calev said. "Come on, Kinneret. He'll listen. He has accepted our friendship."

"He gave up and let you sneak around town with me. It's all been jokes and being children together. This is different. You think he'll be okay with risking his life and his people's lives to get a low-caste sailor's sister back? Hm. I know he's a good man, Calev, but...I don't know."

We took the bend in the dirt road and headed toward Old Farm.

Calev studied the ground. "I trust my father."

"Oh, I trust him too, Calev," Oron said, walking with his chin held high. He touched the shamar yam at Old Farm's gate before each of us did the same. "I trust him to say 'Absolutely not.'"

Calev bunched Oron's tunic in his fists. "Maybe you should go back to the tavern and sleep off your mood."

I put hands between them. "He's right, Oron. Go on. It won't help me make my case if you joke around the whole time."

His lips parted, but he kept silent, shaking his head violently. "Fine. Go on. Be fools. It's not as if I've ever been able to change your mind on anything, Kinneret Raza."

He stormed back the way we'd come, a chunk of my heart going with him.

Calev touched my elbow, his dark eyes were black in the night.

With a sigh, I walked on with Calev. His father would either help or he wouldn't. We had to at least try.

Passing the ritual bath house, carved from a rock outcropping, I inhaled the scent of ceremonial oils and fresh water. Old Farms bathed there once a moon.

Last cycle, hidden in a tall basket, I'd watched Calev participate in the ceremony. He didn't understand why I was curious, but to me the ceremony was foreign, mysterious, something to be studied and treasured. He claimed it wasn't so mysterious, that it wasn't such a huge deal.

But if the ritual was taken from him, if he were Outcasted for getting too close to me after our Age Day, he would miss it then. He might deny it now, but I'd seen him coming up out of the sacred waters. His wet hair showed the shape of his skull and highlighted his large eyes, his nose, and his perfectly lobed mouth.

With his smile, he looked like a creature from the heavens, perfectly glowing and peaceful and happy. A black-robed soul-teacher dripped golden oil over Calev's naked head as he stepped forward. His white tunic, a second-skin over his lean chest and flat stomach, bled water onto the stone floor.

The experience had stolen my breath.

Now, as the square shape of the ritual bath house faded into the dark behind us, I wished I could go there and be blessed. I wanted to be reborn, stronger and wiser, ready for what was coming. But I wasn't Old Farm and I had to find my own path to a blessing.

Fatigue tugging at me, I followed Calev under the cedar lintel and entered the whitewashed stone walls of the Old Farm group house. Clay oil lamps set in triangular niches gave the room a yellow glow. Y'hoshua ben Aharon, Calev's illustrious father, sat at a long table with three other men and two women. Calev's brother, Eleazar, brought his father a leather-bound book, pointed to one of the pages, and said something about barley.

Y'hoshua untucked his beard from between the table and his stomach. "Talk to Ezra. He'll know how to handle it."

"Father." Calev stood in front of the table, his voice taking on what I liked to call *Lord of the Harvest* tone.

Everyone in the room paused to look us up and down. We were a disaster of torn clothing and rising bruises.

Miriam came forward, spindle-stick in hand, and whispered Calev's name. Her wide gaze drank him in, and I hated her more at that moment than I ever had an innocent person. It wasn't her fault she was set to be the one to share his bed and feel his kisses.

Her lips were thin though. I bet her kisses would be as delightful as mouthing two nasty, little eels.

"Where have you been?" Y'hoshua pushed away from the table, knocking over a bowl of black figs. He put his hands on Calev's shoulders. I hadn't realized Calev was the same height as him now. "Are you injured? Who did this to you? The harvest should've begun sunset yesterday."

"It's my fault." My bells jingled as the people seated at the table spoke to one another quietly. "I took him out on my boat. We sailed near Quarry Isle, and the oramiral's men took my sister as punishment for coming too close to their territory."

Y'hoshua's hands fell to his sides. "But you're not seriously injured, my son?"

"No, Father, I'm fine, but Avigail—"

Y'hoshua pulled Calev toward his room. "Then you must make ready for the ceremony." He pushed him through the double doors, still talking as he turned away. "You will lead the first ceremonial cart. You have the best voice for the singing, my good son."

He was chittering about the harvest ceremony? Now? "We need your help, Chairman Y'hoshua. Didn't you hear me?"

Calev's father wove through the crowd, back to the table where four people at once talked about the harvest feast and about the family who'd earned the honor of driving the cart carrying the first sheaves of barley for the blessing.

"Wait!" Calev tried to follow Y'hoshua, but a woman with thick eyebrows held him back.

She chattered to another man while they removed his sash and dagger. "Your harvest tunic is the perfect shade. It will set off the gold of the ceremonial scythe."

I swallowed a bitter taste in my mouth and stood straighter. What could I say to get these people to stop fooling around with clothing and be serious?

Calev looked at me, his jaw set, as the eyebrow woman tugged his headtie off and replaced it with one the color of a harvest moon. Taking the woman by the arms, he gently, but firmly moved her away.

"Give me a moment, Rachel," he said, marching toward his father in the adjoining room. "Father. Please, listen. We need to go after Kinneret's sister now. The oramiral—"

Y'hoshua's face grew stormy and Eleazar backed away. "No, we do not need to go now," Y'hoshua said. "You have a responsibility to your people, Calev."

"As if I don't know that, Father." Pain colored his words. "I'm proud of who we are. We are the kind of people who help others. If you'll just send a group to Quarry Isle—"

"We have never, in over five hundred years, harvested without the chairman's eldest performing the ceremonial blessing. You have a vital role to play, Calev. We will do what we can for the girl after the harvest."

My heart shot into my throat like a cannonball. "After the harvest? She could be attacked for her portion of food while we wait. Strangled while the others sleep! Children are found dead all the time—especially smart ones who stand to gain apprentice spots come test day. The oramiral lets it all go to chaos. You know this!"

"I know how life on Old Farm is." Y'hoshua's voice was a crack of lightning. "We have an agreement with the amir and her lord, the kyros. Dealings with the oramiral are a part of that. Believe me, I detest the man. I visited the quarries once." His eyes brightened like he had a fever. "And never again, if I can help it. The man…he…" Y'hoshua gritted his teeth. "At every quarter meeting, I argue against his treatment of the slaves, how he should free them after seven years as we do, but the amir will not agree to it. And I will not push her. If we don't make our way of life our top priority, we lose it." His cheeks above his beard flushed and he took a step toward me. Calev looked ill as his father pulled him close to his face. "We haven't held on through Quest knights and kyros and amirs and coast raiders and northern men by losing our focus for those foolish enough to tangle horns with men like the oramiral."

I choked on a sob, stunned.

Calev called my name.

Turning, I pushed through the crowd of Old Farms and headed for the door. As I fled from the house, a voice snaked through the chaos.

"…she's going to turn him into an Outcast. I know it."

My sandals pounded the dusty path as I ran toward the town gates.

*An Outcast.*

I imagined Calev in a torn tunic shoveling muck out of a horse's stall. Beyond the stable, he stares at a window. Candlelight illuminates the shapes of his father and brother laughing and handing food across the table. His gaze drops to his bare, dirtied feet and he thinks one name.

*Kinneret.*

I wouldn't do that to him.

I would never try to pull him away from his people or urge him to forget what they held important. But somehow, some way, I had to get Avi back. My lungs burned and tears pushed at my eyes, wanting to fall.

That man. Y'hoshua ben Aharon.

I'd thought of him as a step-father of sorts. He'd given my parents and myself a fair amount of business—sending surplus grains to ports down the coast—despite how his people saw us and our ways. I couldn't believe he didn't care about Avi at all. He knew Calev was close to us. It wasn't as if he didn't know every time he sent his son to study with Old Zayn that I would most likely be there. But our relationship with Calev wasn't enough to put us above a harvest celebration.

A tear leaked from my eye and I dragged a quick hand over it, erasing it.

*Fine.*

I'd go to the amir on my own. I'd remind her of the constant service my parents and I'd provided for Jakobden's trade and economy. It probably wouldn't work. She'd probably serve my impertinent head to the kyros on a silver tray next time he came to visit. But I had to do something.

The massive doors into town were rough under my fists. "Entry!" I shouted up at the man in the tower.

Leering, he cranked the gate open a slice, and I slipped through. "Hurry up, scrapper," he called down.

Calev ran up behind me, his hair tangled and his sash still missing. "Kinneret!"

When I walked on, he grabbed my sleeve.

"Wait," he pleaded.

"I'm going to see the amir."

"You can't. It's late. She won't see anyone right now. Let alone…"

"Let alone a low-caste like me?" I laughed meanly.

"That's not what I meant."

"It is." I turned and rubbed more salty tears from my face.

Calev let out a growl of frustration and began mumbling under his breath. "He loves to dress me up and show me off, but he never listens when it's important."

He was talking about his father.

I took a breath. "He does sometimes. Like when that soul-teacher died and you named his replacement."

"Okay. Once, he listened. He probably had Isaac in mind for the position anyway. Kinneret." He touched my sleeve. "Tomorrow, we can go to the amir together." His words hummed like a good drum. I closed my eyes, reveling in their comfort.

"All right. Tomorrow." It was selfish. Dangerous. But we could handle it. I wouldn't do anything that would show my feelings for Calev. We'd just make a reasonable argument, touching on Avi's future contribution to the amir's town and maybe play on her pride. The oramiral took one of her people without proper cause and all that.

In tense silence, Calev walked me to the tavern's undercroft. I gave him a quick nod before shutting the door to his concerned face. I didn't want him to see me cry anymore. If I was ever going to be respected, I couldn't weep like a child. Even though everything inside wanted nothing more than to crumble against Oron's snoring form and do just that.

As I lay down to sleep, Oron rumbling at my feet, I sighed. I shouldn't have snapped at Calev. He didn't think I was less than him because of caste. When we were still children, he'd struggled with it, but he'd risen above the prejudice.

A memory tugged me away from my cold, dark fear for Avi.

When Calev and I were ten years old, we stole a bowl of tatlilav from the old tavern's kitchen.

In that memory, Calev had held the container of fermented mare's milk in both hands. "I could've bought this, you know."

I'd shamed him with a look. Even then, I'd been good at that.

He stared at his sandals. "I'm only saying…"

"Stealing is more fun and you know it."

Taking the drink from him, I gulped the almond-tasting alcohol. It warmed my throat on its way down.

"True." Grinning, he took the bowl back. When the horse milk touched his tongue, he spat and made a face like he'd just tasted dung.

"Not your favorite, huh?" I said. His face was too funny. Like a rooster who'd had his tail plucked.

The tavern's back door banged open, and Calev and I yelped as the hefty keeper shouted, "Ah!"

The tatlilav ended up in the dirt, the bowl overturned beside a set of broken wagon wheels.

"What is this?" the keeper demanded, his gaze on Calev.

I stood between them. "You can't prove anything."

"I wasn't talking to you, scrapper. Witch." The keeper made a circle on his forehead with his thumb, the Fire's sign.

My cheeks burned hot as the manure-scented, summer air.

"My father is Old Farm's chairman," Calev said. "He…needed a drink and—"

Furious at the keeper and my own humiliation, I pushed Calev back a step. "His father will pay for the tatlilav."

Calev scowled at me. "*I* was talking to the merchant."

"So?" I crossed my arms.

"Step away, low-caste, and let the Old Farm speak," the keeper said.

My gaze flew from the man to Calev, who didn't look like himself at all. Haughty. Proud. Separate.

"Yes, low-caste," Calev said, his chest moving up and down too quickly. "Don't interrupt."

"What?" I was going to be sick right here, on their feet, on my feet, on that delicious bowl of tatlilav we'd dropped.

Calev's face fell. He put a hand on my arm. "I'm so sorry. It's just you always interrupt... and I thought maybe—"

The keeper growled, but his eyes had gone soft. "Go on, the both of you. Before I change my mind and have your hands lopped off!"

I started to argue, but Calev pulled me down the dusty road.

"Mind your companions, Old Farm!" the keeper called out.

At the town gate, Calev urged me into the wall's shadow, his eyes bright in the darker space. People passed, on their way to the market, to their homes, to business, and all their faces seemed to turn to us and wonder why someone like Calev would be talking to someone like me. I shuddered.

"Say you forgive me." Calev was pale. His hand tightened on my arm. "Please."

My stomach twisted.

Calev leaned his forehead against mine. His eyelashes were so, so long, and his breath was warm and soft. "I don't care about castes and you know that. If anything, you should be high and me low. I'm the one who forgets my own mind the second we get in trouble."

I thought of his grimace after tasting the tatlilav. "You can be pretty dumb sometimes."

"Often," he said.

"Daily."

Leaning back, he held up his hands. "Deserved."

"But only when you're awake," I said, eyeing him.

"Are you finished?" he asked.

"For now."

The memory faded as I rubbed my forehead. Calev wasn't perfect, but he was *good*. I closed my eyes, thankful I had him on my side.

My throat tight, I reached under the bedding on Avi's side and retrieved one of her collected seashells.

My heart snapped like it might break into two. I clutched my shirt, breath hitching as the tears I'd fought poured down my cheeks.

The shell's outer surface was sharp and rough, bitten by the shore rocks. But inside was unmarred, smooth and fragile.

If the oramiral destroyed my sister's sweet soul, he was as good as dead.

I'd murder him slowly, painfully.

I was still plotting when dawn burned through the cracks in the door.

# CHAPTER NINE

ON OUR WAY TO THE amir's manor house, Calev and I passed the Holy Fire worship house and its minarets. It was meant to mimic the look of Akhayma, the Empire's capitol city. The spindly towers seemed to hold the sky up, making a tent of blue above us.

My sandal crashed into a mud puddle. I growled and swished my skirt, slinging brown onto the vegetable seller's cart.

"Eh!" The seller threatened me with an onion, then with a respectful nod, offered the vegetable to Calev.

I was too tired—body and soul—to care about a veg seller's slights. My elbow and side throbbed from the fight with the oramiral's men. And it was nothing compared to the chill of Avi's absence.

Calev veered left, out of the way of my muddy stomping. His hands were scratched up and one was swollen and red.

"The amir, of course, honors the Holy Fire, but it's not a true priority to her," he said quietly. He'd been giving me information since we met at the tavern. "She only really believes in battle tales, high-caste bloodlines, and her treasury."

"I'm going to work her pride."

Calev grinned. "Ah. Yeah. We could even throw in some of the slanderous remarks the oramiral's slaves made against her."

"They didn't—oh." I smiled, whispering. "Yes. I must've forgotten. We told the oramiral's men they shouldn't take a Jakobden citizen without the amir's approval, and they said *The amir can approve this.*" I made an obscene gesture.

Calev choked, almost laughing. "That might be taking it a shade too far."

A high-caste man, a hooded falcon perched on his arm, blinked at us and stopped mid-stride. "Old Farm, you should demand the low-caste walk behind. Don't shame your family."

Face clouding, Calev started toward him like he was going to fight him—not a winning plan. Before he could make whatever wonderfully brave, albeit asinine move he wanted to make, I dropped two steps behind.

The falcon's owner moved on and Calev heaved a sigh. "This is why you didn't go with me to the archery contest," he whispered over his shoulder.

"Nah. It's your insufferable company," I said, my humor falling flat. The breeze pulled the hem of Calev's tunic back toward me as we started forward.

It's not like I'd wanted to skip the contests the amir held for the harvest. Calev always nudged elders aside so I could stand beside him and actually see the competitors' yellow and black fletched arrows hit the targets lined up along the horse track.

But we couldn't do that anymore. It was too formal of an event for us to appear together. His father would never have approved. Not anymore. Worse, someone could report us to the amir. Someone like Berker. Then Calev and I both would be well on our way to being Outcasted. I couldn't put Calev in that position for a contest. I wouldn't threaten myself either.

"We're growing up. We're not knee-high anymore. I won't be the reason you're Outcasted."

He stopped and faced me. "That's not going to happen."

"Calev. Think about it. You, an Outcast? It would kill you."

I stared into his honest eyes, thinking of him sitting beside his father and Eleazar as they brainstormed ways to curb root rot. I'd been there, waiting to speak with Y'hoshua about what ports he wished me to visit. Calev had pounded on the table, pushing his points as his father argued with Eleazar bouncing between the two stances. But they'd broken into joking before it could turn into a fight.

If Calev were Outcasted, he'd never be allowed in his home ever again. At best, he'd be with the livestock, mucking stalls and sleeping in the open. At worst, he'd be on the streets along with me, begging.

"We need to fight the system," he said, eyes blazing.

The anger in his eyes made my chest swell, but I had to tamp it down. Rebellion had to wait for another day. "Think I don't know that? But first, we save Avi." I waved him to walk on, so I could trail him like a pathetic little donkey.

I couldn't wait for Ayarazi. Silver in my hands. The world at my feet.

"We will," he said. "I promise you. When this is over, I'll demand that my father listen."

"We need a back way in to fight the system. Something subtle," I said. "Someday we'll figure it out. If you yell about it, everything will be ruined."

Calev blinked. "Did you just suggest being subtle?"

"Told you we're growing up."

He smiled. "Sure."

"Thank you for doing this." My tears reflected in his eyes, and I looked away.

"Avigail is mine too," he said. "My family. You know that."

A light glowed in my chest. *His family.*

I remembered how quickly they'd become friends when she was small.

Once, when Calev and I were eight, I'd dragged him from Old Zayn's weather lessons and down to the boat. Father was arguing shipping prices with a farmer's agent who pointed at the marks on his wax tablet. Father did pretty well hiding his shock at Calev being there. The agent pulled off his straw hat, frowning at the bells on my sash. Calev took my hand and I squeezed his fingers, my pulse beating in the tip of my thumb.

A muscle in Father's jaw twitched. "They're young yet," he said quietly to the agent. "Now about the grains…"

The agent put his hat on and went back to arguing.

Onboard, Avi hurried over. "Kinneret, play the shell game with me."

"I have things to do, little girl."

"I'm only two years younger than you!"

Calev took one bright shell. "How do you play?"

She stole the shell back.

"Come on," Calev said. "I'm good at games. At home, I win all the time."

That didn't surprise me.

"Well," Avi started, "you throw the shells. Like this." She tossed them into the air. "Andguesshowmanylandupsidedown—four!" The little crescents and circles clattered onto the uneven decking, only two of the four showing their shiny insides. "I win!" Her eyes narrowed. "No one beats me."

She threw the shells again.

"Six!" Calev called out.

Avi glared. "Five!"

All six shells landed belly-up and Avi's mouth dropped open. "Kinneret is right. You are lucky."

Calev put a hand on her shoulder. "Will you play with me every time I visit?"

Avi grinned. "Deal."

I shook off the memory. I had to focus if this little impromptu meeting was going to accomplish anything.

The walls of the amir's manor house loomed above us. They were made of the cloudy, white stone from Quarry Isle, the sole product the oramiral exported, the material Avi began cutting and hauling last night.

I walked faster.

Wondering if I was about to stride right into a death sentence—although it wasn't technically a law, low-castes never pleaded their case here—I rounded the corner and followed Calev into the amir's courtyard.

Smoke from a fire crawled into the blue morning sky, and a slave tethered a dun mare to a post outside the mud-brick stables.

At least the amir didn't force her slaves to wear the high bell over their heads. They wore a large, copper one on a metal ring around each ankle. Three more slaves carried baskets of what looked like mushrooms and olives from a storage shed. Like worker ants, they made a line, each one eyeing me—the obvious intruder in my many bells, just one measly step above their status.

Where Calev's home was a simple but large stone structure, the amir's enormous place rose three full stories above the churned earth of her courtyard. Made of the same white rock as the outer walls, it boasted arches with orange stripes over a patio done in mosaic tiles.

Manning the arched openings, two fighters wore onion-shaped helmets that pressed one strip of metal along their noses. Long, sharp yatagans hung sheathed at their sashes beside the ten bells that marked them as middle-caste.

I glanced at Calev, wondering for the millionth time what it would feel like to be an Old Farm and free of the system of slave, worker, warrior, leader. As part of their ancient agreement with the kyros and his amirs, Old Farms were considered high-caste from birth, though they didn't have to wear the bells. They'd worked hard to make themselves indispensable to Jakobden by working the soil in ways that were as much magic as my salt prayers.

When Calev—recognized here from his father's dealings with the amir—received a nod from the guards, we walked into the cool receiving hall.

The absence of the sun's soaking heat made me shiver. An ozan sang quietly of an ancient warrior's battle at sea, his voice warbling like a bird's. Men and women in silk draped the lower half of the walls like curtains. We waited at the door near the Fire in the bronze bowl. The flames flickered and sent the smell of oil into the air. Calev pricked his finger with his dagger and dropped his blood into the Fire. I passed a hand respectfully over the dancing orange and blue, feeling the heat on my skin.

Inside the main section of the receiving hall, Chairman Y'hoshua sat at the end of a long table, opposite the amir. Tapestries covered the top half of the walls. Colored threads wove together to show former amirs' conquests of borderlands, fleets of boats fighting the Great Expanse's waves to search for foggy, lost lands like Ayarazi, and bloody battles with western Invaders.

"You agree to our terms, Amir Mamluk?" Chairman Y'hoshua said.

Calev sucked a breath, frozen in the act of sheathing his dagger. "I didn't know he was here."

"Obviously." This wasn't good. Y'hoshua would stop our supplication before it could even get started.

The amir cut an imposing figure, dressed in red leather the color of blood. I loved the color red, never bought or stole clothing in a color too far from it, but this was a darker shade. Deeper. I swallowed.

She regarded Y'hoshua's beard with cool eyes. "I agree to all except the price of your barley."

"What should I do?" Calev whispered.

"It is a fine crop," Y'hoshua said, "and will make a great deal of silver in trade for us and for you."

"I will not pay like a trader." The amir's braid pulled at her light blue eyes. She cocked her head. The single, pure silver bell at her forehead—tied to a thin strip of leather similar to Old Farm men's headties—reflected the arched windows' morning light.

"Maybe you should get in there," I hissed back, ignoring a house slave's shushing noise.

The amir was too light-eyed and fair-skinned to be of the kyros's race and born high-caste, so at one point in her family's history, one of her ancestors had served as a slave. Now, she ruled this area, with only the kyros outranking her and far enough away to be more dream than reality. She was pretty much my hero. Not because of blood, but because of her power.

"You hold those lands because of my generosity, and the generosity of the kyros's ancestors," the amir said. "Do not forget, Chairman Y'hoshua ben Aharon."

My stomach twisted. I hadn't expected to like her voice. But it was beautiful. It rang like the bell she wore and made me want to hear her sing.

"I would never forget, my lady. And I thank you for meeting me here."

In the past, the ruling amir met the Old Farm chairman in the fields. Before Amir Mamluk, no Old Farms were permitted in her household. They were welcomed into town and highly respected in agreements and trading, but not allowed here, in the home of the highest ranking member of the kyros's ruling class.

Y'hoshua's face was like carved stone. "But, as I said, it is a fine crop."

"One-third finer than last harvest?"

Calev stepped out the shadows. "Yes."

The house servant sputtered and quickly announced us. "Calev ben Y'hoshua of Old Farm and—"

I poked the man and shook my head. My presence only added problems. I wanted to stay in the shadows for a bit longer, see how this panned out. The servant's face darkened. He looked ready to throw me in a cell.

"We remember so they remember," I said quickly, drawing my gaze to his bells, then touching a finger to my own.

He took a breath and nodded slowly. "The amir might not like this. You must be quiet, and still."

I nodded. "I'll be as inactive as your mind."

"What?"

"What?" I echoed.

"You said—"

"I thought we needed to stay quiet."

"Yes," he said sharply. "Quiet."

Y'hoshua's loud voice rang through the room. He stood. "Son?"

Calev bowed to the amir, then gave his father a nod. "Amir Mamluk, what my father says is true. This barley is indeed one-third finer. My brother Eleazar ben Y'hoshua developed a new way to fight root rot and the crop grew more golden than in years past. If you cannot agree to the number my father has set, perhaps we could agree on last year's price plus one hundred extra workers—your fighters or any men or women you see as fit—to weed our fields after spring planting."

The servant beside me made a little *Hm* noise of appreciation.

"Pretty quick, isn't he?" I whispered.

Y'hoshua turned an impressive shade of red.

The amir's eyebrow lifted as she stared Calev down. "It is a delicate balance we set here."

Calev stood straight under her burning gaze. "We are thankful for that balance. Gratitude sings the loudest note in our ancient ways, my lady."

"And we know how Old Farms love their old ways." She grinned like a fox and her fighters laughed lightly.

Y'hoshua and Calev bowed their heads a fraction, and a small smile drifted over one side of Calev's mouth. I hope he enjoyed the moment, because I'd bet his father would strap him good later. No way Y'hoshua would let this slide. Proving my point, he glared at Calev and his nostrils flared.

The amir stood, shoving her chair back with a screech. Y'hoshua hurried to echo the movement, though his chair made no sound.

"We are agreed, Chairman Y'hoshua ben Aharon."

Calev and Y'hoshua made the Fire's sign, forming a circle on their foreheads with their thumbs. The amir copied the gesture.

Now was the time to bring up Avi. I willed Calev to read my thoughts. But he acted like he was going to leave with Y'hoshua, waiting as the amir called for her scribe. The Holy Fire flickered in its bronze bowl and sent out a snap.

Looking at the now empty table—the amir and the chairman had gone to the scribe's podium to sign their agreement—I tried, and failed, to imagine a world where someone like me could sit there. How much silver would it take to make Salt Magic as acceptable as the Old Farm ways and the Holy Fire?

Calev was waiting too long to broach the subject of Avi. I had to speak.

I untied my salt from my sash and bent, pretending to adjust my sandal as I tucked the bag into the corner away from the servant's prying eyes.

Not waiting on the servant to announce me, I walked into the room.

# CHAPTER TEN

THE HOUSE SERVANT CALLED OUT.

"I'm Kinneret Raza, Pass sailor," I squawked, saving him the effort.

Y'hoshua's eyes narrowed as the high ceiling grabbed every smack of my ratty sandals and threw it back at the tiled floor.

Amir Mamluk had taken a seat in a tall chair on a raised platform.

I bent at the knee and raised an open palm to her in respect.

"Chairman Y'hoshua ben Aharon, is this another of your surprises?"

"No, my lady." His face was stormy. "I don't know what brings Kinneret Raza here."

"A low-caste sailor…" The amir wasn't even looking at me and I still felt the threat, all the possible words she could utter and ruin me.

Maybe I should've planned to tell her about the map to Ayarazi. The tales about her ruthlessness could've been false. *She might believe me.* Calev said there was no chance of her taking Old Zayn's tale as truth. But maybe he was wrong.

"I am sorry for the interruption, Amir Mamluk," Calev said with one of those smiles of his. The amir smiled back. Someone would have to be dead not to smile back at Calev. "But we do have another topic to discuss, if you are willing. It is a matter that needs immediate attention."

The amir's eyebrows lifted, but I couldn't tell whether she was angry or interested. "Immediate?"

Y'hoshua raised a palm and the amir turned her attention to him.

"Yes, Chairman Y'hoshua ben Aharon?"

"The sailor has had an unfortunate run-in with the oramiral. I do value the sailor's talent. Even young as she is, she has scouted two new ports for Old Farm. She is very skilled. But her current situation is nothing that concerns my son."

It was like hands pushed down on my shoulders and I had to fight to stand.

Calev's eyes flashed. "It does concern me, Father. And the amir, too."

"Yesterday," I said, "we sailed past Asag's Door, near Quarry Isle, and Oramiral Urmirian's men boarded our craft and abducted my sister, Avigail Raza."

Leaning back, the amir rested an elbow on the arm of her chair and adjusted the leather collar of her military vest. "I believe your father is correct," she said to Calev. "This should not concern you. Now, Chairman Y'hoshua ben Aharon, you may leave and I will have a little talk with your son."

Y'hoshua nodded curtly at Calev. "He does seem to think he has this in hand." And with that, he left.

A buzz reverberated inside me. I spoke louder. "I have brought many of your noble visitors safely across the Pass from Kurakia, Amir Mamluk, and I run many of the merchants and area farmers' surplus goods. My sister will follow in my footsteps to become another valuable member of your township. We work under the protection of your fighters, for the good of your township." I wanted to add the slurs Calev and I had thought up, but the words didn't want to come.

The amir's fingers lighted on the snakeskin sheath of her personal dagger. Her nails were stained with orange spices I'd only taste if I found Ayarazi. "The work you do, it is coppers to me. Have you ever kaptaned a full ship for any of my tenant farmers?"

"No, but I—"

Shaking his hair out of his eyes, Calev took a small step forward and his father grumbled something under his breath.

Burned silhouettes of tiny lemons and barley stalks decorated the edges of Calev's sash. That article of clothing alone cost as much as a cartload of grains. The amir's gaze followed the shining hem, an approving smile ghosting over her mouth. I stood taller. Calev had thought out what would impress her. He was truly was doing his best to help Avi.

"My lady," he said, "Kinneret Raza runs surplus for the headland farmer Matan..."

I winced. "Actually—"

The amir slapped a hand on her throne. "Do not interrupt those higher than you, sailor."

My face burned as the amir looked again to Calev.

"You see, Calev ben Y'hoshua? You shouldn't encourage this one with your admirable kindness. She grows too bold for her station. It could mean trouble for the both of you." Her icy gaze nipped at me. "This one has talent. I've heard as much. But she would do well to earn her silver and rise in the accepted way, avoiding overly close association with upper-castes until she is ready. You know the kyros requires me to protect high-caste bloodlines. You must not mix unless the low is proven and rises, or you will both be Outcasted."

Calev went gray around the mouth, and I shivered.

"With my condolences on the young girl—one should not begin as a slave, then return to it after honorably working—please go on your way and give my best to your father, Calev ben Y'hoshua."

Just like that, she threw Avi's life away.

My heart choked as the amir motioned to the servant to lead us out. Her ozan began singing of her great-great-grandfather's journey to the North.

I wanted to blurt out my knowledge of the lost island of silver, but in this painfully formal room full of narrowed eyes and high brows, I couldn't say it. It wouldn't matter. None of these uppers would believe me.

I imagined Avi's small, thin body curled into mine during the night, her open-mouthed breathing. Where did she sleep now? In the open air slave quarters on Quarry Isle, along with a mass of others, men desperate and women angry. They'd probably already taken her tunic from her. They would steal her food. She wouldn't be able to fight back in such a crowd. They'd take everything she had.

I looked frantically at the approaching servant, then at the amir. "Please!"

The ozan didn't quiet. The amir didn't turn toward me.

Calev's gentle hand warmed my arm and raised his voice. "Kinneret will be the Old Farm kaptan for the next shipment of barley," he said loudly. "Old Farm is confident in her abilities and what should be a quick rise in caste."

*What?*

He held his fist to his neck. "By my word," he swore, "or my throat's blood is yours, my lady."

The ozan's tune fell away.

I put my head in my hands. A throat's blood oath. It was binding until one or both died. If he didn't follow through, the amir would slit his throat in front of everyone in Jakobden and Old Farm and not even his chairman father could do a thing to stop it.

But I forced my chin up. This was my chance to help Avi. I couldn't take on the oramiral without the amir's fighting sailors and ships and coin. Calev had thrown his life into the deal. I pulled in a breath of the manor house's spicy air. I had to back him up now. There was no other choice, as mad as it was.

"It is true, my lady," I lied.

The noblewoman stood. She was taller even than Calev's father. "When I hear from Y'hoshua ben Aharon's own mouth that this girl will kaptan his ship, that she has the protection of

Old Farm, and therefore my own protection due to the old agreements, you will have the coin and fighters you need to take your sister back, Kinneret Raza." Her smile said she knew that would never happen. "I hope you are wise in this choice, Calev ben Y'hoshua. A public execution of an Old Farm would be dramatic indeed."

Blood lust colored her features.

The room spun as we followed the servant to the courtyard.

The ozan's lilting voice carried more tales of heroic deeds. As we walked, he sang of a man slaying enemies with a lion fighting at his side.

Outside the manor house walls, I raged ahead of Calev, my sandals splashing, and my arms like flapping wings at my sides.

"A throat binding, Calev? And how do you think I'm going to kaptan your ship? Your father won't even bend his precious harvest schedule to save my sister's life." I kicked at a basket of leeks and a girl in a white hair wrap swore at me.

"It's not as simple as a change of schedule. It is about a holy ritual. It's not matter of mere inconvenience."

"Yes, it is."

"No, Kinneret. It's not. And you know it. If we wait on the harvest any longer—and there's no way they'll harvest without me at the ceremony—we could lose crops, which means less food for everyone on the Broken Coast and beyond."

"I don't care if it means less food." I grabbed his tunic. "Don't you get it? She's probably the youngest slave. She'll be stepped on, pushed down. Or worse. There are men there, Calev. Desperate men, out of their minds. I have to go after the map to the island."

"The oramiral's men could take you too."

"I don't care. I have to try."

"I know, but maybe we should wait and think about this."

"Really? Wait on what? Silver is my only card to play. Your father is no help, or if he does help, it'll be too late and Avi will be—"

He covered my hands with his. "Kinneret. Calm yourself."

I pushed away from him. "Ooo, using your big man voice, huh?" I huffed and started my raging down the road again. "Save it for your field workers. I'm sailing out now. The wine jug with the map is out there, waiting for me. If I find Ayarazi on my own and return with the purest silver the amir has ever seen, she'll flay the oramiral alive if I ask it and Avi will come home again."

"Can't you wait one day?"

"Oh, and your father is going to let you walk out of Old Farm when it's over? And after today? I don't think so. He'll want you there for the full harvest. You know the fields. And you're better at getting everyone to work their tails off than anyone else. If I were him, I'd want you there."

"He will want me to stay, but I'll sneak off. Eleazar will cover for me."

I lowered my voice as we came to the town gate. "You'd leave right after the ceremony? Even if you know I'll use Salt Magic for this trip? Because I can't simply wait for a good wind. Avi is dealing with only the Fire knows what this very second. The men there will take more than just her share of food."

"I will leave as soon as I can. I promise you. I love Avi too."

I wanted him to come. He was my good luck.

My rage cooled as I stared at his face, full of his promise. His throat bobbed, his skin smooth, the same skin the amir would slice open if I didn't kaptan Old Farm's barley ship.

"Will you wait for me?" he asked quietly so no one would hear.

I pressed my lips together. I needed all the luck I could get. Finding the map would be easier if I had another diver. Oron was terrible under the water.

"Yes," I said. "I don't like it, but yes."

"Come to the ceremony tonight."

I couldn't do that. His father was furious with me and I with him. Besides, the word Outcast echoed through my mind. "No. I need to ready the boat." I touched his hand quickly. "I hope your rituals go smoothly. I'll meet you at the dock tomorrow."

Before I could turn and see his dark gaze following me, before I chanced those eyes urging me into more trouble, I stalked down the road. Zayn's words played in my memory again and again like a prayer chant, promising a good life for Avi and me.

# CHAPTER ELEVEN

ORON WAS DRUNK. ABOARD OUR boat, he swayed on his wide feet, one sandal tucked inside a circle of extra rope and an eye swollen shut from struggling against the oramiral's slaves.

"I'm not worthless, my dear, um…my…Ki…Kin…"

"Kinneret." I held up a hand to block the early sun. My bruised cheek thumped with pain, but the rest of me had stopped hurting as of this morning. I was still in a mood though. Calev hadn't shown yet and I wondered if his father had anything to do with it.

"I was going to say that," Oron said. "I needed a second to think."

"Get off the boat, Oron. I have places to be. Avi isn't lounging in a kyros's tent. I have no sun for your nonsense." I swallowed against the fist in my throat.

He plopped himself onto the rope and crossed his arms.

"Fine. Stay aboard," I said. "But keep out of my way."

By the time I'd hauled anchor, his snores echoed off the boat's sides. I looked down at him and sighed. He didn't usually drink so much this early. I supposed he was worried about Avi and handling it in his own way. A stupid way.

As I let out the sail, someone shouted from the hill beyond the dock.

Calev.

His tunic flowing at his sides, he ran down the path and pounded up to the boat. He grabbed the side before I'd floated a foot off.

Tossing a sack and himself over the side, he said, "I'm sorry I'm late," then looked to Oron, frowning. "He can't hold his alcohol."

"It's not for holding. It's for drinking, silly," Oron mumbled, turning over.

"Did you tell your father about the oath?" I asked Calev. I shuddered, and rubbing salt between my fingertips, whispered to the sea and edged the tiller, a motion more familiar to me than walking.

Calev watched me work the magic with a wrinkled brow. "No. You thought I would?" He handed me a wheat cake from his bag and tossed one to Oron.

"Ow!" Oron scowled, then noticed the cake lying beside him. "Ooo." He gobbled it up and closed his eyes again.

"I didn't know what to think," I said. "It's not like you make a throat's blood oath every day."

Oron whistled like a sick bird. "This is getting interesting. Maybe I should consider consciousness…"

I glared at him. "You're not as funny as you think you are."

Calev leaned toward me. "The oath won't matter when we find the island. The amir just needs to be convinced you're worth her time." He grinned and my heart flipped.

Oron wiggled his fingers. "Oooo, listen to the optimist."

With Calev standing beside me and not judging me for using Salt Magic, and the sea like green glass beyond him, something bright like hope sparked in my heart.

On alert for the oramiral's ship, we made it to The Drift before the sun had fallen two fingers closer to the horizon.

Talking with Calev, Oron managed to make himself useful on the sail's lines. "So, let me get this straight. You promised the amir that our girl here was set to be the next Old Farm ship kaptan in hopes that the amir would consider Avi as a person worth rescuing."

"That about sums it up," Calev said.

"And the amir is waiting to hear from your father on this, even though your father knows nothing about it."

"He'll agree to it."

Oron snorted. "Delusional. And they don't even have drink to blame."

"We're assertive," I argued.

"Even if it kills you?"

Calev and I answered together. "Exactly."

"Did Y'hoshua punish you?" I asked Calev as I dropped the stone anchor off the side.

He looked at the water. "No."

"Well, that is one thing, hm?" Oron tied the sails down.

"Not really," I said. "When he waits to punish him, it's always worse. So he didn't say anything during the harvest rituals?"

"Not a word," Calev said. "Acted like nothing even happened."

Not good.

AFTER DROPPING THE STONE anchor off the side, I skinned off my shirt, skirt, and sash, leaving my small clothes on. Calev peeled his tunic from his back and I averted my eyes from his bare chest and the loose short pants that hung on his hipbones. I couldn't sit around and enjoy the view. It was time to find the map.

Avi needed us. And she needed us now.

The sun-drenched water below the boat glowed like spring grass and lemon peels. As we searched, the light stretched fingers down through the open water, all the way to the broken boards of yet another sunken vessel.

All day Calev had been amazing at holding his breath under water, amazing for a non-sailor, that is. But his lungs were no match for mine.

Before I could crawl, I'd been in the ocean, chasing fish, learning the tide's pull, becoming a Pass sailor. It was why I never feared the rocks or the storms. They were a part of me as much as my own shortcomings—quick anger and stubbornness.

Kicking my bare feet through the chill water, fighting the Pass's rough hands, I swam through a hole in the side of a ship even older than the one we'd already scoured. Calev would likely need to go up for air very soon.

In the ship's crumbling hull, barnacles like rotten, boiled potatoes sat on stacks of cracked crockery plates. Mostly, the space was empty. The sea had claimed what the looters hadn't wanted. There wasn't a wine jug in sight.

Near a long stretch of what used to be part of the deck, the boat's figurehead angel stuck one wing out of the mounded sand, its stone feathers gone green and black at the edges. Past that, a small, walled-in area—probably the kaptan's room—held the skeleton of a bed, a fork, the encrusted remains of iron lanterns, and an astrolabe.

Where was my wine jug? Where was Avi's ticket to freedom? Sadness welled inside my chest, pushing and more painful than the need for oxygen. I had to get to Avi before it was too late.

There was a tug on my toe and I turned to see Calev pointing up. Dying light drifted through the broken vessel's decking and striped his face. Tiny bubbles huddled beside his fine nose and in the cleft of his chin. He gestured to his chest. He needed air. I nodded, and he twisted, swimming back to the boat and leaving me in the wreckage.

The tides would turn soon, making it that much harder to swim and sail against the sea's push to flow out to the Expanse. It also meant another sundown, another day, and with it, Salt Wraiths. I had to hurry.

We hadn't checked the tumble of wood to the right of the kaptan's quarters. Oron was waving the signal stick at me under the water, but I ignored it. Swimming through a cloud of algae-eating creatures no bigger than dust motes, I ducked under the leaning parts of a doorframe. A table, only two legs remaining, hogged the space. A lead plummet rested in my distorted shadow. I tucked it into my top. If I could manage to clean it up, it'd be better than the one weighing my sounding line now. The four transoms of a Jacob's staff poked out from under the table. I didn't want that. It was iron, and only the Fire could make use of it now that it had been under the sea for so long. I'd have to keep using my old wooden one to measure the angle between the horizon and the sun or the Far Star.

Oron and Calev had to be panicking by now. Hot fingers tore at my lungs.

*Just one more look.*

Letting the water tug me to the dark corner behind the mapping table, I reached out my fingers. Then a warm hand snatched my ankle. I nearly inhaled the entire Pass.

It was Oron, his hair like squid tentacles around his wide face. He waved a frantic hand for me to follow. With one glimpse at the unexplored corner, I finally obeyed my lungs and my friend, and headed to the surface, my feet like a tail behind me.

"Didn't you see the signal?" At the surface, Oron roughly wiped ocean from his face and hefted himself up the hook-topped ladder that Calev held steady against starboard.

The signal stick—berry-dyed and beaten to bare spots like a bad donkey—sat on the side of the boat, dripping wet. Below the ladder, I treaded water and pulled air into my neglected lungs.

"I want to go back down," I said.

The sky was the orange of Kurakian chicken and the purple of spiced wine, the memory of the last like pines and flowers on my tongue. I bit my lip.

Closing my eyes, I hated myself. I was a monster for thinking of my stomach, rather than Avi's.

"We still have sun," I said.

The sea lurched me sideways, and I grabbed the ladder, my legs flying in the water.

"No." Oron leaned over the side of the boat as he worked himself back into his tunic. "It's nearly sundown."

Calev, on the other hand, was taking his tunic off again. "I'm going with you. This is no time for cowardice."

I smiled sadly and dipped under the choppy waves to wait for him.

Like an arrow shot into the water, Calev dove into the sea. For me. For Oron. For Zayn. For Avi. And I loved him for it.

Where would I be without Oron and Calev? I might've found the map on my own, but it would've been so much harder. I wished I could do something for them, but nothing that wasn't stupid came to mind. Anything said wouldn't be enough. I didn't have any items to give them to show my gratitude.

Calev came up in front of me and grinned. It took everything in me not to wrap my arms around his neck and press my mouth to his. I wanted to kiss the tiny scar at the side of his full lips. Instead of making a complete fool of myself, I dashed through the water, aiming for the map room.

THE LIGHT IN THE UNDERWATER room was no longer a diffused, golden glow. Because the sun had fallen, swimming into the small area was like walking into one of Oron's blue glass gaming pieces. Like my shadow, Calev stuck to my side as I maneuvered past the table and the tools to the corner. Praying for the absence of eels, I felt around the darkness.

Smooth shapes. A tube—*ah*—the neck of a vessel. Two of them. Two jugs.

Sharp nests of twigs surrounded the containers on their broken shelves. Seeing what I was about, Calev pressed forward to help me uncover our finds.

No large cracks marred the jugs, at least none visible in the twilight. As we tucked them under our arms and kicked back to the boat, I spared a thought for what might actually be left of a map that had lived in salt water for around one hundred years. Probably depended on what it was made of. Parchment. Vellum.

The Quest knights used vellum, calfskin, for religious writings. My father had taught me that much in our talks between spearfishing and sail-mending. He'd explained the kyros had faith, but his views differed somewhat from the Old Farm's religion, and also the Quest knights, who'd controlled Jakobden before the map's existence. The details of everyone's belief systems was lost on me, but I remembered Father's description of Quest knights' holy writings, words ringed with paintings as colorful as Meeka Valley flowers. So if the map was important to them it would probably be vellum too. Did it last under water? I doubted regular papyrus did, being made of plant material.

Oron helped us one by one into the boat, his big eyes drawing a line between the jugs and the darkening sky.

I squeezed the ends of my curling hair, hurrying so I could tug my skirt and shirt back on. Something about being half naked near a similarly half naked Calev made me feel very, very dangerous.

"What do you think the map is made of?" I asked.

Popping his head through his tunic, Calev opened his mouth.

Oron cut him off before he could say anything. "I see you're finally wondering what could possibly survive a century under water."

Calev ran his hands along his skull to press the water from his dark head. I tried very hard not to stare at the angle of his jaw and the slender bulge of his arm muscles under his damp tunic sleeves.

"The map is likely parchment," Oron said. "Made from animal skin. Not papyrus." He hurried over with me to the jugs. I was glad his gaze wasn't worrying over the sky anymore. He was focused on our goal now, like me.

I lifted the first gritty container. It was heavier out of the water. A blackened plug clogged the jug's mouth.

Oron raised a hammer. "Shall we crack it open or do you think we can get the plug out in a more graceful manner?"

I jerked the metal tool out of his hand and knocked the neck of the jug, breaking the top from the container. One of the handles, embossed with a Quest knight rose, came off along with the neck and rattled along the deck. I peered inside the jug.

Darkness.

My heart in my stomach, I looked up at Calev and Oron. "It's empty."

Oron twisted, then shoved the second sea-grimed jug into my hands.

It was empty too.

Knees shaking, I stood. *Is Zayn wrong?* Or was the right container still out there, under the waves? I looked out over the orange-tipped waves.

"Kinneret," Oron said. "We need to get to shore."

Calev set a gentle hand on my arm, his fingers cool and damp. "We can come back tomorrow."

I nodded.

Night peered out of the East. Oron began tugging the anchor up, his fingers white on the rope. Dripping arms and legs of water, the line marched from the Pass like regimented fighters. I couldn't blink. I just stared, Avi's braid in my mind's eye.

Calev stepped closer.

Hugging my arms to myself, I tried to stop shaking.

This was one more night added to Avi's time at the quarry. One more night in a slave's bell brace. A shudder crashed over me. One more night surrounded by people who would cut her throat with a sharp flake of stone for her share of bread and oil.

I spun and knelt near the jugs. What if the map wasn't parchment or papyrus? What if I'd missed it? What if was an object or something I hadn't thought of yet?

Upending each container in turn, I shook them out to check. Nothing.

"What is it?" Calev asked, probably thinking I'd lost my mind.

Oron let the sail out. "I need your salt work to get us moving, Kinneret." He frowned at the pink sun sitting on the waves. "Now."

I raised the hammer and smashed both of the jugs.

"What are you doing?" Calev asked. "We need to get back to shore. Becoming Infused out here won't help Avi."

Ignoring him, I shuffled through the pieces. The first container's insides were like the outside, red-brown and unmarked, nothing like the ones in the amir's hall that were blue glazed and covered in lotus flowers and phoenixes.

I lifted a big section of the second jug's body and flipped it over.

Blue.

I held it up to Calev, struck dumb.

He wrinkled his nose. "Why is the inside glazed?"

White scratches interrupted the color someone had painstakingly slicked inside before firing the thing in a kiln. There was a long line and several notches like tiny mountains. On the left, a snaking strip of white. To the right, another.

My mouth went dry. I smiled, laughed as the world seemed to open up in front of my eyes.

"This is the map."

Oron appeared at my side. "And I am the kyros. And Calev is my pet donkey."

I glared. Calev glared.

Oron held up his hands. "What? I thought we were having a bit of pretend to ease the pain of crushing defeat."

I pushed him out of the way to find the rest of the pieces. *Not that one. No.* This one was blue, but not marked. *Ah.*

"Look." I held the bit I'd found against the other marked piece. They fit like lovers. The new section showed a thumb-sized triangle. I ran a finger over the serpentine lines. "This is Jakobden. This, Kurakia." Touching the tiny mountains, I said, "This is the Pass." My finger found the triangle. "And this. This is Ayarazi."

Oron's hand went to his mouth and Calev made a sound like a sigh.

"You did it," Calev said. "You found it." He shook his head. "I knew you would."

I gave him my best smile because he deserved it. He looked away from my mouth and swallowed.

Tucking the map pieces into my wide sash, I stood. "Now let's get out of here."

# CHAPTER TWELVE

THE WRAITH CAME ON FAST.

Years ago, when Calev and I first began sneaking out together, we finagled our way onto Old Farm's full ship right before dawn. The sun yawned over the fields and dock. With him behind me, I scrambled up the mainsail mast. It hadn't been easy. The night before had seen a strong rain and every climbing post along the tall beam was slick as olive oil.

Calev pointed out the dark backs of seals sloping out of the orange-tinted water and I leaned to look past the rigging.

I slipped. It was a long fall and should've broken my back like what happened to Abraham, former scout on the Old Farm ship. But even though the fall didn't break me, it knocked every bit of air from me faster than I could scream.

And now, in this breath, in this moment, the wraith was that quick.

That unexpected.

Though now I was nearly an adult, I screamed like I was a child again. We didn't have a second to scramble to the cabin or light the lantern.

A scraping sound leaked from the spirit's gray-white, sparkling shape. It looked like a flash of starlight, then took on an almost human form, became shifting sands of salt, sometimes with arms or legs or a mouth, but always with reaching fingers.

Its presence pinched at my reason, instead of smashing it like the other wraiths did. It was a pinpoint of a feeling. Clear. Strong. Focused. But, though the wraith's warped emotions were unmistakable, they remained nearly impossible to fight. It was like trying to dig an inking out of your skin.

Some wraiths were like this, subtle and intelligent. From the stories, they usually had specific revenge in mind and once completed would give up their Infusion victim.

A shiver rattled me.

Ranging high near the moonlit husks of clouds, the wraith's shape unfurled and snapped like a banner. Its emotion smothered us.

Oron stood staring, caught in his fear.

*Wouldn't his blood look beautiful like a Kurakian scarf around his neck?* the wraith said into my mind.

*No,* I answered back, silently, whimpering like a fool.

*But he doubts you. Always doubts you.*

The spirit talked on, convincing, luring. I sucked a breath, grabbed Oron, and thrusted him toward the hull. I turned to Calev.

Like a hawk, the wraith swooped low, then high, and hovered, ready to strike its prey. Its arms—wings now—were white smoke, tattered strings of diamond salt as it dove for my dearest friend.

My heart smacked my chest and I lunged toward Calev. The wraith shot forward, the moon poised dead perfect, a spotlight for this sick player and his tragedy.

Everything happened at once.

The wraith's moonshadow struck across the deck and glanced against Calev's bare foot.

Or did it?

There'd been no time to watch for the wraith's Infusion light, to see if it had soaked into Calev's body. I snatched Calev's sleeve, missing a good grip on his arm, and pulled him back, half a second from Infusion myself. I grabbed the lantern.

Wrestling the tangle of my thoughts and those of the wraith's, I rushed toward the opening to the hull behind Calev. Inside, I pressed into him and he shoved against Oron. None of us could hear, I was sure of that. The whipping sound of the wraith masked all other noises of the water against the sides and our breathing.

The pinprick, knife-slice of black thoughts bleeding into my reason, my shaking hands found my flint and knife. I set the lantern outside the hull's opening, on deck, and lit the wick with a speed I didn't know I had. Orange, silver, and black flames danced inside the glass, illuminating the decking, the mast, our lines.

I looked up.

The wraith was gone.

The night only held stars and the moon and the memories of clouds. No wraiths. Dropping my hands, I choked on a sob, my cheeks burning with shame at what I'd thought about blood and death.

I spun to Calev. "The wraith…it's gone."

He blinked and wobbled. He put a hand on the boat's side.

*Is he Infused?* Had the wraith crawled into him? There was no way to tell, really. The Infusion light was invisible until the wraith's revenge or blood lust was satisfied, slaked. Then the light would leave the mouth, vomited like a sickness.

My skin cold, I fisted a hand in his tunic. "Calev? Can you hear me?" My heart buzzed and flopped between my ribs like a beetle on its back. "Calev!" I shook him hard.

Oron shouted too, his voice tight, his eyes white and scared in the near dark.

Calev's gaze fell past my face to the deck beyond the hatch, like he couldn't see me.

Oron pushed us both out of the hull. He held my fishing spear. "Get him off the boat, Kinneret. Throw him over. Now. A waste, a loss, a grief, but we won't go down with him."

I stuttered, then found my tongue. "Oron! Shut it!"

Calev raised his head. "I'm fine. Stop. Stop yelling." He pressed palms to his temples. "I'm fine."

But his face was green around the edges and pale everywhere else.

I put a hand around his wrist, feeling the comfort of his pulse beneath my fingers. "You're certain?"

His beautiful lips stretched sweetly, weakly, a sad excuse for his true smile. "I am." He touched his thumb to my forehead and smoothed a circle, making the Fire's sign in promise.

I closed my eyes. "Thank the seas."

Oron was frowning when I opened them again. "To shore, my fellow looters." He shook his head. "I've had my fill of thrills. I want nothing more than my mat below the tavern and Kinneret's consistent snoring to keep me company."

"*My* snoring?" I laughed, still shaking. "We'll go to the amir in the morning." I hung the lantern on its hook. "If I show her the map and offer her a cut of the silver, she'll help me take Avi back from the oramiral. The map will win her over."

Calev nodded, but his mouth was tight.

"What?"

"I don't know how you'll keep her from taking it all, from claiming Ayarazi's mines and the horses the stories claim are there."

Oron laughed, his arms tucked around his stomach. "I like how you both believe the place truly exists. This is a fantasy, Kinneret. You place your faith, your sweet, foolish faith in fantasy."

"And what do you suggest I do? Sail up to Quarry Isle and just ask kindly for my sister with a bow and a palm to the sky?"

"Thieves we have been before, my kaptan. Thieves we could be again."

"Speak plainly, Oron. I'm tired."

"We could sail to the northeast end, where they never go because of the sea serpents, and sneak onto the island. We could call up a wave to distract them at the southern end and get our girl over the wall."

"Call up a wave? What do you think I am? I can't work the salt that well."

"You do it better than any I've ever heard of," Calev said quietly. His gaze flicked to the salt pouch at my sash.

"Old Farms are not exactly Salt Magic experts." I raised an eyebrow, said a prayer, and blew my handful of salt into the slow-moving wind. A splash sounded from port side, a night fish jumping.

Calev held up his palms in defeat. "Still."

Oron sat on the bench beside me. "Still." He looked up. "Or we could go to your aunt's. Perhaps she could help."

Calev raised his eyebrows. "The one in Kurakia?"

"No," I said, longing for the comfort of Aunt Kania's strong arms, which had always reminded me of the black roots of the Topa tree that grew in that red and dusty country across the Pass. "She'd be no real help in this. I will handle it. It would take too much sun to get there and for what?"

They let the matter drop, and we sailed roughly through the rocks and the swirling current. We took one hard hit against Tall Man, but otherwise remained sound as we reached the bay.

"Calev, you don't think the island exists? You think Oron's dumb plan is better?"

"No, but it'll be difficult to keep the amir running down the road you choose."

"You are the key, Calev." I squeezed my hands together as Oron caught the dock with his foot and lowered a bumper to ease the rub on my boat's side. "You will stand as witness to her promise to take only a portion. A third of what we find. She won't ignore your witness."

Tossing the anchor overboard, Calev said, "First, I have to make you Old Farm kaptan."

"That can wait." I had no clue how we'd solve that problem, but it had to wait. This was silver beyond imagining. The amir would at least hear us out.

We lowered the gaff. The stitches we'd made to repair the sail had loosened dramatically. It was a wonder they held at all during the trip. We'd fix it later. I didn't have the silver or the sun to resew it now. Oron rolled the sail and tied it as Calev and I ran hands over the side where we'd knocked against Tall Man. No holes.

After grabbing his patchwork sack, Oron jumped out of the boat. "Luck to you both. I'm to brew and bed." His stocky shape faded into the night-shadowed road that led to town where some sad drinker was about to *misplace* his beer.

Calev and I climbed onto the dock and lit a lantern. We sat, one set of knees touching to make a crescent of our legs, with the map pieces between us.

I ran my hand over the glazed markings. "If I understand this correctly, the island is hidden past the northern edge of Kurakia. If the scale of Quarry Isle is tuned to the scale of the Spires' location, Ayarazi should be at least three leagues from the farthest trade route I've ever heard tell of."

My mind flashed an image of the water separating Avi and me right now. The wind. Her arms tucked around her sides. The look in her eyes. I squeezed my own eyes shut and swallowed the invisible glass in my throat, pushing the worry and fear away to concentrate.

"I think you're right," he said. "Do you know anything about the waters up there? Don't they connect the Pass to the Expanse at some point?"

I pulled at my bottom lip. "The chill you feel sometimes on the Pass comes from that direction. The wind too, mostly. There's a good chance the waters will be even worse than those on the Pass. Blue. Cold. There are more rock formations the farther north you sail up the Pass, so it's a guess the area will be challenging to run. A lot of underwater threats."

Calev's brown eyes found mine. "Cold. Rocks. Northern wind and abandoned sea waters. It's beginning to sound like one of Savta's tales."

His grandmother told stories around the community fire at spring planting and at the harvest celebration. Skin like a raisin and a voice like wine, she totally pulled me in with the Old Farm legend about the frozen birds of the far North that thawed once a century when the poppymilk flower bloomed and released its enlivening pollen.

"Which story?" I asked. There could be something in the tales that helped us get through this. After all, we had all thought Ayarazi was only a legend.

His eyes, unblinking, raised the tiny hairs on my arms. "The demon Asag."

"The eddy in the Pass is named for that story."

"Yes. But this is more than just an eddy. Asag is supposedly a horned demon that controls rocks that hide in the sea. He can make the water boil, killing everything near him."

"Cozy."

"And if the possessed rocks and hot water don't ruin you, his hideous face will. It's said that if you look at him, you die."

A shiver slid over my back. "Any way to fight the creature?"

"I'll have to ask."

A ruthless amir grabbing for my silver.

My innocent sister twisting and screaming in the hands of a madman.

Salt Wraiths and legendary sea monsters.

I looked down at my hands, which suddenly didn't seem as strong as they'd always been.

Calev's hand covered my knuckles. "I've seen you sail through the Spires in the middle of a winter storm. You can do this."

I found his eyes. There was no trace of glazed madness from the wraith. He was my Calev. Solid. Blessed. So very, very strong in spirit and body. I squeezed his hand, not caring whether he read into the touch or not.

He leaned forward, a slight, small movement, but my heart betrayed me and danced like the violet nightwingers flying dazedly around his head. Purple nets of light lay over his straight nose and the sweep of his dark hair. Goosebumps tickled my legs, and he reached a hand up and ran his fingers down the back of my neck, multiplying the feeling. My ribs rose and fell too quickly. He would notice. He would know. Why was he touching me?

"Kinneret." He breathed my name like a prayer. "You are so much *more* than anyone else."

I tried for a casual laugh, but it bloomed into a sigh. "More?"

"Your drive. Energy. Your spirit. You are fire, my friend."

*Friend.* My heart died a little.

He didn't notice, his hand leaving my skin, leaving me cold.

"We should go," I said.

My knees trembling from his touch, we started up the path, the way Oron had gone.

My stomach swam at a sudden thought of Avi. I had let worry for her drift away for a moment. I was lower than the dirt on the sole of my sandal. I had to stay focused. My good, sweet sister needed all of me.

Calev's gaze drifted back to the darkness of the marsh surrounding the shining rocks of the sea coast. The skin around his eyes tightened, and his lips parted like he might say something.

"Will you walk me back to the tavern?" I tried to talk to him like I'm sure his Intended did, all shy flirting. I wanted to go back to talk of me being fire and his fingers finding new places to rest on my body.

His gaze snapped to me, his eyes wide. "Really? You haven't actually asked me to walk you home since you were eleven years. To steal honey from the brewmaster, yes. To sneak into the guardhouse, yes. But a walk under the moon just for company's sake?" He raised an eyebrow like a question mark. "And what is that voice you're using?" He elbowed me gently.

Heat pricked at my cheeks. I was foolish to push him. He didn't feel that way about me. Maybe if I found the silver, saved Avi, and became a full ship kaptan, but now, no.

"Never mind. I will meet you at the amir's gates at sunrise."

I stormed away before I could fall into the moonlit trap of his beautiful face and strong arms. It wasn't a snare laid for me anyway.

Calev called out, but when I didn't answer, he laughed and said, "Tomorrow, fire friend!"

Yes. Tomorrow. It all hung on tomorrow. Avi's life. My heart. Silver, death, the sea and me.

# CHAPTER THIRTEEN

T HE AMIR STRAIGHTENED IN HER tall chair. My bag of salt safely stowed under a rock outside, I bowed to the bowl of Holy Fire and rushed to keep up with Calev as he approached the dais. We held up our palms in greeting.

"I'd thought to see your father when my men told me an Old Farm representative had arrived," the amir said in her bell voice. "No problem with your throat-blood oath, I hope."

I snorted. Her nasty grin said she hoped no such thing.

"Kinneret," Calev hissed out of the corner of his mouth. I threw him a glare.

The amir laughed. "You two are amusing. I'll admit that. But I hope you don't think on her as a potential Intended, Calev ben Y'hoshua. Even if she does take on the role of Old Farm's full ship kaptan, until she's paid to remove," she eyed my sash, "*many* bells, you must refrain from your body's obvious desires."

"No, my lady, I…" Calev stammered.

I wanted to turn into water and soak into the amir's expensive carpets.

"There are times," the amir said, looking down at her own hand and talking very, very quietly like she was being more reflective than actually making a statement. "When I think we should permit high-castes to do as they please. Not marry lowers, but perhaps simply take them to bed and be done with this sort of situation—if we could be certain no caste-mixed children would come of the temporary union. My predecessors would've fought such a notion, but I take a clean view of the body's needs."

I bit my tongue. She knew nothing about us. Yes, I wanted his warm lips on my neck, but it was only an extra layer of beauty on our secret world.

"Don't sneer at me, girl," the amir said, finally acknowledging that I could take part in the conversation.

"No, my lady. I would never."

"Of course you would. Your kind love to sneer."

My kind. "You believe because I'm low-caste, rising only a handful of generations past slave, that I—"

Calev smiled like sunrise at the amir, blazing through my rant. "I will fulfill my promise, but today my friend Kinneret Raza has a proposition for you."

"Please no more supplications concerning this one's sister. I'm bored of this conversation."

"Don't you need silver to continue fighting alongside the kyros to increase his dominion?" I asked, my pulse galloping.

"What does a Pass sailor know of the kyros's business with me?" Her eyes went to the servant behind us. She was going to dismiss us.

Her singing ozan hummed a sour-sweet tune and took up his oud, ready to do his job by singing to ease the growing tension.

Changing tactics, I looked at Calev, smiled, then addressed the amir. "Forgive me. I know nothing about politics. I do know that a leader such as yourself would beat me if I didn't share my knowledge of a possible adventure worthy of all the poetry in the world."

The amir's face lost its hard edge. Her lips softened and her eyes widened. "Speak."

"I imagine if you braved uncharted seas and found a lost place full of silver, people would sing your songs for an eternity."

Her body didn't move, but her fingers gripped the chair's sides. "And what is this place, sailor?"

"Ayarazi."

Steel returned to the amir's eyes. "Calev, your friend has seen too much sun. I will hear your father's promise that she is Old Farm's kaptan by the end of this moon cycle, or I will watch your throat-blood enrich my soil." Clapping her hands, she stood.

I pulled the map shards out of my sash and ran toward her with them shining in my outstretched palms.

The fighters by her dais rushed toward me, helmets reflecting the window's light and their arm-length yatagans drawn and ready.

Calev shouted my name.

The amir stared down at me, but held up a hand to stop them from running me through. Her guards halted, and I lifted the map shards like a sacrificial lamb.

The curved tips of her leather boots quivered as she walked down the two steps to meet me. A smile cut through her mouth.

"Correct me if I'm mistaken, sailor. You believe this is a map to Ayarazi, an island only known from stories, an island filled with mystical horses, green forests, and caves lined in the purest silver."

My heart scratched up my throat. When she said it like that, in her ringing, polished voice, the whole thing sounded about as reasonable as wearing a fur coat in the Kurakian desert during high summer.

I blew out a slow breath. "Yes."

A glint brightened her eyes.

"And, my lady, I am willing to guide your ship and your fighters to the island indicated on this map for only one half of the total amount of silver gleaned."

"Half?" She looked to Calev. "Was this your idea?"

Calev whitened around the mouth. "No, my lady, but I do believe Kinneret Raza. She found the wine jug—the pieces there—in a wrecked ship not far from Quarry Isle. Old Zayn—

forgive me, I don't know his family name—insists that his ancestor worked as a scribe for the Quest knights."

Calev filled her in on the tale. The amir listened with thinning lips.

The amir's gaze whipped to a dark back corner, where a man had come in. "We have three days until our trip to Kurakia, yes?" the amir asked.

It was Berker. *Fantastic.*

His mouth fell open as his gaze went from my torn skirts to my face. "What are *you* doing here?"

"Kaptan Berker Deniz, you forget yourself." The amir's eyes flashed.

Berker cleared his throat and the surprise left his features. "Yes, my lady. My apologies. We do indeed have three days until our journey to Kurakia. I do wonder if you are aware who sullies your presence."

I rolled my eyes and Calev's hands fisted at his sides.

The amir's fine brow wrinkled. "Enlighten me."

"This low-caste sailor is the one I told you about. She works to seduce the high-caste Old Farm, Calev ben Y'hoshua, into marriage. They've been caught together more than once."

My heart knocked as I looked to Calev, who was blushing furiously.

"Only talking," I blurted.

Calev squeezed his eyes shut and tilted his head back.

*Why can't I keep my mouth shut?*

Steepling her fingers at her trim waist, the amir said, "Kaptan Berker Deniz, I have spoken with Calev ben Y'hoshua on this, thank you. They are not yet of age. The boy knows I'd hate to see him become an Outcast."

Berker bowed. "Thank you for safeguarding our stronger bloodlines and more capable minds." His gaze slid to me.

Calev put a hand on my arm, holding me back.

Even if I died for it, I was ready to rip the man's eyes out.

Calev's fingers tightened on me. "Shhh," he said under his breath, though he looked as ready to go for the kill as me.

One of the amir's fighting sailors came from the back of the room and handed her a square of papyrus.

She read it quickly. "Kill the criminal," she said to the man. "I don't care if he is the kyros's third cousin."

The fighter strode out of the room, not once looking away from his destination.

The amir turned her attention back to us. "Be at the main docks at sunrise. Kaptan Berker Deniz, Kinneret Raza will aid you as we sail toward the legendary Ayarazi."

Berker's hands splayed like someone had dumped ice-cold water down his back. "What, my lady?"

It was my turn to smile. "I'm going to lead you and the amir's fighting sailors on a quest."

The man's mouth shut like a night flower exposed to sunlight. I almost laughed.

The amir held up a finger. "Ah, ah. Not lead. Just advise."

Berker turned a fantastic shade of purple. "I assure you, the scrapper is lying, my lady."

The amir took a step forward. "Do not use slurs in my presence. Her family served their time as slaves. She is low, but that is all. Also, am I mistaken, Kaptan Berker Deniz, or did you suggest I cannot spot a lie?"

"Of course not. I only meant that you don't need her help. I can take you to the legendary island."

"Oh really? Then why didn't you already come to me with this life-changing information?"

I bit my lip to keep from laughing.

"If it's out there, I can find it for you, my lady."

"Enough." The amir adjusted the tie that held her sleeve in place. "She will advise. Unless she is found to be as unworthy as you seem to think her, Kaptan Berker Deniz."

Calev edged forward. "As to the matter of the riches the group will find, I stand witness that the amir will claim only half of the silver mined at Ayarazi with the other half going to Kinneret Raza, master of this expedition."

Berker's lips pinched together, making them whiten. The amir's hand didn't move to her throat.

"Will you not make the throat-blood oath?" My words peeked out of my mouth like scared children. "My lady?"

Berker sneered. "Don't be insolent, low-caste."

"Silence," the amir said. Her look boiled the flesh from my bones. "I will see you at sunrise." Her long tunic snapped as she twisted and strode back to her chair. "Make ready."

CALEV AND I WALKED OUT of the amir's main hall and under the orange and ivory striped arches leading to her courtyard.

I leaned toward Calev. "She didn't make the oath. And what is your father going to do when he hears about what you're doing?"

"She'll hold to her word. She only believes an oath is beneath her. My father won't do anything. He can't get in the way of the amir's plans. Plus, this shouldn't take so long. Eleazar is covering for me, remember? They'll be so busy with the harvest, they won't have the sun to notice I'm missing."

"Maybe. But how am I going to get us through the Pass and beyond without Berker seeing my Salt Magic?" *Or how our hands brush and my breath catches?*

Chewing his lower lip, Calev said, "You'll think of something. You always do."

I pressed a hand on my forehead. "I hope you're right."

# CHAPTER FOURTEEN

T HE AMIR'S BLACK-SAILED SHIP floated like a wooden fortress at the northern dock. Its pennants, pinned to the top of the mast and the towering prow, flew with the wind, snapping. The amir's seal crouched on each one—a roaring black lion on a field of yellow, ready for a battle with the sea.

But as lovely as the craft was, it was not a worthy opponent for the sea's challenges, nor was the man who now kaptaned it. Berker. He would make all the same mistakes as the kaptans before him.

Sailing a fortress like this one, they tried to force their will on the waters, instead of working with its tides, current, and creatures. If this were my ship, I'd fit it with looser sails. I'd trim the sides, lessen its weight. It'd be a beautiful beast, strong enough to withstand the worst of storms and clever enough to find its way through the waves.

My mother and father had set the idea of the right kind of sailing in my mind. As we crossed the waters with the sun hot on our heads and the hull and deck bursting with fruit, sometimes with sacks of Old Farm's fine grain, or a few less-than-wealthy travelers, my parents poured their wisdom into Avi and me. Let wraiths own the night with the pain they remembered from their

119

lives lost at sea. Allow the current to take the boat four knocks east of the intended route, because it will ease the trip around that rock shelf. Listen to the wind to know when the storm will hit or when the sea will calm and need to rest. The Pass could be a friend, or at least, a respected enemy.

We stopped at the ramp leading to the amir's ship and stood behind a line of her infamous fighting sailors. I leaned right to watch them as they stopped, one-by-one, at the ship's Holy Fire bowl. Each passed a hand over banked coals that glowed like jewels. Pennants of smoke danced over their tall forms and the center of their palms glimmered as they bowed to the Fire. A few touched the center of their foreheads, acknowledging the Fire's potential to give them ideas.

I couldn't even imagine doing Salt Magic in front of so many people. My bag of salt was tucked inside my sash, away from judging eyes, but at some point, I'd have to use it. I only hoped when I did, everyone would be too busy to notice.

On deck, the fighters lined up on either side of the amir and Berker as we boarded the soap-scented ship.

At least they'd swabbed the deck properly.

"Try to remember this is the amir's ship, Kinneret," Oron whispered. "And neither she nor her ship are here for your examination."

I scowled at him.

"You might stay alive longer. That's all I'm saying." Oron shrugged.

Two men fitted a barred cover over a storage space near the prow. I peered in and a giant's sharp, metal finger pointed up at me. "What is that?"

"Mining drill." Oron flicked a hand toward the dark beyond the object. "There are probably five or so aboard."

Those would slow us down for sure. "How much do they weigh?"

"No idea," Oron said. "Calev? Have you used any on Old Farm?"

"We used a different sort on a new well, but I don't know much about them."

We climbed the stairs and stood next to the man-sized tiller wheel as the amir spoke to her assembled fighters. Each wore red leather jerkins similar to hers, but theirs jingled with five bells on each shoulder. Their black sashes secured daggers and yatagans, frog legs, and other charms. Some held battle axes with gold or silver heads meant to deflect blows.

The nearest fighter's axe was decorated with calligraphy in the shape of phoenix heads. Beautiful and deadly—much like its owner, a giant, light-haired woman who would probably lop my head off if I so much as sneezed the wrong way. But that axe of hers...

"You want one, don't you?" Oron whispered up to me.

"I do." My hands never wanted to curl around my small knife and anytime I'd tried a yatagan, it felt too skinny. The handle of that axe wasn't too different from a tiller, and I knew exactly how to handle one of those.

"Just for you, I'll ask its owner where one might find another like it," Oron said, his gaze going up and down the fighter's body.

"Just for me, hm?" I frowned at the woman's impressive bosom.

Oron shuttered his eyes dramatically. "I am the epitome of self-sacrifice."

"My fighters." The amir held her arms wide. "Today we embark on a mission to find Ayarazi, lost island of silver."

A wave of confused murmurs ran through the group.

"You will be richly rewarded if you succeed in following this...temporary kaptan's orders as if she were me." She held a hand toward me and my mouth didn't want to work.

*Temporary kaptan?*

"The title gives you more control, gives you rank. I've decided I'd rather have the one who knows the way fully able to order my sailors. Unless that is a problem?"

"No. It's...no, it's wonderful. Perfect. Thank you, my lady."

Calev elbowed me, his eyes making my knees go liquid.

"Apologies, my lady." Berker looked like his bowels weren't working well. "But she is low-caste and I know for a fact she is a practitioner of—"

"Thank you, my lady," I said, the words coming like they belonged to someone else. My heart beat in my ears. This was my dream. Berker had never seen me practice Salt Magic. He had no proof. And I wasn't about to let him ruin this. I turned to the crew. "And thanks to her sailors who will help me steer this vessel to the northern reaches of the Pass. Haul anchor and tie up the mainsail. I will handle the steering on my own. We go!"

The fighters each drove one fist into the air and hustled to their stations at starboard and port, prow and stern. They were pieces on the playing board and I knew this game better than any.

Giving me a gentle squeeze on the shoulder, Calev spoke in my ear. "My Kinneret, kaptan of the amir's own vessel."

Shivers ran up and down my arms. *Kaptan. His Kinneret.*

I turned, and our breath mingled. The scar at the corner of his lips twitched like he was about to smile. My body thrummed, wanting him to lean closer, a breath nearer, to press his body to mine.

# CHAPTER FIFTEEN

ERKER'S COUGH BROKE THE SPELL. "The sun waits for no one. Let's see what the little nothing can do," he hissed quietly. "It would be sad indeed if the nothing was seen consorting improperly with an Old Farm. Sad if she were thrown to the hull with nothing to do but clean his chamber pot."

I gritted my teeth.

Calev leaned toward my neck and whispered, "Everything will be fine if you can hold that sweet tongue of yours."

It was good we balanced one another like this. When he wanted to leap into something stupid, I held him back. When I was ready to bite and ruin everything, he kept me calm.

Well, he *tried*.

I didn't like tucking my tail between my legs. *Little nothing.* We'd see about that.

Twisting away, I focused on the Pass to learn what the sea had to say about the coming journey. The water was smooth, but an inconsistent breeze whisked through the air and a current snaked beneath the glassy surface, ready to suck us down if I didn't steer the ship right.

I looked to Oron. He nodded in the direction of the wind and I took his advice, moving the wheel a bit so we sat a little more westerly.

Hidden in my sash, the map shards' edges pushed at a spot on my stomach. I welcomed their sharp corners, remembering their promise.

As we cleared the shelter of the harbor, Oron nibbled a skewer of meat—Where had he found that?—and started a game of bones and shells behind me with two sailors who smiled at something he said.

"Only Oron could get fighting sailors to smile," Calev said, walking away to find somewhere to lend a hand.

Tunic sleeves pushed over his elbows, Calev rewrapped a rope with a woman even taller than the amir. Her attention was more on his wiry arms than the task at hand. A hot arrow jabbed my stomach.

We had no more sun to waste. I had to get these sailors moving.

I called out my first orders. "Take us fifteen knocks south before turning north."

"What?" Berker clutched an enormous key and a book with gold lettering down its spine. "But that's hours out of our way."

The sun-warmed cedar wheel heated my palms. I took a fortifying breath. "And how many Pass trips have you made, kaptan?"

"More than you," he spat.

I'd asked around about him, but he'd somehow cloaked his early days in Jakobden. He might've even changed his name, but that was a weak hypothesis of my own. I did know some things though.

"I heard you were a malhatc rope merchant before ever setting a sandal on a boat." I smiled.

His eyes widened.

"Didn't think I'd find out everything I could when I realized how this journey was going to go?" Fisting my hand, I put my thumb against my forehead, but instead of drawing a circle, the

Fire's sign, on my flesh, I spread my fingers in a sudden burst, the dirtiest gesture Oron had taught me.

I heard Oron laugh from far off, but thankfully, no one else had seemed to notice. He had moved away from his game, taking a block from a fighting sailor's hand and adjusting the line. He waved to the sails and rolled his eyes. I was so glad he was here.

Berker gasped belatedly, shocked by my gesture. "Such manners. Suppose I should expect twisted, disrespectful uses of the Fire's sign from one like you. You will learn to behave, sailor, or you will be punished."

"Truly? By whom?" The Pass was moody today. The waves had risen, and they ate at our speed.

"The amir—"

"The amir put me here. I'd guess she won't care that I use the sign to shut your flapping lips. I don't think the Fire cares much either."

Leaving the sailor he'd lectured, Oron pushed his way between Berker and me. "Nor will the amir mind if I ask where the wine is kept. Now be on your way, other kaptan. I have much to discuss with my own lady here."

Huffing, Berker bustled off toward the amir, who stood at the prow with her hair in viciously tight knots. She held her shoulders back as if she could intimidate the sea. The woman was awful, but also kind of fantastic.

Unsteady on his feet, Calev came up beside us. "Rankling Berker again?"

Oron groaned. "Don't start, good luck charm. I haven't had a drop of wine, let alone an amount sufficient to help me tolerate your obnoxiously good nature."

Calev said, "Good luck charm? You're the one who works the least and manages to get the most food. Maybe I should tie you around my neck like a frog's leg." He plucked the last piece of meat from Oron's skewer and popped it between his lips.

Oron rubbed his chin. "It's not a bad idea. I'd have a better view from up there."

"What did you want to tell me, Oron?" I'd asked him to examine their wraith lanterns.

"They have five. They look well enough, though not completely glass like your mother's."

I wished we'd brought mine. Wraith lantern wicks were a complicated thing. Slight color switches at the third and seventh threading, or at the one-third or one-seventh mark across the cloth's expanse, repelled wraiths more acutely, and kept them at a farther distance.

"They keep them in those small boxes, don't they?" Calev asked. The joking slant had fled his lips. He pointed to the dark wood containers poised along starboard.

The odd glint in his eyes told me that last run-in with a Salt Wraith still hung over him. Who could blame him? I'd screamed my face off last time. Only because I'd dealt with the wraiths so many times could I cast off the fear of Infusion afterward.

Once, when a small fleet of us low-caste sailors were shipping Old Farm surplus figs to a port just north of Jakobden's, two wraiths had attacked.

My mother had lit the lantern's expensive, silver-threaded wick with a grace and speed no one else in the world had. Father had Avi strapped to his back. We tried to work the sail and get away, but the wraiths speared from the sky again and again, challenging the lantern's effect on them.

Far enough from those who would threaten Outcasting, we all went to the salt.

A woman in a boat nearby called out prayers and threw handfuls of white, but the sea was sluggish to answer her.

Two middle-aged sisters in another boat huddled together and sprinkled salt over the side of their craft. The wind breezed toward them, but not quickly enough. One of the sisters had been Infused and nearly throttled her own first mate before anyone could lash her to the mast.

I had dusted our salt into the waves, and with one focused prayer, we slipped away, leaving the others to their fate. We were the only boat to get away without an instance of Infusion.

For a good year after, the other small-boat Pass sailors had dipped their heads to me as if I was special.

So even when I, just like everyone else, was scared to shaking by the wraiths, I still had a thread of confidence running through me.

"I wouldn't worry about where they store the wraith lanterns, Calev." I said. "In this clear weather, we'll have no trouble getting them lit and hung before sundown."

He stared at the approaching rocks, Tall Man first, then the Spires, after that, Asag's Door. For a second, the healthy glow leeched from Calev's skin and hair and eyes. He looked like a bad fresco of himself, and my heart clenched to see it. I touched his arm, wishing we were on my boat, away from all of this.

The wish tightened my throat. I jerked my hand away.

No. I didn't want to be away from this. Being kaptan is what I'd wanted my whole life. I could save Avi as a kaptan. And Calev was strong enough to deal with wraiths. He had to be.

I spun. The fighters worked the rigging, the sail snapped and caught, and the ship dipped in the increasingly rough water, then soared high again, my stomach lifting and making me smile.

This was what I wanted. Regardless of the risk. *Kaptan Kinneret. Equal to Calev.*

"So all the lanterns were in good shape?" I asked Oron, double-checking for Calev's sake.

"I think so. But maybe you can take a look at the wicks and see if we should add a threes and sevens stitch." Oron frowned at Calev.

Calev braced himself against the ship. "I'm not worried, if that's what you think. I'm fine." He smiled, but it wasn't his good smile.

WITH THE AMIR'S MEN and women following my orders, I steered the weighty craft around the rocks. The wind at a nice angle, we tracked our way north. I wanted to find the lost island before nightfall. The map shards only gave the vaguest sense of distance. It was impossible to know if we could pull it off.

The sails billowed above us, and I pulled the largest of the shards out of my sash. Calev and Oron leaned over me to look. Calev pointed to a spot we'd see pretty soon.

"What do these raised ridges mean? Do you think they were put there purposefully, or are only a part of the pottery?"

"I think they show some sort of hazard." The wheel pulled at my grip. I tightened my grip and my bag of salt slipped from my sash.

Calev sucked a breath.

I grabbed the bag and tucked it back into place, checking to see if anyone noticed.

"Smooth," Oron whispered as a sailor walked by. He raised his voice. "I think these marks are creatures."

"If they are," I said. "There'd have to be an army of them." Goosebumps tripped down my back.

The scout shouted from the sky cup, his voice carrying from his perch at the top of the mast. "Ahead! Ahead!"

The yellow, sunny day seemed an ironic thing suddenly.

Directly in our path—and any path we could take with the wind the way it was—wrecked ships protruded from the white edges of the choppy water. Like dead starfish, the ships clung to what looked like dark reefs punching through the sea's surface.

Oron grabbed my arm and squeezed. Hard.

Any one of these ghost ships could reach out and break the hull. We'd be food for seastingers. We'd be doomed to rise as Salt Wraiths, twisting and hating for eternity.

"What do they do to salt witches at sea?" I asked Oron, my voice taut, almost breaking.

"Throw them overboard."

Calev stood closer. "You won't go down alone."

"I'm not going down at all. I'll die on this boat first."

# CHAPTER SIXTEEN

ASTS LIKE BROKEN FINGERS. RAGGED sails twisting in the water. Prows, noses to the sun. Wide tillers, jagged from their tragedy. The water in front of us was a labyrinth of debris.

I imagined an errant, wrecked stern puncturing our hull and fighters sliding to starboard, panic jerking their movements. In my mind, a sail reached its triangle of fabric around our tiller until the mighty wood splintered and left us rudderless in the Pass. My head pounded. I went cold from forehead to foot.

And then I was in a memory.

Mother, Father, Avi, and I on the deck of my boat, the sky a green and black calamity raging toward us.

"There are days you must let the sea take you, Kinneret," Mother had said, her voice quiet but strong, like a yatagan slicing the air. "Let the water and the wind, the sea itself, guide you through. Those days, like this one, release your hold on the tiller and your gaze from the rigging. Let go."

The howling storm had raged over us that day. We'd lashed ourselves to the hatch, to the mast, to the side, watching nothing as the rain blinded us. A thousand, two-thousand seconds later, we drifted out of the clouds and wind and water, alive. Humbled.

Reminded that the control we have over our lives only remains in our hands if we sometimes released it from our fisted fingers.

And now, I needed to do the same.

"Loosen the rigging on the mainsail!" I threw an arm toward the black swathe of fabric that pulled us through the water. "All sailors to the sides, positioning beams in hand!"

The fighting sailors had been frozen by the ship graveyard, but they turned, pointed helmets shining, to frown at me now.

"Don't just stand there, fools!" Oron was small in size but not in voice. "Your kaptan gives orders!"

I was already pulling salt from my pouch, hoping I could do more than I'd ever done with the magic and praying Berker and the amir would stay below. Calev shielded me from most eyes, his wide sleeves billowing around me. He watched me scoop a handful of sparkling white, then he nodded.

"Save us, my fire."

My heart rolled over. "I'll try."

I moved to the side, lifting my palmful. The sea grumbled around the dead ships and their rotting limbs. I took a breath. *What prayer should I say?* Why wouldn't the words come to me?

"Kaptan?" a sailor's wide eyes turned toward me as he struggled with the lines beside his friends. "Is that—"

The amir burst from the cabin door, Berker trailing her like a string on her tunic.

I growled.

"My fighters," the amir said. "Do as she says."

Calev said something under his breath, the sound of it harsh and sharp, unlike him.

The amir must've seen our situation from her cabin window. And now she'd see my situation too. Well, what did Old Zayn say? As well hanged for a chicken as an egg. The dead ships in the water loomed closer, raising threatening masts and broken hulls. If I didn't work fast, this would be over. I had no sun for more fretting. Ignoring everything else, I dusted the salt into the breeze and prayed, the words finally flowing.

"*Sea, be with me.*

*Wind, please answer.*
*To take, to give, tumbling currents,*
*Push us, pull us, set us free."*

Some of the salt ghosted into the water, some of it floated back and danced near the sailors' heads, before drifting over the sails and down to brush the amir's cheek.

Our gazes met and my blood pounded in my ears.

# CHAPTER SEVENTEEN

ER MOUTH FORMED WORDS I couldn't hear over the growing wind, but could see and understand.

"This is your skill?" she said. "You are no true kaptan."

The ship shifted under us and we dragged our way past the first drowned vessel.

Some of the sailors gasped. Two turned from the amir to look over the side, as if they could see the magic.

I raised my voice so it would carry like the salt, over the sailors and into her ears. "There are times when we must trust the sea to bring us through. It knows the way."

My mother's words surged through my veins alongside her blood and the bond that no death could ever steal away. I dared the amir to try.

Among folds of Calev's linen sleeve, his warm fingers found my hand. I held tight, hoping his luck would soak into me. His unblinking eyes focused on the amir.

Oron put a fist in the air. "Yes!"

Berker and the amir strode across the deck as the sailors wasted time staring, positioning poles in their hands. We drifted closer to the larger grounded ships with every breath.

"I told you she was no more than a Salt Witch." Berker laughed.

The amir's gaze slapped him silent. But then she loosened the leather collar of her vest and looked to me.

"Sailor, stand down," she said. "Kaptan Berker Deniz takes control now."

We had no sun for this. "We will sink, my lady." We might anyway. I'd never pushed my skill with prayer so far.

She glanced at me, my skirts, my bells. "You've been given your order. Guard!"

A man with a red beard stormed up the three stairs to where we stood, pushed past Calev and Oron, who argued, and grabbed my arms.

Everything slowed to a dreamlike pace and my mind wandered into varying possibilities.

I'd never used salt against anyone. Unless you counted wraiths. But Avi needed me. If I drowned this sun, she would die, by wraiths or by work in the quarry.

I had no idea how the salt prayer would work to hinder or hurt a person. Maybe it wouldn't do anything at all. But my desire, my focus—as Mother had always called it—was certainly there, burning and struggling against the impossible situation. I had to at least try.

Avi was suddenly there, in that same memory of the night we'd escaped the two wraiths. Her cheeks were round as she peered over Father's shoulder, her legs still against his sides. I whispered prayers and sprinkled salt, and her mouth fell open as the sea answered me.

Unlike my sweet sister, I was naturally good at focusing my will and creating strong Salt Magic.

Now was the time to see exactly how strong.

Rubbing the remnants of salt from my fingers, my skin burning under the fighter's rough grip, I whispered a prayer.

*"Go true, winds on the waters.*
*You know me and I know you."*

Calev's eyes widened.

134

Oron's leg flashed out as he kicked the fighter who held me in the knee. "Son of a whoring goat! Let your kaptan go!"

The sky grayed like someone had drawn a curtain on the sun.

Wind curled around my legs, tangling my skirt, and pulled me from the fighter's hands as rain like knives dashed from the ballooning clouds above the ebony sails.

The sea was listening.

The ship turned toward starboard, under my feet, heavy and lumbering.

Calev, Oron, the amir, and I, united in survival, took hold of whatever was closest. I clung to the railing near the wheel. Oron clutched the large bell hung for sounding arrival to the docks. Calev latched onto an empty rope's post toward port, the amir at his side doing the same. A fist of fighters fell to the decking. Some shouted to the Fire, to the power of the sea.

The boat listed to port, then back roughly. Water lipped the edge, salt sea mixing with the fresh rain pooling and dragging across the smooth wood. A sailor slipped and dropped over starboard, legs in the Pass, hands latched to the rim like starfish.

I scurried down to help her back onboard as we twisted past the first of the larger wrecked vessels. A cracked beam reached over the gap between our ship and its own broken body, and I ducked, avoiding its wooden spines. The beam scraped the stern and turned our tail.

"Kinneret!" Calev was running at me, his feet slipping and his face white.

I tugged the fallen sailor's vest and pulled her onto the deck.

The rain went sideways as the sea steered us around another ship with its sails and bedraggled pennants like rebellious daytime wraiths in the storm.

The blowing rain clouded the amir's face. I couldn't tell whether she ordered more fighters after me or if she was clinging to the ship like everybody else. The black and silver lightning blinked over the clouds, then Calev was with me, his hand on my back, his eyes filled with fear.

The ship swung around to avoid two ancient dhows, twice the size of my own craft. Their lines hung from masts and splintered prows like saliva from a wild dog's mouth. Our ship veered close, too close. One snagged our prow and jerked us.

Calev pitched over the ship's side.

He disappeared under the waves even as my hands reached out pointlessly.

My mouth worked, trying to breathe, taking in metallic storm-rain.

Someone screamed. Another shouted.

*Calev. Not Calev too.*

Leaning over the ship, I spotted flesh in the water. Hands. Fingers, wet and pale, holding to a ridge of wood connected to the side of the boat. We lurched backward and Calev's head appeared, the sea releasing him for a second. Near the stairs, a rope and a float hung on a hook. Oron was there before I could finish my thought of grabbing it.

"Here!" Oron tossed it, and I caught the netted float in both shaking, freezing hands.

There was no sun for more salt. I threw the float, praying, hoping, wishing, longing for Calev to reach it, to be able to grab ahold of his chance of seeing another sun.

This couldn't be our end. It couldn't be.

The Salt Magic worked the current of the water and helped us between more lost vessels.

But the float flipped past Calev. He threw one arm out to catch it.

Missed.

In the crash of water, the float blasted back toward him. Letting go of the boat's side, Calev committed both hands to his attempt. Somehow—because he was lucky Calev—he caught it and hugged it to him.

I twisted. Fighting sailors gathered behind me, Oron with them.

"Pull! Pull now!" I shouted.

The rope slid through my chilled, wet fingers, its coconut fibers cutting into my skin. With everything I had, I latched onto it and yanked, the fighting sailors doing the same.

Calev's face cleared the wall.

My heart began beating again. Oron and I tugged him aboard, and I fell onto his back as he lay forward and gasped. I cried and squeezed him, not caring if we wrecked now because he was here with me. He was here with me. Not gone. Not in the sea. Not lost to become a Salt Wraith.

The rain eased, and the sun leaked through the clouds as we passed the last of the dead ships. I stood, hands on my knees, my skirts wet and heavy, and smiled.

*Thanks to you, sea waters. Thanks to you, Fire.*

We were alive. We still had a chance to save Avi. Unless the amir decided she'd had enough of my magic.

# CHAPTER EIGHTEEN

THE PASS WAS A ROAD of silk that night. Watching for wraiths, sailors lit the lanterns. The swinging patterns of orange and silver light almost made me forget the terrible spirits could come at any moment and Infuse us. That they could sweep over us, find a place not cloaked in magic light, and twist our minds so we set on one another like rabid animals.

On the small, raised kaptan's deck, the amir walked up to me, her eyes half lidded. A servant hovered near and offered her skewers of goat's meat. She took two and gave me one.

"Kaptan Kinneret Raza, you may spend the night below with my unit leaders, Calev ben Y'hoshua, and Kaptan Berker Deniz."

"Thank you."

It was unbelievable. I'd thought after the Salt Magic, she'd have me thrown into the hole to suffer the rest of the journey with the rats. My efforts to escape the ship graveyard outweighed my taboo magic. In her eyes, at least. But wonderful as her invitation to go below was, I couldn't leave Oron. Or the fighting sailors.

"I will be fine on deck, my lady."

Calev came out of the shadows, his lips tight and his gaze on the amir. "Thank you for your offer of safety, my lady."

I suppose he'd heard her mention his name.

"Will you sleep below then, Calev ben Y'hoshua?" I asked, using his whole name to show I understood the high-caste ways. I tried to keep any judgment on his decision from my voice. It was smart to take safety when it was offered, and the cabin would definitely be better than staying out here, despite the lanterns. Calev was important to our community. I understood. But it didn't stop me from hoping he'd stay out here with me.

He cocked his head. "Maybe later, my lady. For now, I'll keep Kinneret Raza company."

"For planning purposes only, of course," the amir said in her bell voice as she walked away and disappeared belowdecks.

My cheeks heated and my blood sprinted a lap around my body. "Of course," I answered before Calev could ruin things by standing up for me. I'd had enough fight for one day.

Oron sat on a barrel beside some sailors near the main mast. He'd found a gourd-shaped oud and was plucking the strings like a master.

Clouds masked the sky and blinded the moon. The lanterns were swaying stars that sent comets of gold light off the posts, the decking, and the fighting sailors' varied faces. Some were my age. Most older. Men. Women. Hair like copper, ink, sand. Their flesh was lighter than my own. None with Kurakian blood.

I touched Calev's sleeve. "Want to go down to the main deck?" I gestured toward Oron and the others, who were drinking now and singing sailing songs.

Calev's eyes flicked to the door through which the amir had disappeared and he flipped his dagger casually. Through the cloth of his salt-crusted tunic, his skin chilled my fingers, but his usual scent of sun-heated fields and lemons was a comfort.

"Come on," I said. "You need a little music."

Taking a breath, he nodded, sheathed his dagger, and let me lead him down the short staircase to the main deck.

Oron lifted his eyebrows in greeting as he strummed notes into the night to help us forget the wraiths and the loss of one of our sailors. Oron's smallest finger jumped up and down on the oud's thinnest string, making the instrument quirk high, then higher. I plopped onto a crate of what smelled like flatbread. Sitting next to me, Calev shook his head and moved his jaw.

"Water in your ears?" Other than a three-finger-long scratch down his forearm, he hadn't suffered from his fall overboard. If it'd been me, I'd have lost an entire leg to an errant seastinger.

A woman next to Oron began a haunting accompaniment on an eagle bone flute.

"My head…I feel a little off," Calev said.

I put my hand on his knee to stop his leg bouncing. "It's been quite a day."

"Quite." He gave me a quick grin and tucked his hair behind his ear. A dusting of scruff shadowed his sharp jawline, and my stomach dipped like I'd sailed over a swell.

The tall female sailor from earlier elbowed me. "If I had a man like him look at me like that, I'd have him up and dancing no matter the cost later. Besides, you're a kaptan. For now, anyway." She laughed quietly. "*A wraith's welcome is always a surprise, the sea's embrace a cold one.*"

The traditional sailor's motto had me standing in a breath. Never before had the old words seemed so true. Life was short. I was going to enjoy myself. Just for tonight, while I was still a kaptan. It did Avi no harm for me to keep on living as we worked our way to rescuing her.

"Calev, will you dance with me?" I held out my hands, my heart shivering.

This was a line for him to cross. Maybe I could keep the kaptan status. A low-caste kaptan. Whoever heard of such a thing? But maybe, just maybe…

Plus, it was only one dance. It wasn't a proposal of Intention.

Calev looked up at me. The lanterns poured copper light over one side of his face. His eyes were that deep brown-red of good wine. The kind I'd only tasted when Oron stole a jug. The music, complex and drifting, swirled over our heads, but Calev didn't rise.

And there was Berker, a flash of too-bright silk in the corner, his lips poised to laugh at my public humiliation. I was sure he didn't view my status as anything but low.

I began to drop my hands. Flames enveloped my neck and chest.

Oron added words to his music and crowed so loudly that I knew he was trying to deflect attention from me to himself. Kind soul.

*"He drew her in like tragedies often dooooo, his heart so black and his eyes so bluuuue. She would die before the sea drank the sun, but his smile would be worth it before it was done."*

Then, in one smooth movement, Calev stood.

My heart answered his smile by reaching into my throat and attempting to push me, head first, into his arms.

I fought the urge. I'd gone this far. I wouldn't go further. He had to take the step.

"I'd like that, kaptan," Calev said.

And if it weren't for my sister's plight, it would've been the best night of my life.

Oron shaped his song into a tempting syren's call as Calev's arms circled me. He placed his hands, warmer now, on my back. His palms felt large against the curve of my waist. They sent a slow-moving wash of heat up my back and down my legs. Trying to breathe normally, I lifted my own hands high and flipped them this way and that like swallows at dusk. His gaze locked on my face, we stepped right, then left. His fingers tightened slightly on me and I swallowed, definitely not breathing normally. In rhythm with the leaping, colorful music, we turned as one.

Other couples joined in, bumping us here and there and smiling. A man held a wooden bowl of tatlilav to our lips, each in turn. The drink warmed my throat and loosened my arms and legs. A strand of Calev's hair whipped into my eye, and I laughed as we spun and spun and spun, my body held upright by his strong hands.

Calev's winded voice found my ear. He smelled a little like the salt of sweat and I found I didn't mind it. "They don't teach this kind of dancing at Old Farm." On the last word, someone jostled us and his mouth brushed my ear. I shivered and swallowed.

"N-No, I suppose not." I stepped on his toe and grinned as apology. "It's a trader's jig. Oron taught me."

Hearing his name, Oron tipped his head at us and finished the song with a trill of low notes that had everyone stomping their feet in approval of his skill. Oron set his oud aside and hopped from the barrel.

"Calev," he said, "why don't you favor us with an Old Farm dagger dance?"

My mouth popped open. Did Calev know the traditional steps? I'd never thought about it. But he'd be a perfect dagger dancer with his long limbs and enviable grace.

A blush crept over his nose and cheeks.

I smacked his arm playfully, the tatlilav doing its work to make me bold. "You *do* know how, don't you?"

The man with the wooden bowl offered me another sip, but I waved him off. Oron motioned for the sailors to gather around, then threw two handfuls of salt at Calev's feet.

Berker snorted and left for belowdecks.

We made a wide, seated circle around Calev, who didn't appear to have a choice in this. If he knew how to do this robed-in-secrecy dance, we wanted to see it.

"I don't know if this is a good idea, Oron," Calev said as he put palms to the deck's luminous wooden planks.

Was that the dance's starting position? I'd heard tales about it. But even though Calev was arguing this, he at least didn't seem haunted like he had earlier tonight.

A long-faced sailor leaned in. "We won't tell."

Another agreed. "This may be our only chance to see this. Would you rob us our vision of the Fire's weapon?"

Good-natured laughs followed. Old Farms, the native people of Jakobden, claimed their dagger skills were why the Bahluk conquerors—the amir's people—permitted them to keep their lands. Today, three-hundred-sun-circles later, we knew the real reason. Silver. The Bahluk conquerors and the kyros that employed them enjoyed the silver brought in by trading Old Farm lemons and barley. None had been able to mimic Old Farm's perfectly sweet, but achingly sour fruits. And Old Farm's barley never wilted in the worst of droughts. Although Calev had surprised me with his speed and agility already on this voyage, his people's strength came from wisdom and careful planning, not physical prowess. The dagger dance was ceremonial, not martial.

"I think it's a fabulous idea." Oron grinned. "You'll either make us laugh at your ridiculousness, or everyone will swoon, wondering if your coordination translates to the bed."

Whoops erupted over the deck and I went a little lightheaded.

Calev cocked an eyebrow at all of us, then looked at me. "What do you say, Kaptan Kinneret?"

A light like the sun glowed through me. Even if it was ceremonial, I wanted to see it. Their rituals tugged at me like the sea.

"Please, Calev ben Y'hoshua, son of Old Farm," I said, "dance for us."

With the smile that could heal all my hurts, the smile that promised we'd get Avi back and keep the amir from taking Calev's throat-blood by making me kaptan of Old Farm's ship, he closed his eyes and began.

With a grating sound, his palms smoothed along the deck in front of him until he was nearly lying face down, then with a movement that seemed impossible, he leaped into the air and landed in a crouch, his dagger drawn with a speed I had only seen in animals.

The group gasped, but quickly quieted as his arm arced, making an invisible line with the dagger before thrusting forward, spinning, thrusting back, and whirling one foot in a high kick that had to be more distraction than attack. Calev's foot stomped once, hard, his eyes flashing and his hair swinging. His feet made a thousand small steps, his dagger like a minnow in the waves of his sweeping tunic.

I didn't breathe once.

The dance took on a dreamlike quality. Wide arm movements. Dramatic slashes. Impossible kicks and defenses against imaginary conquerors.

I was no longer on a ship.

I was no longer a sailor.

I was a Jakobden native, one of Calev's ancestors. I was leaping from trees to slice a Bahluk's yatagan hand. I was spinning, the ties of my traditional headtie snapping and the sun on my blade blinding another bell-adorned attacker. I dug a bare foot into the ground and the scent of fertile earth and tannic, syrupy cedar rose into the air.

Calev stopped, bowed, and the spell broke. His dagger hung at his sash.

The sailors sprung into the air, feet stomping, mouths shouting.

My knees quaking, I went to him. "Calev. I…Calev."

He bent toward me, but instead of kissing my lips, his mouth went to my forehead, to my hairline.

I couldn't stop my hands from wrapping around his body or keep my heart from breaking with want. I was a shivering, ridiculous mess. If he could move like that, he could fight. If his stomach and mind could handle the horror.

"Kinneret, thank you," he said. "I haven't enjoyed a night this much ever in my life." He pressed his lips to my head again and my eyes closed. I wished he could be with me, like this, every day. He hadn't kissed my mouth yet, but maybe he would.

The night was still dark and heavy with promise.

IN THE MIDDLE OF ANOTHER trader jig, the ship halted in a way that told me the promise had nothing to do with anything as pleasant as kissing.

# CHAPTER NINETEEN

I BROKE AWAY FROM THE knot of sailors who'd joined me in dancing while Calev told stories near the brasier's glowing coals. Lit orange, his face rumpled in confusion at my sudden movement.

The deck jerked under my feet. Calev and Oron flew to me.

"What is it, Kinneret?" Calev asked.

"I don't know...but it isn't good."

The ship had gone still again. Maybe we were lodged on a rock.

"What is that smell?" Oron's wide nose wrinkled.

It hit me. Stale salt water. Old fish. Blood. Swallowing, I took a struggling breath, wishing I didn't need air.

"Why are we stopped?" Oron asked.

I ran to the side and leaned over the railing. Black rock jutted from the sea and crowded around the ship, gripping it, holding it still in the battering waves. "We're stuck on an outcropping."

"We've run aground," a stocky sailor said.

"But our last depth reading..." The ship shuddered. This wasn't only an unexpected reef. This was something...more.

I turned and faced my sailors. "Take up your weapons!"

Heat rose from the water, steaming against my arms and making the ends of my hair curl more tightly.

Calev pointed. "It's boiling. Kinneret, the sea, it's boiling."

His eyes went wide, and the waves lashing at the ship gurgled like black stew in a cauldron.

I couldn't speak. I'd seen many horrors on the Pass, but never this.

Fish, some small as a fist, others larger than our hull, floated to the surface with dead eyes and cooked, white flesh. The smell was overwhelming.

The stocky sailor and the rest made the Fire's sign on their foreheads, ran hands over the Holy Fire, praying and holding tight to battle axes, bows, yatagans, and lucky frog legs.

Oron grasped my arm. "What is this?"

Calev and I looked at one another. In unison, we said, "Savta's monster. Asag."

"To the cannons!" I called out. "Everyone else, to port side and starboard!"

The amir's men and women rushed belowdeck to the cannons and hurried to the sides of the ship.

"Raise your bows, your blades!" I shouted. "Get into position, then close or shield your eyes. Aim for the sound. Use the noise as your target!"

Calev nodded. "She speaks the truth! Quickly now, cover your eyes. Use your sashes, or a strip from your tunic."

My pulse drummed in my temples.

"A demon will rise from the water," I told them. "If you look at it, you will die. Listen to its screams and aim true, aim high. Stay side by side so we don't injure one another. Courage, all!"

A pounding noise echoed from under the ship and we rose into the air, only to be dropped.

My stomach dipped and my breath caught.

A shrill ringing poured through the night.

Calev, Oron, and I ripped strips of cloth from our clothing and handed them out to white-faced fighting sailors. We found two bows and three quivers full of green and black fletched arrows. I was glad Calev and Oron both placed in the amir's archery competition in the past.

The quiver on my waist and the bow in my hand, I ran to the amir's room, pounding down the stairs, knowing my life was ruined if she didn't make it through this whole and sound.

Before I could knock on the leopard carved into her door, she pulled it open, her eyes like tatlilav bowls. She held a gold tipped bow. The black fletching of her arrows stuck out from the quiver at her waist.

As I handed her a strip of cloth for her eyes, I said, "My lady, the monster Asag is rising. He controls the rock of the seabed and holds your ship. You can't look at him."

Berker came up behind me. "Asag is a story. The low-caste lies. We've run aground."

"Then how do you explain the dead fish, the boiling water?" I spat.

A vicious smile spread over the amir's face. "We will shoot toward its noise." She pushed past Berker and I, and strode onto the deck, tying the cloth I'd given her over her eyes. Winding around the ropes and sailors and masts, she never took a bad step.

With Berker at my back like a malevolent shadow, I found Oron and Calev. The water collected into a bubbling mountain and two night-black horns, glossy and twisted, broached the surface.

I shut my eyes.

The demon rose, making a sound like glass breaking, roaring out a cacophony like one thousand men being flayed alive.

"It is your Salt Magic that's brought this curse," Berker said.

"Your mouth is the curse! Now find something to do! Cannons, fire!" I shouted over the din, my throat burning. My order was echoed, and the weapons below boomed from the ship's windows, shaking the deck.

As I pulled the bowstring back and wished I'd spent more time practicing my aim, hot tears seeped from my eyes and hurried down my cheeks to hide under my chin. A vibration pounded in my feet.

*The rocks. The rocks he controls are moving.*

A sailor called out, and I tried to turn to see who had fallen, who was screaming over the scream.

*So much noise.*

My lungs shuddered as I sucked a foul breath of fish and death.

Someone bumped me. Calev said my name from a few steps away, and then the amir's voice was beside me.

"I will end this demon," she hissed as her arm moved against mine.

She fired arrow after arrow, her string whipping the air beside me.

I tried and failed to keep up with her as Asag's rocks rolled the ship roughly to starboard, then seemed to let go. We bobbed and floated free, the deck moving beneath my feet, as the demon shrieked, rising like the moon over the boiling, deadly water.

I heard splashes and shouting. Someone, maybe more than one, had fallen from the deck.

"Fire!" I shouted and again the cannons boomed, fewer this time. It had to be frightening to reload and light them while peeking from under a blindfold.

The ship lurched.

The screaming ceased.

A rhythm like a hand drill buzzed from the center of the deck. Asag's rocks were drumming their way into the hull. We had to end this now or we would all become wraiths.

Out of arrows, I kept my eyes to the decking as I rushed to starboard and yanked a whaling spear from the side. Careful not to look toward the creature, I spied Oron handing off arrows to fighting sailors. Calev shot the last one he had and lifted his headtie. His eyes found me.

"Take up spears!" Flashes of pain blinked through my ears. The noise was unbelievable. "Wait for my word!" I handed another spear to Calev and found the amir's side.

My spear was heavy and slick with seawater. The clank and drag of more fighters arming themselves with spears interrupted the demon's screaming. The grinding coming from the bottom of the ship halted.

"Now!"

I threw the harpoon.

Holding my breath, my pulse hammering in my throat, I prayed.

Asag let out another heart-shattering scream, sending me to my knees. The amir laughed, her foot dragging against my leg.

Then there was only silence.

I stood and opened my eyes.

Only a spill of what looked like oil and ashes marred the water's smooth surface. A dead squid and a school of boiled silver fish floated beside it.

The amir tore the cloth from her eyes, her bell ringing lightly. "I killed the demon Asag."

I could've argued. I knew in my gut that I'd killed it. But the amir's pride worked to keep her on my side.

"They will sing songs about this, my lady," I said.

She smiled, but I couldn't smile back. The deck held five dead fighting sailors, their eyes blackened in their sockets and their skin gray, slayed by the sight of the demon. More had fallen overboard when the rocks harassed the ship. Two corpses drifted past Asag's remains.

My eyelids shuttered closed, open. I spun to see Calev and Oron, hands clasped in victory like old friends.

Despite the loss, we had won.

But that night, while a dark-haired, mostly silent fighting sailor named Ekrem manned the wheel and a crowd of others sewed the damaged sails, cleaned, and brought our ship back to a functioning level, sleep didn't give me rest like it should've.

I tossed and turned, never comfortable, drained, but strung too tight from the day. Giving up on sleep for a while, I stared at the busy sailors who moved like barley stalks blowing in the fields and took comfort in Calev sleeping sitting up beside me. Finally, my body gave out.

Avi found my dreams, and her pain turned them into nightmares.

Slender hands bloodied by work.

An empty belly.

A man's calloused finger tracing her jaw. Her shudder.

A longing stare toward the Pass as she prayed I'd come for her.

I WOKE. EXHAUSTED FROM my fitful sleep, my body trembled as the sails and the bruised light of morning came into focus. Oron, Calev, and myself had slept on benches beneath a cracked Wraith Lantern, too exhausted to fear anything anymore. I raised myself, slowly, painfully, and took a selfish moment to enjoy Calev's sleeping form.

His eyelashes rested in two crescent moons on his cheeks, and his fine nostrils edged out as he breathed. His collarbone was a smooth line above the zigzags of his tunic collar. I clutched my fingers to resist touching the skin there.

My longing must've woken him. Calev's eyes opened and I smiled.

"Good morning, Kinneret."

The sky was purple through the stitching in the jib sail. "To you also."

Oron snorted and rolled over as we made our way to relieve Ekrem at the wheel.

"Will you see what you can do to mend the wraith lanterns?" I asked the man, looking up, and up, into the fighter's stern face.

His arms covered in leather braces, he made the Fire's sign on his forehead—which I took as a *yes*—then he woke a handful of sailors to help him.

I claimed the wheel, my hands still shaking from the dream.

"Are you all right?" Calev asked.

An ornately carved, wooden box on a support stood next to the wheel. It held the compass and somewhat protected it from all the metal in the ship, metal that often disturbed its readings of our direction. Calev opened the compass box's lid and peered in. He gave me a nod to indicate we were on course. I checked the fact against Zayn's compass that I'd kept in my sash through everything so far.

My shaking stopped as I adjusted my hands on the wheel. "I'm fine. Just…nightmares."

Three fighters, two big like Ekrem and one more my size, but with nine times the muscle, approached and held up palms to me in greeting.

"Kaptan," the stocky one my height said. "What do you wish for us to do?"

"Loosen the mainsail. The wind wants it."

The Salt Magic had worn itself thin and I had to wiggle us around an outcropping of algae green rock to the East. The ship took an age to lip its way to where I wanted it to be. My boat would've already been around the rocks and halfway to the horizon.

"Why the frown?" Calev ran a hand lightly over a row of battle axes strapped to the wall.

Someone had cleaned the slime and blood from them. I was a weakling. After the demon's attack, I couldn't have cleaned one thing if the Fire Itself had asked me.

"The frown is because this ship lumbers like an old, fat man. He's always jostling into things and listing too far."

"Hm." He put a hand to his mouth.

"What's so funny?" Hands on the wheel, I widened my stance and eyed him.

He shook his head. "No. You won't drag me into an argument, kaptan."

Lightning snapped through me at the term. I'd never get tired of that title.

"I will drag you in and you know it," I said, half grinning, half scowling. "Now what are you laughing at?"

The stocky sailor rushed up the stairs and showed a palm to me. "Kaptan Kinneret Raza, our amir wishes to speak with you in her cabin. Her...other kaptan is there too." The man's mouth pinched like he'd sipped old tatlilav.

I had a feeling he wasn't too fond of Berker. *Join the crowd.*

I rubbed the tense rocks of muscle in my shoulder. "Any guess on the purpose of this meeting?" He probably wouldn't tell me. His loyalties were with the amir.

He leaned in and whispered, "The other kaptan sees you as a Salt Witch. I'd watch yourself around him. Stick to what happened and how you saved us and the amir will dance to your tune."

My shoulders relaxed and I couldn't fight my smile. I glanced at Calev, who raised his eyebrows.

"Thank you, sailor. What is your name?"

He sucked a little breath. "It's Ifran, kaptan. And I-I thank you for caring enough to ask. You know, when I passed my palm over the Holy Fire when we first boarded, the Fire gave me a thought."

"You are blessed," I said carefully. He seemed nice, but plenty of people claimed their ideas came from the Fire. Few really did.

"He told me you are good."

"He did?"

The sailor nodded.

I just stood there, mute, as the man hurried away.

Calev elbowed me. "I bet that made up for the old man ship a little bit."

"Yes. A little."

Wanting to think a minute, I called another to relieve my place at the wheel, Calev trailing me. I went to the ship's wide, copper salt pan, where seawater was exposed to sun and allowed to breathe back into the air, leaving the precious salt behind. It was mainly for cooking and salting the rare, edible fish we managed to catch, but of course, I had other uses for it. I scooped a handful and refilled my pouch.

This leadership, this charge, was what I'd always wanted. I'd longed for respect. A ship to kaptan. Equality with Calev. He'd danced with me last night.

But now, staring at my hands and thinking of how much they looked like Avi's, all I wanted was my own craft and Avi on it, with Oron and Calev at my side in any manner they saw fit. I wanted safety.

I toyed with the ends of my sash as I made my way back to Calev and the others on the dais. The endmost bell was cool between my fingertips. "Strange…"

"What's strange?" Calev nodded in a friendly way to the enormous blonde fighting sailor with the beautiful battle axe, the weapon I'd envied. She was cooking some flatbread in a pan over the brasier. Her looks were very plain, ugly even, but orderly. Nose neat above thin lips. Eyes with very scant lashes sat a bit too far apart.

"I never wanted safety before," I explained. "I craved adventure. Wealth." My gaze flicked to Calev's strong cheekbones and chin, tanned from a life in the fields. "And…other things. But not safety."

"When did you last feel safe?" he asked.

It had been years. "At my aunt's home in Kurakia."

There was a time when I longed to flee Jakobden with Avi and live with Aunt Kania. But my life was sailing. My life was in Jakobden. I loved Jakobden's olive and lemon trees, and its Broken Coast, full of challenges. I had to be on the sea, my sea. It was home, where I'd lived with my mother and father. And it was Calev's home too. I couldn't leave him anymore than I could stop breathing.

"You've never told me much about your aunt," Calev said.

"I haven't seen her in forever." Aunt Kania's tower house with its four-story mud brick walls lorded over her nearly barren field of cattle brown as dirt and chickens even browner. "She lives outside Kurakia's capitol. With far too many chickens."

"Can there ever be too many chickens?"

"If you can't get from door to yard without stepping on a dozen, you may have a few too many."

"I bet chickens make for soft stepping stones."

I cocked my head as we neared the amir's quarters. "Soft, yes. Quiet, no."

"Well, not the proud ones. But what about the humble ones, willing to sacrifice their comfort for yours?"

I snorted. "You're starting to sound like Oron." I knocked on the amir's door.

Oron appeared at Calev's elbow and threw his dreaded locks out of his face. "There is no such thing as a humble, quiet chicken."

Two lines formed between Calev's eyebrows. "Except those on your plate."

A laugh sprang out of me despite my sadness and worry. "That's horrible."

A voice rang out from the sky cup, high above the black triangle of the mainsail.

"Land!" the scout shouted.

I grabbed Calev's tunic, my fingers cutting into the fabric. *Ayarazi.*

Running to starboard, I looked ahead. There, on the horizon, was an island that sloped like the back of a horse. It was too far to see the colors of the land, to judge it desert or forest, fertile or barren, a simple stretch of rock or a lost island of silver.

But my heart leaped at the sight of it.

Until it disappeared.

# CHAPTER TWENTY

I BLINKED. BLINKED AGAIN.

"Where did it go?" Calev ran a hand over his face and frowned.

A corner of the island came into view. But I couldn't discern its edges.

"Not good." Oron muttered something else and rubbed the frog's leg hanging from the string around his neck.

A mist thickened and gathered on the surface of the water. As the rising sun glowed orange on the fog, the island seemed to disappear again.

"This is why no one's found it." I began climbing the mast. I'd get a better look from the sky cup.

The scout peered down at me. "Kaptan?"

"I'm coming up. Make room."

A wind like glass shards tore through my hair and across my arms and cheeks. I tucked my head down.

Oron called up from the deck. "Just so you know, from now on, I am deemed forever correct in every assumption."

I scowled down at him. "And what assumption are you talking about now?"

Calev narrowed his eyes at Oron.

Oron crossed his muscled arms. "The one that involves frigid weather mixing with the hot and humid air to which we are accustomed and what it will do to us. The assumption that we are about to freeze our important bits off in the middle of a wet, cold nowhere with no opportunity for one last huzzah."

Looking to the sky for patience, I crawled into the cup. The scout scooted to the far side of the mast that ran through the middle of the perch, giving me a clear, or in this case totally unclear, view of where the island used to be.

"It's still there," I called down, looking again. "It's hidden in a weird reflection between sky and sea." I directed my voice at Ekrem who'd taken the tiller. "Keep our course trained toward the last sight of the land."

I'd thought it would be good to have a high view like this, a view my own boat never could permit, but it'd been worth nothing in this case. As the scout tripped in trying to get out of my way so I could climb down, I cursed this fat, old man ship again. I missed my boat. I'd already have been at the island by now.

The second my sandals hit the deck, my arms were stiff with cold and my hair crusted in ice crystals. Oron and Calev huddled with everyone else, around the brazier. It was ridiculous. One bumping the other. None getting enough heat from the metal bowl to thaw their fingers.

"I don't need everyone on deck. Go below deck and out of this weather. Except for you, please." I pointed at the stocky sailor, Ifran. "And Oron. Calev, would you give the amir my apologies for not answering her summons, and tell her to get her tail up here."

With smooth steps, the amir mounted the stairs and came to my side at the tiller. Berker walked near her, his eyes sour and sharp. A heavy cloak covered his shoulders, but the amir faced the biting wind like a sparring opponent, her grin sharp.

"Speak," she said to me. Her voice might've been like bells, but sometimes they were scary bells.

Berker's gaze traveled up and down as he studied me. Planning my death, no doubt.

I raised my chin and looked the amir and him in the eye. "I saw the island. It is approximately twenty-two knocks northeast."

Her elegant brow reached toward her headstrap and its grape-sized silver bell. "And the island is now…"

"It's there. I saw it. So did the others. This mist and the light are just masking it."

She pressed her lips together. "You saw this too, Calev ben Y'hoshua?"

"I did, my lady." Calev ran a hand up and down my arm and I shivered from both the cold and his soft touch.

Berker tensed. He'd seen the gesture.

Calev and I were getting brave lately. I didn't have time or brain room to consider what that might mean.

Oron swished back the last of a cup of wine. "The island was there, my lady. And if we're to find it again and do any silver mining, you might want to give us some more wine to keep our hands from freezing solid."

The amir's hand landed with a crack on Oron's cheek. My pulse thrummed in my fisted hands. She was definitely not my hero anymore.

"Insolence," Berker hissed at Oron.

Oron straightened and wiped his bleeding lip. He gave a deep bow. Calev held me back.

"Is that the medicinal wine my physician dosed for your twisted back, dwarf?"

Seas, I wanted to punch the woman.

The amir looked like she believed Oron had a bad back about as much as she believed we'd seen the island.

Berker sniffed. "He's taken more than three times the amount he was prescribed. But we've allowed it, considering his…condition."

Instead of being put out like I would've been if someone spoke about my stature like it was a disease, Oron beamed and headed back to the wine barrel to refill his cup.

The amir's jaw tightened. "If there is an island in the middle of this, get us there, Kaptan Kinneret Raza. I will be at the prow."

Berker remained, unfortunately, and the amir walked away, her head held high. Calev went with Oron to get a rag for his cut cheek.

The deck looked more slick. *Ice.* The wind died off and the sails drooped. We were becalmed.

"Lucky for you, the amir likes you, sailor," Berker whispered. "Don't get too comfortable. I will set everything to rights as soon as we find that silver."

I did my best to ignore that stupid grin of his. "Unless you freeze to death first, hm? To the oars!" I ordered the sailors. A chill like needles pricked my throat and nose.

Calev returned. "The rowing will keep us warmer. So that's one good thing."

I grinned at him, shivering. "I can always count on you for the light in the dark."

Leaving Berker with his plotting, Calev and I started toward the sailors leaving the deck.

The amir's voice stopped us. If I hadn't already been frozen, I would've frozen then. "Calev ben Y'hoshua, please keep me company here," she said.

Berker was one step behind us. "Yes, you should keep yourself away from the low-caste vermin."

Calev spun. "She's not—"

I hit his arm gently and he squeezed his eyes shut. "Just go," I whispered.

I broke away and started down the ladder to belowdecks.

"Be sure to empty the chamber pots in our and the amir's quarters as soon as you can be spared," Berker said. "Calev ben Y'hoshua will dine with his high-caste equals now."

Scrambling down the ladder, I held my tongue. Now wasn't the time for angry words. Soon as I had some silver to my name, Berker was going to eat every single one of his insults.

BESIDE THE FIGHTING SAILORS, I was pretty close to worthless at the oars. My wiry arms were nothing to their limbs of cedar. I pulled alongside them, and we tugged the ship closer and closer to the spot where we'd last spotted the island. The bitter mist sliced through the openings in the ship's sides, flaying us with a cold that rattled teeth and turned bones to ice.

We hadn't gone far before five men and women had developed a chill so debilitating that they couldn't row any longer.

"Kaptan?" A woman with red-brown hair similar to my own turned around on the bench in front of me. "Should we stop?"

"No. We must get through this. And the movement will keep you warm."

As the ship lurched slowly through the water like a wounded beast, worry scratched at my mind. If this lasted through the night, we'd all freeze to death. I'd forever be known as the low-caste kaptan who threw an entire amir's guard into the next life as wraiths.

"Stronger!" I gripped the oar's worn grain and pulled, my shoulders moaning. "Faster!"

Oron appeared beside me, smelling like charcoal and wine.

"You could help, you know." I jerked my chin at the open spot beside me. Ash blackened his cheek. "What have you been doing? Sleeping in the braziers?"

"The mist is thickening."

I swallowed. "Not what we needed to hear, Oron. Here." I stood, my hands throbbing. "Take my place. I'm going to get everyone down here. More bodies means more heat."

On deck, I shouted to the sailors manning the wheel and compass. "Everyone belowdecks. If we stay close together, we might keep from freezing to death. You," I pointed to the man at the compass, "stay and watch and take note of our direction as best you can. Watch for the sun. Climb to the sky cup to check for land when you deem it best. Switch with a crewmate when you need warmth."

I ran to the amir's quarters. The lady, Berker, and Calev sat around a rough wooden table laden with brass cups, shell bowls half-filled with figs, and wide plates of dried goat's meat.

"I ordered the crew below decks to stay together for warmth—"

"You've arrived at the perfect time to clean the table for us and the pots in the side chamber," Berker said.

I looked to the amir.

Her gaze, cold as the fog outside these wooden walls, ran over my face and hands. "Yes. A bit of simple work may do you good. You don't want to forget where you've come from, sailor."

Taking a deep breath, I went to work.

Calev's pained stare never left me as I cleared plates, scraped leftover bits into the bucket by the door, gritted my teeth, and tried to remember this was all for my sister. Calev had his part to play and I, frustratingly, had mine.

The amir, Berker, and Calev went to speak to the sailors, who flowed down the stairs opposite the amir's quarters and flooded into any available space around the oars, cannons, and sleeping quarters.

The last of them cleared the stairs' slats and I, bucket in hand, climbed to the deck. A skeleton crew operated the ship, Ekrem at the wheel and compass and a few others manning the lines and blocks.

The wet clouds of the mist danced across the deck like ghostly sails. My bones shook, and I gripped the bucket's handle tightly to keep from dropping it. My nails had gone blue at the tips. I knew I should be miserable, but my heart raced at the unfamiliar feeling of true cold. This was adventure.

I smiled sadly, wishing Avi could be here. Well, if we survived this.

"Kinneret Raza!" Ekrem's light eyes narrowed and he pointed into the white.

Blue, green, and black appeared between the plumes of cold mist. I dumped the bucket's contents over the ship's side and ran to Ekrem, a warmer air teasing across my chest and arms. Feeling crept back into my fingers and toes.

"My lady!" I shouted, leaning this way and that, to see if the colors were what we wanted them to be.

Ekrem said a quiet prayer. "It is Ayarazi."

The island materialized as everyone crowded onto the deck.

The sailors made the Fire's sign.

The amir cursed.

Calev and I joined hands, releasing one another before anyone could see.

Waves crashed and sprayed water over a line of gray rock and bright coral. The island rose, green and cool, behind the barrier. Plumes of spray rose from a waterfall that graced a far off peak. Near a blanket of purple growth on a low hill, a ridge of stone made a scar across an emerald valley. There was movement, tiny spots of dark in the landscape.

The coast's vicious teeth had one gap. We could fit.

Maybe.

If everything went the way I wanted it to. If this fat, old man ship listened. If the salt heard my prayers. If I had all the best luck.

"Calev, I'm going to need you by my side. On deck. Every second. Without your luck on this, we are dead."

"But I'm not good luck."

I pinched his lips shut. "You are."

# CHAPTER TWENTY-ONE

I GNORING BERKER'S LOUD MUTTERING ABOUT what my status would be in the afterlife, I whispered over the salt. It dusted back to its home in the cold waters surrounding an island that, before today, had only existed in bedtime tales told in my father's rumbling voice.

"And the silver threads through all things on the island," he'd said, adjusting the blanket so that Avi had more than the small amount I'd given her. I remembered watching fire smoke dance through the small hole in our hut's roof. "The color runs in the waterfalls, the rivers," Father said. "Grasses grow there, more than you've ever seen even in summer near Old Farm. The green is laced with the precious metal. A handful of grass would weave beautiful sashes for my little ones." He'd touched our noses, a press, each in turn. "Forget the wraiths, children, and dream of the horses there, every color. Pick your favorite and ride her across the sloping valleys and through the rivers, kicking up silver water."

My heart shied from the memory like a beaten dog.

The whites of the sailors' eyes showed as they put hands to the lines and stared at the rocks.

"Wait for the lag!" I called out.

Oron stood beside the mast, his gaze focused on the red leather jerkins surrounding him, making certain the fighting sailors carried out my demands in perfect harmony. He put his face to the wind and leaned into it. He was feeling the wind and the sea's intent. Oron was the best sailor alive, aside from me. We both felt the Pass and the Fire in the waters and wind like music and soft hands, urging and pulling. *With him helping me, we might just make it.*

I turned to say as much to Calev, glad to break away from thoughts of my broken family, but the spot behind me was empty.

"Calev?"

The stairs held only Ifran ordering another sailor to tighten the line that ran with its mates to the rippling black shell of the mainsail.

When I spun back around to check our progress toward the gap in the breakers shielding the coastline, Oron's hand was cupped at his mouth. I could only catch a bit of what he was saying.

"...tracking too far West...the fore lines should be..."

He was right. We were off. I'd been searching for Calev instead of listening to the sea and the wind. The mining drills weighed more than this ship should've been carrying. Poor old, fat man of a ship.

"Tighten the lines, but keep all hands on them. I need them fully released at my word," I called out over the deck.

Oron gave a quick nod and whipped around, gesturing and working the lines, moving like a moth between the glint of the metal and the white of the ropes, the fighting sailors buzzing and tugging lines around him. I eased the wheel around, feeling the tug of water below.

We were at the mouth of Ayarazi's natural bay, with teeth on both sides—rocks poised to tear us apart. *Please stay sound, fat, old man hull.* Asag's rocks had nearly ground it open.

Where was Calev?

There, past Oron, at the far end near the prow. He walked up behind the amir, something in his hand. From my vantage point, the object was partially concealed by the whipping ends of the amir's vest.

I needed him here beside me. I needed everything. The ship shuddered as we brushed a rock and a wave splashed over the side. Sailors shouted and grabbed holds.

"Calev!" I bent my knees as the ship lunged through the tight gap. "Pull all lines tight! Hold on! Wait for it!"

Calev had dropped away from the amir, coming up against the side of the ship, braced on the wall. From his right hand, his dagger blinked at me.

My insides turned to ice. What was he doing?

"Kinneret!" Oron was at the base of the stairs, below me. "The sails?"

I counted silently to myself as the ship righted itself and readied to bump—hopefully a light glance—past the last of the rocks lining the gap in the island's rocky coast. My hand on my chest, I counted. One, two, three, wait…ten, eleven, twelve. I couldn't let the wind take us in a jerk to port or starboard. We needed no wind at exactly the right time.

Now. "Release the lines!" My heart clanked against my chest and my throat ached from yelling.

The sailors moved as one. The blocks wiggled as the lines ran through them. The sail billowed and the lines flipped into the air. The ship ducked like a tall man going through a doorway. We listed hard, very hard, to port, and I fell to my knees, my head smashing against the wheel.

Ifran screamed as water crashed over the deck in successive waves. I stood, but my legs didn't want to hold me. The ship seemed to go forward and backward at the same time. I knew that feeling. Whirlpool—a roiling swirl of deadly water. And we had no sails.

Beyond the ribboning current, the water eased onto a black sand shoreline. If we somehow finagled our way through this, we be on shore. We couldn't catch wind fast enough to keep from being sucked under.

The salt would have to do it.

"Get the sails up! Go! Now! Now!" My throat burned from ocean salt and shouting.

Oron's face appeared next to mine. "Ifran split his head against the side." He turned and shouted directions to the sailors, who grabbed at the lines and caught them one by one.

My eyes searched for Ifran in the mayhem of the ship. I couldn't lose another fighting sailor. These men and women had risked their lives to follow me into this madness. Ifran had been brave enough to give me advice against the amir's wishes.

Ifran lay beside the anchor's launching hole with the angry whirlpool churning right below. His dark head was a mess of blood.

"Calev!" He looked at me and blinked. "Help Ifran, please!" I shouted over the chaos.

I was fairly certain if it hadn't been for the ship's jerking and the blood, the white of bone and tendon would've shone through the wound. I ripped another strip from the bottom of my skirt and handed it to another sailor. "Take this to Calev. Tell him to wrap the man's head."

Calev did as I asked. Beside him, Oron leaned in and made the Fire's sign on Ifran's forehead to bless him.

"What is this?" The amir loomed over them, her voice loud, one hand on a tied line and the other on her dagger hilt. Berker stood at her side like an attack dog. "Stop wasting time with what is replaceable." She jerked a chin at Ifran's body, then looked to me. "Get us to that island, kaptan." With a booted foot, she shoved Ifran through the opening and into the sea.

My body buzzed, my mouth open.

Calev reached for him, but it was too fast, too late.

The amir whipped around and shouted at the fighting sailors to trim the fore stay sail.

A smear of black-red marred Calev's tunic and Oron's sash.

"This is a quest for silver," Berker said. "And you, *Kaptan* Kinneret Raza, are about to fail. Now get us to shore!"

The ship spun like a child's string toy.

The amir shouted in anger, gripping the line tighter.

Calev grabbed the side and Oron fell to a knee.

Ifran was lost to the sea. He would become a wraith, his spirit lost, angry, set to Infuse and receive his vengeance on the living. It was my fault.

The ship rotated again, and the sound of cracking wood snapped through the air. By my guess, we had only a few seconds before we suffered too much damage to make it out of this whirlpool.

Scrabbling for the salt in my pouch, I turned away from the amir and whispered to the sea.

*"Release us, waters of salt and sin*
*Let us breathe another sun*
*Our lives await, and also our kin."*

The wind surged and lifted the nose of our ship out of the whirlpool, but it wasn't enough. The current sucked us down again and water swamped the deck. Fighters shouted out and everyone looked to me. But there was nothing left to do.

We all knew it.

We were going down.

Calev ran to me.

"Kinneret, I should tell you—"

With a mighty lunge, the sea spit the prow upward. Every man and woman fell hard as the prow led the rest of the craft free.

Calev and I tumbled against a large crate. I regained my feet first, but he quickly joined me. The sky was blue and clear above us. The water roared.

Oron whooped and threw a hand into the air. "We're out!"

The fighting sailors let up a great yell of celebration and the amir stormed into her cabin. Berker stood staring at Calev and me. The other kaptan's lip curled and he mouthed something I couldn't discern.

"Throw anchor!" I began cranking the anchor's line out myself, Oron and Calev helping.

As the fighters lowered the sails, I finally took a breath.

In front of us, Ayarazi, lost island of silver and the key to my sister's life, rose like a dream made real.

# CHAPTER TWENTY-TWO

THE SAND WAS SOFT AS down under my bare feet. My sandals dangled from my fingers as I followed the amir and Berker toward the low, grassy perches of land overlooking the beach.

Disembarking from one of the small boats that took us from the full ship to shore, Oron threw himself to the ground and lay on his back. "Sweet land, I do not care if you are rich or poor, you will do. You will do."

Calev threw his head back and sucked a deep breath. The sun smiled on the hollows, curves, and lines of his throat. My fingers twitched. I wanted to run fingertips along Calev's smooth skin and feel his pulse and know he was all right.

The scent of the beautifully rich growth rose like perfume into the air. The grasses smelled like mint. "My father told me the grass on Ayarazi was threaded with silver."

I bent to see for myself as the party moved beyond us, climbing the rise and entering a vast meadow. The blades of grass cooled my fingertips and a shiver ran over my arms. The place was colder than anywhere I'd ever been. Not frigid like that mist, but crisp—a shade colder than Jakobden's winter. Squinting, I plucked one blade and held it to my face. Tiny rows of sparkling silver ran through the veins of the plant and gathered at the edges to create a frame.

"Beautiful," Calev said.

I turned and handed the blade to him. "It is, isn't it?"

He smiled with half his mouth. "I wasn't talking about the grass, Kinneret." His gaze slid over my head and nose and chin.

My cheeks grew hot as Calev grabbed my hand. His eyes were honey and wine. My throat bobbed as I tried to talk, but his eyes and the cool breeze and the promise of this all working out had stolen my words. He touched my cheek.

"Sailor," Berker barked from above. The amir and her fighters had gone on, so they weren't around to correct his address.

Calev's eyes sharpened. His head snapped around. "Address the kaptan properly."

He'd taken the words right from my lips.

Berker stared us down. "You are no longer a kaptan, scrapper. You led us here. It's over now. I'm the only kaptan on this journey." He began to walk away toward the line of sailors, heading toward the mountains. "Funny how the chill gets in your bones so quickly," he said over his shoulder. "Someone might die in such an unforgiving climate."

My temples pounded. *That man.*

"Don't worry, Calev." I squeezed his fingers and climbed the rise to join our party, noticing that Oron was already snoring on the sand behind. "I'll have a fight with Berker before this is over. And I will win."

Calev leaped up behind me, and we started through the silvery green, the cold breeze in our hair. "I don't doubt it, kaptan."

A smile pulled at my lips as I slipped a rope from a fighter's pack.

The amir was leading the group toward the closest mountain. As we caught up, the scar of rocky ground branching through the meadow appeared to our left. I tugged Calev's sleeve and nodded toward it.

"I think we should look there first. It may open into the ground. Plus, it'll be easier to check for silver than drilling into a mountain."

"Let's go," Calev said.

The air, fresh as clean water, spun down the green mountain and swept over the valley where we ran. The grass whisked our legs, and a light shone inside me. The journey here had been so terrible that I couldn't help but hope we'd find the silver quickly and without too much trouble. If I showed the amir what she could hope to gain, she'd give me any amount of fighters and let me take the ship to the quarry to reclaim my sister.

The land sloped upward, and flat, gray rocks mingled with the grasses and led to the seam I'd spotted from the ship. Turns out, it was less of a seam and more of a set of openings into the earth. At the crest of the rise, the ground broke open. Two more such openings sat nearby. I went to the largest and peered inside, Calev beside me, breathing heavily after our run.

I ran a hand over the dark opening's walls, feeling a slimy cold. "I can't see anything. We should get inside."

There weren't any rocks near the opening for me to tie the rope around. I kicked at the dirt at the cave's open ceiling and my toe hit a root.

"It's from that elder there," Calev said, pointing to a needled tree a stone's throw away.

"Elder." I laughed. "You Old Farms."

"What?"

I shook my head. "Nothing. Think the rope'll hold me?"

"Definitely."

I helped Calev with a double figure eight knot and made a loop for my legs as well. Thankfully, there were enough roots and drier ledges for grabbing and I made my way down without Calev having to hold my weight. In the dim, the rope pulled taut and I knew I had no more length for exploring.

"What's it like?" At the top, Calev got onto his stomach and his hair fell over his face.

The walls were a light brown, or at least what I could see of them was. A line of black ran crookedly through the rock ledges, giving me false hope.

"It's just a cave. No silver."

"Come on back up. We'll check this next one."

With a sigh, I maneuvered my way out of the cave and into the next. After I laced the rope around a stump, Calev went down into a third crack in the island, but still, no silver.

I untied the rope and coiled it around my arm, my heart weighing more than a boat full of Ekrems. Calev rubbed my knee and gave me a half smile.

"I really thought it would be here. That black scar in the first opening looked right from what I've heard."

"We'll find it. I'm lucky. Remember?"

My heart lifted a little and I dusted myself off. My calves shook with fatigue, but I didn't want to stop looking. To rescue Avi, I needed the amir's fighters. And the amir wanted silver. It was both as simple and as difficult as that.

Calev walked beside me as we worked our way through the grass. The strands of light gray in the growth blinked teasingly.

Calev broke off a hunk of shining green-gray and sniffed it. "Is this the island's idea of a joke?" He looked at the blade closely, his eyes nearly crossing. "It's really just dots of gray on the surface. I was sort of hoping we could get a scythe out here and reap the rewards, so to speak."

I grabbed a piece and scratched at the silvery spots. "Don't get a big head. You're not that lucky." The sun had slipped off its zenith and a sudden image of Avi's golden-brown hair flashed through my thoughts. "How much silver do you think the amir will need before she agrees to send fighters with us for Avi?" I should've clarified that in our agreement.

"I'd guess once we locate a seam and begin drilling."

"We never talked about how many would stay to mine and how many would come with us."

Calev clicked his tongue. He was more worried than he wanted me to know and my skin itched with the need to leave now. "You should talk to Ekrem about it. He respects you."

"He does?"

"It's obvious."

"And he might know the right way to bring it up with the amir."

"What's going to happen when your father figures out where you are?"

"We already talked about this. He can't do much of anything. She is the amir and she asked me to go."

I raised an eyebrow.

"That's not what I meant anyway," I said. "How is he going to react? Will he get over it when you return home?" Home. Such a chaos of wonderful and horrible. I thought of Miriam and a muscle in my back balled up.

The ground dropped away and I fell into the earth, pain ripping up my leg.

# CHAPTER TWENTY-THREE

K INNERET!"
I gripped at everything, anything, and my buzzing fingers latched onto a mound of wet earth and grass. My feet dangled above darkness. I'd fallen into the opening of another crevice.

Calev grabbed my wrists and helped me up, his eyes wide and his fingers strong. "Are you all right?"

He patted my arms, my head, then held my face softly. I turned my mouth toward his parted lips and a shiver danced over the backs of my legs.

A burning sensation drowned all the good and I looked down to see a tiny stream of blood leaking into my sandal.

I lifted my skirt a little and Calev knelt to inspect my wound.

"It's just a cut." I was lightheaded, but I wasn't sure whether it was from the fall, the blood, or because Calev's mouth was very near my thigh.

He cleared his throat and stood. "Doesn't look serious," he said, blushing.

It wasn't. Just a nip. I spun to face the crevice I'd so gracefully found.

"Should I tie the rope off?" Calev's head turned.

I bent and leaned over the yawning mouth of the cave. Plant life obscured most of the light, making the walls black. Calev moved behind me and a beam of afternoon sun hit the opposite wall and glinted back. Just a wink. Probably nothing.

"Do you see anything?" Calev asked.

"It's hard to tell." The surface inside alternated between smooth and rough. My hand slid over a slick spot and something sticklike stopped its progress. I ran fingers over the object imbedded in the smooth area. Its end curled like a fern's leaf and my heart danced.

"Silver."

"Where?" Calev pushed against me and shoved his hand into the opening. "Ah! I feel it! In some calcite crystal, I bet. Like the mine between Jakobden and the capitol."

"This shallow, it won't be that much labor to free it. A shaft dug. A pulley system. Picks. We don't even need those drills. We'll have to set up a smelting station. Nothing we haven't seen. There are people enough in Jakobden who could mine it and work it into useable pieces." I stood and pulled him to his feet. "You'll help me, won't you? I'll need you to make an appearance now and then to keep the amir in check."

I was already seeing Avi rescued and our lives moving into a place of full bellies and smiles and respectful nods from the men and women I'd sailed with during this trip.

"Of course." Calev grinned. "This is amazing. I never thought…Ayarazi."

A herd of horses in every color of a northern autumn forest pounded past us, whipping us with the force of their passing and shaking the ground under our sandals. Burnt ochre. Yellow and orange. Deep purple like my sail. Their tails and manes snapped like pennants as they galloped, the sun flashing from the silver hiding in the white and brown of their hair.

The look on Calev's face was pure joy.

We had done it. Found the lost island of silver. Grabbed the only chance to save my sister.

A laugh bubbled out of his mouth, and he covered his face with one hand, shaking his head in disbelief. Another laugh, and the deep sound melted over me, warming me in the brisk air.

My mouth wanted to taste his neck, and my body longed for the heat and strength in his arms. I wouldn't make the first move. He knew how I felt now, surely, and I wasn't about to make a fool out of myself even if it was all I could do not to leap onto him. His hair lifted in the breeze, and the sun reddened his browned cheeks.

"Kinneret," he whispered, taking my hands in his. His lips forming my name was worth all the silver under our feet. "You slay sea demons, fight storms, sail like none other, and work magic in a way that makes it holy rather than the abomination so many want to deem it. Why do you even bother to be my friend?"

He laughed, but at the word "friend" my chest clenched like the air was suddenly poisonous. I forced myself to breathe normally. Avi needed me. Even more than Calev did, it seemed. Shaking a little, I pulled my hands away.

"I need to show the amir the silver. Avi needs me now."

Calev's brow and mouth torqued out of line. Then he nodded slowly and followed me toward the slash of red-clothed fighting sailors heading up the hills.

When the group was within hearing, I called out to the amir, wondering where Oron had gone. "We found the silver!"

The fighters spun, eyes wide, and shouted. Everyone began talking at once, patting my shoulder and Calev's, and offering congratulations.

"Well done, kaptan!"

"I didn't doubt you'd be the one, Kaptan Kinneret."

"Thank you." I showed my palm to each in turn and handed out smiles like gold dumplings at an Age Day celebration.

The fighters parted for Calev and me.

"Do you want me to talk to her?" Calev asked. "Because I don't think you do. She is a vicious woman, but she respects you.

She doesn't seem to care that you used Salt Magic. You got us through with only a few losses."

"No. I'll talk to her. I-I can't believe what she did to Ifran."

My mind speared me with images of Ifran, of the woman who'd admired Calev, and the handful of other sailors we'd lost. Their faces, pale, bloodied, shocked by Death's arrival, would never dissolve from my memory. I pressed a fist to my throat, making my own throat-blood oath.

"I will never forget those we lost," I said. "I will say a prayer for them every day I sail the Pass."

Calev blinked and made the Fire's sign on his forehead, his thumb circling the center of his headtie.

It was the very least I could do for them. How was I going to face the woman who'd kicked Ifran into the water before he was even dead?

I could barely stand to look at her proud gait and the back of her red leather vest. I wanted to make her pay for what she'd done, but she was also Avi's savior. I couldn't take the amir down without also destroying Avi's chance to escape the quarry. My stomach curdled and I gritted my teeth. There wasn't a thing I could do about it.

For now.

The amir walked, back straight and head held high, about ten knocks up the foothill. My feet began to complain. Then my head. My stomach. The excitement of everything was fading in my fatigue. I didn't want to waste sun eating and sleeping. But soon, I'd have to listen to my body, or it would shut down.

At last I was at the amir's elbow. Berker walked right beside her.

"My lady." My throat was dry and I could barely talk. I needed rest and water. "The silver is just there."

I pointed as she stopped and looked at me, disdain clear as the sky in her eyes.

"What do you know about silver mines, sailor?" Berker wrinkled his nose.

The amir faced him. "You will call her kaptan, Kaptan Berker Deniz."

"But, my lady, that was only a position for our journey here. That time is over. She should know her place. She is—"

"Enough," the amir said, her bell voice cutting instead of pleasing.

Berker's throat bobbed. "Yes, my lady."

Calev and I exchanged wide-eyed looks. I fought a mean grin, then decided to let it loose. Forget Berker. He deserved the treatment he received.

Pointing the way we'd come, Calev squinted against the sun. "Do you see the outcropping on that far slope, below the mountain with the waterfall, my lady?"

"I see it, Calev ben Y'hoshua." Lines formed around the amir's mouth as she frowned. She took a very deliberate breath. "Did you spot the metal yourselves?"

Nodding, I said, "In one opening, raw silver sits in calcite. It's an easy site for a mine, my lady, and one that'll make the both of us very rich." My voice sounded hollow on that last word.

Calev whispered in my ear. "Are you unwell?"

I smiled, my mind whirring. "No, I'm fine."

Calev spoke to the amir about traditional mining methods, and my thoughts turned inward.

Though I was more tired than I'd ever been and desperate for food and water, I actually felt as though I'd been healed of some horrible sickness. The gnawing need for silver, wealth, power and status, it was silent inside me. I had Calev, at least as a friend, and Oron, and with the silver and the amir's help, Avi's safety. Once I had my own quick and sturdy boat under my feet again, I'd be complete.

I studied my hands. They still looked like my own. My hair was still red-brown and unruly. A strand bounced back after I tugged on it. I appeared the same on the outside, but inside I had changed completely. I was no longer a ravenous fire, needing kindling and something to devour. I was the steel made in the fire, hard and strong, but quiet until the sharp edge was needed.

And though things seemed to be trotting along the path I'd forged, I had a distinct feeling I'd call out for that cutting blade inside me very soon.

# CHAPTER TWENTY-FOUR

GROWING PINK, THE SUN FELL out of the blue sky and hid shyly behind the jagged mountain peaks of Ayarazi. I rubbed my sleep-crusted eyes and sat up from the carpet of grass near the silver outcropping. The amir had insisted on seeing the silver herself before she would believe our story, so while the crew repaired the damage the ship had sustained during our trip, Calev and I led her around. Satisfied, the amir had called us together to eat. Finally. Most had fallen to sleep soon after.

For a part of our meal, Oron had crafted a salad of greens he claimed were safe to consume. Said they were the same ones we had at home, only smaller, tougher. I'd enjoyed the fresh food, a contrast to the hard bread and slightly sour wine. None of the others, except Calev, had munched on Oron's creation. Calev had gone so far as to add a plant his Savta had once described in her stories as having a healing power to it. After the others had their fill of food and of laughing at our green-eating habits, everyone fell asleep, exhausted from the journey.

I smiled at Calev's sleeping form. He argued sometimes with Oron, but he was kind to the man, backing him up around the others. And though Oron claimed to love pity and the shower of undeserved attention it reaped for him, I knew he wanted true friendship. I hoped he saw that he'd found it in Avi, me, and now, in Calev.

Snores rose into the air around the camp, and I was glad of it. As soon as that sun came up, we'd be on the water, headed toward Quarry Isle and Avi. If the amir kept her promise.

I popped my knuckles and patted the salt pouch on my belt. I was ready for a fight with the oramiral. Maybe I'd get the chance to take a hand from the man. He needed something to remind him he wasn't the only power in the world.

My whole body was jittery. No way I could go back to sleep.

As the last of the sun's blush faded, an odd glimmer lighted the foothills and the spray in the distant waterfall.

I shrugged it off. The island was full of things I'd never seen before. Instead of the tiny, violet nightwingers we had at home, Ayarazi's evening air was colored by floating silver moths, big as my hand. The ocean crashed magnificently against the barrier surrounding the island, a louder sound than the Pass's constant grating against Jakobden's Broken Coast. And no night insects seemed to be coming out to sing. The nightwingers at home zipped near ears, a familiar sound. But here, there was only the occasional pounding of horses' hooves, the waterfall's rush, and the sea hammering the rocks.

The inland light glimmered again, and I found my feet walking toward its inconsistent illumination.

It was strange to be alone on land. I'd been alone on the Pass many times. But on land, I'd always had Avi, Oron, or Calev. I stretched my arms wide, inhaled the clean air, and said a silent prayer for my sister into the moonlight. The moon actually looked lovely when you didn't have to worry about Salt Wraiths. That was land's only advantage over water. The earth didn't talk to me like the sea did. It wasn't an extension of my own body and spirit and heart. Ayarazi was beautiful. Awe-inspiring. But I was ready to get back out on the water.

The land dipped down before coming to the waterfall, and as if it'd heard my thoughts on land versus sea, the thick grass tripped me. With both hands, I caught myself and cursed my stupidity for walking into the night with only the moon, enormous insects, and a mysterious light to keep me company. I'd walked a good forty knocks from where we'd camped. If I hurt myself way out here, it'd take Oron and Calev a long while to find me.

Nearing the waterfall, I tugged everything off, except my underclothes, and made my way through a heaped circle of moss-covered, round stones to the pool. The cold air brushed over my exposed skin and I shivered. Beside my sash with its compass, salt pouch, and dagger, I knelt on the rocks to wash dirt, salt, and sand from just the edges of my skirt, shawl, and shirt. I didn't want to get them too wet or I'd be shivering all night. As the spray found my cheek and neck, I gasped. I'd expected the water to be cold like the air here, but it was warm as sunshine. I rubbed my gritty clothes, scrubbing the journey off the ruddy fabric. My face was rough with salt and sand too. I needed a bath.

I slipped into the cloudy pool. Goosebumps exploded up my arms and a heavy sigh left me. Perfect.

A dark shape came out of the darkness and my heartbeat shot into my ears.

Lunging for my dagger, I held it up. "Who is it?"

Calev's dark laugh rumbled from the shadows.

My eyes closed in relief. "You scared the life out of me."

He knelt beside the pool, a grin pulling at one side of his mouth as he took in my bare shoulders.

My cheeks burned. I tossed my dagger back onto the rocks and took a step back.

"It's warm. The water. I thought I'd take a bath." I swallowed.

"Not a bad idea." Standing, he began to shed his tunic, pulling the long, now tattered fabric over his head.

My heart lost its hold on any kind of rhythm, clacking wildly fast and slow and everywhere in between. It's not that I hadn't been in underclothes with Calev before now, but something about the moon and new environment made this…different.

Bending at his trim waist, he slipped off his headtie, his sandals. His chest and shoulders were smooth and curved with lithe muscle and bone. He straightened, his eyes going very serious and a cocky grin tweaking his lips.

It suddenly seemed as if there wasn't enough air. I turned around. "I don't know if this is a good idea, Calev...I...if we—you could become...well, I can't stop worrying..."

Water splashed and lapped around my crossed arms as I faced the waterfall, spray cloaking me.

"How about we stop worrying and enjoy this hidden moment on this legendary island."

He was right behind me.

Every inch of my skin caught fire, and I couldn't breathe let alone form a response to this insane statement. His hands found my arms, and he brushed hot fingertips from my elbows to my shoulders. I shivered. My stomach dipped.

"Kinneret..."

His lips rubbed against the tender skin on the back of my ear. A molten heat in me twisted high, snaking into my arms and legs. I couldn't take his chest against my back anymore or his breath in my ear. It wasn't enough. The golden heat wanted more. I wanted more.

We couldn't do this. I would not do this to him.

"Calev," I said, gritting my teeth, "you'll be Outcasted if anyone sees us. We were fools dancing on the amir's boat. I won't be your fun for one night, then left to pine for you."

He spun me around. "Do you really think that's how I feel about you? That you're one night of pleasure for me?" He swallowed, his gaze going to my lips. "Even if you weren't a kaptan now, which will please my elders, I would still want you forever. I know that now. I could never only be your friend."

"I'm not really a kaptan. The amir was humoring me to get here. Until I can convince your father to take me on as Old Farm's kaptan—"

Calev was shaking his head, smiling. "I don't care about all of that. All I want is you."

He braced my head in his hands and kissed me.

My fingers covered his and my argument dissolved into the mist around us. I pressed into the kiss. His lips tasted salty and sweet and warm and wet from the waterfall's spray. He drew my top lip into his hot mouth and let one hand slip around my neck, back to front. His fingers paused, moving against the pounding pulse in my throat. His stomach brushed mine and what had been a molten glow inside me became a raging storm of heat, uncontrollable, consuming. His skin dragged over mine, and storm tossed my heart into blind joy of red flames and whipping lightning strikes of pleasure. I pulled back, gasping and grinning, to see his smile, that smile I adored, and his hair, curled and dark and soaked against his beautiful, lucky head. Drops of fresh water dotted his brow and the side of his nose. He was a creature from another world, as foreign and alluring as Ayarazi itself. Before I could throw myself back into the kiss, a branch snapped beyond the pool.

My mouth went dry and my heart stopped.

The amir appeared out of the shadowed moonlight.

Calev's eyes went wide and blank.

A fever gripped me and prickled against my temples and palms. I started to speak, to address her politely to cover our crime, but before I could utter a word, Calev dove under the water. He came up out of the pool to stand beside the amir.

Silver flashed from his hand. It was so dark, so difficult to see. The amir grunted, an ugly sound, and fell to the grass. Her feet jerked, she moaned, then went still.

My arms went cold. "Calev, what—"

He turned, and a wavering light poured out of his mouth and dissolved into the night. The blankness in his features melted away, revealing his kind eyes and soft mouth. Blinking, he looked from me to what appeared to be my dagger. It dripped blood onto his shaking fingers.

Bile rose in my throat.

He'd stabbed the amir.

# CHAPTER TWENTY-FIVE

MY HAND WENT TO MY mouth. "Calev."

Dropping the dagger, he stammered, saying my name, then hers, making incoherent noises. "I didn't do this. Kinneret. The amir is dead. I didn't...what happened?"

I was cold all over and not only because of the temperature.

"You killed her. Did you plan this?" I couldn't think. My thoughts whirled, dark and slippery as eels.

Calev ran a hand over his wet, chilled head. "No. Of course not. But I don't even remember having that dagger. Why would I..."

With her dead, I had no one to send fighters to get Avi. Berker would take charge now and Avi would be left to die. He'd, at the very least, Outcast me for the magic and take a hand for good measure. Calev would be put to death for murder. Old Zayn would blame himself, even though it wasn't his fault. It was mine. And Calev's. But why?

My lungs fought for a breath that wouldn't come. "Why did you do it?"

"I'm telling you. I don't know what happened."

A black knowledge swept over me.

He'd been Infused.

The light that had left his mouth was a wraith's Infusion—the evil will that possessed those touched by a wraith's shadow.

Ever since that night on my boat, he'd been Infused.

"It all makes sense now."

"What? Talk to me, Kinneret!"

The occasional darkness in his eyes, unblinking. The times he'd stared like Death itself at the amir.

I swam to the side and climbed out, careful to avoid the bloody dagger in the grass. Shivering, I picked up my skirt and used it to clean his hands, looking into his face.

He was pale. Too pale.

"Calev. Listen to me. You were Infused. Remember the night in my boat? When the wraith flew over us? Since then, I've seen odd looks in your eyes. You acted strangely toward the amir. I didn't know…it was always something quick, gone before I could realize…"

"Infused?" He swallowed, allowing me to keep holding his hands. "But it's been so long. Can it work that way? And why would I wish to hurt one person?"

I pulled away from him and lifted his tunic. Helping him pull it over his head, I said, "I've never seen it happen that way before, but I've heard of it. The wraith felt different that night too. Do you remember?"

He shook his head. "I don't." His gaze flicked to me, his eyes widening. "I don't remember feeling the wraith at all."

"That's not uncommon. Lapses in memory. No recollection of being Infused. The wraith, this one felt…intelligent. Sharp, focused." I dressed quickly, my pulse like a frightened rabbit leaping and screaming in my head.

Calev put his hands over his face. "Do you think it meant for me to specifically murder the amir?"

"I just don't know. But it seems that way."

"If Berker and the amir's fighters see this, if they find me here…"

"You're dead. Old Farm or not. We'll find another way to help Avi. Somehow. Some way." Moonlight draped like death shrouds over the sloping hill leading to the camp near the silver outcropping. "We have to get off this island before they wake up or they'll take you to Jakobden for a trial and you'll be sentenced to death. First, we'll hide the...body."

Calev looked to the sky and heaved a shuddering breath, nodding.

We put hands under the amir's arms and shifted her into a clutch of thickly leaved brush past the waterfall.

"They'll see that someone dragged something through here. Look at the mud," Calev said.

"We don't have the sun to worry about it. We have to go. Now."

His gaze followed my own over the meadow. That strange glistening, silver light undulated around a boulder near the first rise and over the camp.

"They'll never believe I was Infused," he said. "I wouldn't believe it. I would never believe the Infusion could be aimed at one person." He rubbed his face. "Fire, help me." Making the sign on his forehead, he trembled.

"We'll sneak into camp, wake Oron, and take one of the small boats from the beach."

Running alongside me through the damp grass, Calev took heavy breaths between his words. "One of the small boats? On the Pass? But they're even smaller than yours and they don't have sails."

"It's not as if you, me, and Oron can run the amir's ship. It takes twenty to do that. The small boat is our only choice. And I have Salt Magic." We'd probably die. But I had to give it a go. There was nothing else to do.

"What about a Wraith Lantern?" Calev asked.

I'd never been so cold. My fingers were ice, my feet frosted. "We'll steal one from the ship."

Muscles and tendons in Calev's cheek moved as his lips pressed together.

He was right to be scared.

WHEN I SHOOK ORON AWAKE, he shouted, "I paid you already, you muck-mouthed, goat-herding—"

I slapped a hand over his lips.

Calev and I looked from Oron to the fighting sailors and Berker. Surely Oron's broken dream and shouting would wake them. But none stirred. Strange.

The sun was already painting the sky and readying for dawn, and these fighters trained every day at dawn. But now their chests rose and fell in sleep. A few looked pale. Two at the edges of the camp ring moaned and held their heads in their sleep.

"Is everyone ill?" Calev whispered, his face blue in the almost-dawn.

We didn't have the sun to wonder about this miracle that might save our lives. I pulled Calev and Oron toward the path to the sea. "It doesn't matter now. Oron, there's been an…accident."

"Why are you tugging at me? What are you talking about?" Oron jerked his arm free.

"We've no sun to explain. Come. Please."

With a nod and one last look around camp, he followed Calev and me across the meadow.

The sea crashed, promising both challenge and escape. The full ship bobbed in the waters just before the whirlpool. In the shoreline's pale sand, the five small boats that had brought our party ashore lay like beached whales. Together we pushed the closest one into the lapping waves.

As we climbed in, Calev explained everything to Oron.

Oron paused in rowing, and his oar nearly slipped out of his hands before he caught it.

I took over rowing with Calev.

"No one will believe this story, Calev." Oron frowned.

The ship loomed above us, and I snatched a grappling hook from the bottom of the boat and threw it over the side.

"It also doesn't help that Calev has the throat-blood oath with the amir," I said.

Oron held the rope steady as Calev and I climbed.

The sea gave a heave, and the rope slid across the side of the craft, catching on a porthole. It jerked under my grip and I clung to the ship, Calev and Oron swearing in chorus.

"Hold on," I called over my shoulder.

Calev still held to the rope, but he'd lost his foot-over-foot grip. The waves came in like a bully again, stomping against the ship. There was a storm somewhere out at sea. I tumbled over the side and onto the deck, then I checked on Calev. He slipped a yard down and his head banged against another porthole.

"I could use some help here," he said, his words tumbling under the sound of the waves on the hull.

Oron fought with the rope, his weight shifting the small boat. "I don't think it's going to go well for your lucky boy if he ends up in the drink right now!"

Yanking salt from my bag, I tossed some into the wind.

*"Peace under the waters and above,*
*I wait for your will but send prayers still."*

The sea eased into a quiet swell, gentling like a guilty horse, and Calev turned his face up, nodding thankfully.

"Hurry!"

I reached a hand down and after three more upward thrusts, he grasped it and slipped over port side to land next to me. He rubbed his skull.

"You're all right?"

"Fine. Fine."

He was anything but.

With my dagger, now clean of the amir's blood, I cut the rope holding a large Wraith Lantern to the mainmast. Calev caught it neatly, the sun an orange hill at the edge of the sea behind him.

A shout echoed from the shore.

Berker and two fighters stood on the sand, a battle axe and a bow raised. The man with the bow suddenly doubled over, coughing. Berker wiped a hand over his own forehead like someone with a fever.

"They're ill," Calev said, gripping the lantern. The ship listed, but he bent his knees and kept his feet. He was becoming a sailor.

"Exactly what I was thinking." If they were, we'd have more sun to find a way around the whirlpool. But if the sailors were sick, what about Oron? He'd stayed the entire night with them.

At the side of the ship, Calev and I leaned over to check on Oron. He looked up with imploring eyes.

"Do hurry, sweetings." His tunic billowed in a gust of salty wind. "They're sending arrows in place of prayers this morning."

Proving his point, an arrow zipped past my head.

I tied the lantern onto my sash. Calev steadied the rope as I climbed down to Oron, and when my feet were in the teetering boat, I looked up.

We were headed back out to sea. That frigid mist was going to hit us hard. "We need a blanket," I called up to Calev.

Nodding, Calev disappeared, then came over the side with two hefty woolen bundles under one arm. Another arrow flashed past, grazing his leg and bringing a scant amount of blood to the surface.

"Throw the blankets down!" I held out my hands.

Oron and I caught Calev's stolen goods with outstretched arms as more shouts rode from the beach and over the surf. We tucked the blankets under the benches as two more fighting sailors ran to join Berker. If I squinted hard enough, I could see gray around their eyes and mouths. Definitely ill.

Gray.

Silver.

A spark lit my mind as Calev's weight hit the boat.

He and Oron grabbed up the oars.

"Did you see the strange light last night?" I untied my sash.

Calev rowed on the side opposite me, across the boat's belly from Oron and me.

"No." Oron's gaze flickered between the sailors on the coast and the whirlpool we headed toward. "The only thing I saw was the black behind my eyelids, a lightless heaven."

The sailors nocked arrows and raised them high. A bead of sweat dragged down my temple.

Berker probably hadn't found the amir yet. He most likely suspected we planned to tell another party about the silver.

There wasn't sun enough to talk about my guess why the fighters and Berker were sick. "We have to go southeast and slip past the whirlpool. There might be a way to lip around it."

A volley of arrows splashed short of the boat as the sucking sound of the whirlpool reached my ears.

I caught bits of Berker's shouts. "...the whirlpool reaches too far..."

My oar didn't want to move in the water, and my arms trembled with fatigue. I felt for my salt pouch. Nothing but a bit of dust. I'd thought there would be sun to refill it.

The whirlpool's blue-green and white waters churned all the way to the black rocks of the breakers leading to the Pass.

"I think we can make it," I whispered, one hand in my pouch and one on the oar. A road of water, unmoved by the whirlpool's deadly current edged the path toward the breakers. If we could line ourselves up with that...I turned to Calev, my mind thinking twenty things at once. "Did you not see the light last night?"

He faced me, tugging his oar, his eyes tight. "I-I...no. Just you. I..." His words tumbled together and a red flush lay across his fine cheeks.

I'm sure my own blushing matched his.

"Oh ho," Oron shouted over the water. "Don't believe you've shared all your adventures." He tried to smile even as he glanced at the whirlpool. His features tightened.

Still blushing and full of ripe fear, I joined Calev to help him row.

"What?" Calev asked, shifting on his seat. The look on his face reminded me of when we'd been caught leaping from the Old Farm stables' roof onto his father's favorite steed.

"Your color tells me even more than the fact that you can't sit still over there, young man." Oron laughed, then yelped as another volley of arrows zipped into the air.

"Hush, you two," I said. "There was a strange silver light around the island last night, around the camp. Only us three ate your greens, and we're not sick. I think the light is poison somehow. The greens must give us some temporary protection."

Oron twisted and lifted his eyebrows. "Though not from arrows, I'm guessing."

One of the sailors' shots hit the hull. The arrow's yellow and black fletching colored a spot not two fingers from Oron's elbow. His face whitened.

"We have to go back," he hissed.

I nodded, my neck tight. "The fighters are weakened. Maybe we can get back to shore, fight them off or trick them, and disappear into the hills. If I can watch the tides turn, I might spy a path past the worst of the whirlpool and plan a way out."

"You're the most valuable to them, Kinneret," Calev said, his flush gone and confidence giving his words legs again. "Because of what you did to get us here. You stand with me beside you and we'll wave a surrender."

His reasoning was a little flawed considering I was the one Berker trusted the least, but I agreed. We had no choice anyway.

"Reverse stroke, Oron," I said. "Calev, pull hard."

I did too and our boat swung around, putting our backs to the shore.

"The only surrender I know is the formal one done at the harvest contest at the amir's field," I said.

Visions of men on swan-necked steeds decked out in tasseled saddles flashed through my mind.

"It's the only one I know too," Calev said. He met my eyes. "Ready?"

If this failed and the fighters aimed well, this could end with our blood coloring the boat and Oron lost in the whirlpool, destined to become a Salt Wraith. He'd never have the strength to row out and he certainly didn't have the talent with magic.

I steeled myself, not allowing my hands to shake as Calev gave them a quick squeeze, but my heart galloped.

We stood as one and raised our hands, one arm bent and angled toward the other in the sign of surrender.

# CHAPTER TWENTY-SIX

**S**URRENDER!" I SHOUTED WITH CALEV.

The sea lifted the boat and turned her west as we edged away from the whirlpool. On shore, the fighting sailors held their bows high, and the arrow tips glinted in the sun, poised to strike. Voice contorted by the sea's noise, Berker shouted something. The fighter on his left let one arrow fly.

Calev shoved me to the boat's bottom and threw himself over me. My elbow hit a bench seat on my way down and pain splintered my arm. The boards under me reeked of old ocean water.

On top of me, Calev's body jerked.

He grunted, and the hand that clutched me to him loosened and fell limp. I pressed it against my shoulder to make him hold me, but his breath came out in a hiss.

A cold knowledge crushed me.

Then Oron was talking. Shouting rose from the beach. We needed to get back to the oars. The current was pulling us toward the whirlpool again.

I eased my way out from under Calev, settling him, stomach down, in the boat's belly and taking his head in my hands.

"Where exactly is he hit, Oron?" My voice was strangely calm.

Calev's beautiful brown eyes fluttered open and shut. "I'm all right." He sucked a breath and his body shivered. "It's my side."

I couldn't breathe.

Oron had maneuvered his bulky self around an oar handle to view Calev from the back. Oron's tangled locks fell over his wide nose as he crouched to see the point of entry. Calev was shaking in my hands, his knees butted against my own. The boat dipped under us, the tide now taking us too close.

I met Oron's gaze over Calev's heaving form. "We have to row. Now."

I leaped up and grabbed the nearest oar, Oron doing the same. The whirlpool was a slurping, sucking monster ready to devour us, more dangerous even than Asag because no weapon could force it to change course. I could feel my will draining, like a wraith sweeping over me. Without more salt in my pouch, more strength in my gut, and more confidence in our chances, we'd never make it.

It was as if we weren't rowing at all.

The current sped across our path, tearing a wide ripple between us and the shallow water leading to the shoreline. Calev made a noise, and I dug my oar deeper into the waves and strained the wooden handle back. Every muscle in my arms and back and neck screamed. We weren't going to make it.

"Kinneret. The salt." Oron's voice was dry and cracked. He knew I didn't have anything but dust.

With one last haul on the oar, I wedged the handle under my arm and struggled with the pouch strings. The boat tossed with only Oron to row it. Calev's arm dropped to the decking with a knock. He groaned. My blood screamed, my heart hitting my ribs painfully.

*Not my Calev too. Please not my Calev too.*

Salty grit under my nails and in my palm, I tossed what little magic I had into the air and shouted to the sea.

*"Send us out,*
*Send us beyond.*
*We know not your depths,*

*And want not your charms.*
*Out, out, out, out.*
*Please, sea,*
*Please listen to me."*

I grabbed the oar and slammed it into the water. The boat turned its nose a subtle fraction toward the sky. Rowing and heaving and praying aloud, we dragged at the boat. The current fought us. The salt hadn't worked. I'd shouted, and anger never got anyone anywhere with the salt. I closed my eyes and put everything I had left into one last tug on the oar.

Then the craft began to edge out of the current.

Tears or sweat or maybe both poured down my face. As Oron whooped, and with a few more pulls, the tide brought us ashore.

All my thoughts turned to Calev.

Oron leaped from the boat and joined the others in pulling the craft out of the waves. One sailor vomited beside the boat. They were still suffering from the silver toxin.

Berker was snapping and lashing out commands I didn't hear.

I dragged Calev up and put his good side against mine, his arm over my shoulder. He mumbled something and I kissed his forehead, not caring for even a breath if anyone thought anything of it. If they tried to Outcast him for this, I'd kill them all. Twice.

I supposed I should remove the arrow from Calev's back and staunch the bleeding. I draped his body, chest down, over a patch of blue-green grass. Like rain drops, blood trickled from the place where the arrow's shaft sunk into his skin, more of it oozing from the top of the wound. He panted like a dog with sun-stroke, his breaths short and labored.

Purple rings circled Berker's eyes—probably from the poisonous silver light—as he yammered on.

"I didn't intend for the fighters to injure Calev ben Y'hoshua, but this is your doing, sailor," he spat. "As soon as the amir returns from her walk, I will inform her of your attempt to steal away and find a new associate to help you take all the silver for yourself."

My jaw ached from clenching my teeth. At least he didn't know the amir had been killed.

The silent fighters beside him shuffled their feet and mumbled with one another, voices low and worried, faces tinged with gray and yellow sickness.

"I don't have sun for your blathering, *Kaptan* Berker Deniz." With my dagger, I pressed sideways into the arrow shaft sticking out of Calev's shivering back. The wood snapped and left a shorter length that would be easier to grab and pull.

Berker *tsked* at my words and stormed toward the camp, his tunic whipping around his ankles. The sailors stayed with us.

I looked to Oron. Sand cloaked his chin and shoulder. He brushed it away impatiently. "This is the worst sort of place to treat such a wound," he said.

"But we're near the ocean." The sea had the most magic. Its salt would be Calev's best bet against this wound. I put a hand near the arrow. Calev's torn tunic was rough under my fingers. The patterns in it made my tired eyes flinch. "Do you think it's a good idea to take it out now? He's still awake."

Oron knelt. "He won't be when you do the job." He began tearing Calev's tunic away from the wound.

One sailor hissed sympathetically and two held Calev still.

I grasped the arrow shaft.

"Hold it and him still while I make a cut." Oron unsheathed his dagger.

I tried to keep breathing as Oron sliced the blade through Calev's skin, making a cut two fingers long.

Oron met my gaze. "I have to touch the arrowhead. I need to see if it's stuck in bone or bent from a muscle contraction."

I squeezed my eyes shut, then opened them and nodded.

Calev shouted as Oron's finger slipped into the bloody wound. Oron tilted his head, his tongue between his teeth, and Calev went limp.

Pulling his digit free, Oron stared grimly into the grass and sand. "It passed between two ribs. I think it may've nicked his lung, but we won't know unless he…"

"Unless he what?"

"Unless he stops breathing well, smells of pus, and dies."

I blew out a harsh breath. I would focus on doing what we could, not what horrors might happen. "Now what do we do?"

Oron was eyeing the fighting sailors. "Since it's not stuck in bone, we can pull it free. But I need something to loop around it. Anyone have a length of wire?"

A fighter with a voice like a raven said, "Would fishing line work?"

Snatching it, Oron began muttering. "If he dies, Y'hoshua ben Aharon will have me in his fields working off the blood price until the sun goes black."

I tried to swallow, but my throat didn't want to work. "The fields aren't his."

"Oh, don't you start too. I know. I know. Old Farm belongs to all at Old Farm. Everyone is equal and all that." He snorted. "But you don't see any other Old Farm boys meeting with the amir, now do you? They exist in a caste system as we do. They're only more skilled at masking its uglier side."

He was doing his best to distract me with an argument. "If Calev dies, we all work in Y'hoshua's fields until *we* die. It'll be one big celebration."

Oron worked the line into a loop and eased it into the wound. "Remind me to educate you further on what is enjoyable and what is not. Considering this journey you were so keen to embark on, plus your take on working in fields, I feel you've quite forgotten the basics."

The arrow's shaft trembled from Calev's unconscious shaking, and my palms grew damp.

Oron held tight to the fishing line. "Take the shaft and when I call it, pull straight away from the point of entry."

My throat convulsed. "Aye, aye, kaptan."

Oron gave me a wry look. A breath later, he said, "Now!"

We yanked the arrow from Calev's back, a wet noise making my skin cold and damp.

I dove back toward Calev and covered the bleeding wound with the torn square of his tunic. The sea blew behind me, pressing along my back like a friend's hand. Squeezing my eyes shut, I only thought of Calev's smile and how my heart swelled when I saw it. There were no words to this kind of desperate prayer. My heart thudded in my fingertips.

Oron kissed the top of my head like Calev's Old Farm soul-teacher.

The immediate threat over, my mind flipped from rescue to rage, and Oron misinterpreted the look in my eyes.

Keeping one hand on the cloth at Calev's back, he touched my shoulder with the other. "There's no blood from the boy's mouth. A good sign. He's only asleep from the pain."

Good. It was time to settle something.

My vision went red.

I spun and stood in one motion like Calev had in his dagger dance. My eyes searched out the fighter who'd loosed that arrow.

I found him.

Dark hair. Light eyes. Very, very tall. *Ekrem.* I paused. Wait. I liked Ekrem. I hadn't realized he was the one who'd shot at us. The truth stung. Next to him, the blond woman with the beautiful battle axe frowned.

"You." I raged toward Ekrem, pushing the others out of my way. Ekrem didn't back away from me. I shoved his chest. "You hurt the most important member of Old Farm. Your life is worthless."

They didn't know about the amir. I could use her shadow to scare him. I wanted all of them scared. Of me. Of us. So they'd help me with Calev and help me sail away to Kurakia.

The plan grew roots in my mind. Maybe my aunt could heal him. I'd seen her heal a man with a head injury that had left him sleeping for three solid years.

"You know I was under orders, Kaptan Kinneret Raza. Kaptan Berker Deniz outranks you."

Ekrem's stiff leather vest was hot under my gritty palms as I pushed him.

"Well, when the amir hears of this," I said, "she'll have you drawn and quartered. Your head on a spike. Or sent to the quarries."

My hands fell to my sides and all my energy drained out of me.

The quarries.

With the amir dead, how was I going to get Avi back?

Maybe my aunt would think of a plan for Avi. At least she was probably still alive at the quarry. Maybe. Calev could die at any minute. He could be dead already.

The rage in me blinked away. I fell to my knees, knowing my shouting did zero.

Ekrem offered a hand, but I pushed his fingers away. Beyond us, the whirlpool's eddies smoothed from white and blue-green into a dull blue. The sun was a white circle a finger from its zenith. The tide had changed. The whirlpool had calmed a bit.

I faced the sailors, my eyes specifically trained on Ekrem. Maybe his guilt would move him toward my goal. All had to be done before Berker returned either with news of the amir or simply with the trouble he liked to cause me.

"When we left," I said, standing, "we weren't trying to do anything against our agreement with the amir." It was true, but obviously since Calev killed the amir, it hardly made sense. But they didn't know that. "Kaptan Berker Deniz is simply misinformed. Now, I need two of you to come with us to Kurakia, if you will. My mother's sister is the only one who can heal this son of Old Farm. If he dies, I guarantee one of your number will die for it, either in the fields under the sun or by the amir's rough hand. Your amir will suffer too. The kyros also knows and respects Old Farm. He won't let the amir's mistake hinder his ability to make silver from lemon and barley trade. Now, who will row our boat and do their duty to Jakobden?"

The light-haired woman spoke up. "We must wait for the amir's orders."

Oron nudged me. "Kinneret, what exactly are you doing?"

"Stay with Calev. I have a plan," I whispered to him.

"We cannot wait," I said to the woman. "To wait means death for this Old Farm son."

Ekrem raised his blue eyes and nodded.

I took a breath. "Good. I need one more volunteer. We need two strong sailors to row. I have a Wraith Lantern. We'll be safe. I am your kaptan."

The light-haired woman cocked her head and breathed out through her nose. Then she raised her palm and bowed.

A weight dropped off my back. "Good. Your name, please?"

"Serhat, kaptan."

I nodded. "You two, lift Calev ben Y'hoshua. The rest, give up your water skins for our journey please and shove us off the shore."

Movement in the distance caught my eye. My heart contracted. Someone was headed here. I licked my lips and hurried to take the water from the sailors who weren't coming with us.

"Hurry now, please."

Ekrem and Serhat, who'd mostly regained their healthy color, leaned Calev up and put their heads under his arms. They lifted him and I tucked my shoulder under one of his thighs to help get him to the boat. Another sailor joined me, grabbing the other leg. The other two men took oars from the next small boat and placed them in ours.

Once we had Calev settled on the floor of the boat, we hopped out to push the heavy craft into the water. It took way too long to get the boat deep enough for us to board.

The people approaching were taking shape now, getting closer. Three? Four? We jumped into the boat, and I held up a hand to shield my eyes from the sun. Berker's bright tunic caught the light. A smear of darkness marred his sash.

*Blood.*

My heart stopped.

The amir's blood.

*They know.*

I spun to face Ekrem and Serhat. "Row hard. We must make the tide to steer around the whirlpool's tight fist."

Oron took up an oar across from me. As he raised his eyes to the beach, his cheeks fell flat and his mouth dropped open.

"Kinneret."

"I know."

Thankfully, the sailors didn't seem to notice Berker and the others trickling onto the beach. Serhat rowed with eyes trained on Calev, who'd begun bleeding again at their feet. Ekrem kept his gaze on me, probably seeing how I measured up in this unconventional situation. The man probably wondered why he'd agreed to this.

I twisted on my bench seat, trying not to hear Calev's labored breathing above the splash of water and the wind whistling through the metal rings that kept the oars moving in the right place. The whirlpool remained smoother than it had been when we'd first tried this. I had no more salt in my pouch, so I scooted to the side and cupped a handful of ocean.

Throwing the water high, allowing the sunlight to sparkle through it, I called out a prayer and a wish and hoped it was enough. My tingling fingers and toes told me I was too worried to do proper Salt Magic. This would have to be mostly skill and brute strength.

Our craft touched the lip of the whirlpool's hungry mouth.

"Hard to port!" The boat rocked, but the current didn't yet have us. "More! I need more!"

We rounded the island side of the pool, going counterclockwise. The second we slipped from that arc, we had to row with everything to rip free and head to the opening in the breakers.

"Starboard! Row hard to starboard! Reverse on port! Go! Go!"

I tugged at my own oar, the boat shuddering and tossing under me. The handle stuck and the water drew hands over the oar's tip. I cursed and swore and gritted my teeth and hauled on the paddle until it, and the work of the others, finally pulled us another shift away from the pool.

At the gap in the black rock barriers and billowing waves, Oron and the sailors followed my directions like they could read my thoughts. My back and arms cramping, we dashed through the pass, unbroken.

That obstacle crossed, my gaze flew back to the shore's inky sand.

Neither the amir's fighters nor Berker were there.

Oron pointed behind and east of us.

Berker and ten sailors had boarded another boat and obviously followed our lead in getting around the pool. There were more fighters than oars, and some drew arrows from quivers on their backs. They were slow to nock them. Berker's mouth opened wide like he was shouting. His hands jerked through the air as their boat crested an incoming wave near the gap. He fell back and only his head showed above the craft's side.

"He's trying to get them to fire," Oron whispered to me.

Ekrem turned. "They will not attempt to hit us, Kaptan Kinneret. I did not intend to strike the Old Farm. The wind took my shot."

Serhat nodded, her blond braid shifting over her shoulder.

I swallowed and cleared my throat. "Why won't they attack?"

"Because you showed loyalty to Ifran. The amir did not. Kaptan Berker did not. We value loyalty above all."

His words steeled my heart. What could I give Ekrem and Serhat for all this? I had nothing. Nothing but a trip across the Pass to foreign Kurakia, a trip that would most likely involve thirst, hunger, and to top it all, Salt Wraiths.

Still rowing, sweat pouring down my back and temples, I did my best to look calm and deserving of his service and his mate's. "I will reward you in any way I can, though the prize may only be friendship and a place to lay your head at the end of all this."

Not taking his hands from his oar, Ekrem closed and opened his eyes, nodding his head in acknowledgment. Serhat gave me a grim smile and went back to her rowing.

"Kinneret," Oron said quickly, his eyes shining. "You have given me more tales than I ever thought to hold in my heart."

"It isn't over yet," I said. In the shadow of the boat's side, Calev's lashes drew black lines against his sickly pale cheeks. "Calev better live through it with us." A vice tightened around my chest and I gripped the side to keep from falling.

"My wish too, kaptan. My wish too," Oron said, his voice rough as the waters and his gaze on Calev's shivering body.

My throat burned with the need to scream.

I straightened my shoulders, ignored the struggling boatload of Berker and his fighting sailors behind us, and gave the order to drift into the Pass's main current.

AFTER TWO DAYS RIDING A current, Kurakia's coast, barely discernible at this distance, was a calligrapher's practice stroke on the eastern horizon. We had to reach its shores before Calev's body stopped fighting and I lost my best ally in my fight to get Avi back.

# CHAPTER TWENTY-SEVEN

CLOUDS SHROUDED THE MOON AND drew a blanket of pale blue over the looming shoulders of Kurakia's coast. My body shook with fatigue as the others took a break from rowing to sleep. With one hand on our makeshift tiller—simply an oar I held out the aft end of the little boat—I did my best to use the currents to direct us toward my aunt. The Wraith Lantern scattered light over my arm as I scooped another handful of ocean water, threw it, and whispered magic.

The white-black sea shushed against the boat, and I dipped fingers into the water, my heart easing just a little. There hadn't been as many rocks coming from Ayarazi to Kurakia, thankfully. It'd been two nights on the Pass, but it felt like an eternity.

A wet cough and a moan sounded from the bottom of the boat. Calev.

With a small rope laying wet at the bottom of the craft, I tied the tiller oar to the stone circle anchor sitting at my feet. Edging past Oron's slumped and sleeping body, I leaned toward Calev and touched his cheek. His skin was sticky and cold. He opened one beautiful eye.

Swallowing, he tried to talk for the first time since we'd removed the arrow on Ayarazi's coast. "Where...is that...Kin..."

I pressed my palm gently against his jaw, my heart seizing. "I'm here. You'll be fine. We're almost to my aunt's. She'll fix you. Just rest."

He'd managed to drink from Serhat's water skin earlier and worked down two bites of minced fish Oron had miraculously netted. Hope burned in me like wildfire, out of control and raging through any common sense I'd picked up through my short life. I refused to sleep, thinking if I let that fire rest, it might go out.

"Kinneret," Calev rasped.

"I'm here."

His eyes went wide and rolled before closing again, like he was trying to see the two sailors that surrounded him. "Do they know I killed the amir?"

I sucked a breath and touched my fingers to his lips. A prickling sensation ran over the back of my neck. Serhat slept, mouth open and her eyes firmly shut. To my left, Ekrem also lay still, but his chest wasn't rising and falling like a sleeping person. It was dark though. Surely he would've said something if he'd heard Calev.

Calev seemed to be sleeping again though, or lost in pain, so hopefully he wouldn't repeat his question.

At some point I had to tell Ekrem and Serhat about Calev's Infusion and the murder. Would they still value my so-called loyalty when they learned I'd helped their master's killer escape? If they rose against us, we were lost. We could never fight them off with Calev so badly injured. I couldn't carry him on one shoulder and flee or fight.

As I crawled back to the tiller, a Salt Wraith dragged across the moon.

Raising the lantern high, I hissed a warning to the others. "Wraith. Block your ears. Stay low."

The rest, except Calev, stirred and crouched on the bottom of the boat between the bench seats, their fingers jammed in their ears.

This wasn't the wraith that had Infused Calev. This felt like ones in the past had, all raging, nonsensical hate smashing my reason into splinters. Gritting my teeth, I shook harder as the grating anger skinned me alive. Thank the Fire the lantern glowed strong and true.

Oron and the sailors winced against the wraith's attack, eyes shuttered and shoulders tensed. The wraith whisked its charcoal-white, glittering shadow over us and Calev jerked awake. I crawled to him. His cheek pressed against the boat's bottom, and he gave me a small nod, reassuring me. A muscle worked at his jawline. He was feeling the wraith, as we all certainly were, but he was still him, still whole in heart.

Checking Oron and the sailors, I lay down, my head resting on Calev's tunic-swathed calf, and his sandal's edge butting into my belly. I breathed him in, pushing the angry thoughts out, out, out.

Finally, the wraith's shadow disappeared.

The sky was clear.

"No more?" Oron scratched his head, making one tangled length bob.

I sat up and squeezed my hands to try to stop their shaking. "All clear."

"Too bad. The whole Wanting To Kill Everybody thing was tamping the whole Our Future Is Looking Pretty Crap thing down really well."

I shot him a look.

"Kinneret," Oron whispered, his big eyes watching the fighters settle into their rowing. "This whole business with the yatagan-eyed wiseman and the golden axe-wielder," he nodded toward Ekrem and Serhat, "it's…we should've left without them. Not that I don't love the blond's looks of death. They're like rich dumplings that turn your blood to sludge as you grin and take another helping."

Sunlight crept over the hills of the Kurakian shoreline.

Ease washed over me. We'd made it. "Hush, Oron. Please."

"Pardon me for interrupting your moment with the sunrise, but we need to—"

"You did not tell us your truth." Ekrem sat up.

My hands strangled the oar I was using as a tiller.

Eyeing me without a hint of emotion on his rugged face, Ekrem tugged his vest into place and splashed a handful of water over the back of his neck. His voice was loud over the water shushing against Kurakia's red sand shoreline.

"I heard Calev ben Y'hoshua mumbling in the dark. The Old Farm murdered the amir."

I went cold as he and Serhat stood in unison.

"Yes, but..." What was the best way to explain this?

Oron raised his thick eyebrows in an *I-told-you* look. I curled my lip at him.

My oar slid easily from the water, but I dragged it slowly into its ring like it weighed four Ekrems holding nine Serhats. Oron and I began to row us closer to shore. He gave me yet another look, his lips pale and his throat moving in a swallow.

Both fighting sailors stood in front of us with arms crossed, pieces of their hair like whips around their stern faces. Their oars sat on their benches like a sign of rebellion. My stomach felt empty and full at the same time. If I didn't word this wisely, the little chance we had to save Avi was over, not to mention the rest of our lives.

And there was precious little hope of rescuing Avi. What could we do? Even if Ekrem and Serhat spared our lives and stayed by our sides, what could five people do against the oramiral?

Nothing.

"Please. Just..." I didn't know what to say.

A shudder ripped through me. I pressed my lids closed and tears bled out of my eyes. I was losing her. And Calev. If the fighters didn't believe our story, Oron and I too would be killed.

What was the point of trying?

My oar slipped from my hands. I opened my eyes as Oron jumped in front of me and caught its handle before it could disappear into the water.

"Kinneret," he said softly, holding my oar with two white-knuckled hands, "you must move forward. If you don't move forward, the worst will happen. If you do move forward, it may not."

I took a jerking breath, wiped my eyes, and took the oar from him.

"Before we left Jakobden," I said, looking around the fighting sailors to the Pass, to the challenges we were leaving behind, "Calev went with me and Oron to get the map to Ayarazi." My gaze flicked to Ekrem. "You heard about the map, yes?"

He nodded.

"After our dive, Calev was Infused. I didn't realize it then. He was still Infused on Ayarazi. The wraith ordered the amir's death. I watched the Infusion light leave his mouth." Unblinking, I met their gazes, showing them the truth in my eyes.

From my periphery, I saw Oron nod across the boat from me, his eyes swiveling from one sailor to the other. Calev lay silent and shuddering between the bench seats at the bottom of the rocking craft.

Ekrem's chest expanded, and his vest creaked like a saddle as it stretched over his broad build. He exhaled very, very slowly. I turned away from him to peer over my shoulder. The shore crept up behind us. The sailor looked to his crewmate. He was asking her what she thought. It all sat on her shoulders. Calev. Avi. Oron. Me.

Serhat stepped onto her bench and leaped deftly over Calev.

"What are you doing?"

She leaned into Calev's face, her body glancing against my back.

"He can't answer your questions now," I said. "When my aunt—"

The sailor held a hand up to my face and I shut my mouth.

She brushed a large hand over Calev's askew headtie. Her finger touched the line of pale skin that normally hid beneath the cloth. I tugged at my oar, twisted slightly in my seat. A word sneaked out of Serhat's mouth, but I couldn't understand it. Turning her fair face to me, her gray eyes found mine, and I swallowed. Her mouth was a line and her eyes cold as the mist surrounding Ayarazi.

"If your aunt can heal him, we will talk then."

I took a breath and glanced at Oron. So we had time. No promises, but we had time between now and their decision whether or not to avenge their amir.

I'd take it.

Giving her a terse nod, I drew my oar into the boat and hopped into the knee-high seawater to drag the boat onto the shoreline. The others pushed and shoved along with me, sweat blooming on our brows. Already the Kurakian sun was a burning brand on my cheeks and arms. Sand squelched into my sandals, but I didn't mind. We had made it to my mother's homeland.

# CHAPTER TWENTY-EIGHT

KIRTING THE WALLED CAPITOL CITY of mud-brick tower houses with their grass-topped roofs, we wove down the path cattlemen used to take their beasts to market. A small crowd of black-skinned Kurakians surrounded us, their clothing bright with purple and red dye, but dusty. Calev rode my and the sailors' shoulders, and Oron led the way.

He elbowed one cow, headed out of the city perimeter like us. "Get your massive hind end to the side, beast."

A woman in a one-shouldered dress and elaborately braided hair laughed with her friend. The bare-chested cattleman at the cow's long-horned head gave us a scowl and *chit-chitted* at his animal to move it along more quickly. The cow bellowed, and the owner drew a whip from his loose pants and cracked the beast lightly.

"How far away is your dear aunt's bastion of healing, Kinneret?" Pushing the tentacles of his hair out of his face, Oron squinted at the horizon of scrubby Topa trees and dry sloping land. "Or have you tricked us all and are luring us into the Kurakian desert to die slowly out of spite?"

I took a heavy breath of spice and manure, and adjusted Calev's legs on my shoulders. Gripping his ankles, I tried to speed up. I could tell the fighters were keeping their pace slow because of me.

Oron's question sparked an idea. I'd done my part to keep the fighters safe during the sun they'd spent with me. Maybe if I brought up a few of those instances, they'd be more likely to believe Calev's Infusion was truth instead of lie.

"If I'd wanted you dead," I said, "I'd have slit your throats as you slept last night."

That would remind them of what Calev and I were. On their side. Good people.

We cleared the city's uneven wall and started up a steeper rise toward the countryside.

A cloud of red dust spun into the air and Ekrem coughed. "Good for us you stopped at simply slaying our leader, hm?"

Oron snorted. "For one normally so quiet, you certainly know how to craft a verbal strike."

"Striking is who I am," Ekrem said. "I am a hit. A cut. A slash. A blade and a bite."

I looked over Calev's leg at the fighter, then turned to see what his crewmate would say, if anything at all.

She raised her gaze from the patches of scrub grass along the path, to Oron's frowning face. "A kick and a cry of rage. Always, always, always coming for our enemies."

Goosebumps dragged over my arms.

I'd heard the fighters' creed before, tales about it from my parents. But I'd never heard it spoken in all seriousness by those who upheld its intent.

I had to win these two to my side. When Calev was healed—because I couldn't even think about my aunt failing in that—I needed these fighters to help me somehow rescue Avi.

Calev moaned. My plotting dissolved into the sting and burn of fear.

I rubbed my thumb over the bone at the bottom of his ankle. "Soon. We'll get you help soon."

The sun lashed its rays down on our heads and the bare shoulders of the Kurakian men who continued on the path to the next city. We went west and left the crowd. A Topa tree, resembling a hand rising from the dirt, crowned the next hill.

"There," I said. "My aunt's place is beyond that tree."

"Into the hand of the Fire," Oron mumbled, quoting the first kyros's three-hundred-year-old address to his conquered Jakobden natives. "I wonder...should we hope our young man here is delivered into that hand or left behind to fight with us?"

It was a good question. If Calev survived, he'd only live to be injured again if he stayed by my side like I knew he would. Was it selfish of me to wish for that?

"Oh, don't look too torn," Oron said, touching my sun burnt arm. "He would come with us no matter what you tried to do to prevent it. The man is quite in love with you, I fear."

My heart leaped and bumped into my ribs. After what happened at the waterfall, I'd guessed Calev did have feelings for me, but I thought maybe it was only lust for what he couldn't have. But then again, if I did survive this to become a real kaptan... Wait. He'd killed the amir. I'd been by his side. We were both doomed to die in the worst way if we ever returned home.

"What's to fear?" I asked, my voice trembling. "Who cares about caste anymore? It's not as if we can ever return to Jakobden. Calev's Infusion has set us on a path out of our home country. And I don't...I don't know..."

My words tripped and fell back inside me. For once, I had no real plan.

"Is this it?" Ekrem said.

"Yes. We're here. The ancient homestead of the Turays, my mother's family."

My aunt's farm looked much the same as the last time I'd seen it, holding my mother and father's hands with Avi trailing along behind us. A low, dirt wall surrounded scrub, three large Topa trees, the hen house on short stilts, a brick oven, and Aunt Kania's four story, mud-brick tower house. Dodging green-throated roosters and black-brown hens, we carried Calev through a gate crafted of sticks and knotted rope.

"You weren't joking about the chickens." Oron nudged an especially curious one away with his sandal. It clucked and spread its wings, flying the short distance to a hen house ramp.

Desperation for what to do about Avi and worry for Calev threatened to burst through my skin, but I tried to keep my voice light. I didn't want to douse the fire of hope inside me or the others. "I never joke about chickens."

Aunt Kania appeared from behind the second hen house, her skin dark and polished as Topa wood, as Mother's had been. A basket balanced in the braids of her head. Above her traditional, red Kurakian scarf, her wide smile faded as she studied the load on our shoulders.

I wanted to run to her, to bury my face in the bright pink folds of her one-shouldered dress and breathe in the tangy scent of dust and the cool, green smell of healing ointments. It would remind me of Mother. I knew it would. It would be comforting and wonderful.

And a waste of sun right now.

"Greetings, Aunt. I'm sorry it's been so long." I held my palm up as we did in Jakobden, and she quickly dipped and shook her head in the Kurakian greeting. "My friend needs you. He took an arrow to the back. His lung might be injured too."

She tossed the basket to the ground and hurried over, her red linen scarf flying behind her like she had wings.

"Get him to my rooms," she said.

Her Kurakian accent lengthened the vowels of the Jakobden tongue—the language everyone knew, the trade language.

As we walked through the rough arches underneath the tower house and headed toward the ladder, I lowered Calev's legs and let the fighters manage him in the narrow space.

A lot of rushed instructions, sweating, and fretting later, we had Calev on my aunt's top floor.

Aunt leaned over him as he lay on her striped rug. We gathered around, a smelly group for sure.

One ear on his chest, Aunt listened and clucked her tongue. "Not good. Not good."

My skin went cold.

Oron grumbled something and walked to a corner, his hand over his mouth. Serhat and Ekrem helped themselves to a jug of water on Aunt's table and sat on her stools.

Aunt reached toward a set of shelves under her hammock near a wide, open window. Withdrawing a crock, she met my eyes. "He will probably die."

I shivered. Kurakians never did coat the truth with syrup.

"But he's strong." I knelt beside Calev. His hair was soft, despite its sandy grit. His parted lips had lost all their pink-plum color. I drew my finger along their perfect edges. His breath was warm. "He's the eldest son of the elected leader of Old Farm."

Tilting her head in a maybe sort of gesture, Aunt said, "A strong bloodline. Will it be enough?"

Using a water skin and a fold of linen, she washed his wound. He stayed asleep, his face pale but not gray. Not the color of death. The unguent she tucked into the arrow's hole smelled like cinnamon and pepper and green plants. Taking a handful of salt from a pouch on her belt—a pouch much like my own—she began her magic.

Rubbing her palms together, her hands moved like fish darting up and down as she whispered prayers in Kurakian. I spoke nothing of the language. My mother had done her best to teach me. I had zero talent for languages other than my own.

Sitting cross-legged, she rocked back and forth. The grass mat beneath the rug crackled with her movements. Dusting sea salt over Calev's back and into his hair, she prayed over and over, her words blending together and lilting like she was very nearly singing. I couldn't look away from her. The sounds. Her hands. The salt sparking in the light from the window.

"Does Salt Magic work on land?" I asked.

Aunt shrugged. "Who knows what truly works? Could be coincidence when things go our way. Could be prayers. Maybe magic. Some things I know work, but…we do it all, just in case."

With a final word, she placed one hand at the base of Calev's skull and the other below his wound. I'm not sure if it was my fatigue or the fire in me, longing for his return to good health, but it seemed as if the air around her hands and his body shimmered.

Calev's back moved in one deep breath. A deeper breath than I'd seen him take in a long while. Since the boat, at least.

Then Aunt looked up at me. The fighters remained silent. From the room's back corner, Oron breathed entirely too loudly. Calev wasn't breathing loudly enough.

"Now we wait." She took my wrist in her warm, dry hand. "You rest, my niece."

If I slept, what would I wake to?

"Wait," I said.

As Aunt stood, I grabbed a handful of her dress. I had to tell her about Avi.

Wrinkles formed between Aunt's scant eyebrows and she eyed the rest of our party curiously. "You have a story to tell. I have Kurakian chicken to share. Wash, then we'll eat and you'll tell your tale."

Taking turns at the rocky, struggling creek outside Aunt's walls, we did our best to wash our travels from the creases in our arms and the backs of our necks. We hurried back to the tower house, following the spicy scent of the food she'd cooked for us in her outdoor oven. She'd laid a table fit for an amir near Calev's resting form. I crouched to run a quick hand over his clammy cheek.

"Don't stop fighting, my Calev, my luck, my friend," I whispered, my heart beating sluggishly in my chest.

Someone touched my back, and I jumped and turned to find Aunt's kind face smiling sadly.

"He must indeed be lucky. To have such a friend as my Kinneret. You are your mother's lightning strike, her beating heart."

I swallowed. "I was."

Aunt jerked her head once. "No. You are. She lives in you and your sister."

The word turned me inside out. I fell into Aunt's arms, crying like a child.

"The oramiral took Avigail. I was searching for Ayarazi, for a map Old Zayn had heard about and we ran too close to Quarry Isle and the oramiral's men boarded our boat and they took her from me. They took Avi to the quarry."

Her gasp jerked my head off her chest. "Ah, no. No." Her arms tightened around me.

"It's all my doing," I said. "All my fault."

She made shushing noises into my ear, and I tried to quiet, knowing I was making a fool out of myself in front of the fighting sailors.

Pressing her mouth closer to my ear, Aunt whispered, "It is not your fault, child. Tell me. Tell us all."

The dinner forgotten, we sat around the table as I poured out my tale of Avi and the map and our travels and the island of silver, coming back around to Avi. Oron's interpretations punctuated my descriptions.

"The oramiral's mind is not sound." Aunt lit a powdered stick of incense in the center of the table. The resinous scent of myrrh cloaked the musk of animals wafting through the open window. I hated that she used the expensive stick on us. It was meant only for the most important events. "The amir should take him from that island and put another in his place to run the quarry. It is a shame, really, that the madman has no one to care for him and keep him from hurting people."

Serhat's forehead wrinkled. "You don't blame the oramiral for the way he beats his quarrymen? The way he—outside of battle—steals children, men, and women for slaves?"

Aunt stood, the folds of her dress slipping into vertical lines like a rushing river. Her eyes were sharp. "At least he takes them in his confusion and is not like you and your amir, who take slaves with clear heads merely because of battles won and lost."

The fighting sailors pushed away from the table, faces pinched. "You question our honor?" Ekrem's voice punched out and up toward the grass roof.

Oron hopped off his chair and made a short wall between them and Aunt Kania. "We're in a strange situation here, my

223

friends. We won't agree on everything. Kinneret cannot tolerate too much spice in her dumplings, but I would bathe in it if given the opportunity. We must band together in the face of our differences to save this Old Farm innocent and Kinneret's sister."

"I don't believe the Old Farm boy is innocent," Serhat whispered, her words slithering into my ears.

I waved my hand and accidentally knocked over the incense. "He was Infused! You must believe me. Why would he want to kill the amir? The amir supports her people. A new amir may not." I wouldn't bring up the throat-blood oath he'd taken. They most likely already knew about it, but if they didn't…

Aunt's brow wrinkled. "What are you saying? Jakobden's amir is dead? This young man," she pointed at Calev, "slayed the amir? The one who managed peace between our country and yours?" She spun to face me. "Is this true? Was he Infused? Why was he alone with the amir on the waters?"

"He wasn't alone. And it was on land. The Infusion…it-it was different." I shook my head trying to think of a way to explain. "The wraith that Infused him felt sharp, cunning. It wasn't all crazy rage. It was fingers in your thoughts instead of kicking feet. Calev didn't hurt anyone until he had an opportunity to kill the amir on Ayarazi. I was the only witness."

Her mouth pursing, Aunt walked on shaky legs back to her chair. She put hands on the woven back and leaned in, breathing heavily.

"Could it be?" she mumbled. "If it is, we might have a chance."

"Could it be what? Chance to do what?" I asked.

She motioned for everyone to sit again. The sailors frowned and began to argue.

"Tut tut. Enough of this. What has happened is bigger than our arguments." She pointed to Oron. "The short one is right."

Pulling his tunic against his arm to show its shape, Oron's mouth twisted. "I prefer well-muscled, but go on."

Everyone sat and leaned in to listen as Aunt began to talk. We couldn't help themselves. Aunt possessed the most rich, lilting voice.

She eyed each one of us in turn. "Have you heard of the Tuz Golge? It is most likely a bad idea to mention it in your Jakobden lands, but it *is* a tale of your amir. The one your friend slayed. The woman is, was, far older than she looked, I'm certain. The Luk warriors always did age well."

"She was old?" I asked. The amir's skin had possessed a few wrinkles, but she'd been beautiful still.

"That's just frightening." Oron's eyes went wide.

I scowled at him and he held his hands up.

"What? Old women who look young?" He shook his head. "That's like offering up a carton of mangoes for sale, then giving your customer a crate of prunes."

I punched his shoulder. Hard.

Talking to Aunt Kania, I pointed at Oron. "I'm sorry I brought him. You were going to say something, Ekrem?"

Ekrem nodded, but kept glaring at Oron, a promise of death etched in his features. Oron really needed to learn to be quiet. "If your blood is purely Luk," Ekrem said, "you live much longer than most."

"Does that mean you and Serhat—"

"No." Serhat brushed the incense powder I'd spilled back into its dish. "We are of mixed blood. Desert race, northern blood, and Luk, of course. Almost all are mixed now."

Aunt Kania handed a bowl of chicken around the table. "Amir Mamluk once had a husband."

"He was taken to the quarries, wasn't he?" Oron licked his lips and tucked into the food.

"Yes." Aunt ran a thumb over the side of her mouth. She didn't seem to want to eat. Me either. "He gambled," she said, "and was sent to the quarries by his own wife."

Both fighting sailors shifted a little in their seats and frowned. They considered gambling a soul fault, same as families who'd never served as slaves, never ridden a horse, or sailed. It was akin to performing Salt Magic.

"You have no problem with my use of the salt," I said, wondering how they'd bypassed this soul fault of mine.

They looked at one another quickly, then Ekrem said, "You used it to save our lives. You have shown your loyalty to our crew mates. We…have decided we may be wrong about Salt Magic."

Oron snapped his now spice-stained fingers and talked around a mouthful. "Enough about customs. Let Auntie talk."

"Most believe the amir's young husband died at the quarries, but he did not. He escaped."

"Escaped from Quarry Isle on his own?" Oron snorted. "It's surrounded by chalk cliffs and seastingers and the worst waters of the Pass. Not to mention the bevy of guards with those terrifying spears."

"Not impossible," Aunt said. "He is the only person I know of who found his way out."

My heart soared out of my chest and thudded in my heads and hands. I slapped my palms on the table, shaking the dishes and bowls. "If he escaped, so can Avi."

Aunt tilted her head and clicked her tongue. "Slow, my child. Slow."

"But if you know the story, you know how, right?"

"I don't know how he did it."

I sat back, closing my eyes against the pounding in my head. "Then why tell us? What does this have to do with anything?"

"The amir took a new husband, and though he did not live long, the man at the quarry heard of it. He escaped, only to die in the waters of the Pass."

"He became a wraith."

"The great and terrible wraith called Tuz Golge."

"And you believe Tuz Golge Infused Calev and forced him to kill the amir?"

"There used to be tales of Tuz Golge on our shores. Tales of the sky-clouding wraith the size of a full ship's sail that would scour travelers' minds, looking for a link to the amir. But that was many years ago. Nothing has been heard of the wraith in a long time."

I dug at the wood grain of Aunt's table, eyeing the bowl of sea salt on the shelf beside the window. "He was waiting for an opportunity to kill the amir. It was revenge."

Ekrem stood, turned toward the back of the room, and ran his hands through his hair. "I trusted there was an explanation, but this…"

Serhat spoke softly. "You told us truth, Kinneret Raza. Your man was Infused. He is an innocent."

Her crewmate whirled. "And we have no one to punish for this outrage."

"I thought you hated the amir after what she did to Ifran," Oron said.

Ekrem put his hands on the table and faced Oron. "Disagreeing with her decisions is one thing. Murder is another."

Aunt pushed my bowl of chicken toward me like she wanted me to eat. "It is. There is nothing now you can do to punish Tuz Golge. He has what he wants. A dead lover. But you can gain information from him."

"He could tell us how he escaped from Quarry Isle." The idea chilled my bones.

"Whoa, now." Oron got up and began pacing. The hot breeze through the windows tossed his hair and tunic. "Good woman, you expect us to meet with a Salt Wraith *on purpose*? To question the thing?" His eyes couldn't grow any larger.

Aunt grabbed his sleeve as he walked past. "To save my sister's daughter, I do."

Oron closed his eyes. After a breath, he nodded. "For Avigail. Sweet, strong Avigail."

Pressing my fingers into my temples, I inhaled the food's scent of orange spice and the incense. I had to do this. I had to confront a wraith and speak with it. I looked to Calev, lying on the floor. I needed Calev to heal and be strong enough to help me.

"Tell me what to do, Aunt."

# CHAPTER TWENTY-NINE

W E DECIDED NOT TO MOVE Calev for the night. Aunt and I washed him and wrapped him in a clean pair of loose Kurakian pants, leaving his back and his wound bare. I tried to sleep beside him, but all I did was stare at his eyelids and pray they'd open soon.

The others slept on hammocks at the other side of the room near the ladder leading to the courtyard. Aunt curled up in her own sling of netted fabric above the shelves. The night was noisy with cattle lowing, people snoring, and roosters unwilling to wait until dawn to give a shout.

Aunt had told me when the moon reached its height, she'd wake and show me the Salt Magic needed to converse with a wraith.

I swallowed. Never thought I'd need to know a horrible thing like that.

The moon glowed through the window. It had to be near to time.

Aunt slipped from her hammock onto a low stool and to the floor. "Come."

Had she heard me? Or did she just wake herself up. I couldn't decide which was creepier. Aunt was a comfort half the time, and a full-on scary mystery the other.

I took a breath and ran a finger down Calev's proud nose. I touched his lips, his bare shoulder. He was just so beautiful. The wound didn't look any better though. If anything, the puffy red around the entry had grown more swollen.

"Refill your salt bag first." Aunt looked to her bowl on the shelf.

I shivered under her warm hand and did as instructed.

Prepared, we walked past the others in their hammocks. Oron grabbed my hand and I jumped.

"If you can, give that spirit a kick to the babymaker for me, kaptan," he said. Then he rolled over and resumed snoring.

A smile pushed at my mouth, but my lip trembled and I bit it, holding back emotions good and bad.

Aunt climbed down the ladder that passed through a hole in the floor, and I trailed behind, down one level, another, the last. I marveled that the structure was made of only the earth. Each floor was thicker than two Orons placed side by side. When my feet hit dirt, I spun to see which direction Aunt had gone.

My pulse tapped nervously against my wrists. Aunt walked into the night, a stately column of bright fabric and braids, surrounded by the still shadows of her cattle in the moonlight. The night smelled like a storm, metallic and heavy, though no clouds plumed overhead.

Beyond her gate, we found a spot to sit beside the twisting trunk of a Topa tree. The old leaves, crushed under my sandals, smelled like vegetables. Cool, rainy, tart. Aunt pulled a handful of salt from her pouch and jerked her chin at me, her big, black eyes shining.

"You too."

Reaching into my bag, I did as she instructed, then sat with salt cupped in my hands like a baby bird.

With her free hand, Aunt removed the whip from her leather belt. It was her status symbol in Kurakian society. Finer whips, those with more tassels, more gems, more decoration, spoke of more cattle—the only measure of who you were here on this dry land. The whip snapped as she lashed it over her head. I jumped. I didn't have a whip.

"You will use your own physical representation of pride." Her white teeth showed behind a chilling smile. "Show the spirit your confidence, your core."

Her eyes closed, she began speaking low, murmuring words into the night. The hairs on my arms lifted. She laid her whip in her lap and clapped her hands together. The salt she'd held ballooned around her and hovered before falling like waterflakes to her nightdress.

Her magic was already working. This wasn't any small lesson on using the salt. She was trying something. Now.

"But there aren't any wraiths here," I said. "On land. I thought you were only going to teach me."

Her gaze flicked to my face, faster than her whip's strings. "If I do this right, we will hear a wraith, even at this distance from the sea waters. If you follow what I do on the Pass, the wraith will fly to your boat and you will not only hear its true words, but see its face."

Ice jolted through me. "The spirit's human face?"

Wraiths' humanlike form showed only white, crystalized shadows where the face would be. My flesh shrunk against my bones. What would it be like to look at a dead man's face? A dead man who'd been tortured through a death at sea? Through drowning? The very worst way to die?

Aunt didn't answer me. She kept on hissing and mumbling in Kurakian over and over, the rhythm of her words matching that of the night insects around us. *Rumrumrum, ruuuummmmm. Rumrumrum, ruuuuuummmmm.*

With salt-dusted fingertips, she drew a circle, starting at the small, curling hairs escaping her braid and falling onto her forehead and going all the way down her cheek, across her chin, and back up again. She ran one finger along the inside of her lips.

When she said something that sounded like *Nat-kooroo-turumtah*, her voice was no longer hers. Or, it was, but it sounded as though it belonged to someone five times her size, with a much deeper tone.

The insects went silent.

The wind rushed through the Topa in a sudden gust.

The sky was clear though the air still smelled like a storm.

Invisible splinters pinched the skin around my spine and along my ribs. Aunt said another word. Another. Her voice rang in my ears. The prickling hit me again. The wind. Once. Twice.

Then I heard it, the wraith.

It started as a noise so far-off, so quiet, I wasn't sure it was even a noise. Maybe my own heart or lungs, but the noise grew legs and ran into my head, thrusting a spear into my thoughts.

There were no words, only intent, specific intent that my mind shaped into words.

*What do you want, Salt Witch?*

"To hear your voice," Aunt said in the Jakobden tongue.

*I have no need of you.*

"We want to speak with Tuz Golge."

Humor. Sickness.

*One chooses one's own death.*

"This one here witnessed the Tuz Golge's vengeance played out on earth."

*No business of mine. I leave you to it.*

"Wait!" Aunt held up her salty hands and nodded.

Sweat broke over my scalp. There wasn't time to think. I had to learn how to do this, for Avi, for me.

I raised my hands and threw my salt into the leaves of the Topa, into the night. Closing my eyes, I let the salt fall onto my face. Grains danced on my lips.

"I ask you to stay," I said, my voice strong and clear in spite of the fear of the invisible presence lurking around us. I opened my eyes.

The wraith wailed.

My aunt stared at me. Her eyes went up and down. "Release him, Kinneret. I know what I need to know."

A frown pulled at my lips. But she'd wanted me to try to keep him there, hadn't she?

"Now, Kinneret. Release him."

I blew the rest of the salt lining my palms into the air beside us. "Go and find rest," I said.

The wind gusted once more. The prickling sensation fled and my shoulders relaxed. The small part of the wraith that we'd managed to call over land was gone.

Aunt tucked her whip into her belt, stood, and offered her hand. One thousand questions in my head, I took it and started back toward the courtyard.

"Why did you let him go?" I said. "What did you find out?"

She made a noise like a hum. Mother had always made that noise and now Avi did. It was a noise like she was thinking.

"You are the strongest Salt Witch that breathes, Kinneret."

I stopped. "What?"

"You are. You held that wraith, made him cry out."

"I'm not a witch. I'm only using prayers. Using the salt the Fire gives us."

"Same. It is the same."

"Not to me."

Then she stopped too, her hand on the top of her stick gate. "Maybe that is what gives you such power."

"What?"

"Don't fret about it. You are who you are. I am who I am. It is what it is."

I rolled my eyes. Kurakian wisdom. More riddle than reason, Father always said.

# CHAPTER THIRTY

B ACK AT CALEV'S SIDE, I let the tears come.
Everyone else was sleeping, so they wouldn't see my
weakness. I simply lay there for what felt like days,
praying and wishing and longing for Avi's voice and Calev's grin
like a thirsty man on a salty sea. I didn't want to know what a
wraith's voice sounded like and I didn't want to think about
having strong magic right now. I wanted sunlight and freedom
and everyone safe and happy. Avi and Calev were my fresh water,
my life source. I had to have them back. Without them, I'd shrivel
and die like a fish out of water.

"Please wake up," I whispered to Calev, my throat aching.
"Aunt says we can control the wraith who Infused you. It knows
how to get Avi out of Quarry Isle. Wake up and we'll go. We'll go
get our girl."

A sob took my breath, and I sucked air through my nose,
trying to keep quiet. I put a hand on Calev's forehead. The bare
skin felt odd bare of its normal headtie.

It was more odd the way heat rolled off his skin and into
mine.

I jerked away. *No.*

His cheeks looked like they'd been slathered with fat, waxen and swollen.

"Calev? Can you hear me?" He was so hot. I lifted his arm to see where the arrow had punctured his body. A firey red glared back at me and yellow pus leaked from the center.

The wound was going bad.

I ran to Aunt and shook her shoulder hard. "Calev's getting worse."

She licked her dry lips and blinked. "I told you he might die."

A spear went through me at her bluntness, but she smoothed my cheek with her rough fingers and I knew she was just worried too. I grabbed my shirt and squeezed the fabric between my burning fingers.

"You have to save him."

Swinging out of her hammock, she sighed. "He has to save himself."

With a stone mortar and pestle, Aunt ground bitter smelling herbs and animal fat into a poultice for Calev's souring wound.

For hours, we nursed him.

Poured fresh water over his lips, only to watch it dribble to the floor. Wiped his flaming face with cloths.

His eyes never opened.

I ran a fingertip over the slight bump in his nose, as familiar to me as my own features. He inhaled slightly, a ragged, weak breath and my own chest clenched, wanting to breathe for him, to be strong for him. I hovered a hand over his wound and heat blared through Aunt's wrappings. The skin around the strips of linen had reddened even more over the last hours.

Her herbs and our prayers weren't making him better, but that didn't mean I was giving up.

*Please, Fire. Let me keep him a while longer. We still have so much to do. Let him see Avi safe. I need him to help me save Avi. Please. Please. Please.*

My hands shook as I stared at him. His face became Father's, then Mother's, and I was a child again, losing my parents.

I ran to the window and threw up everything in my stomach.

It was all going wrong, so, so, so wrong. If I failed now, Oron would never stay here with me and my aunt. He loved the sea like me. Zayn would die alone, blaming himself for our end. My sweet, little sister was lost to a horrible, disgusting life at the quarries. I clutched at my hair, squeezing it to the roots and welcoming the pain. And now, I was losing my love, my Calev, my smile and my luck. My lungs fought a breath and I fell to my knees, Aunt's hands on my back and her whispers in my ear.

As dawn cut the room with light and Aunt took to her hammock, I curled up next to Calev, resting on his outstretched arm. His dry palm lay against my mine own and I cried until I was an empty husk.

This entire trip had been for nothing.

I'd found silver I couldn't use. I'd thrown Avi from one hell into another.

I could never glean information from Tuz Golge. I hadn't even known Calev was Infused. I was clueless, a fool, a stupid, stupid low-caste with no chance of the life I'd dreamt of. The sleeve of Calev's loose tunic pressed wrinkles into my forehead.

I was an idiot and all of this was my fault.

# CHAPTER THIRTY-ONE

HEN ONE OF CALEV'S EYELIDS lifted. Gasping, I put a hand on his cheek.

"Calev?" I whispered.

His eye closed and I sagged, lying next to him.

Seas, what could I do?

If it weren't for Avi, I'd wait here with him forever. Avi needed me to at least try to rescue her. I could never live with myself if I didn't fight for her. But if I left, would Calev wake up and not find me? What if…my eyes blurred…if he died while I was gone and only had Aunt, a stranger to him…

My chest wanted to split open. This was a pain worse than anything that an arrow or a yatagan could cause. It seared and gnawed and swallowed me whole.

Calev made a small noise.

I sat up.

He opened his eyes, blinked, then closed them.

I touched his shoulder. Was Aunt's magic finally working? "Can you hear me?"

It was little more than a hiss, but I heard the word.

"Yes," he said.

The room spun for a breath and I took a gulp of air. "You're going to be fine. You're strong."

"Fine?" he croaked, barely loud enough to for me to hear. "Not sure about that."

I laughed through tears. "Stay quiet. Rest. Next time you wake up, you can talk more. All right?"

He must've agreed because his eyes flickered once, and not long after, his breathing evened out in sleep.

Aunt's magic was healing him.

I don't know how much of the night passed as we slept there, but when I opened my eyes, I saw Calev's smile. Pale, weak, but real.

The wildfire in me rose and dried my tears. "How do you feel? Any better? Can you breathe well?" I touched his shoulder, then pulled away. She'd healed him. The magic had actually worked. I could hardly wrap my mind around it. I was scared to say it aloud and risk it not being true.

Calev laughed quietly and winced. Moving so that his forehead braced against the stripes of the mat, he said, "I am better. Much, much better." He put his palms against the mat and began to push himself up.

Scrambling to my knees, I supported him. "You can't get up yet. Rest. Later you can get up."

With a nod, he let me lower him back down. The effort must've sucked him dry because he slept again almost immediately.

The gray light of near dawn and Calev's rustling woke me. He was trying to sit up.

I lodged a hand under his arm, too afraid to say much and realize this was a dream. "Don't rush it. I don't want you dying on me again." Fear sharpened my words.

Shaking his head, he braced a hand on his knee, and I helped him sit.

His wound was clean and smooth. Still red and a bit swollen, but healed. Aunt's magic was strong. I squeezed Calev's hand, then let go, knowing if I kept touching him, I'd throw myself at him like an idiot.

His ebony hair fell over one side of his face as he swallowed. "I need a drink."

I had to grin as I scooped water from the bucket near Aunt's hammock into a wooden cup and handed it to him. A part of my own thirst was quenched.

Now to find Avi and complete the answer to my prayers.

The bones above Calev's chest were sharper than they had been before his injury. His stomach, though still muscled, sunk in like a depression between two waves. He sipped the water I gave him, his throat moving as he threw his head back. I hugged myself to keep my arms busy.

He set the cup down. "Now tell me about this wraith."

I did.

And to refrain from staring at Calev's bare chest, to keep from crying with relief at his healing, I allowed my eyes to stray to the window's view. Behind Calev, night lightened into day. A purple-white glow laced the edges of the Topa tree where Aunt and I had spoken to that wraith, where I'd learned…what? That I could control a spirit? That I had enough Salt Magic to glean information from the legendary Tuz Golge?

I shared all this and more—everything—in hushed whispers with Calev. Before he could say anything back, Oron flipped out of his hammock and landed flat on his back.

"Creations of the Devil," he spat, rising and dusting his hands.

Then everyone was awake.

"You should not be up yet." Aunt scowled at Calev and patted at her braids, which had grown fuzzy during the night.

The two fighting sailors eased out of their hammocks, the bells on their shoulders jingling, and looked Calev up and down. My insides going cold, I put a hand on my dagger. In a second, they could be on him and he could be dead.

"Ah," he said. "They know what I did."

I nodded. My finger circled my dagger's cool hilt, and the wind from the window tugged at my curls.

Oron smirked. "That they do. I strongly suggest you explain your side of the story before they decide your handsome head would be a fine decoration for their sashes."

The sailors advanced on him, step by step. Aunt's room went from cozy to cramped.

Unhitching himself from the wall, Calev held out his hands and lowered his chin a little.

"I had no fight with your amir. I hated what she did to Ifran, but aside from that, she was Old Farm's friend."

The three stopped, within striking range from one another.

Ekrem's eyes were calm, but Serhat stared at Calev with death in her face. They traded a look, then Ekrem said, "Because Kinneret believes you, we do also."

Serhat's jaw tightened and she turned her head away.

Ekrem's words made me stand taller. I took my place at Calev's side, Aunt and Oron muttering at both ends of the room about how the sun wasn't even up yet.

"So you'll go with us?" The question was one I'd asked Calev so many times, the words so familiar to my lips. But I was far from anything truly familiar now. In Kurakia. Making plans to deal with a wraith. Asking loyalty from high-caste fighters. "To meet with Tuz Golge and break my sister out of Oramiral Urmirian's quarry?"

"We are your fighters now, kaptan. Command us at will."

Aunt made a shushing noise. "Never thought I'd see a girl with no cattle to her name command two of the amir's. If you've never ordered beasts, how are you to order men? Now, go down to the courtyard, let my animals out of the gate and wash yourselves to eat. Gather some eggs while you're there and gain some advice from those hens as you do."

Advice? From hens?

"I'll ready some oatcakes and dried beef," she said. "We'll treat the farmer's wound once more, then you can be on your way."

The fighters climbed down the ladder, Serhat's head disappearing from view as Oron walked over and grabbed my arm and Calev's.

"You're certain about meeting with the Salt Wraith? Calev, talk sense into her."

"I trust her," Calev said quietly. "And I'm not a sense-first man. I'm more of an adventure-first, challenge-obsessed land lover." He grinned.

I elbowed him gently, my cheeks warm, then patted Oron's hand. "There is no sensible way to do this. We have to grab this opportunity, this one small, dangerous edge on the situation, and go."

"Go?" Oron held both hands up. "Just like that?"

Calev and I nodded in unison.

Oron gusted out a breath and folded his hands behind his head. He turned away. "Foolish youth."

Aunt's steady hands urged us toward the ladder to do as she'd instructed. "Yes, small man. They're so ready to give up the short life they've had."

Calev went down the ladder and Oron stepped down behind him, looking up at me. His wine-dark eyes were bright in the strengthening dawn.

"I'm not so sure about your aunt's sanity, but in this instance, the woman is right."

"This is our life to live, Oron. And I won't do it without my sister by my side."

He swallowed loudly and continued down the rungs. "It's not as if I meant…all right then. But Fire help me, I do not wish to die on the sea or at the oramiral's hands."

"I know, I know," I said, passing through the last floor before the courtyard. Dust from Calev's sandals rained on my head as he came down after me and I didn't dislike it at all. I was just so glad he was alive.

"I'm guessing that you, Oron, prefer to die in a feather bed with a woman's arms wrapped firmly around you," Calev said.

I leaped from the ladder to land in the courtyard, narrowly missing a hen who squawked her annoyance.

Oron grinned. "How well you know me."

Calev laughed and tucked his hair behind his ears. It was strange to see someone in an Old Farm headstrap without a fine, embroidered tunic. The blue Kurakian pantaloons made him look taller.

Oron's mouth tucked up at one side. "I think I'll grab some eggs while you two…wash." He jerked his head toward the pump well that the fighters had left to open the gate.

Laughing, Calev and I zigzagged, laughing, through chickens that brushed along our legs and beat wings at our feet. At the well, he insisted on pumping the water and allowing me to cup handfuls of lukewarm water to throw over my face and hands. I went ahead and doused my head too. The day wasn't going to grow any cooler and I was already sweating. Calev winced a little but managed to toss a handful at me. I got him back right in the eye.

Calev went quiet and still.

"What's wrong? Are you feeling your wound? Should I get Aunt?"

"It does hurt. But that's not… We shouldn't be laughing and enjoying ourselves while Avi is…" His throat worked and tears burned at the corners of my eyes.

My chest caved in as I tried to keep breathing. "We *should* laugh. It's hard, but we should. She would want us too." I squeezed out the ends of my hair and kept my face turned toward the ground. The sadness in his eyes would make me cry like last night and we didn't have sun for tears. "We need some smiles and laughter to give us strength for what we're about to do."

"I don't know why it always surprises me when you say wise things. After all our lives, it shouldn't. You're right. If we're going to deal with the darkness of a wraith, we need all the light we can rouse."

I looked at him then. His black hair shuffling over his bare shoulders. His honest, red-brown eyes, the eyes that always held a spark of mischief. His hands on the pump, ready to help me with more water if that's what I needed. I pressed my eyelids shut and tried to sear the image of him on my mind. I never wanted to forget this moment. It was the light I would need to face the creature that twisted my good Calev into a killer.

# CHAPTER THIRTY-TWO

THAT NIGHT, THE MOON OPENED its eye over the horizon and stared at us as we gathered on the Kurakian beach. The sea was the pale blue of ice, stretching out from the shore in one solid, clean mass under a steady wind. My heart ached to sail on it. I couldn't see our boat yet, but it was there somewhere. Tiny, and a sad, little thing to ride on into the night, but it would have to do. My hands clenched with the need to feel a tiller's worn, wooden grain and tug a coconut fiber rope. Beside me, white light cloaked the fighters' emotionless faces, Aunt's braids, Calev's wavy hair and strong nose, and Oron's smirk.

"I don't know if you've noticed," Oron said, putting a fist under his chin, "but that's not the boat in which we arrived, dear kaptan."

Aunt was smiling. The sailors made appreciative grunts and nodded, pointing to a wooden craft with two masts bobbing in the shallow water off the shore.

My heart jumped. "Did you do this?"

I squinted and the two lateen sails wrapped against the masts reflected a flash of pale moonlight. Long ties at the boom fluttered in the breeze.

"I have much," Aunt said, still smiling. "Cattle. A home. Chickens. And no children. No man. No woman. I'm glad to have the chance to help my sister's children."

Her lips tilted down at one side and she took my fingers in hers gently. She stroked the back of my hand with her callused fingertips and the child inside me wanted more than anything to run back to her tower house and curl into a hammock.

"Get our Avigail safe," she said. "You can do it. I know you can."

My throat was hot and dry. "If I fail..."

Aunt *tsked* with her full lips. "It is not good luck to talk of that."

"We should have a shamar yam." Calev picked up two shells from the sand and studied them with a look of concentration. He tossed one down and cupped the other, his serious eyes meeting mine. "I don't have paper for the prayer, but I can speak one into its hollow and secure it to the mainsail with my headtie."

Aunt elbowed me. "You are right. He is lucky. He knows how the world works."

"Thank you. For everything." I hugged her, my arms and hers tight and strong. She smelled so much like Mother, like dust and green things and spices from the land that was foreign, but somehow familiar to me.

I didn't want to let go. I was dying to let go. Because every minute we waited, Avi spent another in the quarries.

Aunt thumped her hand on my back. "Go. Go on now."

When I pulled away, tears wiggled down her beautiful, sloping cheeks. She wiped the moisture away impatiently, frowning.

"And the Wraith Lantern?" I asked.

Surely she'd thought of that. But if she hadn't, maybe we could get one at the market. Aunt had never been to sea. Kurakians hated the water. She might not realize how many wraiths roamed the skies. Though we meant to meet with one, more than that would be suicide.

"It hangs from the center mast." She gave a nod.

Oron looked impressed as we neared the craft, our feet splashing into the cool, rolling water. One sail ruffled loose like a woman's skirts. "Kurakian-style sailcloth," he said. "I haven't seen such handiwork since I worked on that northern ice wine ship."

"Kurakian craftsmanship on an ice wine route?" I lifted my newly filled bag of salt from my sash to keep it from being doused.

Chest-deep in water, we made it to the boat. Aunt took hold of the fore and Calev went toward the back. Aunt had sewn a tunic for him out of one of her plain, dusky blue work dresses.

"The kaptan had a fondness for the women of this land." Oron hefted himself into the craft as we steadied it. "He appreciated their many…skills."

Calev snickered along with Oron and I threw a look at them. Oron wasn't talking only about sailcloth.

Aunt shook her head and smiled, helping me up. Though I didn't need the assistance, it warmed me to have her hand at my back, ready to be there if I slipped. I hadn't had an older person take care of me since Mother and Father died. Unless you counted Oron. But he was as much trouble as he was help.

The fighters crawled aboard and gave Calev a hand up without exchanging a single word. How deep did their loyalty to me go? Was it really enough to forgive Calev for killing their leader? There wasn't much I could do about it, so I pressed the worry into the corner of my mind.

With one last wave to Aunt, we rigged the sails and tracked a line away from her tiny shape in the shallow waters. I'd never be able to thank her enough for saving Calev. If her idea to meet with Tuz Golge worked and we discovered a way to get Avi out, I'd be further in her debt and happy to be there.

Oron lit the Wraith Lantern while Calev whispered a prayer into the shamar yam and tied it to the mainmast. The orange, silver, and black flickers from the lantern's wick passed over their faces, illuminating cheek hollows, accentuating noses and whites of eyes.

The Pass was a wide road of white and black beyond our boat. I'd need to see clearly if we were to get to the place we'd first met Tuz Golge. We had to keep the lantern lit in case we had to deal with another wraith.

The moment I thought the word, one swept away from the moon toward us.

Ekrem took the lantern from Oron and held it high over our heads. The crystalized spirit drifted over our sails, its evil intent lashing against my thoughts like a desert lion's claws. Sweat dripped down my nose as I plugged my ears with my fingers.

Oron sat next to me, Calev on my other side. "Can't you control this one too?" Oron shouted above the wraith's sweeping noise and its accompanying hissing whispers of murder and rage. The whites of Oron's eyes and teeth were bright in the near dark.

"It will leave," I yelled back. "I'm not wasting any salt."

The wraith pressed on my mind.

Fury.

Blood.

The taste of blood.

Salt in my mouth.

Flesh in my teeth.

I opened my eyes when something warm brushed against me. It was Calev. Fingers in his own ears, he'd scooted closer to me and his elbow touched my back. He lay his forehead against mine and I inhaled deeply, breathing in the scent of him—sun-warmed earth and lemons—to wash away the wraith's sour wrath.

The shadow dusted over us once more, then seemed to leave. The blood-lust was gone. I took my fingers out of my ears and looked at each of my crew in turn.

The fighters were hunched over, their heads brushing their knees. Making the Fire's sign on his forehead, Oron crossed his thick legs.

Calev gave me one of those smiles. "We made it through."

Warmth flooded my stomach and I turned away to focus on my words.

"The Tuz Golge's attack will be different from that," I said as we found spots to sit around the decking. "Some of us know how he feels inside the head. It's a sharp thing. Intelligent. Difficult to block out."

The headsail, the smaller of the two triangular sails, lagged a little. We needed to jib and track toward Jakobden's angry coast, and the wind was cooperating.

"Hopefully my Salt Magic will control it, but keep your ears plugged and your mind alert in the case that I fail."

At my command, Oron lowered the headsail and Calev and the fighters tucked it away. "Take a line, everyone," I said from aft. "We need to jib. When I shout, let them run through your fingers." Everyone but Calev knew exactly what to do, but I didn't want to single him out, so I called out directions for all.

When I shouted, they did as asked, and the ivory sail flipped high over the mast. We took control again and brought the bottom of the sail back to the boat's side. We tied, Calev tying right alongside us like a real sailor. I smiled.

The only thing loud now was my heart. It shivered like a scared dog at the thought of how exposed we were and how reliant on the small lesson I'd had with Aunt. We were almost to the place where we'd seen Tuz Golge.

Black water lapped on all sides and the wind stayed steady. With Oron's clever help, Calev's good eyes, and the fighting sailors' strength, we easily wove around a high ridge of shining rock.

And at a calm stretch— —as calm and open as the Pass can be— I started calling for the wraith.

Sitting cross-legged, across from Calev's encouraging face, I raised my dagger and carved a circle in the air about my head. I whispered the words Aunt had given me, "*Raturookumruntarah. Rumininah. Rumininah. Buruqnahrumtilrirah.* I listen. I understand your cause. I understand your cause. Speak to me, and I will hear you in your empty place."

The Kurakian words tripped out of my mouth and caught on my lips with quick turns in emphasis and hard sounds. It was not a beautiful language. It had only been my aunt's lovely voice matching the calming din of night insects. My own pronunciation lacked skill.

Would it work?

As Aunt had instructed, I began chanting the amir's name. "Mamluk, Mamluk, Mamluk."

Her former sailors' heads snapped up and they glared before blinking and seeming to resign themselves to the situation. They knew as well as I this was no time for anything except completing this horrible chore and living through it.

Then my head seemed to crack open.

Tuz Golge slipped into the mercury light over our heads. Roughly the shape of a man in a flowing tunic, the edges of his spirit-self leaked into the sky like spilled poison. The lightest part of him fogged the place his face should have been. His shadow, impossibly large, blotted out the moon and a sick light rained down, a fitting match to the twisting evil in our thoughts.

I went from enjoying the smooth beauty of Calev's skin to imagining the press of a knife separating flesh from bone. Blood in patterned lines down his cheeks and chin and throat.

His eyes closed and he lifted his face, swallowing hard. Oron's voice called across the abyss of bloodlust, toward the man I loved more than any other.

"Kinneret." Oron's voice scratched against the wraith's planted thoughts. His fingers were in his ears, the sailors beside him, shaking and eyes wide open.

Sucking a salty breath, I stood. I tore my dagger across the wind that blew my skirts around my legs.

I would not let Tuz Golge take us here.

I could do this.

I sheathed my dagger and took salt from my pouch. I spread the grit from the insides of my wrists, over my sleeves, and onto my collarbone, to my pulse points. The wind rose and tossed my hair wildly. The sea rolled as I knelt.

I slapped my hands together and shouted to the wraith.

"I ask how you escaped the quarry!"

Hissing. Nonsense. Garbled words, a mix of Kurakian and the Jakobden tongue.

But behind the power and the hate and sharp mind, panic danced through the sounds. Uneven. Low, then loud.

Realization flooded through me as the wind sheared against us and rocked us hard in the water. Calev killed the amir. Tuz Golge owed us. The boat righted, and I knew exactly what to say.

"Speak in this tongue," I said. The salt thrummed against my flesh like a thousand tiny hearts beating in the same rhythm as my own. "We have done your work. We have slayed your wife. You owe us obedience."

The hissing grew into snarls that matched the rising wind. Calev and I slammed into one another, both grabbing for the mainsail mast as the sea grew angry. Oron and the fighters latched onto the sides of the boat, their faces like yesterday's ash. My salty fingers grated against the mast and one of Calev's hands. I pressed my forehead against his. He was whispering. Eyes closed and one hand on the shamar yam. He was praying.

*Nothing!* Tuz Golge shouted into my thoughts. *I owe nothing!*

My words hadn't moved him like they should've. What was I forgetting?

The wraith's sharp intent pushed against my will, drowning it in darkness and pain and the desire to unsheathe my dagger and slide it along Calev's face to destroy the beauty Tuz Golge would never again possess.

I fisted my hands and pulled myself against the mast, squeezing it with my arms, trying to feel the boat under my sandals and the wood against my skin instead of the hate, the hate, the hate.

Calev's lips moved fast as nightwingers. Sweat became diamonds on his chin, tangled in the beard he'd grown over the last few days. He brought his hand from the prayer shell to his mouth, touched his lips once and began praying again.

*The salt! Aunt lined her mouth in sea salt!*

I ran my first two fingers along the insides of my lips.

My skin puckered as I shouted, "Yes, you do owe us, Tuz Golge. You will listen. I am Kinneret Raza, born on these waters, slayer of the demon Asag, conqueror of the lost silver island, and you will speak with me!"

The intensity of rage and inky fingers of mind control flattened and cracked. My will, like a small orange sun, squeezed into the small, broken places, shining through the cracks in my thoughts. They brought memories with them.

Calev. Chin held high. Teeth gritted together. Determined face. His laugh at the well. The velvet of his hands on my waist at the waterfall. The feel of his lips, his mouth smiling against my neck.

And Avi. Strong, long fingers on the sail's ties. Stubby nails. The dimple in her otherwise fierce face.

I would be fierce for her.

For Calev. And Oron. And these two warriors who'd risked all to help us.

The orange sun of my will blasted through the broken lines of the wraith's twisting hate.

The wind settled.

*Speak, Kinneret Raza.* The wraith hung still as death over our heads. *What would you ask of me?*

Everyone stared.

"Is it talking to you?" Oron asked, taking a step.

The fighters relaxed their hold on the boat and put hands to the battle axe and yatagan at their sashes, as if weapons were any use against this threat.

I gave Oron a nod and he stepped back again, crossing his arms. His mouth pinched up and Calev stared.

He reached a hand out and I took it gladly.

I closed my eyes and let the salt thrum against my skin and spoke silently to the wraith.

*How did you escape the oramiral's island?*

*Why do you desire this information, sailor?*

*Tell me.*

A laugh, dark and bitter like soured coffee. *I didn't. I died. In the waters. You know that.*

*Tell me.*

*I gathered fallen bamboo on my treks up the stairs to the slave quarters. It is open air. But you know that. Your sister, yes? She hides in the shadows there? She slaves for the oramiral?*

I wasn't about to bend and give him knowledge he had no right to. *How did you escape?*

*I removed my tunic, ripped it down the middle, tied it to the bamboo I'd lashed together with rope I'd stolen from the guards' storage bins, and I created a glider.*

*Details.*

*I made a sturdy length of framed fabric and sailed off the slaves' castle walls into the air and down over the Pass.*

My concentration faltered. A sail? For the air? But how would that work? How would you catch the wind and then direct yourself with only a long strip of framed fabric?

Like someone had drawn a blade across the tie between my Salt Magic and Tuz Golge, the sense of the wraith left my mind and floated away.

The sky was clear of spirits and a bank of blue-black clouds gathered.

He was gone. I collapsed onto the deck. Bamboo and a tunic? That was the great information I'd risked everyone here to get?

I couldn't breathe. It would never work. My Avi was lost.

# CHAPTER THIRTY-THREE

ALEV OPENED HIS EYES. "WHAT did he tell you?"

It was then I noticed my hands were shaking. I hid them behind my back, but Calev grabbed them gently and rubbed the backs with his thumbs. "You should be scared. There are times when I've wondered whether you're human like the rest of us." He smiled grimly as he kept on stroking my hands, flipping them over and starting on the palms, massaging them now and pulling me closer.

It was a trick and I knew it, but I let him tug me into the circle of his arms. My shaking grew into a full-body tremor.

My mouth pressed into the soft blue fabric of the tunic Aunt had made him. His chest tensed under my lips and the strength there, both in muscle, and beneath that, in heart, gave me hope.

"I was afraid I wouldn't be able to handle the wraith. It was all on me. And—"

"And it wasn't sailing. Or anything else you've done before this sun."

He held me tighter as I felt a hand on my back. Oron.

"You did well, my kaptan," Oron said, peeking at me and smiling with tears in his eyes. "You used what your aunt taught you, claimed your status with the spirit, and gleaned information

257

from the other side. Very well done. I would've messed my tunic and leaped overboard, so all in all I'd say the evening has been a resounding success."

Ekrem pressed fingers into his temples, shaking his head. Serhat glared like she was upset she hadn't attacked the wraith and Oron might serve as a good second choice of target.

I looked down at the X stitching along Calev's short sleeve. "But…the wraith talked about things I didn't understand. I don't think it's going to help Avi."

"Maybe we can make sense of it." Calev stepped back, and I turned away to look out over the waters.

"He said he made a sort of sail out of bamboo and his tunic. He jumped from the top of the slaves' castle quarters and the sail helped him soar through the air, to the Pass."

"How would sticks and fabric hold a man?" Oron rubbed his chin. "And I think we should decide on where to make landfall. That brewing storm looks almost as threatening as Tuz Golge."

He was right. Those clouds, snipped and billowing, meant lightning and high wind and slashing rain.

But where could we go?

Not home. We would be questioned by the amir's men and women who hadn't left on the journey. They may have even received a rock dove, telling all, from Berker by now. If they didn't yet know, Calev's father and kin would question him on his lengthly disappearance, his clothing, his scar. The story would come out, then what was left of the amir's retainer would strap us to horses and rip us to pieces.

We couldn't go straight to Quarry Isle. As much as I wanted to get to Avi, we had to plan if we were to emerge with her alive, instead of full of the oramiral's canon shot and spears.

Ayarazi? Definitely not. Kurakia again?

"Kurakia is our only choice." I untied the rope that had helped flip the sail. "We'll use this storm-blowing wind to take us east."

But when we landed, what then? Tuz Golge's idea made no sense.

The wind gusting brightly, the storm chased our boat neatly back toward Kurakia. The speed made my blood sing through my veins. Normally, I would've been light and happy during such a successful sail, but now, no. We were racing to nowhere. I had no answers and was no closer to rescuing Avi. Plus, soon the amir's absence would be taken as something out of the ordinary. We'd planned on three days away. It had been seven. Maybe eight.

I rubbed at my eyes, my knees dipping when the hull slapped the water. The kyros and Old Farm would send men and women looking for the ship. Kurakia was the closest known landing spot. Aside from Quarry Isle. And Aunt couldn't protect us. Her city-state of Lutambiarum would give us up without a thought. Calev's father might try to protect him. But maybe not. Calev had committed the crime. He was guilty. If they didn't believe us, he would be condemned to die. If they caught us here, no one would speak up for the fighters, Oron, or I. We were good as dead.

I finished my bowl of Kurakian chicken and licked the orange spice off my fingers. Though my soul hung somewhere low as my feet, my stomach couldn't be ignored. Besides, I needed food to get my mind working.

Calev pushed his now empty bowl to the center of Aunt's table and leaned back in his chair. "A sail. For the air." He put his hands on his elbows and sighed.

Oron finished Aunt's remaining store of tatlilav and belched loudly. "Let's try it." He hopped up and slapped his thighs. "I've lived a good life. Strap the bed linens to me and toss me off the roof."

He started toward the hammock he'd been using, assumably to grab the linen sheet tangled in the woven coconut ropes. I stood and snared his arm.

"Though I'm impressed you've matured enough to offer yourself, we're not throwing you off things," I said, looking to Aunt and Calev for help.

The fighters were down in Aunt's courtyard, training with their beautiful, flashing weapons. No matter. They wouldn't care about Oron's impending doom.

Aunt cleared the wooden bowls from the table and wiped her mouth with the back of her hand. "You will find the answer, Kinneret."

Oron tugged his sleeve free from me. "We already have. Me. The roof. Fabric." He began flapping his arms like wings.

Calev laughed, though his eyes were sad. None of us could stop thinking of how long Avi had been gone now.

"Oron, exactly how much did you have during the meal?"

Oron eyed him. "Are you asking about alcohol intake or would you also like to know food consumption for weight considerations?"

"I think he's talking about the tatlilav." I asked.

He held his hands up. "Well, I want to be sure to provide such information as our Old Farm friend sees as necessary for tossing men from roofs."

Calev grinned.

Oron rubbed his chin. "I believe I imbibed around three bowls each of tatlilav and chicken." Patting his slightly round stomach, he added, "Just about perfect for a would-be eagle, I think."

"Eagle?" Calev said. "I'm thinking more of an overgrown, extremely ambitious chicken."

Aunt rubbed the clean bowls dry over her water bucket, laughing quietly.

I gave Aunt a quick hug, passed Oron and Calev, and started down the ladder.

"Come on then, bird of questionable descent. We must check your wings," I said, the rungs smooth under my tired hands.

Oron, Calev, and I dodged chickens and pecking roosters and walked out of Aunt's courtyard and into the patchy grass of her fields.

"We will sneak into the slaves' quarters. Then, because we'll no longer have surprise as our ally, we'll glide off Quarry Isle." I nodded, more to myself than anyone else. It was a ridiculous plan, but the only one I had.

"You're the kaptan," Oron said.

We were fools. "We need bamboo," I said, heading toward the creek. A clutch of green shaded a cow and her calf. The mother turned her head to look at us with big eyes. One of her arm-length horns brushed benignly over her young's bony spine.

"Better not anger her. She could skewer and kabob us without moving a hoof." Oron stepped behind Calev and eyed the cow.

I looked to the sky and shook my head.

Calev put a hand on the first group of stalks we came to. Their light brown lengths reached higher than the roof of Aunt's tower house. Lime-green leaves fluttered in the dry breeze.

"Has your Aunt cut any?" Calev asked as we snaked through the small forest. "Saplings grow right out of their harvested elders."

Oron chuckled. "Spoken like a true Old Farm."

"It's true." I pushed some fallen branches back to look for stalks at the base of a broken trunk.

"What?" Calev cocked his head and crossed his arms.

I laughed. "Don't get defensive. It's just how you all are. You call mature trees and plants *elders*." A smile pulled at my lips as he raised his chin. "Old Farms see growing things as they see people."

Eyebrow lifted, Calev took a step toward another bunch of smaller trees and shrugged. "Our mindset has worked so far, wouldn't you agree?"

"Yes, yes, Lemon Prince," Oron said, taking a small, green-handled saw from his sash. We'd borrowed it from Aunt's tool rack outside the henhouse.

"I don't enjoy that title, Oron, and you know it." Calev frowned as he cleared thorny brush away from the base of the head-high stalk Oron had found.

"That's exactly why I used it." Oron grinned in Calev's face.

Calev glared at him.

"Be careful, chicken-eagle, this one will be manning our escape boat after we fly from the quarry slaves' quarters roof." I held the stalk steady as Oron ran the steel teeth back and forth.

Calev's gaze snapped to me. "What?"

"I can't risk the oramiral getting his hands on you."

"First, he won't take me. I'm Old Farm. Second, what makes you think I'm going to stay in the boat while you blast into the quarry to battle trained fighters?"

I stood and put hands on my hips. "First." I couldn't keep the bite out of my voice. "You are an Old Farm who murdered the amir. You don't need to borrow anymore trouble. Second, you just try to keep me from going in there after Avi." My blood burned under my skin. "Just. Try."

Oron stopped sawing. "Whoa, there, kaptan. Remember who the enemy is here."

"It's the oramiral," Calev said slowly. "And I will not watch as you, Kinneret, pointlessly subject yourself to possible capture."

"Pointlessly?"

I gritted my teeth and stared at Calev, who'd raised up and matched my glare. His red-brown eyes were on fire and it made my blood even hotter.

This was my rescue mission and my sister and my magic that had gotten us this far. He was not going to lash me to the mainsail to keep me safe like I was a child. I didn't care who his father was or how old his blood or how smart he thought he was.

"You think I'm pointless?" My voice coiled and raised its head like a cobra.

"Acting like you are a fighter is pointless when we have two actual fighters in our party. You are the sailor. You should stay in the boat. That's the safe choice. The smart choice. And you well know it, Kinneret. You're being obstinate."

My head was about to come off. My fingers itched and trembled. I wanted to lunge at Calev and shake him until he felt how impossible it would be for me to perch in safety a stone's throw from where my own sister was being held by the worst man in the world.

"Kinneret." Calev put hands on my shoulders and I couldn't breathe I was so frustrated. "Kinneret. Just admit I am right. Oron can stay with you. The fighters and I will rescue Avi if it's possible. If it's not, you being there will make no difference and only risk your life too."

Then we both went silent. Like the eerie quiet before a storm. Anger and love and frustration and everything we'd been through rushed through me, burning me, jerking me, setting me on fire. Calev's mouth didn't move. His eyes were black stones and his chest rose and fell like he was about to—

Oron put his hands between us and tried to push us away from one another. "All right now. You two are either going to fight or…well…we don't have the sun for any pleasant diversions, if you'll recall. No matter how long it's been coming," he muttered, finally succeeding in shoving us each back a step. "Now help me cut this ridiculous tree so we can make the ridiculous wings."

I swallowed, my throat dry and scratching. "Fine."

Calev's jaw tensed and he turned back toward Aunt's house. "Fine."

WE ENDED UP CUTTING FIVE stalks taller than Calev and headed back to the courtyard to meet Aunt. Calev kept stretching like his healed wound was bothering him a bit. It was amazing the wound didn't still have him half dead and on the floor of Aunt's house. I wished I could heal like Aunt Kania.

She greeted us with a white-toothed smile. "I'm very interested in this. I have meditated and think this may actually work."

Oron tossed a hand up. "Oh. Well. She meditated. We must be on the right path then."

I elbowed him sharply.

"Ow!" He rubbed his arm.

With sweating brows and heaving chests, the fighting sailors gathered around our bamboo and a stack of fine, silk robes on a straw mat at Aunt's feet.

Calev knelt by the stalks and grabbed two, bent them. "They'll give and hold like the gaff that holds the sail on a boat, right?"

I nodded. "That's what I was thinking. If we lash those two together, they'll be the size of the gaff on the boat you gave us, Aunt."

She held up a length of draping red silk. Sun glinted off its smooth surface and the wind lifted it briefly as the fighters each took a handful to spread it out.

"I can cut this to fit the framing." Aunt turned her head a little like she was considering where and how to make the cut.

"Will silk be strong enough?" Oron asked. Standing beside the fair-haired fighter, he fingered an edge of the rosy fabric and scratched his hair.

"Oh yes," Calev said as he tied two of the stalks together. The muscles and tendons in his forearms worked smoothly, beautifully, like sailing ropes under his browned skin. "Silk is very strong. And light."

"Light being fairly important if this rig is meant to keep two people in the air for over four hundreds yards or so," Oron said. He looked at Calev, then me, like we might start in on one another again.

"Why two people?" I asked.

"We have only so much of this expensive silk. And just four good stalks." Oron kicked the fifth, exposing a splintered edge on the underside. "Two for each…glider. A fighter can stay with me in the boat, in case we're boarded."

"Stay in the boat?" Ekrem frowned. "We will infiltrate the fortress. We are masters of such maneuvers and should be involved in the recovery. I see that we will need to glide out. They'll surely know of our presence with the slaves once we're there. But Serhat and I should execute the plan."

Oron held up a hand. "If the oramiral's men see the boat and take it, then where will the rest glide into? A friendly seastinger's jaws? A relaxing Pass current that will take them down to a wraith's death?"

The sailor's mouth pinched up.

"He's right." I wanted to pick up on his thinking. I wanted to go in to get Avi. She'd be so frightened, so weak. She needed me.

"Oron and one fighter will stay with the boat. Calev, if you insist on going in, you and Serhat can come with me. I will fly out with her and Calev, you can fly out holding Avi's hands to the glider's supports. When thinking of weight, the plan makes sense."

Calev threw me a dark look, but nodded. "I agree."

Oron put a hand over his heart. "They agree! The impossible is possible."

"Cut here. Here. Along this place too. And you two," Aunt said to Calev and Oron, "saw the fifth stalk into two pieces. You can suspend the piece from the support frame for the handle as Kinneret explained in her plan this morning."

Aunt handed the silk off to the fighters who began cutting with silver shears in the places she indicated. Oron and Calev traded jokes as they followed her orders. Then Aunt took my arm and led me away, toward the well where a rooster strutted around the stone base, his throat green as Ayarazi's meadow in the baking sun.

"What has happened between you and the Old Farm?" she asked, her brown eyes seeing right through me.

I glanced toward Calev. His smile made me smile. "Nothing. We...had an argument. He wants to protect me. And I want to lead."

"Ah. You love one another."

"Well, yes. But not like that. We can't..."

"Oh, yes you do. And him too. And you can. You just have to make decisions. There is always a choice to make. If you choose to live outside your land's caste rules, so be it. I think you two do not care to avoid difficulty anyway. It is not too much to think this attitude will carry you through to loving one another, to mating."

The sun seared my cheeks. I put a hand up to cover one and turned away. "I didn't say anything about mating. We don't talk like that in Jakobden," I mumbled, my tongue not working quite right.

Aunt laughed and steered me back toward the group. "But there are children enough in Jakobden. Talk or not, there is mating going on."

I shushed her as we neared the group and Calev gave me a look with a question in it. My cheeks were definitely getting too much sun.

Aunt leaned toward my ear. "Don't let that beautiful man escape you, my Kinneret. You are brave. You take him and you make beautiful babies. Do not allow something as simple as caste deny a real love. It comes once, sometimes twice, in a lifetime. I should know."

I couldn't take my eyes off Calev. *Once in a lifetime.* I believed Aunt. There was no one like him. I couldn't bear to lose him. He was my luck, my heart, the blood in my veins, and somehow, some way, I would have him.

# CHAPTER THIRTY-FOUR

Y OU'RE CERTAIN YOU WANT TO go first?" I cupped my hand
at my mouth and called to Oron.

From the grass and stick roof, he waved a hand. "Yes!"

He lifted the sideways sail of red silk and bamboo over his head, his body looking tight with the effort. The wind noticed the glider and gave a tug. One of Oron's feet jerked forward and he caught himself before toppling off the roof.

"Go!" I punched a hand in the air.

Calev shouted suggestions about reaching arms as far out as possible and the fighters cheered. Aunt covered her face with her hands.

The wind took the glider as Oron's feet lifted from the roof. He began to fall the five stories down to the straw we'd gathered into a massive pile that covered most of the courtyard. He was going fast. Very fast. Then the silk cupped the air and seemed to slow Oron's descent a fraction.

Oron swore. Loudly.

Then he began kicking and thrashing. "I don't want to die! I'm rethinking this. Save me!"

His leg movement lurched the glider sharply down on one end and his graceful descent became a typical fall. Fast and ending in pain.

We ran to him.

The glider flipped over his head and landed bottom up. Oron was face down.

I turned him gingerly and his face was coated in dust. A long piece of yellow straw stuck to his cheek.

"Am I alive?" he asked.

"Yes, you fool. You're alive. If you hadn't lost your nerve, you'd have been fine."

Calev leaned over and pushed Oron's hair out of his eyes. "I'm going next."

I whipped around. "You are?"

"Yes." Calev and the fighters lifted the glider and headed toward the ladder we'd set against the outside of the house.

I pressed my lips together. Today was not going to be dull.

AS IT TURNED OUT, CALEV was the best on the glider.

"Go!" I called up to him from his perch atop Aunt's roof.

There was something in the way he leaped forward and into the air without hesitation, the way he kept his body light and still as the silk eased his descent to the earth. As the straw-strewn ground came up to meet his feet, he went into a run, holding the glider aloft and steady with his lean, strong arms. When his momentum was gone, he lowered the glider to the ground behind him.

The fighters and Oron stomped their feet in praise for his skill. Aunt missed the excitement. She'd gone to the market to gather some dried beef and root vegetables for our journey.

"That will never grow tiresome." Calev ran a hand over his wind-tossed hair and did his stretching thing again, moving his torso around to ease the discomfort in his healed wound.

I didn't smile like he did when I took my turns with the glider. I liked my feet on a boat deck, the water shifting and familiar under me. To have nothing beneath me…

Calev laughed as we leaned both the gliders we'd created against the courtyard's mud wall, near the gate.

"You look a little green," he said.

"I feel a little green." My stomach rolled like a sea swell. "You think the gliders will hold two riders?"

"I do. But we shouldn't over-test this fabric. It's all we have."

"Agreed."

The others washed and drank at the well in the middle of the yard. We had to go now.

I swallowed and crossed my arms over my stomach, the cutting scent of soap rising over the miasma of cow dung and chicken feed. Aunt had kindly washed our clothes after our first set of practice flights and allowed us to dirty her extra robes and tunics. I inhaled the clean smell and Avi's face floated through my mind's eye.

She'd helped me with washing every sundown as long as I could remember.

Splashing. Smiles. The way she pinched up the side of her mouth when a dab of tar sealant wouldn't come off her skirt. I remembered her putting her underclothes on her head once and doing her version of a trader's jig. Father had snapped at her, but she'd giggled with me when he finished lecturing. His fussing made her cry when she actually deserved it.

*My Avigail. My sister. My only family.*

The sudden hot burn of tears pressed behind my eyes and I turned to face the Topa trees beyond the gate and wall.

"Ah, Kinneret," Calev said. He put a hand gently on my back. "That oramiral…" His voice went low and menacing. "We will take her back."

Suddenly, strangely, the courtyard blurred and I couldn't breathe, I couldn't take it anymore. I needed all of Calev or none of him and I was tired of worrying about what would happen if I did get him, of what would happen under the threat of being Outcasted. My skin itched and my heart thunked erratically.

I spun to face him and my emotions exploded into a jumble of anger and fear. "Don't make promises you can't keep."

Calev's eyes widened like I'd slapped him, and no wonder. I was acting like a maniac, but I couldn't seem to stop myself.

"All right," he said. "But we—"

My hands rested on his chest. His tunic was both soft and rough beneath my fingers. "I know." I took a heavy breath. My lungs didn't want to expand. "But don't lie to me. And don't try to touch or kiss me again. I won't make you an Outcast. You'll have enough to overcome without an unconventional union."

The words spilled out of me without my direction.

"I…I don't think I can take the beauty of your attention, only to have it ripped away from me when, or if, we return to Jakobden." I was shaking all over then. My hands. My heart. Voice.

Calev blinked quickly and leaned away a hand's width. "What do you mean, if we go back to Jakobden?"

"You will be tried for killing the amir. I hope we can convince them that you were Infused. Your father will help I'm sure, and the amir's fighters we have on our side, but the kyros will be involved." I grasped his tunic and stared up at him, willing him to understand the danger. "You may have strong luck, Calev ben Y'hoshua, but this. This could mean your death."

He put his hands over mine, then his mouth tensed and he dropped them to his sides again. "You're the only one who believes I'm lucky." His grin was sour-sweet with sadness. "I only believe in the Fire's will for my life. Well, that and the arrogance of my father." He laughed quietly.

"Don't make this a joke. I'm tired of joking." I released him, my thoughts flying like wild birds. I'd never wanted to move from Jakobden, but now…it was the only way. As long as I could work the sea, it would be fine. "I want to rescue Avi, then take you and her and Oron and whoever else wants to come and go to a place where no one knows us. We'll sail far, far away. To the Great Expanse. To a new land."

Calev's head swept to the side and he clenched his fists at his sides. "I can't leave my family, my people, Kinneret. I am Old Farm. I will always be. It's who I am. Like the sea is for you."

A chill poured over my skull and back. He would never leave Jakobden. I'd known it already. I'd only been denying it the last few days. He would remain at Old Farm. Even if it killed him. Even if it kept us apart, in a way we could never be joined as husband and wife. The cold seeped into my chest and shook me hard. No matter what I did, I would lose him.

If he returned and was killed for slaying the amir, I'd lose him. If he was pardoned, he'd have to marry his Intended. It wasn't really his fault. But after all this, if he wanted to remain Old Farm, he'd have to do as they wished in marriage. He said he was Old Farm and would always be. His first loyalty was to his people. Not to me. Not to the love sprouting between us.

I would never wake up to find Calev sleeping beside me in our own home. I would never carry his dark-haired babies in my belly. I would never feel the length of his body against my own. He would keep secrets with another woman. I would be outside their world. Another type of outcast. Like I'd always been. Kinneret. Scrapper. Low-caste. Witch. I'd lost all chance at kaptan when I'd crossed Berker.

Even if we were considered innocent of conspiring to kill the amir—which most definitely was not a certainty—I'd never kaptan the Old Farm ship. Of course, Calev wouldn't have to pay with his throat's blood for that promise he'd made to the amir because she was dead. But I would pay instead. I would never lead a crew and run a full ship across the Pass. Honestly, I didn't so much care about that part anymore. I wanted my own small craft, a business so I could purchase food and supplies for Avi and me and Oron. I longed for Avi's safety, our freedom, and Calev. But I would never, ever have him because he refused to leave Jakobden and its caste system.

Feeling numb, I pushed past Calev. "Oron! Ready?"

Oron tucked his dagger into his sash. "Yes." He gestured toward the fighters at his side.

Ekrem took a drink from the well cup and set it on the stones.

Serhat nodded at me. "We are prepared, my kaptan."

Calev came up beside me as I gathered a bedroll and opened the gate for the fighters who'd lifted the gliders.

"Kinneret. What is it? What did I say? We'll be fine at home. Father will speak for me. These sailors will speak. You had nothing to do with it. You only fled to protect me. Kinneret! Stop! Look at me!"

But I didn't, and the others were wise enough to simply follow us in silence. I left Calev standing, open-mouthed, at the first turn of the path leading away from Aunt's estate. She'd agreed to meet us with the food on the beach where the boat waited, under watch of a boy she'd paid to do the job.

When we were far enough from Aunt's place that Calev was a dark smudge on the horizon, Oron tugged my rolled sleeve.

"Is he not coming with us?" he asked.

Ekrem grunted as he adjusted the glider on his shoulders. Although we would definitely need to find a way to fold the creations to make for easier running and climbing on the island, I don't think the sailor's grunt resulted from carrying the thing. He was upset Calev wasn't with us. I knew enough of military operations to realize missing an operative was not the best.

"He'll come." I set my gaze firmly on the slim path pointing toward the sea's shushing tide. "He loves Avi enough to risk his life for her."

"Then why are you mad as a squashed bee?"

I glanced at Oron. "He likes to risk his life. It's pleasurable for someone as lucky as him. It's the drudgery of sun-to-sun sacrifice he won't be a part of. Not for anyone."

Oron's mouth became a tiny circle as he lifted his eyebrows. "Oh. I see. Doesn't care to run off into nowhere with a lowly non-Old Farm girl who just happens to hold both his heart and his—"

ALISHA KLAPHEKE

"Oron." I glared at him. "I have not mated with him. Not that it's your business."

"Doesn't matter. You hold all the balls in this game." He snickered at his own stupid joke. "The boy won't be able to leave you alone."

"I disagree, Master of Love Experience." I walked a little faster.

"Point taken," Oron grumbled.

Guilt niggled at me, but I didn't apologize. No one asked Oron to get involved in this. And he was wrong. Very wrong. I didn't hold any power between Calev and me. Calev held all of it. In the way his smile made me shine. His caste, allowing him all kinds of choices and respect from everyone. And in the potential mates he probably had clamoring around his father at Old Farm. Miriam, for one. A bitter taste slicked over my tongue. I wondered if she had taken that trade trip north yet with her mother and father. Too bad there hadn't been many reports of wolves.

I shook my head to clear it. We were headed to Quarry Isle to break Avi free. All my focus had to pinpoint on that. If I wasn't my best, and the rest along with me, today's sun would be the last one we'd see.

# CHAPTER THIRTY-FIVE

THE SUN WHITENED THE UNDULATING road of the Pass. The heat rolled over our heads as we neared the oramiral's island. We'd opted for an afternoon escape as the slaves were forced to work from the middle of the night until the sun was directly overhead. They then had sun to rest and eat.

Oron tugged at his tangled, thick locks of hair. "I still think this is madness. They'll see us coming a mile away."

In taut silence, Calev helped me tighten the rope that curled the largest of the triangular lateen sails, adjusting our track a bit. He opened his mouth to say something and I shot a glare, closing that pretty mouth of his. Rocks like tombstones crowded the water to the West. A hazy block of white and brown and green, the island hulked northeast of us.

We were ignoring Oron. It didn't work.

As the island grew and eventually loomed over us, I threw the anchor overboard into the shallow water. The anchor's splash was unheard over the crash of the Pass against the island's rocky crust. There was no movement in the watch tower directly over us.

"Just because we don't see them, doesn't mean they don't see us." Oron knotted a rope, making a circle at one end. He threw it over the nearest tall rock at the base of the island.

Calev strapped one of the gliders to Ekrem's back with some extra rope. We'd undone the lashed strips of bark and coconut rope that held the two main bamboo supports together on each of the gliders and folded them for easier maneuvering while on the island.

"I'm borrowing this," I said to Oron as I turned him around and untied his broad sash.

"Hey!" He slapped my hand. As the sash came free, he grabbed his dagger before it hit the deck. "Where am I supposed to keep my blade?"

"Up your nose."

Oron snorted. "That wouldn't do at all, kaptan. My nostrils are far too small for such an endeavor." He *tsked* and looked to the fighters and Calev. "I'm worried our kaptan has had too much sun. Perhaps we should put this mission off until moonrise?"

"Oron." Calev put his arms out and I, with Serhat's help, ran Oron's sash over the glider on Calev's back and knotted the ends of the stained, green fabric on his chest.

"Kinneret." Calev's words stirred my hair. He smelled warm and spicy. "Look at me."

I would not.

"Please." The word was filled with such longing, my gaze flew to his before I could stop myself. He tilted his head and spoke softly as the others steadied the boat against the rocks with bumpers. "Don't shut me out. We need to—"

"We should disembark, kaptan," Ekrem said.

Before Calev could say anything else to make my heart beat too quickly, I leaped from the boat and onto the tiny black rocks and clear seawater of the island's coast. The stones crunched under my feet as I put a hand to my warm dagger hilt and eyed the ascent we were about to attempt. The sun lay on my exposed forearms like a blanket of flame. I turned to see Calev directly behind me. He knotted his headtie. The glider on his back made him look like he had red wings, like he was some creature sent to torment me with his unattainable beauty. But he couldn't have been sent from any hell. He was too good.

Well, he was until he decided we had no future. I gritted my teeth and ripped my gaze away from him.

Behind Calev, Ekrem stared at the cusp of the cliffs above our heads. A sea bird soared out of a messy cliff face nest and dove into the Pass.

From the look I'd snagged when we were close to the island searching for the map, I knew a spindly path was around here somewhere. It led to the main path that stretched between the slaves' open-air quarters, the quarry, and Oramiral Urmirian's fine shelter made of the same rock he quarried.

"Where's the path?" Ekrem's broad shoulders blocked most of the glider on his back from view. Only one red and brown-green edge stuck up behind his ear.

Lichen-covered rocks rose like discarded stone doors at the base of the cliff.

"Maybe it's farther east than I'd guessed," I said, climbing over a fallen boulder. I jumped over a tide pool of hand-sized lime seastingers. "Watch your step," I called over my shoulder.

I rounded another collection of head-high rocks. Stepping up onto a smaller boulder, I searched the sea for Oron and Serhat. They had raised the anchor and sails and were working to break free of the crash near the island's base. They had to. Staying close for too long would allow the tide and the rocks to puncture the hull. So we had no way out now.

As we climbed over a natural wall of seaweed and stone, a broad stroke of dirt appeared. My pulse jumped. It rose like a rescue rope until it disappeared into the clefts of the island's side.

"The path! Here." I waved a hand.

A shout punched out from the watch tower far, far above us.

"They've spotted our boat," Ekrem said. "They'll fire on them."

Calev hurried to catch up to me, eyes black with fear. "Go, Kinneret. We'll use the boat as a distraction. Just go!"

Agreeing, I stormed up the path. The sandy dirt ribboned through crevices and past alcoves where sea birds nested. If one flew out, I'd fall to my death on the rocky beach below.

"Don't look, Kinneret," Calev said, his voice breathy as we rushed higher and higher and higher.

"Don't pretend to care," I shouted over my shoulder. It was mean. Mean felt a whole lot better than scared.

"Quiet, you two," Ekrem said from the back. "We should be nearing the top."

He was right. The cliff only reached a jump above us. When we doubled back on the path again, the rocks that had surrounded us dropped away and exposed a valley of extremes.

The quarry was a dip and a crescent of white in the green hill directly across the valley. The oramiral's house coiled at the base of a black rock outcropping, snug and formidable. It was made of the same stone as the amir's abode, but this house lacked the columns, mosaic portico, and treed courtyard. To our left, far above the rest of the island's structures, watchtowers included, the slaves' turreted castle tower rose into the blue sky.

I could smell it from here.

*Avigail.*

My feet pounded the path, and we neared the slaves' quarters without anyone stopping us. But two guards stood sentry at the entrance. Ten foot tall spears stood at their sides and bells hung on the oramiral's well-known contraptions above their heads. Their shoulders looked every bit as broad as Ekrem's.

I spun, grabbed Calev and Ekrem by the sleeves, and dragged them into the brush off the path. At the island's edge, a man with a bell jangling over his head, raised his arms.

"He's shooting a crossbow at Oron!"

Calev's face was fingers from mine. "We have to get into the quarters now. Oron knows how to evade crossbow bolts."

"And how exactly does one do that?"

"They're well out of range, kaptan," Ekrem said. "He will go farther out. If you don't mind my suggestions, kaptan, you should cross the path and head, hidden in the brush, up that side of the path. Calev and I will sneak up this way. When you are near the guard, throw a rock and distract the guards. I will take them down with Calev's help."

Calev frowned. "But I'm not a fighter."

I could tell he hadn't wanted to say that. And really, the way he'd moved in his dagger dance had shown he was at least capable of the action.

Ekrem put a hand on his shoulder. "I saw you with your dagger onboard the amir's full ship. You know your way around a blade. Simply strike flesh instead of air."

"Oh, simply strike flesh." Calev shrugged dramatically and rolled his eyes. "No problem then."

I gave Ekrem a nod and squeezed Calev's hand tightly. Too tightly.

"He's right, Calev," I said. "You can do this. You haven't cowered once during this…"

"Hells," Calev said quietly. "Because it definitely hasn't been paradise."

The mention of our ongoing game with Avi hit me in the throat and I had to look up to keep from releasing a sob.

This was a hell. And if we died here…I had to tell Calev how I felt. If the guards caught me or him and he never knew… Though I was still so painfully disappointed in him and burned raw with his rejection, I had to make certain he knew.

"Calev. I love you. I always have."

I didn't give him a second to respond. I took off, running across the path like a lizard and diving into the spindly bamboo trees, crunchy grass, and sandy dirt. Rolling, I came up into a crouch. The growth on this side of the path didn't provide nearly as much cover as Calev's side, but the guards remained standing, eyes glazed in fatigue until I was close enough to see the sweat around the metal straps that held their bell bars in place. The bells hanging from the bars over their heads clanked in a gust of wind. An insect buzzed past my ear and I swatted it as I searched the other side of the path for any sign that Calev and Ekrem were in place. Then I caught a flash of red. Gliders. And if I spotted them, the guards would too. Soon.

I had nothing to use as a distraction. The ground at my feet was nothing but grainy earth. Not a rock to be seen anywhere. Not a fallen tree limb. Nothing. Not even a lizard to throw. I took a deep breath of the searingly hot island wind. I felt like I was being slow roasted in this heat.

That was it.

Fire.

The perfect distraction.

It would keep the guards far more busy than the easy-to-scout-out rock noise. They'd have to deal with finding water in this dry place. If the fire spread, it could eat this entire island before nightfall. Their oramiral would not be pleased.

I smiled.

Pulling my nub of silvery quartzite and my dagger from my sash, I eyed the bushes and ground for kindling. A flaky length of fallen bark from a eucalyptus shading me was ideal for the job. I struck my dagger along the quartzite rock until a spark fell onto the bark. And died. Only a thin line of gray smoke curled out of the bark. Not enough to start a fire.

Groaning, I lifted the tiny stones and leaf debris around my feet. If I could find some fungus…

A man shouted and another grunted. I jumped up to see Calev holding one of the guards from behind with his dagger on the larger man's throat. Blood trickled down the man's front. My stomach churned. Ekrem stood over the other guard, holding the man's hair. Ekrem kneed the man in the face and the man collapsed to the ground. I went hot and cold all over as I ran to them. My heart thwacked my ribs like a sail cut loose of the gaff.

"Did you kill him?" Calev asked, his voice rising.

"Who cares if he did?" I asked, already kicking at the slave quarters' entrance.

Ekrem took over and blasted a boot through the wood. The odor of urine and fear and desperation raked nails over my face.

We ran into the round, open room and were immediately surrounded by men, women, and children with shaved heads, white-dusted faces, and dead eyes. Their slave bells clanged in a mournful chorus.

"Avi?" Where was she? My heart leaped high, dropped, and exploded. "Avigail?"

Calev and I pushed through the seemingly frozen crowd. They were probably too shocked and in too poor of health to even react to our surprise entrance.

"Avigail!" My throat was raw and my nose burned.

And there she was. Slumped and staring up from the bottom of the stone walls.

They hadn't shaved her head yet. Her sunlight hair still gilded her skull like a crown and veil, but her ragged tunic hung loose. She was skin. Bones. A living wraith.

Not meeting her gaze, I grabbed her and tucked her under my chin. My body shook so hard I was afraid I might hurt her. She was mumbling, but there was no sun for this. They'd be here any second.

"Did you hit your guard on the head?" I asked Calev.

Calev ran a gentle hand over Avi's head and down her cheek. Tears were silver in his eyes and hers. My heart contracted and exploded again.

"Did you put your guard to sleep?" I asked him. "We need to fly. Now." Another smell rose, sharp and lurking, over the odor of the slave quarters.

Ekrem worked his way to us, holding his hands out to keep the slaves from his path. He stopped at Calev's shoulder and lifted his nose to the air. "Smoke." He looked at me and my stomach fell into my knees.

My fire had caught.

"Fly. Now." I set Avi a step away, turned Calev, and began tugging the glider from his back. Ekrem did the same with his own.

"Are you going to take her away?" A woman not much older than me leaned toward me as Calev and I worked to lash the glider supports back together. She had bright blue eyes.

Avi whimpered and put a hand of bones on my arm. I touched her skin briefly, keeping my feelings shoved deep down so I could work. I could not look at her now. I'd lose my every thought, every plan.

My hands were worthless as I tried to tie the lashes. "I can't get it!"

Ekrem already had his assembled and was climbing the wall with one good hand and his feet in nooks in the stone.

Calev touched my cheek and edged my shaking hands away. He tied the lashes neatly, his wiry hands quick and sure. We stood. Avi kept a handful of my shirt and Calev's tunic as I hoisted the glider up. The scent of smoke grew stronger. The slaves began yelling and rushing toward the door we'd broken through.

I climbed the wall; it wasn't so high. Ekrem and I helped Calev lift Avi up to join us. We took the glider from Calev then and he climbed up after. The view from the top of the castle wall was chaos. On the path leading to the quarters, a jumble of guards in gray and the oramiral's retinue in yellow fought one another. Fire licked at the trees and grass, spreading down the valley like a river of light.

"They turned on the oramiral's men. Some of the slave guards turned on the retinue!" I shouted and took up the glider.

Now I finally looked Avi in the face.

And I shattered into pieces.

My ears buzzed like an impossible amount of insects had crawled inside to fight and die.

Calev and Ekrem readied the gliders and held them aloft. An arrow zipped past the glider he held. He ducked his head and dipped the silken creation outside the wall.

I cupped Avi's face in my shaking hands. "No matter what, hold on to Calev. Hold on with everything you have left, Avi." I was crying. My face felt cold and wet in the wind.

Smoke like acrid wraiths drifted through the air, choking me as I climbed onto Ekrem's back. Avi did the same with Calev, her foot slipping once behind his bent knee and jerking his tunic. Her elbows were sharp as yatagans at his shoulders. She lay her head between his shoulder blades.

The world dropped away from my feet as Ekrem and Calev jumped from the wall. My stomach floated into my throat. My arm muscles spasmed as I held on and lifted myself up to look over Ekrem's shoulder. Below us, another clutch of yellow-garbed slaves ran up the path toward the slaves' quarters. Slave guards in gray tunics raised crossbows at their former comrades and fired. Some came together with yatagans and spears. The sun flashed off their weapons and the bells ringing above their heads.

"What if the slaves burn in the fire?" I said into Ekrem's ear as he slid his right hand down a bit on the glider's handle bar. "We can't leave them there. Those people…"

I shuddered. Their shaved heads. The empty eyes and bones so sharp under their ashen skin. It was wrong to help Avi and leave the rest.

"But what can we do?" Ekrem's beard scratched against his leather vest as he turned his head to talk to me.

A crowd of slaves—skeletal quarry workers and guards in gray—surrounded the flames and beat on the fire with boots and shed tunics.

"They're working together to put it out," I said, pointing back and down.

Calev and Avi soared above my view of that end of the island. Calev's hair flew behind him like a small cloak over Avi's head. A shiver of hope danced over me. She might make it out of this alive. But the others like her…

"Maybe the oramiral won't regain control of the island," I said. "Maybe—"

"He has weapons," Ekrem said. "And food. The slaves will not win out. Not unless his retinue goes against him."

"Why don't they?"

"They are his children."

My stomach clenched. "What?"

"The yellow tunics are his children from bedding other slaves. He keeps them in his housing. Feeds them. Clothes them. Warps their minds into believing he is a god."

The tattered clouds blurred, and I searched the sky for Calev and Avi.

So much evil existed in the world, driven by greed and a thirst for power. Was I like that? Is that why I'd wanted the silver badly enough to risk all my loved ones' safety?

Looking past us and up, I saw Calev's red glider and the ends of his tunic flickering behind him like blue flame. As we lifted in the wind, then drifted down, down, down, past the island's green growth and sand and black rock toward the speck of Oron in the Pass, I was detached from the earth in body and mind. Like arrows, my pains hit me one by one and lodged deep in my heart.

The look in Avi's eyes, her innocence burned away.

Calev's rejection.

The slaves we were leaving behind.

The fire I started that might kill hundreds.

The rough landing on the water we were about to experience. Fear for Avi in that crash.

Where we might go when or if we made it onto the boat with Oron.

It was too much. I squeezed my eyes shut and let the sea sing in my ears. Whispering. Rushing. Questioning. What would my mother have said to do? My father?

They would've said the same thing they always did when we had a decision. Stealing the sentence from one another, picking up where the other left off, they would've repeated what felt now like the only thing I could remember about their wisdom

"When you don't see where to go," Mother would say.

"Put a hand to your stomach." Father would grin and wiggle his black eyebrows.

"Fingers over your heart." Mother always gently pressed her own to my chest and smiled.

"Think of your choices. The one that make both heart and gut hurt, that is the true path." Father liked to rub his knuckles on the crown of my head and make a funny clucking noise before pulling me into his arms.

I set one hand on my head now, remembering the feeling. The sea waters were flying up to us and the drift over the white caps should've been thrilling. We had escaped after all. We had saved Avi, unless they shot us down with arrows, crossbow bolts, or spears. But as we plunged, feet first, into the chill water, I was far away, in my own boat, beside my parents and a tinier Avi, smelling the orange Mother had bought as a treat at the market, listening to my parents' wisdom, and rubbing a hand over my young heart. Calev hadn't been a problem then. He'd been a surety. Like my family, the sunset, the tides.

My hands released Ekrem as our bodies sunk into the Pass. Above us, both gliders stayed afloat, a red slash against the blue-green sky of water. Blowing air from my nose, I pushed my hands through the sea and twisted. *Where is Avi?* She wouldn't be able to swim in her condition.

Ekrem turned, a dark shape against the inconsistent yellow light, and held out a hand. I waved him on and he kicked, bubbles racing from his sandals, rising to the surface. Spinning again in the water, I saw another shape, this one leaner, lithe and familiar as my own hand. Calev. He jetted diagonally down through the blue-green.

Below him, a ghost drifted deeper, deeper.

My heart stopped in my chest.

Driving my feet back and forth, I propelled myself toward Avi, not caring that Calev was already well on his way to her, because her arms unfurled from her sides like a banner dropped from a cliff. My body went numb and everything was moving too slowly. I drove toward her, but she was disappearing into the dark, Calev her shadow.

Bringing my arms forward, then thrusting them back, I sped forward. Below and beyond me, Calev stopped. His tunic billowed around him like a storm cloud. I couldn't see Avi anymore. Then Calev whipped around and Avi was in his arms. I opened my mouth, forgetting I was in the water and salt puckered my tongue. With a look at me, Calev—his mouth a line and his eyes furious—kicked his feet and swam toward the surface. He was too slow. She'd be taking in water. She was weak. She would drown.

I swam up beside him and put my hands under his elbow and his thigh, pushing him with every one of my surges upward. We broke the surface, Calev and I gasping, Avi still limp.

Oron and Serhat's faces appeared over the side of the boat. Shouts bounced into my ears. Behind us, the island's rock walls curled lukewarm air off the water and threw it back at us along with threats from the oramiral and his men above.

Our sails weren't up. We were unmoving targets.

Oron reached his arms down. "Hand her up. I have your salt here, Kinneret. You can help her." Calev and I lifted Avi as best we could, the boat bumping against us. "Get our kaptan onboard quickly," Oron said to the sailors and Calev. "She has healing to do."

"I can't heal," I mumbled as Oron tugged Avi over the side and I began climbing the small rope ladder.

Calev put a hand under my thigh to heft me up. "You can. You will."

Something thudded into the boat by my hand. A short, wooden shaft. Feathers. A crossbow bolt.

Calev blasted up the ladder behind me, scooping me into the boat with him. We tumbled to the deck as another two bolts banged into the boat's mast and side.

"That's why the sails are down," Oron said, widening his eyes.

"Well get them up now!" I scrambled to my feet and rushed to where Avi lay chest-down near Serhat.

The fair-haired sailor struck Avi's back and water poured from my sister's mouth. On her knees, she coughed and fell forward into my arms. She was light as a bird. Cold as ice.

"Avi? Can you hear me? You need to stay awake. I'm going to sit you up." With Serhat's help, I raised her into a sitting position.

Avi's face was a puzzle of white, purple, and pale greenish.
She wasn't breathing.

Calev and Oron shouted instructions at one another as they raised the jib and halyard. The wind shouldered into the sails and we pushed westward.

"Avigail," I whispered into her face. My hand searched blindly for the salt pouch Oron had kept for me. "Breathe. Please breathe. We have you now. You have to live to help me deal with Oron." I searched the deck. "Where is the salt?" I shouted at Serhat and everyone who would listen. Leaning back down to Avi, I said, "And Calev needs someone to help him irritate me."

"Here," Calev was suddenly there, kneeling and holding the bag of salt. He lifted my hand to his mouth and said a prayer against my skin.

"*May the One who blessed our foreparents, mothers, fathers, bless and heal the one who is sickened, Avigail, sister of Kinneret. May the Shining Pure One overflow with empathy and love upon her, to refresh her, to raise her up, to make her strong, to heal her.*"

I swallowed. "Thank you."

My soul was turning itself inside out. I drew a handful of salt from my pouch. What words had Aunt said over Calev?

It didn't matter. I just had to try. I'd already done things I never thought I could. Father's long, bedtime lectures about thinking on my magic before taking up the salt made so much more sense now. I could still see the worry in his brown-green eyes and the way he tucked my and Avi's sleeping blankets so carefully like he could protect us with mere bedding.

With his caution in my heart and my mother's magic in my veins, I prayed.

"*Salt, blood of the oceans, heal,*
*Wake this one's lifefluid.*
*Feed your strength to her.*
*Enliven, spark, breathe!*"

My arms shook. I pressed my salty hands against Avi's bony chest. A rasping sound came from her mouth and my heart lurched.

"Please, Avi. Breathe. Cough. Live."

Her cheek, her ear, were warming. Her chest rose in another breath.

And she opened her eyes. Tears ran into my mouth as I laughed.

"Drink?" she rasped. I could barely hear her.

Before I could scramble around for fresh water, Calev's hand appeared at her mouth with a water skin. His hand was steady, holding the drink to her chapped and bleeding lips. I cupped her head and helped her position herself better to swallow. After coughing up the first sip, she worked a few swallows down. I put my hand on Calev's, moving the container away, and he looked at me.

"But she's still thirsty." Water droplets shone on his lashes, confusion in his eyes.

"She has to drink slowly. Or it will make her sick."

He nodded, plugging the skin with its cork. "I'm so glad they hadn't yet fitted her with a bell."

I nodded. It would've made our escape and her landing that much more difficult.

"Kinneret." Avi twisted. Her eyes seemed so much larger than before. *Before.* It was like an age ago. "Are we going home?"

Icy fingers walked down my back. We couldn't.

"We're going to visit Aunt."

"And then home?"

"Close your eyes and rest, Avi." I ran a hand over her head.

She nodded and settled against me, her body shuddering in a deep breath. Waves rose around our boat like blue-green hills, blocking most of our view to the island. No more arrows came our way. No more shouting. We'd made it.

Avi was here in my arms and we were headed to safety in Kurakia, where they wouldn't question us about our past. We could start new there, maybe wait until Berker and the rest of the fighters managed to get off Ayarazi and sneak back there ourselves.

"Kaptan!" Oron stood at the bow, one foot on the side of the boat, his hand up to shield his eyes from the white-hot sun.

"I'll be right back," I said to Avi.

"I'll take her." Calev gathered her into his arms. His smile had to be an unguent for her pain.

When I ducked past the rigging, I saw it.

The oramiral's ship.

.

# CHAPTER THIRTY-SIX

M Y HAND WENT TO MY throat. "No."

"Yes." Oron swallowed loudly. "We should arm ourselves."

I laughed hysterically. "Oh yes. With our four weapons. That'll work perfectly!"

Calev came up behind me and put his hands on my shoulders. Past him, Serhat now sat with Avi, who peered over port, her eyes trained on the oramiral's yellow sails.

"Kinneret," Calev said. Corded muscles ran down his arms and I wished more than anything that strength and luck were enough to help us escape our enemies. "Do you have any ideas?"

I breathed out of my nose, my head spinning with worry for Avi. She didn't even seem like the same sister. Wisdom earned through pain had lurked in her eyes as I'd held her. She could not go through imprisonment again.

What power did we have? What advantage?

The oramiral's boat could outrun ours. He had slaves aplenty that were obviously still on his side, both gray-tunic and yellow. The struggle on the island must've switched track and gone his way. As usual, the world did no favors for those in slavery. It was why some respected those who'd been through it and risen to a higher caste with strong business skills or a stroke of luck. Slavery stripped you down and turned you into a lean, fierce version of your former self. The transformation bled into the generations that came after, into children, grandchildren, making them stronger and smarter. But slaves had to earn their way out. Serve consistently, convince visiting merchants and tradesmen to buy their freedom, or impress their owners to such a degree that they emancipated them. And breaking Avi out of the quarry hadn't impressed the oramiral. What would?

Oron held his dagger sideways in the air, surrendering as the ship approached. Ekrem dropped the sails.

"Kinneret, what's in your head?" Calev still stood in front of me now, eyes questioning.

I bit my lip. It turned my stomach, but… "You tell him Old Farm sent you to retrieve Avi."

"Why? He'll need a reason. A strong reason."

"Tell them she's your Intended."

Calev cocked his head and rubbed the back of his neck, eyeing Oron as he came near.

"A good plan. I don't like it." Calev's gaze flashed to me, a question and an answer in those eyes that I didn't have the sun for now. "But it might work."

Our fighters surrounded Avi, their uniforms making a wall of red leather.

"You have your father's ring?" I asked.

"What are you two planning?" Oron frowned and kept his face turned to the approaching ship.

Calev lifted a hand. A gold band, brushed by age and wear, circled his thumb. The Old Farm sigil, a sun rising behind a smooth leaf, was barely visible on the flattened top. His dark eyes glowed and he clenched his jaw. My heart skipped. He looked more like his Old Farm ancestors than ever. The colors that made up his skin, hair, and clothing echoed the brown sand, black soil, and blue seas. His people had survived the Quest knights' takeover, then the line of kyros thus far.

I ran a finger over his ring. My own veins held a tiny bit of Old Farm's blood. My twice great-grandmother had been Old Farm—pushed from the community and made an Outcast because of her affair with my twice great-grandfather, one of the amir's house slaves. I was a jumble of every kind of people that had lived in Jakobden.

A bang, then another, broke us apart. Two grappling hooks housed themselves in the boat. The full ship rose beside us, sails like clouds of tawny poison. Slaves in the same yellow as the sails boarded the ship in a silence that set my teeth on edge. The only sounds were the waves against the hulls and the sour clangs of bells.

The monkey-faced slave that first attacked the day they took Avi sauntered up to Calev, Oron, and me. Rukn. He took Oron's offered dagger and tucked it next to his undecorated steel yatagan. "The oramiral is eager to see you."

My skin burned. "You and your oramiral have sinned and you will pay."

The slave put a finger against my lips. The heat under my flesh shook me.

Calev moved to grab the man's arm, but I beat him to it. My fingers laced around the slave's wrist.

"Why are you even loyal to that beast? You enjoy cleaning up his piss and cooking his meals?" I spit at his feet. "Pathetic."

He laughed. "You know nothing, girl. I am Rukn, master of slaves. You are the one with no future. Well, you do have something keeping you alive for the next few days."

"What is that?" Oron asked quietly.

Rukn's black eyes turned. The slave sniffed down at Oron and grinned at me. "The oramiral has two great talents."

A heaviness draped over me like a sail had fallen from its ties and landed on my back and shoulders.

"One is shaping slaves into weapons," Rukn said. "The second…"

"Bone and shell game strategy?" Calev asked, nudging his way between us.

"A fine hand with the oud?" Oron blinked and strummed an imaginary instrument.

Rukn's grin fell into a grimace.

Where was my sister?

I couldn't stand the space there was between us. I wanted her in my arms as if I could protect her from all this. A stupid thought. Across the wet decking, a wan-faced slave held her quill-thin arm.

Serhat and Ekrem were restrained beside her. They were dead too. We all were. Instead of only losing Avi, I'd thrown Oron and them into the storm. Maybe Calev would get out at least. Maybe.

"Joke all you want, prisoners," Rukn said. "You're dead men. But only after the oramiral has enjoyed pulling every form of scream from your trespassing throats."

"The young girl." Calev jerked his chin at Avi, who shivered. "She is my Intended."

Oron made a noise, then covered it with a cough.

Calev raised his hand and his Old Farm ring flashed in the sun. "I am Old Farm—Calev ben Y'hoshua, son of Y'hoshua ben Aharon—and under the amir's protection, therefore so is the girl. You had no right to take her." Thank the Fire for the strength and confidence in his voice.

*Please let it be enough to save her too.*

The slave's face fell, then he narrowed his eyes. The longer hairs in his eyebrows moved in the sea wind. "Why was she not wearing Old Farm henna if she was so recently Intended?"

"She was sick," I lied. "Unable to participate in the henna ritual."

The slave leered at me, then at Calev. "Why was an Old Farm, and a sick one at that, on a worthless little boat? Why are you here?" he asked Calev. "She's no full ship kaptan." He pointed. "What is your business with these scrappers, Old Farm?"

So Rukn did believe Calev. At least the part about him being Old Farm.

"We were headed to her aunt's home in Kurakia," Calev said. "She's known for her healing abilities."

It was another good lie. Truth made deception easier to swallow. Something about the liar's eyes.

Straightening, one hand on his yatagan, the slave called out to the men at his sides. "Lies. All lies. Take them on board. All of them. And drag their craft." He spun and leaped deftly to the ship, flying over the netted float skins and the slapping waters between the boats. "They won't be needing it."

His loud laugh ripped the veins from my arms, the heart from my chest.

Rukn's men swamped the deck and grabbed Calev with quarry-strong hands. Calev went pale. I reached out and put a hand on his back and tried to piece him and myself back together.

"They believe you," I mouthed.

Untruth on top of untruth.

As they wrestled Calev onto the full ship, Oron whispered up at me. "What are you doing?"

The men tore Avi from Ekrem, whose lips went white in his beard. My heart flapped in useless ragged beats between my ribs. Serhat pushed another slave off her arm and climbed aboard the oramiral's ship on her own.

I pushed away from Oron and around another slave as they dragged Avi across the deck. The slave next to me whipped around and hit me across the mouth.

Wincing, I dipped low and rammed my shoulder into his side, moving forward. "Avigail!"

She shouted my name and her eyes fluttered like dying nightwingers as two hands latched onto my arms and kept me where I was.

"If you injure an Old Farm Intended, you suffer drawing and quartering!" I said.

Oron sucked a breath and glanced at me in question.

"It's true and you know it, Rukn!" I jerked my arms free, but didn't run. There was nowhere to go. "Remember that!"

It was an old law, one the first kyros enacted as proof of good intention toward Old Farm in exchange for the brightest lemons, the best barley, and the silver that came with their trade.

The slave holding me ripped my dagger from my sash, tucked it into his own, and hauled me onto the full ship. He threw me on the bigger ship's deck next to Calev. Blood trickled from Calev's brow and he held a hand against his arrow wound. I licked my lip and tasted blood. I wished it mattered that I was bleeding. That he was. But it would only be the first of our blood spilled.

Oron landed beside us as Rukn called out orders for the lines and sails.

Around a cough, Oron mumbled, "That law doesn't come up very often."

Calev titled his head. "Not too many Old Farm head out to sea with wild, mixed-blood sailors."

He smiled sadly at me. He hadn't meant to insult. I knew him. Humor was his coping strategy. My hands shook as I pressed them against the worn deck.

"Not many Old Farm are exciting enough for wild, mixed-blood sailors," I said.

"I'm beginning to think excitement is overpraised." Oron pulled himself to standing.

Rukn stood atop a set of stairs as his crewmen rushed around the ship, working lines and watching the waters.

"The Intended and Calev ben Y'hoshua will enjoy a cup of wine in the oramiral's quarters below. Tirin, please escort them out of the sun."

"Yes, Rukn," said a gray-shirted slave with a wide brow and deep-set eyes. He lifted Avi with a care that surprised me.

"Sailor," Rukn said as he looked at me. "You and your crew will wait below until the oramiral sees fit to judge your future."

I glared at him. Calev's eyes widened at the black mouth of the full ship's hull. The odor of unwashed flesh and stale water curled between the bars of the opening.

Oron, the fighting sailors, and I walked, with yatagans' points digging into our spines, toward the place that would be our temporary prison.

"This is not the day I thought it'd be," Oron grumbled.

My gaze darted to him as the slaves raised the barred entrance and gestured for us to climb down the ladder into the near dark.

"You thought we'd die in the escape," I said. "So this is better than your hopes."

Oron gave me a withering look before I started down the ladder. "Save your determined optimism for the rats, Kinneret. Their minds might be soft enough to soak it in. Mine is not, although agreeing to this entire endeavor speaks strongly against my argument." He touched his head sharply and held a hand to Ekrem and Serhat. "Please, go ahead. I wouldn't want the amir's own fighters to wait on measly little me."

The ladder rungs were greasy. When I made it to the bottom, I wiped my hands on my skirt. Ekrem and Serhat climbed down to join me. Above, sunlight ringed Oron's head. He turned to Rukn.

"Speaking of," Oron said, "won't the amir be a trifle ruffled if she hears you threw two of her best fighting sailors into a hull filled with despair and possible infection?"

An invisible hand curled around my throat and I put a hand against the ladder as it shook under Oron's weight. It made sense to bring up the amir, to try and use what we had to gain an advantage, but the mention of her title, the fear that the oramiral and all of Jakobden might know we had a hand in her death…

"Enough," Rukn snapped.

The slave near Oron shoved him with his foot, knocking Oron from the ladder.

Serhat managed to catch the small man and he hugged her neck, breathing loudly.

"My savior!" he said into her chest.

She scowled and dropped him.

"That was unnecessary. We could've been lovers, Serhat, my sun-haired beauty."

"I'll admit a strong admiration for your knowledge of the sails and the sea, but you are too little for me," she said.

Oron stood, dusting his tunic. "Don't be so quick to judge by size, you lovely beast. I am more than—"

I hit his shoulder. "We need to think about what we're going to do when we get to the island," I whispered.

Rukn and his fellow slaves replaced the grating over our makeshift prison. The bars from above made striped shadows across Ekrem's crooked nose and reached over Oron's tangled, long hair. Blinking, Serhat stepped away from the light, her vest creaking as she crossed her arms.

"She's right," Serhat said. "If they take us to the oramiral and he does not know the amir is dead, we can play confident and possibly secure our release." She looked to me. "I don't know what we can do for you, though." Oron received a look too. "Or you."

Ekrem scratched at his beard. Calev and Oron had shaved at Aunt's because of the heat, but Ekrem had kept his scruffy growth.

"It's possible they won't hear of the amir's death," he said. "Not ever. After all, if our crew mates were all sickened by the silver fog on Ayarazi, they may be stranded still."

"You two got over it quickly enough. And the rest seemed fresh as lemons when they shot our handsome Calev," Oron said.

"Yes." I chewed my lip. "I think they were getting over the sickness. There was a marked difference in their balance and color when we left."

"Then how long do you think we have before the oramiral hears from Berker?" Ekrem asked.

It was the most important question. We were doomed the moment he got word of the amir's death. "The journey to Ayarazi took us over three days. But that was with a full ship with a kaptan who knew the Pass better than anyone," I said.

"Very humble, this one is." Oron mumbled.

I shrugged. "It's the truth. We don't have the sun for humility." Ekrem and Serhat nodded. "Berker will have half, maybe less of his crew, if my guess on the death toll is right. Many were unmoving when Calev and I woke Oron at camp. And he can't use Salt Magic like me."

The deck was quiet above now, only the sounds of slaves' bells, water, and sail rigging mixed with an occasional shout from Rukn. Was Calev cleaning the filth from Avi's face right now, cuddling her and bringing her back to who she was? I squeezed my eyes shut. I hoped he was, but I wished my hands were caring for Avi. I knew how to help her without injuring her pride. How to joke and tease to take the sting out of needing someone. She was so much like me that way, the pride and independence.

"Kinneret?" Oron tugged my sleeve. "Berker could already be in Jakobden."

I shook my head to clear it. Ekrem stared at the ceiling.

"What is the process once they return?" I asked. "How will they inform the kyros of our…offenses?"

Serhat looked as though she could bore a hole in the side of the boat with her eyes. The move to my and Calev's side still niggled at her. Strangely, I respected her for it.

"They will have sent a rock dove with the message to the kyros," Ekrem said. "Then the bird most likely returned two days later with orders. Berker will be given control of the proceedings as he was the highest ranked when the amir was murdered."

"How will Berker and the other fighters know we are even here?" I asked.

"Because of the fight on Quarry Isle, I'd guess the oramiral's master of doves already sent a bird to the amir's court with a full report," Ekrem said.

"So if we have Calev's luck," Oron said with a wry smile, "we might have a day until the oramiral knows for certain he isn't the one that's allowed to kill us. That it'll be Berker's duty to punish us."

Serhat stepped forward. "Yes."

"Berker will punish all of us as far as he is permitted." I blew out a breath, my shoulders heavy. "It will be death, and not in a way I'd choose."

"You have a way you prefer?" Oron's eyebrows lifted.

"I'd take a heart collapse while sleeping, or maybe by the yatagan," I said.

Oron nodded. "As opposed to drawing and quartering, I guess."

"Exactly," I said. "Or being burned alive."

"Hm. Yes." Oron tapped his chin. "That is not one of my favorites. I'd like an exotic poison."

"Do you have a plan, kaptan?" Ekrem popped his knuckles.

I smiled grimly. The thought that he still considered me a kaptan of anything was no less than a miracle.

"Actually, I do. If Calev and my sister are treated as equals, they may not be as closely guarded. If the oramiral imprisons us near his own compound—I'm hoping for this because he won't be certain what to do once he's heard who Calev is—then maybe Calev can break us out. We can steal a boat."

"And then?" Ekrem leaned toward me.

I met his eyes. "We go to Ayarazi. Mine silver. Buy our way out of trouble. Shove some of it up Berker's—"

The ship lurched, and I bent my knees to keep my footing. Oron and Serhat grabbed the same rung of the ladder. He winked at her, and she pulled her hand away as the slaves lifted the grating over our heads.

"Up, prisoners," Rukn said. "It is time to meet Death."

# CHAPTER THIRTY-SEVEN

WITH PUSHES AND YATAGAN TIPS, they ushered us onto the island. Avi slipped and Calev caught her. My world shriveled around me. The only thing keeping me from screaming until I went mad was the chance that Calev and Avi would be sent home to safety. Calev would figure out what to do about the lie concerning Avi. Somehow he would charm his father into protecting her. They would be safe. I could get through this with that knowledge.

As the slave guards turned us down the path's right fork, toward the oramiral's housing, I peered up at the castle fortress where we'd found my sister. Guards stood at the door, calm and armed, as if the entire fight hadn't even happened, but the earth showed the effects of our struggle. Blackened ground, crisped grass, and trees like a corpse's dead fingers surrounded the path that led to the fortress and stretched up to the quarry.

Plumes of white dust floated from that far-off area. A handful of slaves, small from the distance, pushed metal carts up the hill away from the quarry, bringing the valuable stone toward us, toward the docks, where it would be shipped to the highest bidder.

The sun was a brand on my exposed arms and nose. The oramiral had set the slaves to work during the heat of the day as punishment for the uprising. A shudder made me lose my step and Serhat grabbed my elbow. This was all my fault.

Now instead of Ekrem and Serhat living to serve and fight and be rewarded, they would be killed. Tortured and killed.

Oron too.

I squeezed my eyes shut and opened them, searching for his stocky silhouette in the messy line of slaves behind us. He walked between two large men, eyes scanning the island. Oron wasn't a very brave person, compared to Ekrem, Serhat, and Calev, but he'd stood by us the whole way just like every day since I'd met him.

The day Oron came into our life, I'd been eleven years. The fever had dragged Mother and Father away the week before. It hadn't touched Avi. It had hounded me. I remembered a hearty knock on the door of our hut.

Avi cracked it open, then turned to me. "It's a tiny man, Kinneret."

Oron had edged his way in, taking a moment to touch the *shamar yam* Calev had tied to our lintel. "I heard you have a boat."

I'd thought he was there to steal from us. Head pounding, I'd pushed off my grass mat, grabbed Father's dagger, and pointed it at Oron. "So what if we do?"

He held up his thick hands. "I'm an excellent first mate. I heard you might need one."

"You'd work for a young girl?"

"Oh, yes." His voice had a flat tone to it. It reminded me of the traders from the North. *A filthy bunch of people,* Father had always said.

"I find the female mind far sharper than any male's," Oron said. "And you tend to smell much better."

He was teasing me. I raised the dagger.

"Plus, a woman will oftentimes pity a poor soul such as myself. Seeing as I've been cheated on height."

"So you'll work for me, but only because no one else will hire you."

Oron smiled. "You see, the female mind. There it is again, being sharp."

"Father said northerners were dirty. Will you keep the boat clean as I direct you?"

He'd laughed then, a big laugh that made him hold his gut and put tears in his eyes. "I don't think your good father was speaking of mud or offal. He meant something entirely different."

I hadn't understood him then, but after years spent watching him drink and give ladies coppers for time spent in tavern corners, I'd learned.

Oron was roguish, but he was also quick with the sail's lines like no one. He worked hard when he worked. He had saved my life and Avi's.

Blinking the memories away, I put a hand over my heart. I realized I loved Oron nearly as much as I'd loved my parents and aunt.

Before we entered the oramiral's house, I glanced at Oron again. He clucked his tongue loudly and held up one finger, two, then three. *Count*, he mouthed.

He wanted to keep a count of the slave guards we saw. He hadn't given up hope then.

Had I?

Four yellow tunics walked in front of Serhat, Ekrem, and I. In front of them, two escorted Avi and Calev. Ten—no, twelve—ambled up the path near Oron. I'd seen two at the castle fortress. None stood at the oramiral's wide door, but surely there would be a few inside. I didn't know how many were up at the quarry. It was hopeless. We could never fight off that many. If they could find weapons, Ekrem and Serhat could cut through five each, but aside from them, only Calev was good with a dagger. Avi, Oron, and I were near to pointless. Obstacles really, for Ekrem, Serhat, and Calev.

They rounded us into an entry room with a flat stone floor and a low ceiling.

My sister gave me a brave smile, her sunken cheeks making it a mockery of what it normally looked like. I smiled back, bile rising in my throat. I couldn't wish or pray any harder that she could leave this place with Calev and never set one foot on its horrible shores again.

Near Avi, the biggest of the slave guards had hands on Ekrem and Serhat. Oron stood beside me still and I craned my neck to find Calev's face in the assemblage. He met my gaze immediately and my blood pulsed hard through my body.

He glanced at the slave nearest him. The short-haired woman stared ahead, not noticing us. Calev looked back and mouthed, *I will get you out.*

I nodded tersely, my blood shuddering through my arms, making me want to strike out at these people who thought they could take our freedom at will. What gave them the right to take anyone they wanted and do as they pleased? Just because the oramiral was the kyros's cousin didn't mean he should be able to mistreat slaves, take orphans from Kurakia's muscle shoals to slave outside their own culture, and do pretty much whatever he wanted?

My breath came too quickly. This room was too small. Too filled with sweating people and hate and desperation. How could beautiful stone or silver be worth a ruined innocent's life?

I never thought I'd think it, but now, now I hated silver.

Hated what it made people do. Good people and bad.

"You gave a good fight," the well-muscled slave beside me whispered, eyes trained on the oramiral. "We wish you would've won."

My mouth fell open. I spun to whisper back, to find out what exactly he meant and how that might help our situation, but he was raised to his full height now and gave no indication that he'd even said anything to me.

His hands shook at his sides as he looked toward the dark corridor at the back of the room.

I turned to Oron and the slave on Oron's far side glanced at me. He gave me a terse nod, something that spoke of respect.

A shrill voice came out of a dark corridor in the back of the room. The slave near Oron whipped his head around and a muscle in the man's jaw tensed.

The oramiral's head brushed the ceiling as he walked out of the corridor. What did he do to these strong slaves to make them fear him so much?

The oramiral's chin was shaved smooth, his cheeks sharp and proud. With his slanted eyes and straight nose, I had to admit that, while he had none of Calev's breathtaking presence and his hair had grayed at the edges, the oramiral was a very handsome man. Strange looking, but not in an off-putting way. His odd features made him exotic.

He took a porcelain cup of tea from a skinny little slave walking behind him and slurped its cinnamon-scented contents. His one pearl earring flashed as he returned the cup to the slave's tray and clapped his hands together.

"Ah, the incredibly ignorant fools are here! Perfect."

The ends of his yellow silk tunic billowed as he crossed the room to Rukn, whose deferential bow only made him look even more like an oversized monkey.

Rukn rose and held a hand toward Calev.

My heart punched through a beat and seized up. *Please, don't hurt him. Please, believe him.*

"This one is Old Farm," Rukn said. "He claims the scrap of a girl—taken as punishment for her sister's trespassing in your waters—is his recent Intended."

The oramiral's eyes narrowed and he bit his lip. Hands clasped behind his back, he stepped toward Calev. "I suppose you have your sigil ring?"

Calev lifted his thumb so the oramiral could examine the slip of gold. "I am Calev ben Y'hoshua. Son of Y'hoshua ben Aharon."

"Hm." The oramiral clicked his tongue. "Well, Old Farm. I know this sigil."

The oramiral may've been one of the amir's favorites, but he certainly didn't live by her formal manners. She would've always used his full name. It wasn't a good sign. He wasn't showing proper respect.

"And it's true," he said. "A true sigil." He raised himself up and extended his arms. "I welcome you to stay here the night and my slaves will sail you to Old Farm in the morning."

What about Avi?

Calev's face whitened. "I accept. Do you admit to your mistake with my Intended? Such action is punishable by drawing and quartering by the first law of the first kyros."

"Oh ho. Someone knows their laws, do they?" He smiled. "Does the law consider a different recourse when said Old Farm mounts a full attack on my island without attempting to speak to me first?" He tapped two fingers on Calev's chest. "Would've saved the both of us a great deal of trouble, yes?"

My gut went cold. Calev held his chin high.

"I will honor your claim on the girl," the oramiral said quietly.

He spun as a chunk of my heart stitched itself back together. At least Calev and Avi would be safe. Maybe this afternoon, or tonight when they were busy with the night work at the quarry, Calev could free the rest of us.

"But," the oramiral said, "the rest will die. Now."

My head seemed to float above my body. *No. Not yet.*

"What about torture?" I asked.

All eyes turned to me. Oron smacked his forehead.

But I had a plan. If we could stall our deaths, maybe Calev could get us free somehow. He might figure out a way to get us out if night fell and he had some cover. I just had to stall for time, had to drag this out, or we'd be dead before anyone had a chance to do anything.

"I heard you are fantastic at torturing people." I wondered a bit how mad I'd gone. My voice wasn't shaking nearly as much as my knees. I blinked to clear my light head. "Now you're going to kill us without any excitement at all? Dull."

A small laugh came from the back of the oramiral's throat. "Well now. This one is quite the surprise." He put a finger under my chin. His skin smelled like women's perfume. "But you are only stalling. Are you worth a wait, I wonder?"

I breathed in and out, the sound loud, too loud.

"Fine." He nodded.

Strong hands pushed me from behind and I fell to the floor, my hands striking the stone and sending pain jolting up my arms.

"Stop." Calev's voice only made this worse. I didn't want him to suffer too.

"My apologies, Old Farm, but aside from the archaic law that I will not break because of my relationship with the amir, you have no power here," the oramiral said.

The oramiral grabbed my hair and I clenched my jaw to keep from shouting.

"I think I'll give you my mark. Though I'll most likely throw you into the sea and your wraith form won't show it later, I'd like to claim you somehow. You are so very exciting."

I heard Calev's shouting and struggle as if it was happening far away, in another world.

A chill scratched through me. He was going to throw me into the Pass. I'd become a Salt Wraith. I opened and closed my hands, imagining salt sharpening my fingers and vengeance as my only drive.

The oramiral didn't give me time to pity myself. He flashed a dagger from his sash.

"Stop!" Calev called out again, and I heard the smack of knuckles to flesh. Calev grunted and brought down every Old Farm curse known to mankind.

Avi's crying grew louder.

Oron tried to grab me and was dragged away to the side of the room.

I had to drown them out. To focus and keep the oramiral's mind on me.

Between the oramiral's fingers, an emerald the size of a bumblebee blinked from the hilt. The oramiral glanced at the slave holding me.

"He doesn't need to keep me down," I said. "I'll take your punishment. I'm not afraid of you."

I jerked my arm free of the slave's grasp.

The oramiral smiled wide. The steel blade's tip made a small line down my forearm. The pain was bright like the sun at midday. Shocking and loud and never faltering.

"My sigil is simple. Just a cut stone atop a silver coin." His eyes looked into mine. They were as lovely as a snake's when it tries to charm you before striking. "Fitting, don't you think?"

He turned the tip slowly, pressing it into my flesh, to make one corner of the quarried rock, another, and another, until the shape was complete.

Calev exploded from the back of the room. The oramiral stood and shouted as Calev raged through the crowd. Slaves reached for him with slow hands, almost half-hearted in their attempts. Calev's eyes were storms and his blue tunic whipped around him like wind-churned clouds. He snagged a yatagan from the nearest slave's sash and hurled it at the oramiral.

The man dove right and his laugh echoed off the low ceiling. He caught Calev by the throat as the yatagan clanged to the floor.

My heart jumped and strained as I struggled to my feet.

Oron slipped to my side and pulled me back as I eyed the fallen weapon. "No, Kinneret. It won't work."

Backing Calev against the wall, the oramiral's fingers tensed on Calev's throat. Calev's eyes were unblinking. He kicked at the older man, who deftly bumped the strike to the side. The oramiral pressed his body against Calev's, keeping Calev's legs from moving. The oramiral pinned one of Calev's arms to the wall and secured the other with his elbow.

"Stay out of this Old Farm. I don't want your community or the amir's wrath set on me for injuring you, but if you interfere with my work, I'm within my rights to strike you down, or at least, ruin that face of yours. It's nearly as fine as mine. It would be a shame, really."

His gaze slid over Calev's headtie, down his cheeks, and I struggled against Oron. I could strike him now and he would be dead. If I could make my move before his slaves caught me.

"Impossible odds, Kin," Oron hissed.

The oramiral pulled back and knocked Calev across the temple with the dagger's hilt. Calev dropped to the floor, eyes shut.

Returning to me, the oramiral sighed. "That was delightful. Now to finish this torture you are so insistent upon, my sweet."

Blood was ink on my skin, showing the lines of my pain, the strokes of the man who had started me down this path to death.

But really, this was my fault.

So I forced myself to take the pain of the oramiral's dagger. I ignored Avi's cries and Oron's swearing. I didn't dwell on Ekrem's shouts of mercy or Serhat's sucked breaths and murmurs of my accomplishments to the slaves. I didn't even look at Calev on the floor.

I lived in the pain.

The dagger cut the circular shape of a silver coin into my arm as sweat drained from my hairline, down my temples, dripping onto my chest.

"You should smile, sailor." The oramiral's voice was a caress in the red dark of the pain. "You have demons and I'm cutting them out of you."

My eyes flashed open.

He nodded sagely. "I, too, have demons. I know the look of one who knows she deserves the pain. So smile about it. Smile."

"I won't do anything for you. I'm nothing like you."

"Oh, no? You caused all this trouble for these people, these innocents."

"But I've learned from it. I won't repeat my cruelties."

"Smile."

"No."

His eyes glittered and he lifted the blade to my mouth. "Yes." He slipped the tip into the side of my mouth and nipped the dagger up.

I pulled back, and he grabbed my wrist, the one he'd cut. My head swam. It was a small slit, the one where my lips met, but the pain was so much, too much.

"Now you have a jaunty grin, at least." He jerked me into his face. "I always get my way."

At least Calev and Avi might live. It was the only thing keeping me from crumbling in on myself.

It was the light shining through the pain.

An agonizingly familiar voice came from the door behind us.

The oramiral found his feet and looked over me and the rest of the crowd.

"The message was accurate," the slippery voice said. "My sources said the traitors were here and here you are. Greetings, oramiral."

The voice hung in the air as my ears buzzed and my cuts flamed.

Berker.

# CHAPTER THIRTY-EIGHT

THE ORAMIRAL PUSHED THROUGH US to meet him. On shaking legs, I stood to see them hold palms up to one another.

"Welcome to my island," the oramiral said.

As they traded formal greetings, Calev rose from the floor, rubbing his head. His face was flushed, but when he was standing, he went pale. He started toward me. Swallowing roughly, he heaved a heavy breath and gritted his teeth. His gaze was on my arm, then my mouth.

I turned toward our enemies.

Berker smiled darkly and his gaze slid to me. "That one, Kinneret Raza, low-caste sailor, she killed the amir. She will die today."

"What?" Oron struggled against his captors.

The oramiral's face dropped and his lips parted. The shock changed his features. For once, he looked weak, unsure. He swallowed. "Truly?"

Crossing the room to me, Berker tapped my leg with his shoe. "Did you think you would get away with this, scrapper?"

I wasn't about to tell them it was Calev's hand who struck the amir down. If I could convince Berker and the oramiral that I

311

took Calev against his will, at dagger-point, I could get him out. He could still get away and take Avi with him. If Berker didn't recognize my sister. I didn't think he'd ever had the chance to see her. I'd try to get Ekrem and Serhat out of it too, and Oron. I always had been fantastic with lies.

"I almost escaped," I said proudly.

He sniffed. "I don't think so."

"Oh no? I coerced my first mate, an Old Farm, and two fighters into thinking the amir had gone mad and attacked me first and that you wouldn't believe me. That if I could get away to the oramiral and tell my story, we would set things right. I'm a good liar. It was only the tangle of the oramiral mistakingly taking the Old Farm's Intended as a slave that tripped me up."

Hopefully, Berker and the oramiral wouldn't begin figuring the days or order in which the events happened.

Narrowing his eyes, Berker leaned closer. His breath smelled like fish and tatlilav left in the sun. "Where is that sister you were so determined to rescue?"

This was the hitch. He knew why I'd set out with the amir to the lost island of silver.

"She's dead. We came for both her and Calev's Intended. We infiltrated this horrible island, set a fire as distraction, and broke into the old castle fortress. We saw my sister..." I shuddered for effect and nudged the gash on my lip to increase my pain and wash the color from my face. I stared at Berker. "She was dead in a corner. We took up Calev's Intended and used wings of cloth to glide to the sea."

"Is this a child's sleeping mat? Am I to believe this outrageous nighttime story?" He turned to the oramiral.

"It is true, Kaptan Berker. Parts of it, at the least." The oramiral's lip twitched, and he touched the jeweled dagger that sat once again in his sash. "They sailed through the air on framed cloth supports. It was a wonder. Too bad she will die for it. She is rather clever. And quirky."

Berker raised his eyebrows.

312

"She asked for torture." The oramiral grinned, turning my stomach.

I swallowed bile and cold sweat washed over my back and face. My arm throbbed, but I focused on Berker's face, on the oramiral's. They had to believe this.

"And Ekrem and Serhat." I nodded at the fighters. "They were persuaded to help me because of their duty to the kyros's law. To the agreement between the Empire and Old Farm. In the face of the amir going mad, they felt they had to help Calev. That he was their duty. And the tiny man…"

Oron flinched, but I kept on, guilt gutting me.

"The dwarf is a fool. He believes anything anyone tells him."

"Why bring him along at all?" the oramiral snapped.

Maybe if I spun this well, Oron could find a life here. It wouldn't be one he liked, but a bad life is still better than none at all.

"Because he works the lines like he was born to it," I said. "You'd take him too if you knew his skills. He's the one who designed the gliders. He is dull as a training blade when it comes to people and facts and lies, but with mechanics, he's a genius."

Oron squeezed his eyes shut. Tears ran from under his lids and his chest heaved.

The oramiral clapped his hands, his face grave. "In light of the developments then, I hand this criminal to you." He pointed at me. "Slaves ten and twenty-three, take the Old Farm and his Intended to Jakobden."

The slaves shuffled Calev and Avi toward the door.

Avi sobbed. "Kinneret!"

*Keep your tongue, Sister. Keep quiet. Don't give yourself away.* The prayer went around and around in my thoughts like a miller's wheel. I stood and looked at her, tears burning the cut at my mouth. I nodded once curtly, not wanting to ruin my lie. Her mouth opened and she went limp, fainting in the slave's grip. He scooped her up and took her through the door, into the light.

Calev twisted in the slaves' clutches, his eyes a lightning bolt into mine. It was as if he was saying *No. I won't let you do this.*

I knew my Calev. I knew his thoughts as well as I knew my own. He would get Avi home, even if it meant my death. He knew what that meant to me, to both of us. But he would do everything in his power, to his last breath, to get back to this island before they killed me, and pull me out of the flames.

*I know,* I mouthed. A sad smile pulled at my cut. Blood, hot and salty, poured over my lips and down my chin. Our gazes locked and flames washed through my skin, my muscles tensing. His eyes were brighter, darker, more alive than anyone else's. *I love you.*

While Berker and the oramiral convened, the slaves tried to jerk Calev out of the door, but he turned quick and freed one arm, enough to give him a second to mouth back.

*I will come for you. I will return.*

They pulled him away and he was gone.

I fell to my knees, relief a sweet taste on my tongue. I could withstand anything if I could see them safe, as well as Oron and the fighters.

Ekrem and Serhat could handle themselves in the trial. Because that's surely what Berker would do. He would have to take them back to Jakobden. There was no avoiding it, but after all this, they could handle it with the story I'd given them. Serhat wouldn't want to lie, but Ekrem would lead her where she needed to go. He would slip them both past death, at least. They'd be tortured, but not killed. Ekrem would see to it. He was a survivor. I knew when I saw one, because I was one too.

Until now.

Now I was a sacrifice.

My heart settled into the role. Someone had to take the blame for the amir's death. And if Calev had spoken up, we'd all have suffered the worst of what Berker and the oramiral could think up. It had to be me. It made sense.

"Little man," the oramiral said. "I will take you myself, as payment for my trouble. I could use a fine sailor on my full ship. And I want a set of gliders. They would be rather diverting, I think. Berker, I assume you must take the two fighters who aided in this with you to face trial in Jakobden."

Berker was rubbing his chin, one arm tucked under the other. He hadn't yet fully swallowed the hook. "Yes," he said quietly. "I suppose so."

His gaze flicked to Oron, who'd gone white around the mouth. Oron stared at the flat stones beneath the oramiral's curved-toe slippers.

Berker's eyes widened. "It's all settled then. I won't need to take this girl back. She killed the amir. Coerced the amir's fighters and an Old Farm into breaking the law. She will die now. But first, first I think, she should prove her dagger skills to us. There should be a test of her ability."

The oramiral frowned. "Why do we care how she is with a dagger?"

But I knew. My heart iced over. If they saw how weak I was with the weapon, they'd know there was no way I could surprise and murder the amir. The amir had been the sharpest of fighters in her youth. Though she'd been older when Calev killed her, she was still fast. She'd still had her fighter's sense. If I couldn't prove myself with a dagger, this entire rescue mission would very quickly spin into the abyss like a sucking whirlpool, taking all my loved ones with it.

Maybe if I simply showed confidence now, they would leave off the test.

I stood, my head spinning and my wounds growling and burning. "I'll do it." I smiled and let the cut rip open wider. Blood spilled down my chin and I knew I looked as evil as I needed to look. "I love to show off in front of high-caste weaklings."

Berker's gasp was a nice little gift even though my stomach tried to crawl out of my mouth.

The oramiral shook his head. "She is wonderful. Now let us find a suitable spot for this test."

Berker nodded and started out the door with the oramiral at his side.

THE WHITE WALLS OF the quarry blinded me, the dust coating my throat and my teeth. The sun poured onto my head like molten gold, all the beauty taken and replaced with scorching heat. Sweat ran along my temples and rose from the crooks in my arms as I followed Berker and the oramiral. Their men marched behind us. Their faces didn't give away whether they believed I'd killed the amir or not. They might not care. The amir never did anything for them. She allowed the oramiral to take whomever he chose as a slave.

Like someone needed burning after death, we were a double-line of grim-faced mourners headed into the very belly of the place that had been my sister's nightmare.

I twisted to find her in the crowd. Two large, gray-shirted slaves stood at her sides. One held her arm with spindly fingers. She leaned toward him like he was a friend rather than a captor. Made sense. She was probably still so weak. Bile rose in my throat. *Monsters. All of them.* My poor little Avi. I gave her a sad smile and she blinked like a sweet, tiny owl with wings that had been plucked naked.

I breathed out my nose, trying to keep my rage in check, to keep my story believable. She was my friend's Intended. Not my sister. It was the only way she'd get out of here alive.

Berker's gaze scanned the faces around me. I wished he'd get on with this. I was either going to pass the test or not. Freedom for Avi and Calev or the end for us all.

Standing around frying to death wasn't going to change the situation.

"I'm here. You have the dagger. What else do you need?" My arm thumped with the rhythm of my heart. "Should I put on a new skirt and do a little twirl?"

Berker's eyes went dead. "I'm looking for your target."

Despite the heat, a chill gnawed at my bones.

Calev stepped up and put himself between Berker and her. "I'll be the target."

I couldn't move.

But it was probably good I was frozen. Berker's dead eyes and oddly quiet voice told me his mood was like the first kyros's fireblooms, a technology lost in time. The old stories said when Quest knights rode over the silent explosives waiting under the road's dust, they didn't have time to scream before the sudden flash ate them whole. Berker was waiting like that, biding time to explode.

"Fine," Berker said. He pointed to the far wall of the quarry. "Stand there, if you would, Calev ben Y'hoshua."

He said Calev's full name like it was a curse. *Stupid man. If he knew anything, he'd make sure not to say the name, the name that brought all kinds of luck down on us.* A cruel grin tugged at my lips.

"Old Farms are so brave!" the oramiral shouted, and clapped his hands like an idiot. "I hope your aim is good, sailor!"

Because Calev volunteered himself, they had to go along with it.

"Now," Berker said to me. He handed me a dagger, the amir's jeweled dagger and the same that had killed her, and also, a fig.

"Um, kind of you to offer refreshment, but I can't say I'm overly hungry."

"You will place the fig," he walked toward me, "on your lover's head," he whispered. His breath smelled like old butter and sour wine. "You will spear it with the blade from thirty paces."

I couldn't do it.

I didn't have the skill.

I would kill Calev right here, right now.

"And," I coughed, "and if I don't?" *If I can't?*

Berker smiled. "You'll all be put to death. I think you may be protecting the Old Farm."

I forced my voice not to shake. "Why would he kill the amir?"

"That I don't know. But she was a trained fighter. Seasoned. You are a dock rat. The Old Farm and the two fighting sailors with you are the only ones who could've done it. Since you're lying about your sister, you're doing all of this to protect them

317

both. It has convinced the oramiral. But not me. Failing in this test will convince the oramiral of the truth."

One question bumped against my lips, forcing its way out. "Why do you say my mother was a liar?"

"Your parents and I tested for release on the same day. Your witch of a mother lied to the masters, claiming your father solved our group's assigned problem instead of me. The apprentice masters gave your father and mother the last two spots, and I slaved here for three more years." He spat at my feet.

I tried to hold myself calm, to still my trembling bones, but my teeth chattered. Was he lying? It felt true, though my heart fought the story. My mother had betrayed him and saved my father. After seeing the slave island with my own eyes, I understood some of his venom.

But even if it was true, this wasn't justice.

"I am not my mother."

"No. But when I hurt you, I am closer to feeling satisfied. This is your penance. Your family wronged me."

Shoving past Berker, I stormed toward Calev.

My throat caught at the courage in his eyes.

"You can do this, Kinneret," he whispered, no idea that my world had tipped into madness. "I'll save Avi. I'll come back. Old Farm will not stand for this. I won't let them."

He'd need a boatload of silver to talk anyone into saving anyone from the oramiral, especially if Berker ended up in a power position. Which, as the amir's kaptan, he would. He might even secure the position of amir himself. I shuddered.

My hand shook as I placed the tiny fig on Calev's head. It took every shred of my willpower not to touch his face as my hand lowered. One last touch. One last lightning bolt of joy.

"Berker knows," I said.

"He'll be paid. I'll make certain Old Farm deals well with him. If he remembers that someday I will most likely take the chairman position, he will enjoy having this to hold over me."

I swallowed. It wouldn't be a happy life for Calev. Especially if Berker bought his way to being the amir. He'd have the silver from Ayarazi, and buying people and power was the Jakobden way.

"I will see you soon, then," I said to Calev, my stomach churning.

Calev blinked and a tear ran from his eye. "Soon, my fire."

I grew taller, stronger. I flexed my hand, fisted it, and pressed it against my thigh instead of my heart so no one else would see my declaration of love for Calev. *My fire.*

His lips tucked into a quick grin. My mouth longed to kiss his, to press into the feel and smell and strength of him. I took a heavy, deep breath of the dusty air.

"Sailor," Berker called out behind me. "Now."

The cuts on my arm and mouth throbbed as I put steel around my heart, walked thirty paces back, and threw the knife.

# CHAPTER THIRTY-NINE

T HE CLOUDS HUNG IN THE sky. The waves didn't smash even though the sea cliffs were close by. The birds froze, suspended above us. The dagger rushed through the space between Calev and me. It was a tear in the colors of the world, a flash, an opening to the white, hot torture of knowing I'd killed my best friend, my love.

The weapon's arc bent.

I'd missed.

It was going to hit him directly in the eye. Immediate death.

In that moment of a frozen world, when nothing but the dagger moved, I aged one thousand years. I was an old woman. My body was thin and insubstantial as chaff. Crevices marred my smooth skin, a line for every pain, every crime, every tragedy of my life. Mother. Father. Avi. Oron. Calev. The lines went on and on, from my eyes, along my cheek, to my neck and knobbed hands. But my eyes remained clear. It was my penance in that eternity of a moment—to see Calev's red-brown eyes and the trust glowing from them the moment before I killed him.

"I'm sorry."

His thick eyelashes lowered slowly, so slowly, then lifted again as the dagger landed.

My heart screamed. He wasn't dead. I'd missed wide, but only by a hand. It was enough to prove my lie. Maybe.

Calev's eyes widened. Scooping the fig from his head, he turned to look where the dagger had landed, far to the left.

All my energy poured out of me and I fought to stay standing. Calev was alive. I hadn't killed him.

Giving me a solemn nod, Calev started toward the crowd like all was settled. Hopefully, he'd find Avi and stay with her. I wanted them off this disgusting island now. Yesterday. My head buzzed.

"Well done," Berker said, face void of any emotion. He glanced at two fighting sailors—one stocky, the other with hair like a cactus. "Tie her. Neck to wrists. Wrists to ankles. She has a meeting with the sea."

An invisible battle axe chopped at my temples and the base of my skull. The buzzing grew louder.

It was time to die.

*Please*, I prayed. *If I must become a Salt Wraith, make me a weak one, unable to harm.*

I had to let go of my vengeance. If my heart clenched the hot anger for Tuz Golge for Infusing Calev, the oramiral for taking my sister, Berker for…everything, I'd have the power to Infuse masses and cause the death of countless innocents.

The spiky-haired fighter wrapped coconut rope around my wrists, making a slipknot. Had he realized how easy it would be for me to get out of that? Of course, where would I go?

The fighter glanced over his shoulder at Berker as he gave the ends of the rope to the other fighter, who wove them around my neck. The men tied my ankles. Another slipknot. The rope scratched at my skin as I turned to search for Avi and Calev.

Calev was looking left and right. The wind lifted his hair as he scowled at Berker.

"Where is my Intended?" Calev asked.

My skin itched with worry and the rough texture of the fibers. The man holding onto Oron's arm pushed him through the other belled slaves and the large group of leather-clothed fighting sailors.

Oron stood in front of the oramiral and Berker, and I frowned.

My first mate gave me an odd look, then faced our captors. "Kinneret Raza did not kill the amir. Calev ben Y'hoshua did."

A spear of ice gored me. "No!"

I lunged toward Oron, but the fighters held me. I had to stop him, shake sense into him.

"What?" The oramiral bent toward Oron, but Berker put a hand on his chest.

"What are you saying, dwarf?" Berker said, eyes narrowed.

"Don't worry, Kinneret," Oron said. "Avigail is off the island."

"He's lying!" I struggled against the men's grip.

Oron swallowed loudly, his eyes watery. "I can't allow you to die for Calev, Kinneret. You're too important, too bright, to die for a crime you didn't commit."

My mind would not soak in his words. This had to be a nightmare. I was asleep. This wasn't happening.

"Silence!" Berker waved a hand toward the ground and the slave shoved Oron to his knees.

The men holding me did the same and I hit the ground hard.

"Avigail left with Ekrem and Serhat," Oron said.

Berker smacked him and spit flew from Oron's mouth.

The oramiral straightened and put hands on his hips. "Are you saying the two disloyal fighting sailors escaped? They took the Old Farm's Intended?" He looked to Berker. "Someone please tell me what is happening here."

Berker grabbed Oron by the hair. "Explain."

Oron's throat moved and lines of moisture ran down his face. "They escaped. So they wouldn't suffer when I told you the truth. The Old Farm," he said it with spite, like he'd never cared for Calev at all, like Calev was a stranger, not a friend, "he was Infused when he stabbed the amir. He did it. Not Kinneret.

Kinneret is innocent. Calev ben Y'hoshua coerced us all to help him. With his high position, none of us dared oppose the man."

"No…" I realized then I was sobbing. Avi, Ekrem, and Serhat were safe. But Oron? Calev? They were doomed now. Their deaths showed in Berker's shining black eyes.

Berker grew very, very still.

"What should we do?" he hissed.

The oramiral raised his eyebrows and touched his head, lost.

With a single clap of hands that jolted me, Berker said, "I'm finished here. Throw them all into the sea. And catch the fugitives." He scanned the crowd. "Or I'll throw you all in the sea along with them."

Bells clanking, slaves and fighters grabbed Calev. They dragged us toward the opening in the quarry.

In the crush of sweating bodies, confused murmurs, and the oramiral's shouted commands to make for the cliffs, I found myself within arm's length of Calev, though bound as I was I couldn't reach for him.

A wrinkle appeared between his eyes under his blue headtie. "I'm sorry. I should've told them right away, but Avigail—"

"You were saving her." My throat tried to close around my sobs. "Don't apologize. But…but they'll catch Avi. They haven't had enough sun to escape far enough away yet. Do you think…think maybe your father has sent ships out to look for you yet? Maybe if they find them first…maybe…this is all my fault. All of it. My recklessness and going after the silver and—"

Calev's jaw worked, and his eyes bored into mine. "None of this is your fault. You wanted the silver to change your caste, to improve your life, Oron's, and Avigail's. That's noble. That's a dream worth risk. If anything, this is all my fault. If only I'd moved faster the night Tuz Golge…" He squeezed his eyes shut, then opened them again.

I stumbled on a rock and the fighter holding me pulled me up before I could fall, my wounds stinging.

"I…" Calev was the picture of misery. "I love you, Kinneret."

My heart blazed.

Oron appeared at my side. "As touching as that was, the whole death-confession-moment is entirely unnecessary."

"What?" I choked and coughed dust out of my throat.

Oron shrugged, one slave still holding his arm. The slave grinned.

"We just needed another moment. And a nice distraction. The slaves and the fighting sailors," Oron said, "are going to rise up against Berker."

I froze. My captors pulled me onward.

Calev's mouth dropped open. "When?"

"What do we need to do?" I searched the faces of the men and women around us, but none gave up the game.

Oron licked his chapped lips. "When they take you to the cliff's edge, call up some of your fine Salt Magic, my kaptan." He grinned.

Nothing was funny.

"Don't scowl at me, sweet," he said. "I do think you're too special—"

"That's not why—"

"I think if you're going to die, it should be for one of the many fantastic crimes you actually have committed. It's a shame to take the handsome one's single chance at infamy."

Calev looked offended. "Single chance? I've committed as many crimes as Kinneret. What about falling for a low-caste?"

"Oh, that's not worthy of infamy really," Oron said. "You've missed the good crimes. Kinneret never takes you along for the truly spectacular infractions."

Calev's gaze went to me.

My mouth snapped open, my cut pinching at me. "We don't have the sun—"

Calev interrupted. "What have you done without me?"

I threw my head back. "Fire and Sea, give me patience. Just a few pre-harvest opening runs up the northern coast. Nothing that should be illegal. Now where exactly is my sister?"

Before Oron could answer, we were at the cliffs.

The wind, salty and carrying grit, buffeted my body. The slaves and fighters pushed us toward the edge. My foot kicked a clump of sandy dirt from its grassy perch. The earth fell until it disappeared into the roiling waves and angry rocks below. If the men and women around us were making a show of this, they were certainly convincing.

Calev and Oron tugged and jerked as slaves tied their wrists, ankles, and necks, as mine were. Berker and the oramiral slithered around the right side of the group. The oramiral crossed his arms and smiled like this was all a fantastic bit of entertainment. Both his and Berker's tunics waved in the wind—yellow, black, and red.

"I, Kaptan Berker Deniz, declare you, Calev ben Y'hoshua, as killer of Amir Mamluk of Jakobden of the Broken Coast. I declare you, Oron No Name, and you, Kinneret Raza, as conspirators in this man's terrible plan. I give you to the sea."

I didn't have salt for magic and if I did, I couldn't grab it. My wrists were still bound. Why hadn't they untied me on our walk here? Too risky? So I was meant to be the final distraction. If I created a spectacle, the slaves and fighting sailors could hit Berker, the oramiral, and those loyal to him as they looked on.

The tallest of the slaves eyed me and held Calev over the cliff's edge.

Calev simply closed his eyes.

The muscles in his arms were relaxed and his lips moved in what I guessed was a silent prayer. I couldn't believe how calm he was.

Then he looked at me, and I knew.

He was calm, because he believed I could pull this off. That I could make magic happen and save us all. Respect. He respected me. I wasn't just the one he joked or played pranks with, the person he kissed for fun. He was following my lead.

I laughed.

The people around me frowned like I'd gone mad.

But I was happy, not crazed.

Calev had been following my lead this entire journey. I'd only now seen it. He did love me. And he respected me, believed in me.

I wasn't about to disappoint him.

I chanted under my breath, fast and sharp, as I dug salt from under my fingernails.

*"The Fire and the sea listen,*
*Listen please to me.*
*Your chosen prays*
*Along with me."*

My eyes flicked to Calev, whose beautiful lips whispered.

*"Lift the winds,*
*Bring them from the waves,*
*Bring them high to shield us.*
*With your power, crash,*
*Arise, blast across this field.*
*Remind all who made this sea*
*And the magic in it."*

I stared out at the Pass. A spot on the horizon flattened into a watery sheen, like an air-filled sail. It grew toward us, spreading out and on until the sea below the cliff didn't hold a single wrinkle.

It was wind. Sheering across the water. Rising.

The massive gust roared up the cliff and threw Calev and me back, showering everyone in sea spray.

I laughed as Berker shouted, "Salt Witch!" and the oramiral's tunic tangled him, a fancy net around a surprised fish.

The slaves and fighters rose to standing. They'd been prepared, prepped, for this distraction. Their yatagans, axes, and daggers flashed as they turned on their masters, and those few still loyal to them, with wild howls.

Calev had somehow snagged a dagger and, already freed by a stranger, was running toward me with a face of grim determination.

A fighter cut Oron loose, and he turned to see the oramiral's yatagan slicing down. Oron spun.

Before I could shuffle to Calev to shorten his spring, a hand grabbed the rope connecting my neck to my wrists and ankles.

Berker's face leaned into mine.

"Kinneret!" Calev was almost to me when a yellow-tunic wearing slave flung a hand at him. Calev blocked the strike and moved to hit the man.

Berker twisted the rope holding me. My neck burned. Pressure built in my head.

I was choking.

"Your magic won't save you today, witch," he said.

I fumbled with the rope, trying to breathe, to get even a second of air. I brought my knee up like Calev had at the oramiral's house. It connected with Berker's groin and he growled.

He shoved me off the cliff.

# CHAPTER FORTY

THE AIR TORE AT MY cheeks and eyelashes, my clothing, and hands as I tumbled through nothing. I was headed for rocks or water. Couldn't tell which. If I submerged tied, it wouldn't matter. I would drown. I would still become a wraith.

Fevered, I tucked my thumbs and tried to work my hands free. The rope bit into my skin as I squeezed and pulled and fell.

One hand slipped free.

I pried the other loose, pain lashing over my cut flesh. Straightening, I threw both hands over my head and arched my back to find blue, to find the water, to aim.

And then I was swaddled in the cool blanket of the sea. My head thudded, the deeper water pressing painfully against my eardrums. Green-blue surrounded me. Where was the surface? My lungs screamed for air.

Then luminescence like melted butter slid into view to my left. My ankles still tied, I drove both legs through the water like a fish would, kicking toward the light. I rolled my torso and let a wave of movement course down my body, to my legs. My feet were a tail, a fin.

The light grew.

My lungs sparked and shivered.

I broke the surface with a gasp and swallowed in air, perfect, wonderful air.

Swimming as best I could, I used the movement of the current to drive toward a large rock at the shore. I heard so many noises, broken by the water's sloshing around me. This was taking too long.

Still, I swam. And swam.

I pushed toward the rock, the current helping for a breath, then hauling me out again.

It'd been so long since I fell. My limbs shook with fatigue. If I didn't get to the rock soon and out of the water, I'd miss it all. The battle would already be won or lost.

A heavy swell rose and I went with it, grasping, reaching until my fingers found the nearest rock. The wave crashed and I tucked my head to my shoulder to avoid being bashed senseless against the unforgiving island. Grasping the mussel littered rock, I pulled myself up and scrambled onto the sand. Finally.

*Calev. Avi. Oron.*

Sheltered by man-sized rocks, I used an emptied oyster shell to cut the rest of my ties. Navigating the rough shore along the cliff's base, I searched the beach for the way back up. The sun had moved. I'd wasted so much light.

"Kinneret!"

I whipped around to face the sea and there, among some wide, flat rocks, under the graying sky, sat a boat with yellow, slack sails. One of the oramiral's, half beached, a hole in its side. Avi huddled near the boat's rope ladder. Her arms shook as she tried to pull back the string on a crossbow. Tears streamed down her cheeks.

On the black and gold sand near the boat, Ekrem, Serhat, Calev, and Oron fought men and women in yellow tunics. The oramiral's personal slaves. Ekrem's yatagan and Serhat's battle axe lashed through the air at their attackers. Calev's dagger was a minnow again. The knife cut the yellow-garbed slave here and there and there again as the slave barely managed glancing blows to Calev's shoulder and arm.

Another fighter—no, it was the oramiral himself—raged down the hill toward Avi. His silken clothing billowed and his mouth leaked blood as he grinned at Avi. His yatagan flashed in the sun.

Ekrem had his opponent on his knees at the prow of the craft. Soon, he'd be free to fight, but not soon enough to save Avi.

I ran as fast as my shaking legs would carry me.

The oramiral would get to Avi before me.

There was no way I could save her.

Avi screamed. "Calev!" She saw me. "Kinneret!" Her foot pushed at the base of the crossbow and her fingers strained against the draw weight.

I climbed over the rocks, dodged two dead men.

Oron tried to get to her and suffered a slash from the man fighting him, forcing him back into that life or death fight.

An idea shone in my head. Calev's dagger. It would only work if he acted fast with no questions and only if my guess was right.

"Calev!" I shouted, running. "Your dagger! Northwest, now!"

Without a blink, his hand uncurled in the direction of the approaching fighter. The blade zipped past Avi and speared the oramiral's yellow-swathed chest, right over the heart, with a thick sound. He fell forward into the sand.

The oramiral was dead. Blood poured through his fine clothing as fast as it did any slave's. Caste meant nothing when it came to death.

I smiled grimly. We had done it.

But we didn't have the sun to enjoy the victory.

Calev's attacker grinned at his lack of a weapon as I caught Avi in my arms and threw her to relative safety around the craft's prow. The slave's yatagan arched toward Calev. Just when I thought I'd planned wrong, that my recklessness had once again shadowed a loved one's life, Ekrem finished the man he'd been fighting with one slice across the throat. Ekrem leaped between Calev and the other slave and drove his yatagan into the man's belly.

With a shout of victory, Serhat finished off the man coming at her and Oron scrambled around the back of the man fighting him and stabbed him through the liver. Oron kicked the man into the incoming waves. With that, all our attackers were down and it seemed the gray-clothed slaves had swamped the oramiral's yellow-garbed men on the rise above us.

There was a shout and a cluster of fighting sailors—3 large men—scrambled down the slope toward us.

Oron swore. "It's Berker."

My body went numb. My anger was steel and ready to work.

He'd stolen someone's red leather vest. With a yatagan extended and blood running from a deep cut along his face, he and the fighters who remained loyal to him closed in on us.

"Try to edge them around so our backs are to the cliffside," I whispered as Ekrem, Serhat, Oron, Calev, and Avi gathered near.

Berker and his men came in with knees bent and weapons ready.

"You've already lost," I said, stepping at an angle and silently encouraging Berker toward the sea.

His weasel smile turned my stomach. "No, no. This isn't over. If I capture you, I could convince the rest that you and your little party here must at least go to trial in Jakobden. Isn't it sad? After all you've accomplished, it might still come down to me being high and you low."

Out of the corner of my eye, I saw Calev and Oron helping Avi onto the higher rocks on the cliffside. Ekrem and Serhat stayed close, their blades wonderfully menacing at my sides.

"See?" Berker gestured toward Avi. "Even your most loyal are jumping ship, so to speak. How much easier will it be to persuade the rest of those still alive to follow the laws that have been in place for ages?"

I laughed and rubbed my salty hands together. "I'm pretty convinced I've witched up all the laws now."

His grin faltered.

Reaching my salty fingers toward the shore's rumbling waves, I prayed.

*"Waters, meet me, higher, deeper,*
*I need your cold, your power rushing."*

Berker launched his yatagan at me, but the waves were already growling and swamping him and his men. The shush of the sea muffled their shouting. I let myself float below the surface, hoping the others were safe on the cliffside.

In the water, under the rolling wave, I spotted Berker's flailing legs and his men as they fought to swim. The sea was only listening to me and my prayers now. Their strong swimming did nothing. The current sucked the fighters farther and farther until they were only smudges in the blue-gray. Berker's head dipped under the surface as the water pulled him down. He refused to give up his heavy weapon. He met my eyes, jerked once, and sank and sank and sank.

WHEN THE SEA HAD EDGED away from the shore, Calev retrieved his knife from the oramiral's body, which was lodged between two large rocks.

Soaking wet, I pulled Avi into my arms. I held her tightly, my injuries thumping and complaining. But they were less deep now, still cuts but not bleeding. The sea must've begun to heal them.

"My little lion." I cupped Avi's face as we sat beside the others at the base of the path leading up the cliffs.

Perched on a boulder, Calev and Ekrem were slicking seawater off their heads and laughing. Near them, Oron and Serhat grumbled to one another, but Oron worked a smile out of Serhat.

"I'm so sorry for all of this," I said to Avi. "I'll never put you at risk for something as ridiculous as silver ever, ever again."

She hugged me back, then stared at me. "It wasn't for silver. It was for us. For Calev. Old Zayn. Oron. I know that."

I pressed her sweet head against my shoulder, watching the faint moving shapes above the cliff tops, where the fighting went on.

"Promise you'll stop me if I ever try to do something mad again," I said.

"I promise no such thing, Sister." She pulled away and smiled with all her crooked teeth. "We made it through this, didn't we? If we kept to safe things forever, we'd have no kind of life at all."

"She'll be insufferable now that she's become so wise," Oron said, holding a scarf against a cut.

Over her head, I smiled shakily at him.

"I can't believe it. We're alive." I laughed and my throat felt raw.

Calev held out his hands. "Seems we are." He looked at the rest of the island that rose into the sky. "Unless I'm having the strangest dream ever."

Oron rolled his eyes. "In that case, you'd still be alive, Calev. One cannot dream whilst dead." Oron shook his head, then said to me, "Do you truly want to spend large amounts of sunlight with this dolt?"

Calev's dagger whooshed past Oron's shoulder and lodged in a grassy mound.

Calev raised an eyebrow. "This dolt could cut your tongue out if you're not careful."

"Ooo," Oron said, blinking repeatedly.

The sounds of cheering erupted from the top of the island.

Oron pulled Calev's dagger free. "Kinneret always had a penchant for flashy things."

Ekrem, Avi, and Serhat laughed at that, following Oron as he started up the incline.

"We need to find a boat," I said.

"We'll have to get to the dock. It means going back up. Into that." Oron pointed toward the movement on the cliff tops. The goat path we'd used dangled down the rock and growth like a fraying thread.

Agreeing, we started up the incline.

Before we reached the top, a group of slaves in gray and fighting sailors in red danced down toward us, arms around shoulders and chanting something into the salty wind.

"Kinneret Raza, warrior and witch!"

They were smiling, not judging or threatening. I stopped, trying to soak in this new reality.

"We saw the sea obey you and kill Kaptan Berker!"

"And the Old Farm who struck the oramiral on your command!"

My stomach turned, but I took the praise and grinned with all my teeth. My enemies were dead. I felt a hollow sort of triumph, nothing like what I thought I'd feel. The slaves and fighters gave us another nod and hurried past us to the beach, maybe to get a better look at the carnage.

"That's that, then," Oron said. "But I still want off this dirty piece of rock."

Avi grinned, then flashed her lion look. "An island of silver only my sister can find, enemies dead, and freedom for everyone."

I laughed. "Paradise!"

Oron and Calev echoed me and an invisible weight slid off my shoulders. Avi would use what she'd suffered. Not to become someone else, haunted and anxious, but to grow into a stronger version of herself.

As we walked, Calev elbowed me. A question rose in his eyes, a question that made my heart turn over and my head spin. I smiled.

"You go on ahead," he said to the others. "We will meet you at the western dock."

On the path ahead of us, Ekrem and Serhat rounded a rock that grew grass like a fur coat. Oron and Avi followed them, Oron shouting sailing advice that sounded very much like thinly veiled instructions for the bedroom.

Calev looked at me through his dark lashes and heat flashed under my skin. "I know we don't have the sun for this. But..."

My heart thundered and I put a hand over my chest. I had our lives safely in hand. Was I pushing luck to ask that I have him too?

I reached and touched the skin that met the edge of his tunic. "How will we explain all this?"

"When Oron planned this uprising, he told everyone to hold their tongues until we could talk to them. He has a story to spread. And I think I know—"

I pulled him into a kiss.

He laughed against my mouth, warm and sweet and sour.

"I don't know what's going to happen when we return to Jakobden," I said, "but I refuse to miss out on this."

He leaned into me and dragged his lips over mine. A delightful shudder poured through my tired, injured limbs, making me feel nothing but pleasure. He must have felt the change in me because he made a noise like a murmur and the kiss burned from sweet into spicy. His hands tore into my loose hair. His lips and tongue moved smoothly, roughly, and everything in between over my mouth. I was his fire and he was my luck. Fire help the person who tried to stop us.

"Calev ben Y'hoshua," a deep voice said.

Calev's eyes went wide and he jerked back.

As I turned to see who had said his name, I realized the Fire must possess a strong streak of humor. I wasn't amused.

Because there, on the path, was Calev's father.

Aside from a slight narrowing of his eyes, his face was blank of emotion. His hair, as black as Calev's but with a streak of gray down the middle, fell to his shoulders and his beard was longer than I'd remembered it ever being. A group of Old Farm men and women walked with him, their sashes embroidered with pomegranates and lemons. They were disturbingly quiet.

"Father?" Calev wiped a hand across his slightly swollen mouth.

I crossed my arms and raised my chin. "We are glad to see you, Y'hoshua ben Aharon."

Regardless of the red in Calev's cheeks and the way he had to turn away from his father and his brother as they approached, I wasn't about to cower after all we'd been through.

"We heard word of the amir's missing vessel. I knew you'd end up here, going after this one's sister," Y'hoshua said in his rocky voice.

We needed a story and we needed it now.

Calev blew out a breath, strode to his father, and moved like he was about to embrace him.

Y'hoshua stopped him. "You have some explaining to do, my son. I see there's been a rebellion. Chaos reigns at the quarry—the oramiral and his men are dead—and we've heard some disturbing reports as to the amir and her kaptan, Berker Deniz."

Calev ran a hand over his head. "It is a very long story."

"Very," I added as we trailed Y'hoshua down to the shoreline, where the ruined boat floated beside the bodies.

Moving to a stretch of rocky shoreline away from the gore, Y'hoshua told Calev to make a fire and wait as he explained to Eleazar how to organize the gathering of the highest ranking slaves still alive for questioning. He found someone to send rock doves to Jakobden to inform Old Farm they would be gone another day.

A woman with a coiled brown braid noticed my arm. "Let me help you with that." She pulled a cloth and a small jar from her shoulder bag. With fresh water from a skin, she rinsed the cuts the oramiral had made in my skin. Her quick fingers told me she was used to this work.

Beyond her, Calev bent to pick up two long sticks of bleached driftwood.

She glanced at him, then at me, her mouth tightening. "I'm Miriam's sister."

The name was an arrow in me. I'd almost forgotten she existed.

My cheeks went hot. "Um. I don't—"

She made a noise of dismissal. "Don't bore me with lies."

I jerked my arm away and pain shot up my arm. I finished the knot she'd started in the wrapping. "I wasn't going to lie. It's none of my business."

The girl put a hand on her hip. Her seal ring reflected the lowering sun. "Ha. You don't look at a man that way unless you already made him your *business*."

"Thank you for tending to my injury," I snapped and walked toward Calev, who'd made a spark with his dagger and a flint. A moon-hued blaze flickered in the driftwood bones.

Out of the corner of my eye, I watched Miriam's sister glare at me before heading off the way the others had gone.

Calev and I were alone.

"You're not going to tell your father the truth, are you?" I found a seat on the massive piece of driftwood next to Calev, who prodded the flames with his dagger.

He sat and pushed his hair behind his ear. The fire sparkled in his eyes as he glanced at me. "Of course not."

I squeezed my knees. "Good."

"Have any ideas on what I should tell him?"

I did actually. And if I could stop thinking about that girl's comment, I could fill Calev in.

Calev touched my bandaged arm. "I...oh." His eyes flicked to mine. "That was Miriam's sister, wasn't it? The healer?"

He could probably hear the blood boiling in my veins. "So?" I demanded.

He trailed one finger up my good arm, raising unseen flames under my skin. A grin tweaked his mouth as he leaned toward my ear.

"Miriam is the meanest little snake I've ever known. Just like that sister of hers. I am *not* going to marry Miriam," he whispered.

My heart crashed like a wave into my throat. "You're not."

I tried to make it not sound like a question. I was not going to ask him to do anything for me. I would not beg. He might break my heart, but no one would ever again tear down my spirit. No matter what caste I was in.

His lips drifted over my ear, and gooseflesh spread over my back and thighs. "No. If you'll have me, I will marry you."

"You will marry me."

He laughed quietly, the air ruffling the small hairs around my temples and neck. "Yes. And I will enjoy everything that comes with it. You, too, if you're up for it."

Heat cascaded down my throat, chest, belly, and lower until I thought I might start my own fire and all the work he'd done to make the sea-colored flames in front of us would be an enormous waste of sunlight.

"Oh, I'm up for it," I whispered back, turning to face him. His dark eyes promised a storm I'd happily die in, lightning and all.

"Calev."

We both jumped.

It was his father.

The man had the timing of Oron at the tiller after two flasks of stolen ice wine.

AROUND THE BLUE FLAMES, we wove a story that people would talk about for ages. Calev picked up my line of thought, and we spun that tale like when we'd been in trouble as children together.

Y'hoshua shook his head and tugged at his beard. "So Kaptan Berker found out you had chased off the oramiral when the other fighting sailors were ill."

"Yes. The oramiral killed the amir right in front of our eyes." I let my fatigue play as sadness in my words.

"Turns out, the oramiral was obsessed with the amir." Calev pursed his lips. I was pretty sure he was holding back a laugh.

Y'hoshua nodded. "Many men were. Tragic."

Eleazar came scrambling down the path and spoke into Y'hoshua's ear.

The older man looked at me, the wrinkles around his eyes deepening. Then he gestured for Eleazar to sit beside Calev.

"I…I'm glad you're alive, Brother," Eleazar said.

"Me too." Calev clasped Eleazar's shoulder kindly. "I have some amazing things to tell you about."

"There's sun enough for that later, boys," Y'hoshua said.

"Yes, sir," they answered in unison, their eyes wide and submissive.

I bit my lip to stifle a laugh. Calev looked downright adorable. For some reason, it made me want to smother him with kisses.

"You know," his father said to me, "despite your age, as the last appointed kaptan, you have a strong influence on who the kyros will name as the next amir of Jakobden."

I did know that. And I knew exactly who I'd suggest. "Ekrem will be my choice."

Calev's father straightened and Calev smiled.

"The fighting sailor?" Y'hoshua said.

"Yes. The man is an expert at strategy. He has a cool head. He would be perfect."

Y'hoshua stood, indicating this meeting was over. "Well then. Eleazar has informed me that none of the fighting sailors or slaves will speak about the events that occurred this day or earlier. They wait for their leader, they say. And that," he pointed at me, "is you, Kaptan Kinneret Raza. Never did I think I'd say that to the sweet-faced dock rat that dragged my son into all sorts of trouble."

Calev's face had darkened at *rat*. "Father. I plan to wed Kaptan Kinneret, if she will have me. Please show respect to my Intended."

Y'hoshua's face hardened. "You would risk your place, your place as *my son* to have a low-caste sailor?"

Calev grasped my hands, his face was all hope as he looked at his father. "I would."

His father turned to me. "And you would risk his well-being simply to have him as your Intended? Your sister will suffer too."

I swallowed. "I am a kaptan now. And if that isn't enough, along with the silver we found at Ayarazi, we will manage as best we can."

"You are set on this." The vein above his right eye twitched as he looked at Calev. "Even if everyone at Old Farm and in Jakobden proper refuses to speak to you, work with you, or acknowledge your union?"

"Father, will you really turn away from me for this? Because I'm serious. Don't test me."

A vicious grin flickered over Y'hoshua's face. "If I never tested you, you'd never have become the man that stands here now. How would your voice grow loud enough to be heard at the council table? Without struggle, the body grows weak. With plenty of fights, the body develops muscle. Today, you've shown me you finally have the strength to lead." He smiled, warmly this time.

Calev's fingers gripped mine.

I wasn't sure when she had walked up, but Miriam's sister appeared beside Y'hoshua.

"I can't believe what I'm hearing, Y'hoshua." The poison in her voice put my hand on the dagger at Calev's sash. I was ready if that—

Y'hoshua turned toward her. "Miriam never hennaed her hands. She was never officially Intended."

I broke away from Calev. "I thought—"

Calev jerked my good arm gently. "Hold your tongue for once, Kinneret."

Y'hoshua inclined his head toward Miriam's sister. "I'm sorry for any pain this causes you or your family, but it was Miriam's choice to make me wait for her official answer to my suggestion of becoming betrothed to my son. She pays for that hesitation. Kinneret Raza has earned her way to high-caste in my eyes and she has also earned my son's heart, it seems." He nodded curtly toward Calev's hands on my arm.

I pressed my cheek into Calev's shoulder.

"He listened to me. For once. He really listened," Calev whispered to me.

The girl's face collapsed, but before a cry came out, she smoothed her features and ducked her head respectfully to Y'hoshua. "As you judge, Chairman."

I opened my mouth, and Calev clamped a hand over my lips. "No, no, fire. Behave."

I scowled at him. The girl deserved a little *haha* from me.

"She deserves it," Calev agreed, "but Father won't like it. And things will be much easier with him on our side."

"Fine," I said behind his fingers.

Then I nipped his thumb with my teeth playfully. His eyes widened, and he looked from my face to his father's. I grinned.

We followed Y'hoshua and Eleazar up the path and I spoke with the fighters and former slaves. With Y'hoshua's help, I detailed a plan to get them all off the island for good. The bulk of us left that very day for Jakobden.

We only had one more obstacle to our happiness. The remainder of the amir's court.

# CHAPTER FORTY-ONE

AT LAST, THE MOON REIGNED in the sky above Old Farm's low, stone buildings, stubbled barley fields, and neat rows of dark-leaved lemon trees. I leaned out of the betrothal room's one window and inhaled the night air. All of Calev's people, along with Avi and Oron, were drinking and eating under the stars, around the corner.

Calev would be here soon. I tapped fingers against the smooth, wood ledge. It seemed today the sun had stayed high for far longer than it should've. Of course, every day since Old Zayn told me about Ayarazi had seemed filled to the edge of the bucket. Especially the day we'd returned to Jakobden minus one amir.

After hearing the fighting sailors account matched mine perfectly—a fine bit of work Oron had done there—and Y'hoshua's own affirmation of everything, the court and the kyros's representative agreed to Ekrem's appointment, Berker's falsified martyrdom, and the oramiral's imagined crime of murdering the amir. Yes, on Age Day, I'd not only turned eighteen, but turned Jakobden upside down.

Now, in the betrothal room, Calev and I would begin the process of promising ourselves to one another.

"Pondering an escape?" Calev said.

I turned away from the window as he shut the room's side door, setting the many candles to flickering. Two bronze incense burners released white clouds of scented air that swirled around Calev as he approached. He wore the same thing as me—a plain white tunic. He looked better in the *angel uniform*, as Oron had deemed it, than me. His hair was so perfectly black against the fabric and the outline of his trim waist and strong, long legs showed through the tunic, outlined by the burners' inconsistent light.

He sat on a low stool and pointed to another across from him. "Should we begin?" His voice sounded deeper than normal and his gaze traveled up and down, from the exposed red-brown curls of my head, to my face, along my body, all the way to my dusty, bare toes.

I nodded, strangely shy, and gathered the parchment cone the servants had left for us. It was filled with deep brown henna dye. Calev put his hand in my lap, and I began to draw the symbols of his family on his palm and fingers.

I took a breath to steady my heart and dragged the pierced tip of the parchment cone down his first finger. A flourish snaked into existence, eventually growing into a lemon, a leaf, and a sun that sat in his palm, a palm I knew as well as my own. I started another design, working around his sigil ring and adding curls like palm fronds along his fingertip.

He shivered and his eyes flashed. They looked larger than usual, maybe because he wasn't wearing a headtie. "You're doing that on purpose," he said.

"Doing what?"

"Tickling me. Driving me mad."

Laughing quietly, I dotted the lemon with tiny circles. "I am not. Now quit fidgeting. Everyone is waiting for us outside for the formal announcement. And you still have work to do on me."

A sly smile drew his lips to the side. "I certainly do."

I felt like a host of violet nightwingers had been loosed in my belly. "That's not what I meant."

344

I looked away from his mouth and focused on the barley stalk I was creating on the heel of his hand. His skin was gold in the light of the candles and burners. The scent of beeswax mixed with the earthy, spicy odor of the henna. The Old Farm grandmothers, including Calev's own Savta, had added ginger and clove.

"Kinneret." Calev's breath moved over my hair, warming my scalp.

I kept my eyes down, drawing now on his other hand. "I'm almost finished. See?" His palm and fingers were covered in leaves, swirls, dots, hatched lines, lemons, barley, and even a tiny pomegranate. "Hold still for it to dry, then you can start on mine."

He made a little laughing noise, and I looked up. He gave me that thief's grin of his. "What do you suggest we do to pass the sun as we wait?" he asked with all the innocence of a pirate.

He held my gaze, unblinking. A cool breeze drifted through the window and stirred his tunic, pressing it lightly against the lines of his chest and arms.

My body began to feel very, very warm. His pulse moved in the hollow of his throat.

"We can't..." I started. "I mean, you have to let the dye dry."

"I suppose we'll have to make do with your hands then."

My heart bumped around in my chest, a clatter of noisy thumps in my ears. Everyone was outside the double doors, waiting for us.

"Kinneret, relax." He smiled. "We can just talk."

My heart cracked like a whip.

I was being a coward, fretting over pleasing his father and his people, who waited outside. Since when had I let others get in the way of what I wanted? Since never.

I smiled, enjoying the feel of my blood rising.

"There she is," Calev said.

Leaning close, I ran a finger over his sharp chin. I touched the pale strip of skin that was usually hidden by his headtie. I ran both palms down the column of his neck, feeling the tendons and muscles and the flow of blood through his veins. His Adam's apple moved under my fingers.

A knock sounded at the heavy, wooden doors. Calev made a noise, and I spun, dizzier than I'd ever been.

Avi peered in, her eyes happy and her sun-colored braid hanging over a shoulder. The embroidered seashells on her skirt and the five high-caste bells on her sash reflected the candlelight.

"Sorry." She grinned, her cheeks going rosy above the blue of her clothing. "Just wanted to see how much longer I had to listen to Oron trying to goad Y'hoshua into an argument."

Calev and I laughed.

"We'll be finished soon. Promise," I said.

She shut the door, and I eased back onto my stool, giving Calev my hand. "As much as I was enjoying myself…"

Calev's chest moved faster, his eyes a bit wild. "Kiss me, Kinneret."

"Not yet," I said, quirking an eyebrow. "You have work to do first."

Closing his eyes for a breath, he scooted forward and took up the dye cone I'd tossed to the floor. "Back to being kaptan again, are we?" He made a face.

"We are."

"Such a challenging little beast, aren't you?"

I pointed to my thumb. "I'd like the shape of a sail here." I opened my hand to show my palm. "And a combined shell and lemon design here, if you can manage it."

"Of course, kaptan." He drew the cone's tip across my skin slowly. Goosebumps rose along my arms, echoing the touch.

Calev's black hair hid his face. His hands moved smoothly, his knuckles like knobs and his henna designs twisting to life with his fingers' movements.

Every sweep of new lines and curves drawn on my skin brought another rush of heat, and eventually, my breathing matched his.

Slowly, he raised his head, his eyes glittering and ebony. He met my gaze, then said my name without a sound, dropping the henna.

Standing, we crashed together like waves.

With only the lightest of clothing between us, my hips pressed into his. He kissed me and I tasted honey and lemons. As his mouth moved to my neck, I breathed him in. His hair smelled like sun-warmed earth. My hands couldn't touch him enough. His chest heaving and strong and hot under my fingers, he breathed my name into my shoulder, and I shuddered as sparks danced down my legs.

A cough broke us apart and I felt like I'd been hit by lightning.

Oron coughed once more. "Please excuse the interruption, but Y'hoshua ben Aharon is about as happy as a beached seastinger out there and if you make him wait much longer, it'll be a curse rather than a blessing he bestows upon you."

"Did you stir him up?" I snapped, wanting him to leave. I wanted Calev all over me again.

"That's like asking if it's my fault that Asag fellow was such a grouch. His attitude is a permanent condition, my dear."

Calev studied the floor and ran a hand through his hair.

"Come." Oron grabbed our sleeves and pulled us out the doors.

We stepped into the moonlight, our appearance prompting the foot-stomping and smiles of Avi, Y'hoshua, and the rest of Old Farm. They'd set up tall, brass candleholders along the dirt and stone pathway leading from the betrothal room to the main farmhouse. Violet nightwingers flitted through the honey light, one resting on Avi's shoulder. She tried to kiss it before it flew off again.

Oron released us, and found his bowl of drink, raised it, and drank it down.

Old Zayn stood in the dark shadow of a cedar, his smile white. I gasped, and with a nod to Calev to wait, I ran to him and hugged him tightly.

"Easy, young thing," he rasped, patting me lightly on the back. His hand felt like a sack of tiny bones.

I pulled away and stared. "I lost the compass you gave me."

He grinned. "Ah. Well. It went down during an adventure and I'd say that's more than any compass could pray for, could pray for."

"Did you receive my message?" I asked.

"And the silver too." He pointed to his thick, brown tunic and wide green sash. "I thank you. You are as kind as your parents were."

My eyes burned and I turned, imagining Mother and Father standing beside Y'hoshua, still and solemn. Mother winked. The wish-picture dissipated and Zayn patted my back.

"They are here. In you and your sister. And you make them so proud, so proud. Me too, if you care to know," he said.

I hugged him, a tear escaping despite my best efforts.

"Now go," Zayn said. "Visit me during the winter months, yes?"

"Yes." I smiled at him, then returned to Calev.

Calev took my hand, the henna caking off and scenting the air with cloves and ginger as we walked toward his father.

"Thank you for saving me again," Calev said.

"Saving you?"

"Once, from the sea. Next, from the…everything during our journeys. And of course, now."

"Now."

"Now."

I squeezed his fingers. "You never really needed saving. You're too lucky."

"Haven't you figured it out yet, Kinneret? You are *my* luck. Not the other way around."

Then Y'hoshua was holding one of our hands each in his larger ones, and saying the blessing. He took up the painted glass container of holy oil.

"I think now, that there's no such thing as simply being born with good fortune," I whispered to Calev. "We make our luck."

"You do it well," he said.

I smiled. The night sky's blue moonlight coalesced into the gold illumination of the candles, making everyone look like dreams among the night insects.

"What do you think?" I asked. "Hells or paradise?"

"I think you know the answer to that one," he said under his breath as his father raised an oiled hand and prayed in a ringing tone.

"Paradise. With the promise of hells to come."

Calev's eyes widened.

I laughed. "Life would be dull without any flames to challenge us."

He ran a finger down my palm and kissed my forehead, earning a reproachful frown from his father.

"My thoughts exactly, my fire," he said.

As Y'hoshua rubbed oil into our hands and readied to chant the Old Farm betrothal, I knew I was ready for this. I'd fought hard for this life, an existence stretched between two cultures, and a fantastical blend of exquisite joy and soul-waking pain. There was no greater magic than life itself.

If you'd like to review WATERS OF SALT AND SIN on Goodreads or Amazon, please do! Reviews are super important for everyone.

# ALSO BY ALISHA KLAPHEKE

Need more Kinneret, Calev, and the rest?
Get FEVER, an Uncommon World Novella—told from Calev
and Avi's points of view. (Available on Amazon and also through
Kindle Unlimited)

Visit alishaklapheke.com for more Uncommon World info
and a free prequel, CLAIMED.

# ABOUT THE AUTHOR

During non-writing time, Alisha teaches martial arts (Muay Thai kickboxing, Krav Maga, and BJJ, specifically), loves on her two amazing kids, and travels the world with her ninja husband.

90267372R00212

Made in the USA
Columbia, SC
28 February 2018